Praise for *The* STEADY RUNNING *of the* HOUR

Indie Next Pick May 2014
O, *The Oprah Magazine* "R
Apple "Best of the Mo
BBC.com "Ten Bes
Popsugar.com "Best of the

"With this debut, Justin Go deploys the elements of a caper—an unclaimed fortune, an illicit affair—in an assured literary thriller."

—*WSJ Magazine*

"One of the hottest debuts of the year."

—*O, The Oprah Magazine*

"The plot, with its combination of world war, doomed romance and exotic locations, seems designed to catch the attention of Hollywood producers in search of another *English Patient*. And, indeed, Go's strengths lie in his screenplay-ready dialogue, which feels both naturalistic and specific to time and place. He is a particularly keen chronicler of altered states and the skewed insights that come to the sleep-deprived, jetlagged or hungover. The depiction of Ashley's war experience is particularly unsparing and evocative."

—*The Washington Post*

"Richly imagined . . . a heady blend of romance, history, and adventure . . . War's horrors, love's joys, obsession's perils and identity's complexities. In this affecting and accomplished debut, Go addresses them all, and he does so with intelligence, grace and compassion—and with the realization that resolution can elude us. Riveting and addictive, *The Steady Running of the Hour* compels the reader to reflect on the brevity and breadth of time—and of life."

—*Richmond Times-Dispatch*

"Every work of literature is a story of survival, a battle against fate or a struggle for love. *The Steady Running of the Hour* is all three . . . a multilayered odyssey that clips along and is hard to put down . . . Stories told in present tense are often forward motion without depth, but Go straddles the decades with profound verisimilitude . . . When I finished, I wanted immediately to start it again."

—*Minneapolis Star Tribune*

"Ambitious . . . this is a remarkable work."

—*Booklist*

"Gifted storyteller Go captures a period feel . . . This story is a page-turner and an impressive first work, sure to be appreciated by fans of historical and travel fiction."

—*Library Journal*

"Go's debut is ambitious in many ways: it evokes a time of privileged daring in which British climbers, defying post-WWI disillusionment, climb Mt. Everest with foie gras at the ready; it depicts a love that transcends time and disdains convention; and it fluidly moves between past and present . . . heartfelt."

—*Publishers Weekly*

"The stuff of love's poetry. Go makes you believe their love is unique in all history . . . I read the last 200 pages without breathing."

—*Historical Novels Review*

"A spellbinding historical novel."

—*The Saturday Evening Post*

"Poetic, epic, expansive, bloody with the battlefields of the war, and crisp and daunting with the peaks of Everest. Sweet and haunting, *The Steady Running of the Hour* captures the disconnection of our modern world."

—Interview.com

"Go's intriguing first novel spans the 20th century . . . with vivid accounts of wartime France, pioneering mountaineering expeditions, and an isolated village in Iceland."

—BBC.com

"Justin Go's impressive and ambitious debut is meticulously plotted and researched, and combines the narrative drive of Dan Brown with the literary sensibility of Alan Hollinghurst's *The Stranger's Child*."

—*Financial Times*

"Falls into that rare category of being both compulsively readable and haunting, its figures still insistently real long after you've left their fictional world . . . ambitious, honest and unabashedly passionate . . . a lovely meditation on how men and women meet the world's harsh demands and how they wrestle with their humanity in the process."

—*Shelf Awareness for Readers.com* (starred review)

"Justin Go has written an astonishingly vast, meticulously plotted, and beautifully told novel. In elegant, haunting prose he tells a wartime story that is at once violent and lovely, hopeful and despairing. I won't soon forget Go's passionate, star-crossed lovers and their deeply moving story, set against the riveting, utterly realistic backdrop of the Great War."

—Anton DiSclafani, *New York Times* bestselling author
of *The Yonahlossee Riding Camp for Girls*

"A wonderful time-slip story, beautifully written with a superb sense of place. Go captures the spirit of early 20th-century England perfectly, both in the past and the present, in a novel that is exciting, emotionally engaging and ambitious. I loved it!"

—Kate Mosse, *New York Times* bestselling author
of *Labyrinth, Sepulchre,* and *Citadel*

The STEADY RUNNING *of the* HOUR

JUSTIN GO

SIMON & SCHUSTER PAPERBACKS

New York   London   Toronto   Sydney   New Delhi

Simon & Schuster Paperbacks
An Imprint of Simon & Schuster, Inc.
1230 Avenue of the Americas
New York, NY 10020

First Simon & Schuster trade paperback edition April 2015

SIMON & SCHUSTER PAPERBACKS and colophon are registered trademarks of Simon & Schuster, Inc.

For information about special discounts for bulk purchases, please contact Simon & Schuster Special Sales at 1-866-506-1949 or business@simonandschuster.com.

The Simon & Schuster Speakers Bureau can bring authors to your live event. For more information or to book an event contact the Simon & Schuster Speakers Bureau at 1-866-248-3049 or visit our website at www.simonspeakers.com.

Designed by Ruth Lee-Mui

Manufactured in the United States of America

3   5   7   9   10   8   6   4   2

The Library of Congress has cataloged the hardcover edition as follows:

Go, Justin.
The steady running of the hour : a novel / Justin Go. —
First Simon & Schuster hardcover edition.
p. cm.
1. Young men—California—San Francisco—Fiction. 2. Inheritance and succession—Fiction. 3. Family secrets—Fiction. 4. World War, 1914–1918—Fiction. 5. Mount Everest Expedition (1924)—Fiction. 6. Mountaineers—England—Fiction. 7. Everest, Mount (China and Nepal)—Fiction. I. Title.
PS3607.O22S74 2014
813'.6—dc23   2013027387

ISBN 978-1-4767-0458-6
ISBN 978-1-4767-0459-3 (pbk)
ISBN 978-1-4767-0460-9 (ebook)

For my mother and father

"Strange friend," I said, "here is no cause to mourn."
"None," said the other, "save the undone years,
The hopelessness. Whatever hope is yours,
Was my life also; I went hunting wild
After the wildest beauty in the world,
Which lies not calm in eyes, or braided hair,
But mocks the steady running of the hour,
And if it grieves, grieves richlier than here. . . ."

—Wilfred Owen, "Strange Meeting"

EUROPE.

Scale, 256 English Statute Miles to One Inch.

Kilometers.

Elevations in English Feet. $\cong$ Depths in English Feet.
Importance of places is indicated by
style of type, approximately, as follows:

LONDON, Liverpool, Dublin, *Limerick*.

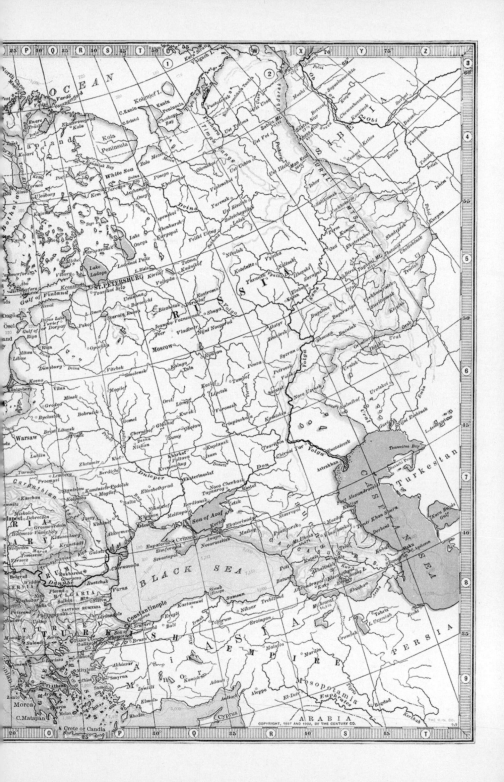

COPYRIGHT, 1897 AND 1902, BY THE CENTURY CO.

THE FORTUNE

The letter came by courier last week.

I knew when I touched the envelope that it was fine stationery. I knew from the paper, the porous surface of pure cotton rag; the watermark that shone through as I held it to the light. The letter is in my bag in the overhead compartment, but I imagine the cream fibers, the feel of the engraved letterhead. *Twyning & Hooper, Solicitors, 11 Bedford Row, London.*

The courier knocked at my door, the letter and a clipboard in his hands. He asked for my name.

—It's a special service, he explained. The sender requested we check ID.

I showed the courier my driver's license and signed the delivery bill. He set the letter in my hands. On my kitchen counter I pulled the plastic zipper of the express envelope. Inside there was a smaller envelope of cream bond stock.

I read the letter standing over the sink.

Dear Mr Campbell,

I am trustee of an estate of which a substantial portion remains to be distributed. Information has recently come to light that suggests a significant connection between you and the named beneficiary. As we could find no current telephone number for you, we have despatched this letter to your listed home address in the hope of making urgent contact.

I cannot stress enough that the proper resolution of this matter is our utmost concern. Accordingly, I would be most grateful if you could telephone me at your earliest convenience, reverse charge, using the direct-dial number listed above.

For your own benefit, please retain this matter in the strictest confidence until we have had the opportunity to speak.

> *Yours sincerely,*
> *JF Prichard*
> *Solicitor – Private Client*
> *For and on behalf of Twyning*
> *& Hooper LLP*

I walked four blocks down Valencia Street to reach a pay phone. Part of the plastic receiver had been smashed off, but when I put it to my ear I heard a dial tone. Three collect-call operators transferred me before I got through to England.

The law firm's secretary answered. She said Mr. Prichard was away from his desk, but I could speak to a Mr. Geoffrey Khan. Khan sounded breathless when he came on the line.

—So you do exist. My God. James will be delighted, I expect he'll be retrieved immediately. Listen—in case our connection is severed, could you give me your current phone number? We had enough trouble just finding your address—

—I don't have a phone right now.

—I see. Well stay on the line, James will be with you momentarily. Tell me, did your grandmother—

Another voice came on to the telephone. The second man sounded older. He enunciated his words with a strange precision.

—James Prichard here. Geoffrey, I can take over.

Khan excused himself and his line clicked silent.

—Mr. Campbell, Prichard said, I'd first like to thank you for calling. If you'll pardon me, so that we may verify we're speaking to the correct individual—just in case we've blundered—could I trouble you to answer a few simple questions?

I pushed a steel button on the pay phone to increase the volume.

—Sure.

—Splendid. I should add that obviously we are not connected with any official enquiry, and you are not required to speak to us, though it may be in your interest to do so. Naturally, any information you give us will be used only for the resolution of the case, and will be kept in the strictest confidence. Would you mind telling me your mother's full name?

—Elizabeth Marie Campbell.

—And her maiden name?

—Martel.

—Her place of birth?

—San Francisco.

—Thank you. And your grandmother's name?

I hesitate. —It was Charlotte Grafton. I don't know if she had a middle name—

—That's all right. Do you know her place of birth?

—Somewhere in England.

—Indeed. Thank you for answering my questions. If I may, I'd like to explain briefly why we're making all this fuss. Nearly eighty years ago, this firm was engaged to draft a rather singular will. Our client passed away not long after the will was completed. Remarkably, the client's estate was never claimed by the principal beneficiary. What is doubly remarkable is that the will set up a trust explicitly required to retain its assets until they could be distributed to this beneficiary, or their direct heir. For a host of reasons, this distribution has never been possible.

Prichard paused. Faintly I heard a woman's voice in the background. Prichard muffled the receiver and replied to her.

—Pardon me, Prichard said. I was recently shown a document that suggests you may be related to this beneficiary. I don't wish to give you false hope, but we've been waiting a long time to fulfill our client's wishes, and this is the first substantial lead we've had in decades. I must emphasize that all this be kept in confidence, for your sake as much as ours. Unwanted attention could be a hindrance to any potential claim of yours.

I told Prichard I understood.

—I do realize, he continued, that this is a lot to digest at once, coming as it does from the other side of the Atlantic. So by all means make enquiries about our firm, look us up. May I ask you something else? Would you happen to know if your family's vital records are extant? That is, do they survive, and do you have access to them?

—I'm not sure.

—I mean in particular not only your birth certificate and the like, but also your mother's papers and most especially any papers relating to your grandmother.

—I doubt it, but I could look. I don't think we have anything from my grandmother.

—I'd be grateful if you could have a look. Geoffrey shall give you a list of the kind of documents we're interested in.

A fire truck rumbled down the street behind me, the siren's whine shifting pitch as it went by.

—Quite a bedlam, Prichard said. Are you outside?

—I'm at a pay phone.

—Ah, Prichard sighed. No wonder Geoffrey couldn't find your number. Well there's a final thing I wished to mention. I certainly don't need an answer now, but I wonder if you might be able to visit London in the near future, at our expense? This case is rather time-sensitive, and much would be expedited by your presence here.

—I don't know. I might be able to go.

—I'd be pleased to see you here. I understand you're a university student?

—I just graduated.

—My congratulations. Then perhaps you can delay your entry into the working world long enough for a jaunt to England?

—Maybe—

—Consider it. I shall give you back to Geoffrey to discuss some administrative matters, including our confidentiality policy and the prospect of your journey. He's your man for all the details. Feel free to contact either of us should you ever need to, of course, but you'll find he's more easily reached.

Prichard drew a breath. It was a moment before he spoke.

—Mr. Campbell, I must advise you not to discuss this matter with your family until you've closely examined your feelings. I do not encourage deception, but if you are party to any portion of this estate, it is through your mother's family, and as such would be yours undivided. Neither your father nor your stepmother nor stepsiblings have any possible claim. Thus I advise the utmost discretion.

—I understand.

—I'll put Geoffrey on now. I shall be forward enough to hope that the next time we speak it shall be in London.

That call was four days ago. They had been long days and it felt good to finally get on the plane this morning. I've never flown business class before. All through the flight the stewardesses offer me food and champagne and coffee, until the cabin lights are switched off and everyone pulls back their seat. For an hour I lie wide awake under a blanket. Then I turn on my reading lamp and take out my notebook.

Barely slept last night. But I still can't sleep on the plane. After all those plans, always waiting for the right moment—suddenly something happens and I'm on a plane to London. Because I didn't have a choice, I just had to go or stay. That's a good lesson.

Tomorrow I meet the lawyers. I couldn't find anything worth showing them, but they wanted me to come anyway. Why?

It doesn't matter. In four hours I'll be in London. That's all I know and that's plenty.

I shut the notebook and lean my head against the cold windowpane.

I wake to a pink sunset streaming through the double glass. Crystals of ice gather on the rim of the outer windowpane, drops of dew carried from California and frozen hard in the thin air. In a break between the cumulus clouds below, a jagged black coastline appears, then terrain of the deepest green. A vast blue-white glacier drops to the sea. Iceland. I'm at the gates of Europe.

Before I left I asked Geoffrey Khan one question.

—Why would anyone leave money to someone who'd never bother to collect it?

Khan sighed. —Even if I knew the answer, I couldn't tell you. Information about our client can be given only at the trustee's discretion. You can ask James when you arrive, but I can't guarantee he'll be able to say.

—I understand.

—However. If I may say something so obvious as not to be a breach of confidentiality—

—Please.

—This was 1924. And these were not people like you and me.

BOOK ONE

⊷⊶

ALBION

Son of the goddess, let us follow wherever the fates draw us or draw us back. Whatever may be, every fortune must be mastered through endurance.

—Virgil, *The Aeneid*, V. 709–10

THE SOLICITORS

⊷═◎ ◉═⊷

Gentle rain falls from a colorless London sky. I thread my way through the sidewalk crowds on High Holborn, checking the street signs against the map in my hand. *Kingsway. Procter Street.* Rainwater gathers in dark puddles, reflecting the white delivery vans, the jet-black cabs and candy-red buses.

I turn left and follow Sandland Street to Bedford Row, a line of four-story terraced Georgian houses with brick facades. Beside the entrance to number 11 there is a brass plaque: TWYNING & HOOPER, SOLICITORS. I push a button on the intercom, feeling dazed and shaky. At breakfast I had two cups of coffee, but they didn't help much. I look up at the security camera. The white columns of the doorway have Ionic capitals.

—Good morning. How can I help you?

—I'm Tristan Campbell. I have an appointment with James Prichard—

The receptionist buzzes me in. She takes my jacket and leads me into a waiting room with a tufted leather couch.

—I'll get Geoffrey right away.

A few minutes later she comes back carrying a tray with a porcelain tea service. The tea scalds my tongue, so I stir in more milk. I look up and see the receptionist watching me from behind her desk. Our eyes meet and she smiles. Absently I page through a copy of the *Financial Times* from the coffee table. I finish the tea and flip over the cup. SPODE COPELAND'S CHINA ENGLAND.

—Mr. Campbell. A pleasure to meet you at last.

Khan approaches with a quick stride and shakes my hand. He wears a slim-fitting suit of dark navy. His brogues are buffed to an impressive shine.

—Shall we go and meet James?

Khan leads me up a tall wooden staircase. Above us are vast murals on the walls and ceiling: a king on horseback heralded by angels; young Britannia with her shield and trident, receiving the tributes of the world.

Two young men in neckties come down the stairs, maroon folders tucked beneath their arms. They nod solemnly as we pass. I look down at my thrift-store clothes, a wrinkled dress shirt and a pair of old slacks.

—I feel underdressed.

Khan smiles. —Not at all. You're the client. We're the solicitors.

We walk down a corridor to a pair of French doors. Khan pauses here, lowering his voice.

—A word before we go in. Naturally you can address him as James, he doesn't stand on formality. But I might suggest you answer any questions—

Khan hesitates.

—As directly as you can. I can say from personal experience that vagueness goes nowhere with James. He sees right through it. Be as blunt as you can with him and he'll be honest with you in turn. How does that strike you?

—Great.

Khan smiles warmly. He knocks on the door and ushers me in. The office is large but spartan. A table with carved lion's feet, its surface covered with paper stacked in neat piles. A leather couch and club chairs. An immense Persian rug. Prichard stands behind the table, a sheet of paper lifted intently before his face. He is silver-haired and wears a tie and waistcoat over a French-cuffed shirt. He raises a hand to us, then paces between the window and the fireplace, his eyes fixed on the page. Prichard signs the sheet over his desk and calls in a secretary to collect it. He turns, beaming.

—If you can fill the unforgiving minute, Prichard quotes, with sixty seconds' worth of distance run—

He extends his hand. —James Prichard. Sorry to have kept you waiting. I suppose London weather is living up to your expectations?

Prichard gestures to one of the chairs; he and Khan sit on the couch opposite. They cross their legs in the same direction. Framed photographs hang on the wall behind them. Above Khan's shoulder there is a black-and-white picture of a group of men in three-piece suits gathered stiffly around a bald man with a white mustache. The bald man's head is tilted slightly to the camera and he holds a pipe in his hand.

—Is that Clement Attlee?

Prichard looks at me.

—That's right. He was a client of ours.

I point at a tall, fair-haired young man in the photograph.

—And that's you?

Prichard nods, but he doesn't turn toward the picture.

—I did very little work on Mr. Attlee's estate. It was handled by the most senior solicitors, but they let me sit in on a few meetings for posterity's sake.

Prichard pauses. —At any rate, how was your journey? Don't be put off London on account of Heathrow. Or British Airways, for that matter. Our charms are elsewhere. What hotel have they put you in?

—Brown's.

—Splendid. Seen much of London yet?

—I got here last night.

—Well, have a look around before you go. The Tower. Regent's Park. The British Museum.

Prichard looks at Khan.

—The confidentiality agreement, Khan prompts.

—Of course, Prichard says. You've read it carefully?

—Yes.

—And Geoffrey tells me you're without your own representation?

—Yes.

Prichard nods. —As I'm sure you noticed, the agreement forbids revealing details of the case to any outside party, which makes advisors rather pointless anyway. Will you sign the agreement now? Without it I should not be able to tell you the details of the case.

Khan puts the thick document on the coffee table before us and offers his fountain pen. I flip to the signature page at the back and scratch out a misshapen signature. Khan calls in a young woman to notarize the document.

—Everything said henceforth, Prichard warns, is strictly confidential. Geoffrey, I can take over from here.

Khan walks out with the young woman, closing the door behind him. Prichard watches me for a moment, as if waiting for me to speak first. He smiles faintly.

—This is quite a long shot, but are you familiar with the Mount Everest expeditions of the 1920s?

—Expeditions?

—You're forgiven. Geoffrey told me you were a history student, but it's hardly the kind of thing one studies at university these days. Shall we move to the desk? I'm afraid I'll need my notes to explain all this.

Prichard pulls out a chair for me in front of his desk and sits opposite. He shuffles among stacks of documents, some of them typewritten, others written in longhand on unlined paper.

—I've been brushing up on the case all week—I warn you, it's quite a headache. I'll endeavor not to bog you down with details, but it's essential that you understand the 'problem' of the Walsingham estate, and the sooner you grasp the problem, the better, for our time is limited. Most of what I'll tell you was recorded by Peter Twyning, the estate's executor. Fortunately he took meticulous notes. The case was a headache from the moment Twyning took it on. And he knew it.

Prichard unfolds a pair of tortoiseshell reading glasses and puts them on. He examines the page before him.

—Our client was a man called Ashley Walsingham. At the age of seventeen, Walsingham inherited a substantial estate from his great-uncle George Risley, the founder of a very profitable shipping line. This was 1913. Risley was childless, and as Walsingham's own father was dead, Risley looked upon Ashley as his grandson. When Risley died, Ashley inherited the majority of his estate. Peter Twyning managed the Risley estate and would later become executor of Walsingham's fortune.

—Ashley went up to Magdalene College, Cambridge, in the Michaelmas term of 1914. Rather bad timing, wouldn't you say? The war began that August and Ashley duly applied for a commission in the army. By the summer of 1916 he was about to be sent to France. In his last week in England he met a woman called Imogen Soames-Andersson.

Prichard looks up at me. —Does that name mean anything to you?

—No.

—A pity. I'd hoped it might. You see, Imogen was the sister of your great-grandmother Eleanor.

I shake my head. —I've never heard of them. Soames—

—Soames-Andersson. Anglo-Swedish—an unusual family. Twyning left pages of notes on the Soames-Anderssons alone. The father was a Swedish diplomat, first deputy to the Swedish envoy in London. The mother was English, apparently an accomplished sculptress. They had two daughters, Eleanor and Imogen. The English side, the Soameses, had quite an artistic pedigree, and the daughters were brought up in the same line, rather bohemian. Eleanor later became a painter of some distinction.

—She was my great-grandmother?

Prichard frowns. —Yes, we'll get to that bit. As I said, Ashley met

Eleanor's younger sister Imogen in August 1916. They had some kind of love affair for a week, then Ashley was deployed to France. We presume the two of them kept in touch. In November 1916, Ashley was badly wounded in one of the last battles of the Somme offensive. He was mistakenly reported dead. Imogen was notified by this law firm of Ashley's death, only to learn a week later that he was in fact alive. As soon as she heard, Imogen went directly to France. She found Ashley at a hospital in Albert, near the front line. They met briefly but had an argument, or so Ashley told Twyning. Then Imogen disappeared. As far as we know, she never returned to England and was never seen again.

—What happened to her?

Prichard takes off his eyeglasses.

—We don't know. I don't suppose we'll ever know. Ms. Soames-Andersson had a reputation for being rather—impulsive, shall we say. At least in Twyning's view. From his notes, I gather he considered her something of a wild card. Certainly he wished she'd never crossed paths with Ashley. There was much speculation on the cause of her disappearance, but nothing was ever proven. Evidently Ashley believed she was still alive, for he told Twyning so on several occasions.

Prichard glances at his wristwatch. He puts his eyeglasses back on.

—I've neglected the most important part. The climbing. At Charterhouse one of Ashley's schoolmasters was Hugh Price, the famous mountaineer. Price took him climbing in Wales, with summer seasons in the Alps. In 1915 Ashley was elected to the Alpine Club, and by the early 1920s he was said to be one of the best climbers in England. In 1924 Ashley won a spot on the third British expedition to Mount Everest. A few days before he sailed for India en route to Tibet, Ashley came to this law firm and asked Twyning to revise his will. Previously his principal beneficiary had been his mother, but Ashley had Twyning amend the will to leave the majority of his estate to Imogen.

—But I thought she was gone—

—She had been missing for seven years.

—You can leave money to a missing person?

—Why not? It's not illegal. It's simply a very bad idea. Naturally Twyning tried to dissuade him from the changes, but Ashley insisted the money sit in trust until such time as Imogen or her direct descendant claimed the estate. He ordered that the trust sit for eighty years. If no one claimed it by then, it was to be divided among various charitable beneficiaries—the Ashmolean Museum, the Alpine Club, a few village churches in Berkshire. This clause was intended to make it impossible for anyone to preempt Imogen's claim during her conceivable lifetime, or for the estate to escheat to the Crown.

Prichard flips over the sheet of paper on his desk.

—Ashley Walsingham was killed on Mount Everest on the seventh of June 1924, caught by a storm during a summit attempt. His mother received her portion of the estate, but Imogen never surfaced. For decades we'd been expecting to distribute the remainder when the eighty years ran out. We'd already drawn up the papers. But last month all that changed.

—You see Mr. Campbell, in the last few years there's been a certain interest in Eleanor's painting, though from what I've gathered it has less to do with her work than her connections. Evidently Eleanor was close to the Camden Town Group as well as some notable French painters. Last month a graduate student was looking through Eleanor's letters at the British Library. She found something that caught her eye, and eventually the letter got passed on to us. We believe it concerns Imogen.

Prichard lifts a photocopy from his desk.

—This letter may clear up why Mr. Walsingham left the money to either Imogen or her direct heir. Not her sister or parents, mind you, but only her descendant.

He pushes the page across his desk.

—The letter was written in 1925 from Eleanor to her husband. The 'C.' mentioned here is, of course, your grandmother. She was eight at the time, and evidently having difficulties in school.

The photocopy is the final page of the letter. The handwriting is florid but precise.

Francis thinks I shall be able to get at least 8,000 francs for Smythe's portrait. Provided it hasn't been damaged in transit – as I fear given its odd shape & the inevitable shoddy crating. He's certain that Broginart will take it as soon as he lays his eyes upon it. I'm not convinced.

Naturally it worries me to hear that C. is again at odds with her best interests. I agree that Miss Evans is rather dense & unsympathetic when it comes to C., yet there is no denying the girl is impetuous & easily distracted. Certainly we've striven to raise her as we judged best, but I suppose it's equally true we've made allowances for her & always shall. Every day she is more the image of her mother, in both appearance & temper.

I laugh to think how I. would consider it another mark of destiny or divine signature that C. is not as we raise her, but as she was born to be. I must also admit I sometimes treasure C.'s obstinacy, having been without I. all these years. But above all, I worry, lest she meet the fate of her mother.

I must go now – the concierge has just announced the intrepid Mme. Boudin. Once again.

Burn this.

Love to all,
Eleanor

I hand the letter back to Prichard. He takes his glasses off and leans back in his chair.

—You understand the implication?

—My grandmother was Imogen's daughter, not Eleanor's.

Prichard nods. —With you her only living descendant. I suppose the letter survived by pure hazard. Legally it's of little use. It doesn't even call Imogen by name.

—It seems clear to me—

—If it's truthful. But it may not be, for any number of reasons.

That's why the law won't rely on a letter like this. We would need more substantial documentation.

—Like what?

—Official documents connecting your grandmother to Imogen. Considering they went to the trouble to hide your grandmother's maternity, one wonders if such papers exist. Failing that, more evidence like this, put together, could be a persuasive argument. But we would need far more.

I take a moment to think.

—Would this Walsingham be the father, then?

—Possibly. It would explain a great deal.

—I don't understand. You think I can find out something about this?

Prichard stands. He begins to pace around the room.

—We are at an impasse. The Walsingham trust was drawn up with great privacy in mind. What the trustees can do by way of investigation is strictly limited. Mr. Walsingham believed Imogen would come forward on her own to claim the estate, and he didn't want anyone probing into their private affairs. This letter certainly suggests why. In any case, the trust explicitly forbids us from hiring third-party help of any kind. For eighty years there have been no probate researchers, no private investigators, nothing.

Prichard stops before a tall window, shaking his head.

—It's exasperating to say the least. And it's persisted all my career. Mr. Twyning always said the Walsingham fortune must sort itself out sooner or later, that with so much money involved an heir must surface. But it's never happened. You're the first outside party that's ever qualified to be told about this trust, and I can tell you achieving that wasn't easy. Even as a potential heir you had to be subject to a confidentiality consistent with the trust, which is why you can't hire outside help any more than we can. That's hardly encouraging, but it's possible the evidence may not be particularly difficult to find. We simply don't know, because we've always been straitjacketed. We know the truth exists, but we're prohibited from looking for it.

Prichard looks at me.

—You've the opportunity of being more enterprising.

He turns back to the window. The rain has quickened outside and sheets of water are tumbling down the glass. A man on the street below dashes for cover.

—The Walsingham case was at our firm when I joined. That was forty-one years ago this March. I should like to have this case settled before I retire, and settled as our client intended. The money wasn't really meant to go to any church or museum. So you can imagine how pleased I was to hear of this letter, and to learn of your existence. Let's say it's one of my legacy cases, and I shouldn't like it to be a defeat.

—I wouldn't know where to start.

Prichard nods. —Let me give you a piece of advice. If there is proof of your relation to Imogen, I doubt it will be in government archives or the like. You can look, of course, but you and Geoffrey already went through that business with your mother's papers, and the one thing trustees have been permitted to do is look through vital records. There's no paper trail to Imogen after 1916. All the usual records have been searched. Nothing turns up.

Prichard taps his finger on the photocopy.

—This letter is the breakthrough. It's the thread you ought to follow. New evidence often opens new doors. In eighty years no one had the benefit of this knowledge, nor had they the freedom you have. Do you follow me?

—It's incredible.

—It certainly is. It's also a mess, and I'm enlisting you to sort it out. You won't thank me, for I've yet to tell you the worst of it. Today is the sixteenth of August, is it not?

Prichard sits down behind his desk and lifts another sheet of paper.

—Ashley Walsingham was killed on the seventh of June 1924. The news appeared in the British press on the twenty-first. As soon as he learned of it, Twyning tried to get in contact with Imogen, but of course he couldn't. Accordingly, the Walsingham estate passed into trust on the seventh of October 1924. You recall it was an eighty-year—

—That's in two months.

Prichard looks at me.

—More or less. If the estate isn't claimed, it passes to the alternate beneficiaries on seventh of October. That leaves you roughly seven weeks. You see why I insisted you come to London straightaway. I grant you, it seems foul luck to have learnt of this letter only now, but imagine if we'd found it two months from now. It's a question of perspective. A pessimist would say you've seven weeks to find what could not be found for eighty years—

Prichard leans forward. A wry smile crosses his lips.

—Mr. Campbell, let me ask you something. You're not a pessimist, are you?

I hesitate. —I'm not sure.

—Spoken like a true Englishman. For my part, I'm confident you can achieve much by October. I don't say you'll find the proof, because we can't be certain it survives. But you ought to be able to trace that which is traceable.

Prichard pushes a button on his telephone. He asks for Khan to be sent back in.

—As ever, Geoffrey shall bring you up to speed on particulars. He's your man for the details. Good luck.

Prichard stands and I spring up awkwardly, following him to the door. He shakes my hand again.

—If I can help, he says, don't hesitate to call.

11 April 1914

Gorphwysfa Hotel

Snowdonia, Northwest Wales

It is four o'clock and everyone but Price is asleep. He had gone to bed right after his bath, leaving the curtain open to look up from his pillow every few hours and watch the progress of the waxing moon over the hillside. The Chamonix guides never used clocks for early starts. Neither would he.

The piano downstairs went on well past midnight and even when it ceased he still could hear the voices. He knew who was talking and could half-follow the conversation, occasionally broken by thumps and bursts of laughter, until finally it softened to whispers and Price fell asleep. His dream started almost at once. He walked into his father's house in Cheshire, but he had his climbing boots on and the hobnails scratched against the floorboards. In the dining room he found the whole family at the table, his parents and brother and even his sister Beryl who had been gone these six years. His mother was in a gown and his father in white tie, but Price was wearing his heaviest alpine clothes, his jacket and felt hat dusted with snow. They told him to sit for dinner, but Price looked at Beryl and she opened her mouth to speak. Then he woke.

Price dresses without lighting the lamp, winding puttees over his calves in the dark. He wants to keep his pupils wide for the ridge. He feels the rope strung up between the posts at the foot of the bed. The flax is still damp. Price coils it and throws it over his shoulder, stepping quietly down the hallway in stockinged feet into the bedroom next door.

Ashley is asleep on his side. His mouth is open and a shock of hair hangs down his forehead. Price shakes him gently by the shoulder, but Ashley only turns his head on the pillow. Price pulls back the blanket. Ashley curls up toward the wall, fully dressed in plus fours and a thick Shetland.

—Kitted before bed?

Ashley grabs the blanket, his eyes still closed.

—You always come too bloody early.

—So does the sun.

Price fetches his rucksack and the two men meet in the foyer downstairs. The checkered floor is littered with boots and Ashley picks them up one by one, holding the leather soles before his eyes. Save for the nailing pattern they all look the same.

—Damnation. Two left boots. Don't even know which is mine—

—Probably neither.

Price lights a candle and they grope among the shadows until they find the right boots. Ashley pulls on his Norfolk jacket and Price dons a misshapen hat. They open the front door, a gust of frigid air surging in.

—Coldest part of the night, Price remarks.

He starts up the path at his usual clip, the white stone of the miners' track bending and rising among brown and green hills. Ashley follows a few paces behind, wrapping his muffler around his neck. They walk along the shore of a narrow lake, the water glowing silver beneath a murky sky. Price glances back at Ashley.

—Who was the last to bed?

—Fraser and Cousin David, I expect. Fraser was still on the rafters when I left.

—Still game for the girdle?

—Of course.

They pass another lake and follow a steeper trail onto the mountain's broad shoulder. The sun is breaking over the ridge to the east, but the great north cliff ahead remains in shadow. Price walks off the trail and the angle of the hill steepens until they stand on the eastern edge of the thousand-foot cliff, its two peaks and soaring buttress high above them. They mean to traverse the whole face.

—Still a touch of snow, Price remarks.

He uncoils the rope from his shoulder. The dampness has stiffened into frost and he takes his gloves off to smooth the kinks before fastening his waist loop. Ashley ties on and anchors the rope around a jammed boulder, paying out handfuls of slack as Price pulls himself across a crack and lowers himself down a smooth gully, sweeping footholds below him of snow and pebbles with the toe of his boot before resting his weight.

They work quietly, Price moving across a band of milky quartz in fluid, rhythmic movements, calling back only occasionally.

—Goodish hold here. Rather damp—

—Frightfully icy. Stay clear of the lower slab—

—For God's sake, some slack, Ashley!

Ashley leads the next pitch and they go on alternating, one man belaying as the other edges westward across the cliff. The rock is freezing and the icy patches leach cold water in the sunlight. Both men climb with bare hands, stopping at times to rub blood into their pale fingers.

They rest on a nose of banded quartz and Price lights his pipe. The wind howls on, pulling swift curtains of mist across the spectacle of mountain and valley below. Suddenly the sun flares over Snowdon, sending a narrow beam of light across the peak. Both men let out a little gasp.

—There she goes, Price murmurs. Sometimes I wonder if we aren't fools, forever chasing foreign peaks when we've hills like these. Are you hungry?

Price opens his rucksack. He takes out his pocketknife and spreads anchovy paste over a pair of biscuits.

—What would you call this view, Ashley? Beauty or sorrow?

—Foreboding.

Price hands Ashley a biscuit. —Oughtn't say that on a climb.

—Sorrow then. With British hills it's always sorrow.

—Why is that?

Ashley looks down at his boots.

—I don't know. All the moors and dark rock and clouds. I expect they were made to suit us—

—Or they made us.

Price stands up, buckling his rucksack shut.

—I suppose you might lead this one—

Ashley edges his way along flakes of rock, his face brushing patches of snowy vegetation. The ledge narrows until he has only the toe of his boot on the rock, then a single nail scratching the flaky ledge. He looks down to the slope of jagged scree five hundred feet below, the calm opal waters of the lake. Ashley hooks the rope over a knob of outcropping rock and spiders along westward, Price belaying with his pipe still in his mouth.

Half an hour later they stand below a chimney of smooth rock, four feet across and nearly vertical. A film of water courses down its walls.

—Looks slick, Ashley says.

—It'll go.

Price steps into the narrow chute, putting his back against one wall and his boots against the other. He pushes upward with his legs and back, his hands touching the walls only for support. Ten minutes later he is on top, belaying the rope over a rock spike.

—Your go.

Ashley moves deep into the chimney and begins his way up, trying to keep his weight on his legs. But the handholds are minuscule, slick ridges smaller than a fingernail.

—You're too far in, Price calls. Get out to the edge!

Ashley does not listen. He pushes upward, his arms growing tired, his bootnails skating against the wet stone. The chimney steepens until he reaches an outcropping of rock that blocks his way. Price is eight feet above him, holding the rope taut as he peers down at Ashley.

—Foothold to the right.

—Can't get there.

—Follow the crack! The left is too slick—

Ashley's left boot searches for the ledge, but he has overreached his right hand and he sinks his weight down on his foot before he notices the pebble on the ledge. His boot skates off and he slides down the chimney, skidding against the stone. Price braces himself and grips the rope, but before it catches Ashley jams his arms and legs hard and stops sliding.

—Are you all right?

Ashley's elbows burn with pain. He puts his weight on his back and rests for a moment. Then he climbs the chimney on the right as Price instructed. He comes over the lip and looks down at his bloody knuckles, one of the fingernails cracked. His left elbow is skinned and his knees are wet and filthy.

—Technically, I suppose, yours was the better route—

Price shakes his head.

—Bloody fool.

They top out on the western ridge an hour later and descend the skyline quickly, reaching the hotel by mid-afternoon. A group of climbers are smoking pipes on a bench behind the building, its white gables sheathed in the gathering mist.

—Was that you two on the girdle? I say Walsy, were you the one who floundered onto the ridge like a trout?

The other climbers laugh.

—We were coming up the west ridge and saw something flop over the top behind us and go flat on a slab. Like a trout coming out of the water. Hardly moved at all, just gazed up at the sky. I said it must be Walsy—

—I consider myself, Ashley interrupts, more salmon than trout.

Price points to a new Ford touring car parked in front of the hotel, its black enamel paint splattered with mud.

—Someone expected today?

—Only stopping by, the climber says. Chap from the Climbers' Club and two sisters. What's the chap's name?

—Grafton, another climber says.

Price and Ashley enter the hotel. There is an odd silence in the foyer. The litter of boots is neatly arranged in rows now, the climbers sent back indoors by the mist. As they approach the door to the smoking room they hear the piano, a slower piece.

—How queer, Price says. Certainly not in the songbook—

Price pushes the door open but halts in the doorway, raising his right hand in a gesture of silence. Ashley cranes his neck over Price's shoulder.

A large group has arranged itself around the upright piano. Climbers sit cross-legged on the floor, a few reclining, others sucking on glowing pipes. The aroma of cheap shag tobacco hangs low. A row of spectators is seated on chairs at the back, among these a few women. Ashley sees only the back of the piano player. A cream blouse, a long dark skirt. Her hands are fair. A silver band is around her wrist.

Ashley and Price stay in the door frame, watching. The piece returns to its theme again, a churning cascade of notes. The music slows, then ceases. The girl lifts her hands from the keys. There is cheering and applause.

—Encore, encore!

The girl swivels on the piano bench, startled by this enthusiasm. She is slender and her dark hair is tied up. There are faint freckles beneath her blue eyes.

—It wasn't anything, she says.

—Marvelous, Price calls. Encore!

The girl smiles and bows her head a little. She flips through the songbook, but her two companions stand up, another dark-haired woman and a man in a motoring duster. The room goes on applauding as the girl stands and makes a shy bow. Clapping on, Price leans toward Ashley.

—She shan't forget this hotel.

The girl and her companions walk out amid cheers. A young man with a pipe in his mouth pulls out the piano bench, starting a lively tune whose lyrics were worked out last night. The audience joins in the chorus. Price clasps Ashley on the shoulder.

—Look here Ashley, I'm only trying to set you on the right course. Plenty of climbers start as fire-eaters, forever biting what they aren't fit to swallow. I daresay I've been as guilty as any fellow. But you must learn to profit from another man's experience, otherwise you're courting disaster. It doesn't matter how skilled you are. I told you the safe route, and you went flailing over some mad path that dropped you.

—I caught myself—

—Barely. A true alpinist doesn't depend on chance.

Price lifts his hand from Ashley's shoulder.

—I've a question for you, Ashley. Which do you suppose takes a man furthest in life—talent, judgment or persistence?

Ashley considers.

—I'd say the salmon possesses all three. And after infinite labor comes to die in the same place he started.

—Be serious.

—Then I don't know. Which is it?

Price takes the rope from Ashley and throws the coil over his shoulder. He starts toward the stairs, shaking his head.

—Which, indeed.

THE BLOODLINE

I come out of the building and walk south toward High Holborn, carrying a cardboard portfolio stamped *Twyning & Hooper*. Inside are the papers they've given me, the proof of what I've seen and heard: the solicitors exist. The fortune exists.

High Holborn is not a beautiful street. Buildings of glass and stone. Throngs of pale businessmen in dark suits, their garish neckties bound in thick Windsor knots. They know nothing about the fortune. A woman staring at her cell phone collides with me, knocking shoulders.

—I'm sorry, I say.

The woman walks past and turns into Holborn Station, not seeming to hear me. I drag my hand against the polished surface of a building to steady myself.

I'd wanted to go to London the moment Prichard suggested it. But I didn't admit it over the phone. After that first call I spent the afternoon sitting in Dolores Park, watching the clouds close over the skyscrapers downtown. I thought about London and Rome and Paris, cities

I'd read about that were still only names to me, dark spaces on a map. It was harder to think about the fortune and even harder to link it to my grandmother. The park turned windy and I walked back toward my apartment. Near the corner of 24th and Capp I passed another pay phone. I looked at it for a long time. Then I picked up the receiver and called Khan.

—I want to come to London. I just need to look for the papers first.

—Splendid, Khan said. Can you be here by Monday?

He forwarded the itinerary an hour later. I went to my father's house and tore apart the garage looking for anything related to my grandmother. My mother's things were all in cardboard boxes stored high under the rafters and I hadn't looked at them since the funeral. I got a ladder and took them all down. Soon there were papers everywhere: bank statements and photographs and old letters. I sat on the oil-stained concrete floor looking through everything. In one box I found my mother's high school yearbook from 1968 and I read some of the autographs in the back, but that only made me feel worse. I shut the yearbook and went through box after box of old linens and polyester clothes. Everything smelled like mothballs. None of it was my grandmother's.

On the highest shelf in the garage I found the jewelry box my mother had once used. It was upholstered in silk and opened with ivory clasps shaped like small tusks. Inside there was antique jewelry that may have been my grandmother's—ancient brooches, long strings of imitation pearls—but there was nothing else. There were no documents of any kind.

My father came into the garage. He looked at the mess on the floor and made a low whistle.

—Looking in your mom's stuff?

I closed the jewelry box, but I didn't answer.

—Listen, he said. I'm the one who put that stuff up there, I know what's where. So what are you looking for?

—My grandmother's stuff. Anything of hers. Do we have her birth certificate?

—Birth certificate? Christ, I doubt it. What for?

—I'm applying for this scholarship for grad school. You need British ancestry for it.

My father shook his head. —I've never seen any of Charlotte's stuff around here. Not any papers anyway. She didn't have much to do with us.

My father picked up one of the letters in the pile and looked at it. It was his handwriting on the envelope. He frowned and dropped it back in the pile.

—Why was that? I asked.

My father shrugged. —Would have been better to ask your mother. By the time I met her, she was one of those ladies who've been divorced for so long, they're completely independent. She told her own daughter to call her Charlotte, which tells you something. I don't think she cared for family obligations. Or any kind of obligation. Maybe in her own way she did love your mother. But they couldn't stand to be around each other more than a few hours.

—Did she go to your wedding?

—She did. She flew out here alone. She wasn't living in England at the time, somewhere else. Maybe Holland? We had some pretty good champagne at the reception and she drank quite a bit. It loosened her up. I remember her joking that the lapels on my tux were too wide. This was the seventies, you know, and she was from a very different generation.

—Do you remember anything else?

My father knelt beside the jewelry box. He opened the lid and looked at the pearls inside. He turned to me.

—At the reception, I danced with Charlotte after I'd danced with your mom. I guess she was surprised that I knew what I was doing. She told me, 'You're the second best of any man I've danced with.' Naturally, I asked who was the best. But she didn't answer. She just said I was a good dancer and she knew we'd have a long and happy marriage. 'Americans don't believe in sorrow,' she said. 'That's what makes you so charming.'

—What does that mean?

He shrugged. —I don't know. I guess she had a pretty hard life. She moved around a lot. The guy she really wanted to marry was killed in the war, somewhere in North Africa. So she married an American instead, but of course that didn't last. You done with these boxes? None of this stuff is Charlotte's, I can tell you that.

We started putting the papers back in the boxes and replacing the lids.

—Listen, he said. You never told me anything about grad school, and now you're taking off to Europe in a huff. What's going on?

I looked at my father. He was up on the ladder, putting the boxes back under the rafters. It was afternoon but he was still wearing his pajama pants.

—Everything's fine, I said.

At least he hadn't asked about my mother. It had been almost three years and whenever my father sensed something was wrong, he always assumed it was her. And she was the last thing I wanted to be reminded of. It had taken a long time to separate her life from her death so that I could think of the first without having to think of the second. Finally I learned to let the small and simple memories float to the surface, as they did sometimes, and I no longer tried to push them down.

So I let myself remember. My mother dropping me off at summer school early in the morning. My mother giving me hardcover books wrapped in gold paper for Christmas, books that I'd pretend I'd never read before. My mother meeting my high school girlfriend and worrying what she ought to wear to dinner, then both of them being too polite and shy as they talked across the table.

There was no use for the other memories. My mother at the

hospital, the trays of food that sat uneaten for hours, both of us looking out the window. Before she was sick we used to talk about anything, but in the hospital I never knew what to say. I'd sit by the window overlooking Divisadero Street and talk as long as I could, stopping when the nurse came to empty the bag attached to my mother's body.

The nurse would leave and my mother would turn to me.

—You don't need to stop every time she comes in. Just keep talking.

—About what?

—Anything at all. I just like to hear you.

I'd talk about the new apartment where I was living; about a trip I'd taken across the Mojave Desert during winter break. My mother's eyes would close as I spoke, but if I stopped they would spring open, green and bright. So I'd go on with my story. And my mother would turn her head on her pillow and shut her eyes again.

In the hospital there was only one thing that made her smile, a simple phrase she spoke like a confession.

You're the only one for me, my mother would say.

Because I was her only child and maybe the only thing that would bind her to this world once she was gone. I don't know what dreams she had for me. She never told me. When I was younger she imagined I would make a good doctor, but in the end she hated her doctors and might have changed her mind.

The two of us were night and day. My mother had no use for the arts or history, and she believed it was easiest to be happy in a practical profession, which was probably true. She had spent her whole life in California and loved it as much as her own mother had hated it. My mother wasn't interested in cold places. She didn't care about stone castles or distant battlefields or cracked oil paintings hung in old palaces. She found it quaint that I loved these things without ever having seen them.

And she almost never talked about my grandmother. I can only remember one time. It was spring break and we were driving up

Highway 1 to visit my mother's friend in Mendocino. Suddenly my mother felt sick from the winding road. This was two months before we knew what was wrong with her. The sun had just set and my mother pulled over at a gas station and went inside to use the bathroom. I got out and took a picture of the lit-up Texaco sign while I waited. When she came back she looked tired.

—Tris, do you mind driving?

I started the car and we pulled back onto the road. My mother turned to me.

—How's school going? Your father said you're taking an architecture class.

—Yeah, medieval architecture. It's a good class. We went to Grace Cathedral on Monday. They've got a labyrinth on the floor, just like the one at Chartres. They say medieval pilgrims went through it on their knees, it symbolized the path to the Holy City.

My mother turned to me.

—Chartres, she repeated. I haven't heard that word in years. Charlotte used to talk about it all the time, she'd go on for hours about the stained glass. The round windows, what do you call them—

—Rose windows.

My mother nodded. We drove around a peninsula and we could see the headlights of the cars ahead making yellow tracks all the way up the coast. She looked down at the dark water below.

—You know it was her idea to name you Tristan. I wanted to name you Michael. But Charlotte always loved the name, and she never had a boy of her own—

—Was she much like me?

My mother pulled her seat back and shut her eyes.

—No. She wasn't like you at all.

My flight for London was leaving early in the morning, but my father insisted on driving me to the airport. I got up before dawn and repacked my bag to make sure I hadn't forgotten anything. I was taking my old camping backpack, the nylon faded and worn from trips in the Sierra Nevada. I wanted to travel light in case I went anywhere after London.

In the main compartment there was a down sleeping bag that kept me warm in the snow and stuffed down to the size of a loaf of bread. My clothes were rolled up to save space. I took a black hardcover notebook kept dry in a quart-size freezer bag along with my passport. In the lid pocket of the backpack I put an LED headlamp that ran on three small batteries, and a pocket book of London street maps.

My father tapped on the door and came in. He looked at the backpack.

—That's all you're bringing? What about a coat?

—It'll be seventy-five all week. The lows are in the fifties—

—You know your stuff. Let's go.

We got into the car and by the time we crossed the Bay Bridge the sun was coming up. My father turned down the radio as we merged onto the freeway.

—Did you see Adam yesterday?

I hesitated. —I didn't know he was back.

—He got back on Friday, he's just been at Lizzie's. I told him you were leaving town, he said he'd try to get ahold of you. One day you'll explain to me how a young guy manages a social life without a cell phone—

—How did you?

My father looked at me and grinned.

—Fair enough. But times have changed. You know how old I was the first time I went to Europe? Twenty-nine, a lot older than you. Seems like you've been pining to go since the day you were born. How's it feel to be finally going?

—A little surreal.

My father nodded.

—Well don't let it pass you by. You've earned a break. Don't worry too much about the grad school stuff. Just soak it in, you only get one first time over there.

When we reached the airport my father turned in to the international terminal and pulled the car up to the curb. There was a strange expression on his face. He glanced in the rearview mirror and pulled the lever to pop the trunk.

—Hold on, he said. Take a look in the trunk.

—My bag's in the backseat—

—I know. But have a look in the trunk.

We got out and my father held the trunk open, grinning to himself. Under the lid there was an old brown canvas shoulder bag I hadn't seen in years.

—You didn't have time to fix that Nikon, did you?

—No.

—I didn't think you would. So you were going off to Europe without a camera?

—Yeah.

—You aren't now.

My father opened the bag and took out the camera. The black finish was worn off the edges of the top and baseplate and you could see the brass showing through, the logo worn but the engraving below still clear. ERNST LEITZ GMBH WETZLAR GERMANY. My father looked through the viewfinder and made a low whistle. He handed the camera to me. It felt heavy in my hand.

—I got to thinking, he said, it wasn't doing me any good sitting in the closet. It was supposed to be your graduation gift, but I was waiting until I got the ninety fixed, and I never got around to that. Maybe you should just take the fifty, it's sharp and fast, and that's less for you to haul around or lose. You know how to change the film?

—Yeah.

—You've gotta pull out the spool or the counter won't reset—

—I know.

I fingered a dent along the camera's baseplate.

—What happened here?

—It got dropped.

—You dropped it?

—I didn't say that.

I smiled. —Well somebody must have dropped it.

—Somebody did. Right on the tarmac at Da Nang in '69. I was younger than you then. Which makes this camera a hell of a lot older than you. Don't lose it.

My father snapped the camera into the ever-ready case. He went through the canvas bag with me, removing the lenses I didn't need, showing me the meter and spare film and lens tissue.

—I got you five rolls each of Tri-X and Velvia. I didn't know if you shoot chromes—

My father paused. He squinted at me in the sunlight.

—You know something, Tris? It was good luck, that camera. You'll take some good pictures in Europe. You always had the eye.

—I'll try.

—One more thing. You were in a hell of a rush to leave. But you forgot to say when you're coming back.

—I'm not sure. It depends whether—

My father grinned and shook his head.

—I'm just pulling your leg. Come back when you're ready.

We shook hands. I walked inside the terminal trying to remember if we'd ever shaken hands before. The whole flight to England I kept the camera on my lap. There wasn't even film in it.

In the days before I went to London I made a list of all the things I wanted to see in the city. By the time I got here there were thirty-two items. They were things I'd read about over the years: museums and palaces, but also pubs hundreds of years old; alleys with strange names, their passage so narrow that you could touch both sides as you walked; blue-plaqued townhouses once inhabited by spies or poets or prime ministers. On my first night in London I was too tired to see any of these things, and when I left the lawyers this afternoon it was too late to start my research. I'll begin that tomorrow.

Instead I sit in Trafalgar Square among the statues and stone lions, among the tourists and the pigeons. I take the lens cap off my camera and point it at Nelson's Column, but the pillar is too tall to fit in the frame. I watch the tourists to see if they'll do anything interesting, but all they do is snap photos of one another. So I walk around the corner to the National Portrait Gallery, a museum full of oil paintings of dead Britons. It suits my mood.

I begin with the Tudors: Holbein portraits I've seen only in tiny reproductions in history books. But here are the real paintings, imposing pictures hung in gold frames in the lofty gallery. Sir Thomas More, the golden collar of his high office around his neck, a paper missive in hand; Catherine of Aragon, her portrait in a round silver miniature I could hide in my palm; the portly Thomas Cromwell, Earl of Essex, seated before a background of blue damask, his eyes sunken in a sinister gaze.

I walk on. Now the Elizabethans, ladies with snowy complexions and domed foreheads; noblemen with ruff collars that cartwheel to their shoulders. I imagine a whole line of these strangers stretching toward me, father and son, mother and daughter, only to end with me, sole survivor and heir apparent. And the fortune. I try to picture its shape. A line of zeros on foreign bank statements. An ancient gated house I've never seen before, room after room of dusty riches that belong to me and yet don't belong to me. A life apart from anything I've ever known. It seems impossible.

The next gallery is the Stuarts. Portraits of the English Civil War: men with flowing hair, steel breastplates. I try to focus on the pictures, but my mind jumps between Prichard and Khan, between Walsingham and Soames-Andersson, a story I can put together until I need the piece that connects it to me. Then it all falls apart.

Beside the staircase there's a wall map of the museum. I'm with the Georgians now. Then the Regency, the Victorians, and finally the Edwardians, many rooms away.

All that matters is the evidence. A sheet of paper that proves Imogen Soames-Andersson is my great-grandmother. Everything else is a distraction. I walk on, trying to repeat this in my mind, but every row of pictures in the gallery points to the same thing, a riddle whose question I can't even name.

You're the only one for me, my mother had said.

18 August 1916

Royal Geographical Society

Kensington, West London

Ashley sits beside Price toward the back of the lecture hall. The room is nearly full, only a few empty seats among the many rows of wooden chairs. Except for the gray-haired men almost everyone is in uniform. Two colonels, a smattering of captains and majors. Plenty of other lieutenants. A brigadier. Ashley holds the program in his hand.

ROYAL GEOGRAPHICAL SOCIETY

SEVENTH AFTERNOON MEETING, 18 AUGUST 1916

THE PRESIDENT IN THE CHAIR

PAPER: 'A CONSIDERATION OF THE POSSIBILITY

OF ASCENDING THE LOFTIER HIMALAYA'

DR A. M. KELLAS

The society president steps to the podium and sets down his calf-skin ledger. He fingers the edge of his white mustache, waiting for the audience to fall silent.

—Good afternoon. Before this afternoon's speech, I have two brief announcements to make. The first is that the anniversary dinner and *conversazione* will not be held in the present year. The second is in regard to the society's house. As you all know, a large part of the premises has been occupied by a special staff employed on the production of the map on the scale of one to one million—

Ashley stifles a yawn. He and Price are here as members of the Alpine Club, their first visit to the famous building on Kensington Gore. They both wear the uniforms of second lieutenants, but Price's khaki is shabbier, for he has already been to the front with the Royal Garrison Artillery. Ashley is on a week of final leave before he crosses to France.

It was Price who had insisted on attending, claiming that to hear about Mount Everest was worth any number of visits to *The Bing Boys Are Here*. But Ashley had been indifferent. In three seasons in the Alps he had seen enough to know he would not exhaust those ranges in a lifetime. The Himalaya were an abstraction to him, pieces of geographic trivia in distant and unapproachable countries.

Then Price had shown him a photograph of Everest. That had changed everything. Everest was not a beautiful mountain, for she lacked proportion or airiness or symmetry, or any of the features that make peaks attractive. But what power she had. She was a brute, a colossal formation of rock and snow risen out of the tallest mountain range on earth, her broad-shouldered ridge running northeast and capped by a monumental summit pyramid. And she was an enigma. No European had ever reached Everest's high approaches, and yet the Geographical Society was holding a lecture to consider whether the mountain could be climbed.

—It's absurd, Ashley had said. The whole world's at war, and they're talking about climbing in the Himalaya?

—That's precisely the point, Price said. It would take years to plan such an expedition. And piles of money. They'd be lucky to go within five years. And who do you imagine will be at the top of their form then?

Ashley shook his head. —If we're alive at all.

—A man survives, Price insisted, by the strength of his conviction. You must believe you won't be harmed, or you shan't come back from France.

Ashley doubted that conviction would make any difference to a grenade or a trench mortar. But he had not been to France yet. He agreed to come to the lecture.

The president begins to introduce the afternoon's speaker.

—The poles having both been reached, it is obvious that the next object of importance on the earth's surface to be attacked by adventurers is the highest mountain in the world.

The president looks up to the audience. He makes a half-smile.

—There are, perhaps I should not say unfortunately, a good many difficulties in the way of reaching it. In the first place, you have to deal with a government which has up to the present time forbidden you to approach within one hundred miles of the mountain's base. In the next place, the mountain itself is probably—though of this we have no sufficient evidence—of considerable difficulty. And there is thirdly the main obstacle, the effect of the rarity of the air at great heights on the human frame.

—As you know, the greatest heights reached at present are twenty-four thousand six hundred feet by the Duke of the Abruzzi's party and twenty-four thousand feet by some young Norwegians on Kabru, one of the mountains nearest Darjeeling. Dr. Kellas, who is going to lecture to us this afternoon, will deal with this question of the effect on the human frame of high altitudes, and there is no one in Europe who can deal with it with greater authority or greater practical knowledge.

Kellas sits beside the president, a small man in a Royal Army Medical Corps uniform making a final appraisal of the notes on his lap. The president welcomes him to the podium and Kellas begins his address, speaking with a strong Scottish accent.

—Under certain conditions, mountaineering can be regarded as a branch of geographical exploration—

Ashley has heard Kellas spoken of as an intrepid Himalayan climber, but he hardly looks the part. He has narrow, sloping shoulders and his mustache is waxed to neat points. His round spectacles glitter like tiny mirrors under the electric lights.

—If these reasons were deemed insufficient, one might bring forward the primeval axiom which subconsciously, at least, is in the soul of every geographical explorer: man must conquer and investigate every spot on the earth's surface. If the difficulties are carefully considered, the conquest should be peaceful, but nature in some of her aspects is adamantine, and even the most cautious explorer may suffer.

Ashley's gaze wanders to a pair of women two rows ahead, the only women in the audience. One of them wears her dark hair unusually short, cut to just below the ears. Ashley can see her slender neck and the lace collar of her dress.

—From the general point of view, the chief difficulties of Himalayan exploration might be summarized as due, firstly, to transport, and, secondly, to intrinsic difficulties of the mountain region. As all tents, equipment, foodstuffs, et cetera, have generally to be carried one hundred to two hundred miles—

Ashley thinks of the six days until he crosses to France. He wonders what the troopship will look like and if the sea will be rough in the Channel, and if they will wear lifebelts in case of U-boat attacks. He wonders if anyone will come to Victoria Station to see him off from England. He had always imagined that someone would see him off.

Kellas directs his voice toward the back of the hall.

—May we dim the lights, please.

The slide operator rouses himself from his chair and the lights are switched off, the long velvet curtains drawn. The operator switches on the projector's bulb and the lantern slide is illuminated. An image of Kanchenjunga appears on the screen, the five snow-capped peaks soaring above a field of jagged scree. Ashley looks toward the girl again. She is seated to the left of him and with his face turned he knows that the others in the room can see that he is looking at her.

—After these preliminary notes, we now come to the consideration of the possibility of ascending the loftier peaks of the Himalaya, mountains over twenty-five thousand feet in altitude, none of which have so far been climbed. We will consider the limiting case as a rule, and the problem might be stated as follows.

Kellas cranes his neck to the screen behind him. He frowns. Finally the operator drops in the new slide. A bleak range of mountains of incomparable scale, a great pyramidal peak towering above them. Ashley leans forward in his chair. He looks at the jet of clouds flowing over the mountain's summit.

—Could a man in first-rate training, Kellas asks, ascend to the summit of Mount Everest, twenty-nine thousand one hundred and forty-one feet above sea level, without adventitious aids?

Two rows ahead, the girl's silhouette shifts. Her head dips as if she is looking toward the floor and her profile appears black against the image on the screen, the fine delicate nose, the small mouth. The girl rises and passes down the aisle, then goes through a doorway that leads to the map room.

—The difficulties of ascending the higher Himalaya must be considered from two points of view: the first physiological, the second physical. The physiological difficulties are indubitably of a very high order, and depend upon deficiency of oxygen.

A new slide appears: a graph with a swooping curve labeled *Percentage Saturation Oxygen*. Ashley looks back to the doorway, a faint light emanating from the end of the corridor.

—How absolutely fundamental respiration is in maintaining life may be grasped—

Ashley rises and bows his head, making for the doorway. The aisle is wide and he passes easily between the rows of seats, going out through the dimmed hallway.

The map room is immense. A vaulted ceiling. Bookcases running floor to ceiling cradling leather-bound atlases. A pair of massive globes upon wooden stands. Rows of oaken map cabinets with wide drawers holding charts on paper and parchment. A map of Tibet is spread atop one of the cabinets, a banker's lamp switched on above to complete the display. Ashley stops here, pretending to study the map. He can still hear Kellas.

—Physical obstructions might be classed as those due first of all to weather conditions, and secondly to the intrinsic rock and snow difficulties of the mountains.

There are footfalls coming from the hallway. Ashley looks up and sees the young woman, the silhouette of her bobbed hair, the tiered skirt cut well above the ankle. He looks back at the map, but the girl comes up beside him and leans against the cabinet. She is close enough that he can hear her breathe.

—You're not interested, the girl whispers, in the problem of oxygen?

Ashley turns to the girl, her face half lit above the green glass shade of the lamp. She has almond-shaped eyes and her hair is cut flush with her jawline. She looks down at the map of Tibet. Then she smiles at him and continues down the hallway. Ashley stays beside the cabinet, waiting to leave an interval between the girl's return and his own. When Ashley goes back to his seat, Price eyes him with curiosity, but Ashley looks straight at the speaker.

—There is, however, one serious difficulty in connection with wind, namely, the low temperature sometimes met with. An intensely cold north or northeast wind might drive one down to avoid frostbite of hands and feet.

The operator drops a new slide. Another image of the pyramidal peak. It looms high above its sister mountains, the plume of vapor singing past.

—Mount Everest or Chomo Langmo, again, at twenty-nine thousand one hundred and forty-one feet. As the latter name was obtained by Colonel Bruce and myself from quite different sources, its claims may be worth consideration at a later date. A pass to the northeast of the mountain, about eighteen thousand five hundred feet high, leading to Kharta near the Arun River, is called Langma La. The mountain may be assailable from the northeast or north.

—While the limited scope of this paper hardly allows the deduction of categorical conclusions, it is highly probable from the data cited that a man in first-rate training, acclimatized to maximum possible altitude, could make the ascent of Mount Everest without adventitious aids, provided that the physical difficulties above twenty-five thousand feet are not prohibitive.

Kellas taps his notes into a neat stack against the lectern. He answers a question from a first lieutenant about the dangers of the sun's rays at high altitude, then the president comes to the lectern to make a few concluding remarks. As the audience applauds, Price cups his hand over Ashley's ear.

—Something interesting in the map room?

Ashley watches the two women rise. The short-haired girl dangles a large handbag from her elbow.

—Look here, Ashley says, see those women? Do you know them?

—I know the one on the left. I've met her husband, chap beside her. He's in the Climbers' Club. Think the wife is an artist. I hope she isn't an interest of yours.

Ashley shakes his head. —It's the other one. She's not an interest, but I've seen her before.

—Jeanne d'Arc over there? Her I don't know. But she's damned pretty, in spite of the crop. Shall we meet them?

Price takes Ashley over and introduces him to the man in the group, a first lieutenant who shakes Ashley's hand with a wry smile.

—Charles Grafton. This is my wife and her sister, Miss Soames-Andersson. Only for the Lord's sake, don't tell me you fellows are in on this Himalayan business too. Give me Lakeland hills any day of the week, no coolies, no bandobast—

Price and Grafton talk about climbing. Ashley's eyes meet Eleanor's and she smiles pleasantly, but her younger sister looks distracted, her attention straying to the image of the peak on the screen, to the other people talking around them. Ashley holds his cap under his arm and the badge catches Eleanor's eye.

—I see you're in the Artists Rifles, Eleanor says. Are you an artist?

—Only a pretender, I'm afraid. I was with the Artists for OTC, but they're putting me with the another regiment when I go out.

Eleanor steps closer and lowers her voice.

—I hope you're not going to France.

—On Thursday.

—How frightful. Do be careful.

—I'll do my duty.

—Of course you will.

There is an awkward pause as the two sisters face Ashley, neither knowing what to say. Price is talking to Charles about the postimpressionists and he draws Eleanor into the conversation so that Ashley and Imogen are left alone. Imogen looks to the side and swings her handbag. She looks at Ashley.

—What did you make of the lecture? You seemed to prefer the map room.

Ashley shrugs. —The slides were rather impressive.

—Aren't you interested in the Himalaya? You are a climber, aren't you?

—Of sorts. But if you ask me, the lecture was a lot of bosh. They won't know anything about climbing at those heights until someone actually does it. There must be some guinea pig. If they mean to climb Everest, that's four thousand feet above what any man has done before. They haven't the slightest notion what it would be like. It can't be studied in a laboratory.

—You'd like to try?

Ashley grins, nodding toward Price. —Hugh would like to try.

—And you wouldn't?

—I would too, Ashley admits. Though not so badly as Hugh, I expect. Are you interested in alpinism?

—I'm interested in everything. And I do find climbing intriguing, but Charles acts as if it's the same as playing rugger, a bunch of fellows competing on a mountain. He'll never tell us anything about it. So when he mentioned there was a lecture on the Himalaya, I insisted he bring us here—

—You wanted to come?

Imogen smiles. —Naturally. Though I can't say I learned much, except that men always want to try the one thing they oughtn't to. But everyone already knows that. From the sound of it, these fellows spend so much time worrying how they'll climb a mountain that they never consider why they do it. Surely there's more to climbing than just boasting rights? Perhaps you could explain it, Mr. Walsingham?

—I doubt it.

—I'd be grateful if you tried. Tell me, when a fellow climbs a mountain, is it the danger he loves?

Ashley grimaces. —God, no. It's not so crass as that.

—The adventure then?

—Not at all. It isn't so vulgar—

—The sport? The competition?

He shakes his head. —Certainly not.

—The mountains then? Or what they hold?

—That's closer. But it's not exactly that either.

—Then you don't know what it is, Imogen hazards. It isn't something one knows, but something one feels.

Ashley looks at the floor, the ceiling lamps reflecting bright on the waxed floorboards.

—Yes, he agrees. That's right.

Imogen begins to rummage through her handbag. The slide operator has shut off the projector and is rolling up the long screen. Price is talking to Eleanor and Charles about Cézanne. Imogen takes a tattered handbill from the bag and gives it to Ashley.

—Here it is. I was given three of these on the street today. Imagine it, three people giving one the same handbill. So I thought I ought to give you one. You see, there's a splendid matinee tomorrow at the Queen's Hall. They're performing Mozart's twenty-third piano concerto, one of the ones he kept to himself. It's very lovely. And there are fewer decent concerts every month.

Ashley thanks her and puts the leaflet in his pocket. He is about to speak when Charles announces that the trio is already late for an engagement. They say their good-byes hurriedly. Eleanor gives Ashley a sympathetic smile.

—Do be careful. Do come back safely.

Imogen touches Ashley's hand as she passes.

—It's only *au revoir*.

The three of them walk out of the hall. Price and Ashley exchange greetings with a few other members of the Alpine Club, then walk out onto Kensington Gore, pulling their caps on.

—What about a stroll?

They cross the road into Kensington Gardens. Price whistles as they follow a groomed path of soft brown dirt. A four-wheeler coasts past them, the horses snorting imperiously. Price stops whistling.

—And what did you think?

—Strange people. The older sister said she hoped I wasn't going to France. Can you believe that?

—I can.

Price scratches his cheek. He smiles.

—Strange or not, you fancy that Jeanne d'Arc. Ashley, I never knew you went in for these bohemian types—

—A man can fancy nothing in six days.

—A man can live a lifetime—

—Spare me.

They sit on a bench beside the path. Ashley leans his swagger cane against the bench and stretches his legs. Price shakes his head.

—Grafton. Of all the fellows to see at Kensington Gore. He hasn't the slightest interest in the Himalaya, and the Climbers' Club—

—The girl wanted to go. That's why they came.

Price looks at Ashley.

—The girl?

—She wants to know about alpinism. Grafton won't tell her any-thing, so she dragged them all to the lecture. She asked me why a fellow climbs mountains.

—What on earth did you tell her?

—I told her I didn't know. Do you know?

—Certainly I do.

—Would you care to explain it?

Price grins. —Certainly not.

THE WORLD'S KNOWLEDGE

Fluorescent light floods the Underground carriage. I listen to the recorded woman's voice announcing each station. *Warren Street. Euston. King's Cross St. Pancras.* I rise.

Sheets of rain lash Euston Road as I run west, holding a copy of the *Guardian* over my head. The newspaper curls with moisture. Black taxis sail by at twenty miles an hour, measured out in fleets by the switching traffic lights. I walk through a red-brick gatehouse, the sandstone lintel above inscribed THE BRITISH LIBRARY. A huge bronze statue of Newton sits in the courtyard, the scientist mining the secrets of the universe by some obscure instrument.

I enter the cavernous building and put my belongings in a locker downstairs. In the admissions office a clerk gives me a number and tells me to wait. When my number comes, I plead my case for several minutes. The clerk grants me a plastic reader's card with a photograph of myself, my gaze directed slightly off-camera.

The library is much bigger than my university library and I have no idea where to start. So I take brochures from a display and sit before the glass tower of King's Library, scanning the leaflets quickly. The British

Library is a legal deposit library, which means it has a copy of every book printed in the UK and many printed elsewhere. It holds 150 million items and there are eleven reading rooms at this site, each specializing in a subject.

I begin in the two-level humanities room. Everything is in rows: scholars seated shoulder-to-shoulder, scores of computer terminals, neat queues of patrons waiting to collect their books from the circulation desk. I follow the perimeter of the massive room, scanning the reference works that line the shelves. The National Union Catalog, ten bookcases wide. Huge and ancient leather-bound dictionaries in Latin and French. I pull the 1922 to 1930 supplement of the *Dictionary of National Biography* and look for Walsingham. No entry.

Walking along the shelves, I reach the geographic reference section. At last I find an entry in a volume of the *Encyclopedia of Exploration*.

Walsingham, ASHLEY EDMUND (1895–1924), mountaineer, was born at Sutton Courtenay, Berkshire, 16 April 1895, the only child of Henry Franklin Walsingham (1865–1909), a textile merchant, and his wife, Emily Symons Fitzgerald (1869–1933). Walsingham was educated at Abingdon School, Charterhouse, and Magdalene College, Cambridge, where he matriculated in 1914. He left Cambridge after a single term and took a commission as a 2nd lieutenant in the Royal Berkshire Regiment. Posted to the Western Front in August 1916, Walsingham survived two years of dangerous front line service, taking part in both the Somme and Third Ypres actions. In the British attack on Empress Redoubt on 5 November 1916, Walsingham was so badly wounded that his commanding officer mistakenly reported him dead. He was later decorated with the Military Cross for his actions in taking a German trench.

From the age of 16 Walsingham was an avid mountaineer, climbing on rock and ice in the Alps to a high standard. He was demobilized from the army at the age of 23, but the war had left an indelible impression on Walsingham, and his failure to readjust to civil life made mountaineering ever more important. An inheritance from a wealthy relative in 1913 enabled Walsingham to live without the need to earn his own income. In 1919, Walsingham attempted to return to his studies at Cambridge, but left within a month and spent the summer climbing in the Dolomites. In October, Walsingham sailed to Mombasa to manage a coffee plantation in Kenya, and although the business was profitable, he found it morally distasteful.

In May 1921, Walsingham again returned to the Alps for an admirable season of climbing, but rather than returning to Kenya that autumn, Walsingham sailed to Aden. He travelled the length of the Arabian Peninsula, often on foot, collecting material for a treatise on the 'lost cities' of the Arabian Desert. In 1922, Walsingham briefly assisted the excavation at Ur under Sir Charles Leonard Woolley, and later at Kish under Stephen Langdon. However, the majority of Walsingham's two years in Arabia were spent searching for the so-called 'Iram of the Pillars' in the vicinity of the Rub' al Khali desert. These efforts were hampered by his weak command of Arabic and other Semitic languages, and in April 1923 Walsingham telegraphed Hugh Price, IRAM VANISHED MEET ST MORITZ JUNE ASHLEY.

Walsingham reached Switzerland by June, and in the following three months he would achieve the most impressive season of any British alpinist to date. In a series of spectacular climbs Walsingham scaled obscure peaks and pioneered new or difficult routes, including a first ascent of Piz Badile by the Badilekante route on 9 July 1923, and a harrowing first ascent of the North Face of the Dent d'Hérens on 2 August 1923. Geoffrey Winthrop Young estimated that among his peers Walsingham was 'the least naturally gifted, the least graceful; also the most driven, most relentless and most indestructible climber I ever saw on a mountain'.

Walsingham had always been a staunch advocate of guideless climbing, but his later ascents were notable for their daring, particularly his perseverance in the face of deteriorating weather;

he developed a reputation as an insular, mercurial climber, his keen mountain sense governed by instinct rather than intellect. Hugh Price later wrote that Walsingham 'was introspective to a fault, except while climbing, where he compensated by never thinking at all'. On several occasions Walsingham is said to have saved his climbing party from disaster, avoiding rockfalls and avalanches, and navigating safe routes under harrowing conditions. On 20 August 1922 he famously arrested the fall of two climbing partners on the Grandes Jorasses, anchoring his rope around the head of his ice axe barely in time to secure the belay.

The initial 1921 expedition to Mount Everest was little more than a reconnaissance, and the climbing party led by Hugh Price struggled to find a feasible route towards the summit. Walsingham applied for a place on the 1922 Everest expedition, but was not accepted despite Price's endorsement, possibly because the committee judged Walsingham's temperament unreliable – he was known as an irreverent, even impertinent climber whose inherent mistrust of authority had been cemented by the war. Walsingham contributed money to the expedition in spite of this rejection, a gesture that impressed the committee and may have won him his place upon the third Everest expedition in 1924. He trained rigorously through the winter of 1923–4, conditioning himself according to the latest athletic principles, and even consulting a professional coach. But the British climbing community, committed to genteel amateurism, regarded such methods with suspicion, with the predictable result that although inexperienced at high altitude, Walsingham was probably the strongest member of the 1924 expedition.

From its arrival at the Rongbuk Glacier in April 1924, the third Everest expedition was plagued by bad weather, and the climbers established their high camps on the North Col only at great cost to their physical fitness. Walsingham suffered particularly from a throat injury, acquired in the war and exacerbated by the altitude. On 4 June Walsingham wrote to Young that he felt 'weaker than a child, sicker than an invalid, and madder than any fiend who ever chopped steps in ice. But certain, terribly certain, that I must and shall make it to the top'. On 7 June Price and Walsingham made an attempt on the summit without supplemental oxygen. Traversing the north face of the mountain, Price was pushed back by snowblindness, but Walsingham insisted on continuing towards the summit alone.

The circumstances of Walsingham's death remain unknown. The onset of a storm in the late afternoon suggests he may have died from exposure, or he may have fallen down Everest's north face, a drop of thousands of feet.

Walsingham was commemorated in a cairn erected near the expedition's Rongbuk Valley base camp, and a memorial was installed in 1926 in the chapel of Magdalene College.

I flip to the front of the encyclopedia and check the publication date: 1951. Then I take a pencil from the reference desk and copy the information into my notebook. Walsingham's name gives no results in the electronic catalogue, so I call up a half-dozen books relating to the 1924 expedition. This is only the beginning; I spend all day in these sunless rooms. In the morning I read of the Everest expedition in the South Asian room, under portraits of turbaned Mughal emperors, resplendent with their swords and jewels. By noon I'm in the microfilm room, paging through newspaper indices for references to Walsingham and Soames-Andersson. There are many newspaper articles from 1924 on the expedition and Ashley's death, but they all parrot the same information with no mention of his private life. In the afternoon I'm in the manuscript room, begging a librarian to let me see the letters of the artist Eleanor Grafton, née Soames-Andersson.

—It's a special allocation, he says. You'd need a letter from your university and then you would have to receive approval from the library.

—But I'm not affiliated with a university.

—Then you've no chance.

I plead further with the librarian, explaining that I'm related to the author of these letters. The clerk listens impassively.

—Even if I wanted to, he says, I couldn't give you the letters. There are procedures here.

I return to my seat and stare at the desk in frustration, twirling the pencil in my hand. The pencil is dark purple and engraved in white capitals: THE WORLD'S KNOWLEDGE. Piled before me are five books on the expedition, two books on the war, and a photocopy of the only relevant clipping I'd found in two hours of microfilm research. It is from *The Times* of London, dated October 13, 1924.

EVEREST CLIMBER'S ESTATE IN LIMBO
HEIR TO SHIPPING FORTUNE MISSING

The Times has learned that part of the estate of Mr. Ashley Walsingham, who died on Mount Everest in June, has been placed in trust after a failure to locate the principal beneficiary.

Mr. Walsingham was heir to the estate of his great-uncle George H. Risley, the famed shipping magnate who made his fortune as founder and managing director of Moor Line Ltd. The value of Mr. Walsingham's estate is unknown, but sources in the City say that Mr. Risley's estate must have been 'considerable.'

The missing beneficiary's name has not been revealed. The law firm handling the case, Messrs. Twyning & Hooper, has declined to comment on the matter.

Mr. Walsingham perished on Mount Everest in an attempt on the mountain's summit. The King paid tribute to the explorer, saying 'he will ever be remembered as a fine example of a mountaineer – ready to risk his life for his companions and to face dangers on behalf of science and discovery.'

The small display on my desk illuminates. A message glows in green letters: PLEASE CONTACT ISSUE DESK.

I show my reader's card at the issue desk and a woman hands me a green cardboard box labeled *Grafton, Eleanor S.A.: Personal Correspondence 1915–1931*. On the way back to my desk I pass by the reference counter, but the librarian I spoke to is gone.

The box holds seven envelopes, all addressed to Eleanor's husband Charles, who seems to have been stationed with the army in Palestine from late 1916 onward. The letters discuss Eleanor's art career and various financial matters, with frequent references to specific individuals, but I can make little sense of these. Many people are referred to only by a surname or first initial, and the difficulty is aggravated by the unfamiliar handwriting.

I study the letters, learning that Eleanor went to Sweden in late 1916 and my grandmother Charlotte was born there. I read on. On the second page of a letter from December 1916, something catches my attention and I read it again until I feel sure of its meaning. I copy the passage into my notebook.

> *It seems certain now that we shall need to send at least*
> *an additional 2,000 kronor to refit the Ejen house in haste.*
> *Apparently Mrs. Hasslo consulted several joiners & workmen,*
> *and as the house was never intended as a winter residence, and*
> *the season is bitterly cold there, it will require substantial refitting.*
> *At a minimum this includes a new WC and stove upstairs, new*
> *double-glazed windows, new doors to the outside, the addition of*
> *insulating materials to the attic, &c. The remoteness of the location*
> *also accounts for this sum, as the workmen shall have to stay on the*
> *island until the labour is complete, and this incurs a surcharge.*
>
> *The winter stores & building materials have already arrived*
> *on site; with luck much will be done before we arrive. Mrs. Hasslo*
> *confirms the doctor in Leksand is highly regarded. As for the*
> *nurse, I believe even if we don't engage one from England we shall*
> *have to bring one up from Stockholm or a similar distance to get*
> *someone worthwhile. All things considered, I think we should*

*feel more comfortable with an English nurse – the sensible thing
is to hire someone soon & have her arrive by the end of January.
If we begin advertising now in London, I imagine we can secure
someone both experienced and capable, and hope she is willing to
travel.*

*It's been agreed we shall pay nothing for the refitting, nor shall
the winter's expenses be split – Papa insists on paying it all. We
may, however, find it best to pay now & be reimbursed later to
ensure the work is completed on time.*

I take a large atlas of Sweden from the reference shelf and flip to the
overview map. Running my finger along the towns and villages I find
Leksand, 150 miles northwest of Stockholm.

I turn to a detail map farther back in the atlas. A few miles from
Leksand I recognize the name Ejen, printed in italics over a mass of pale
blue water. Ejen is a lake. A small island is pictured in the center of the
lake, but the island isn't named. I make a photocopy of the map.

I call Prichard from a phone booth outside the library. His secretary tells
me he isn't available and I'm transferred to Khan, but when I describe
the letter to Khan he tells me to hold. A few minutes later Prichard's
voice greets me cordially. I read the letter to him from my notebook.

—I'm afraid, Prichard replies, that I'm not sure what you're getting at.

—Eleanor says 'before we arrive,' even though Charles wasn't going
with her to Sweden. He was in Palestine all of 1917. And she says
her father was going to for pay for everything, the expenses wouldn't
be split.

—I don't see—

—Imogen must have gone with her. That's the only thing that would
explain it all. Why go up north to winter in a remote house that'd never
been used in winter?

—One moment, please.

I hear another voice speaking in the background. Prichard responds, muffling the receiver. The other voice disappears.

—My apologies, he says. As regards the letter, there could be other explanations. Someone else might have accompanied her.

—But it makes sense. Eleanor would tell everyone she was pregnant. That'd be expected, she'd been married for years. Then Eleanor would go to Sweden with Imogen, and after Imogen's child was born, Eleanor could raise it as her own. Isn't that what women did then, if they got pregnant before marriage? They went away and came back without the child—

—I suppose some of them did. But why go to all that trouble if Imogen wasn't coming back to England?

—I don't know. I haven't figured that out yet.

—Did you read all that was there?

—Yeah. There were seven letters, and one of them was the one you showed me in your office. This was the only thing I found.

—Then by all means, keep looking. Your letter is certainly interesting, but you'll need something more definitive. Unfortunately, I've a client meeting shortly. I shall let you research onward with my blessing. Do stay in touch.

I hang up the phone and walk onto the road in the rain, still holding the notebook.

19 August 1916

Queen's Hall

Marylebone, Central London

The concert concluded, the musicians fit their instruments in velvet-lined cases. The audience stands. Some chat idly in the aisles; others file out toward the exit. The murmur of conversation grows steadily.

Ashley sits in the last row studying a Great Western Railway time-table. He has already seen Imogen. He is waiting for her to notice him on her way out. Ashley takes a fountain pen from his pocket and circles the 9:38 from Paddington to Didcot.

Imogen takes the seat beside him. Her eyes fixed on the stage, she leans toward him and whispers.

—So it is you.

Ashley puts the timetable back in his tunic pocket.

—One might imagine, he says, that you were following me.

—Did you enjoy the concert?

—Immensely.

—Then why sit at the back?

—I came in late.

—And why were you late?

Ashley smiles. He looks away down the aisle.

—I was outside, he admits. Wondering if I ought to come in.

—I'm glad you did.

An elderly woman with a cane tries to squeeze by them in the aisle. They rise to let her pass. Standing now, they do not sit back down.

—I cross on Thursday, Ashley stammers. I mean that—it's a splendid day. What do you think of a stroll?

Imogen agrees. Ashley says they could go to Green Park or even Hyde Park, but Regent's Park is closest.

—We'd as well go to Regent's Park anyhow, Imogen says. It's the loveliest, and there are French gardens, if we tire of the English. Though you are going to France. Then again—

Imogen lets the sentence hang. She bites her lip and gazes toward the exit. Ashley watches her expectantly.

—Pardon?

She shakes her head.

—I didn't want to say it. I suppose you shan't see gardens there.

They are in Regent's Park, walking among the ordered fountains and linear hedges, the afternoon sunlight golden on their faces. Ashley looks at the empty stone planters and frowns.

—Not quite the same without the flowers.

—But one remembers what they looked like.

Imogen walks forward and touches a planter.

—Here were the crocuses. The oddest name for the loveliest flower. The purple hyacinths were here, surely. And the daffodils there, and behind them the geraniums and dahlias—

Ashley walks beside her, swagger cane clasped behind his back. A group of wounded soldiers in blue hospital uniforms walk by, followed by a pair of nurses. Ashley talks about his officer training and Imogen mentions that she is studying for the entrance examinations for Somerville College.

—You've my sympathy, Ashley remarks. I had an awful dread of my Cambridge little-go, made it that much easier to run off to the army. Are the Somerville exams difficult?

—Not exactly. But I'll be taking the scholarship papers, so I'll need a decent score. Of course, it's easier because I've studied for them before.

—You have?

Imogen nods. —It's a rather embarrassing tale. But you have to understand, Mr. Walsingham, there was so much confusion. No one would have raised an eyebrow if I wanted to study art or music like Mummy or Ellie. But I wanted to know things, to be a part of life and not simply imitate it. So I got it in my head that I must go to Somerville. There were endless rows with Papa, but in the end I went up for the Easter exams anyway. Naturally I hadn't studied nearly enough. I could manage the English or Greek, but my Latin was weak, and maths was pure misery.

Imogen glances at Ashley, knitting her brow.

—You see, it just felt so wrong. Sneaking out to Oxford on my own when Mummy had practically bent over backwards to put Ellie in the Slade. And when I got there it was nothing like I'd imagined, the colleges practically empty save for cadets. The exam was four days, staying in the most frigid rooms at Oriel, for you know they've made Somerville a hospital. By the third morning it just seemed absurd, with the war on and rebellion in Ireland, that there I was quivering in bed at the thought of algebra—

—You didn't finish them?

Imogen sighs, shaking her head. —But I'm going to take them again. I've had a few months to knock about London and think things over. That's quite enough. Sooner or later one realizes it isn't enough to be clever, to have even the finest ideas. One must do something, one must create some corner of goodness in the world, however small. For a few weeks I was convinced I should be a midwife with the Quaker relief in France, but as soon as I told Papa he said perhaps I ought to go to Somerville after all.

Ashley laughs. Imogen smiles, shaking her head in mock indignation.

—He was quite right, she protests. No doubt it's easier on the nerves than war nursing, but I can hardly stand to see someone with a bloody nose. I only wanted to do something useful. The trouble is that I'm simply not trained for anything. So I'll have to learn more first.

—Starting with algebra?

Imogen wrinkles her nose.

—Good Lord, let's not speak of it. If I suddenly dash behind a tree, it's because I've seen my tutor, Mr. Blagdon. He thinks I'm in bed with fever.

They walk out of the gardens onto broad green lawns. Ashley looks at Imogen.

—I've the impression your people are different from mine. Certainly your sister seems an interesting woman.

Imogen shrugs. —I don't know. Ellie and Charles do go around with a certain set that share certain ideas. But their marriage is rather ordinary. My parents are the same. Papa's very conventional, it's only that he married a woman nothing like him.

—You say he's a Swede. But you were born here?

Imogen shakes her head. —Ellie and I were born in France. At the time, Papa was posted to the embassy in Paris, that's where he met Mummy. Apparently it was quite a romance, though you'd never guess it to see them now. Papa was young and very dashing. Mummy was studying sculpture at the Académie Julian.

They pass into the shade of a huge willow and Imogen sits down beside its trunk. Ashley hesitates, then takes a seat beside her, not very close. He grabs a fistful of grass and tosses it into the air idly. He looks at her.

—I'm confused, Ashley admits. So are you English or not?

—That's the question, isn't it? I spent my first years in France. We moved to Berlin when I was five, and we only came here when I was nine. After that Mummy refused to leave England again. When it comes to languages, my French is good, mainly because I've kept it up by reading. My German is decent, but my Swedish is rather disappointing, and Ellie isn't much better. I can speak Swedish if I have to, but I can't write it to save my life. With English—

—You haven't a foreign accent, Ashley interrupts. But you don't speak the same as an Englishwoman. It's something in your phrase.

Imogen nods. —I've heard that before. Of course, on paper I'm Swedish. But I hardly know the country. I've scarcely seen Stockholm. And if I had to pick a city, I'd take Paris over London in a heartbeat. Oddly enough, I'm quite attached to Berlin, because it reminds me of my childhood. I don't know what all this adds up to. I'm not French, I'm not a proper Swede at all, and I'm certainly no German.

—Then you're English.

She smiles. —If it pleases you.

They talk in French awhile and Imogen tells Ashley that his accent is good. Playfully they exchange a few phrases in Greek, a few whispered rhymes in German.

—Not so loud, Ashley warns. They'll think you're a spy. Come to think of it—

Imogen winks at him. —Spies are everywhere. But I spy only for myself.

Ashley leads Imogen along the park's narrow lake, drained for the war, and they pass the new postal hutments where the mail from France is sorted. They sit on a bench before a large field.

—Would you mind terribly, Imogen says, if I asked you why you joined the army?

—For the uniform. I thought I'd cut a fine figure. And I got tired of getting white feathers every time I rode the tram.

—You don't like to be serious.

—Not always.

—Try to be. I want to know.

Ashley looks at her quizzically. —You may have heard this, but the country's at war. There was hardly a fellow in my college that didn't join.

—Do you always do what the other fellows are doing?

—No.

—I didn't think so. Mr. Walsingham, I'm not trying to be difficult. I may have certain ideas about the war or the army, but I'm the first to admit they could be entirely wrong. One can't listen only to people like Mr. Russell any more than one can read the *Morning Post*. So I want to know why you really—

—I was bored at Cambridge, Ashley says abruptly. I supposed there had to be more to life than endless Latin. And I was fool enough to worry I'd miss something if I kept out of the war.

—But you told Ellie you wish to do your duty.

—And I meant it. After all, one can't live only for oneself. I've tried that, and it isn't any good.

—Is going to war your idea of living for others?

—It could be.

—And killing people?

Ashley hesitates. Imogen shakes her head, touching his sleeve.

—I'm sorry, I don't mean to put you in the dock. We scarcely know each other and already I feel I'm fouling everything up—

—It's a fair question, Ashley says. I suppose the answer is that we ought to kill only in order to save others.

—It seems a poor trade, killing one person to save another. How would you know you were really saving anyone?

—I suppose one never knows.

Imogen looks at Ashley, narrowing her eyes.

—You'll forgive me, but you don't seem particularly bellicose for a solider. I always imagined soldiers being so certain about everything.

—No thinking man can be certain about anything. Least of all anything complicated. And the war is damned complicated.

—And climbing?

Ashley smiles. —No. That's simple.

They fall silent. Ashley squints at the orange-red sun dipping into the water. Imogen looks at her hands.

—They say it's very bad in France.

—I know.

—Do you think it's as bad as they say?

—It must be worse.

—You know, Ashley. You don't have to go—

—Of course I do.

She shakes her head and puts her hand over Ashley's. Her palm is cool and the softness of her hand thrills him.

—You can do anything you like. That's all I've been trying to say. I simply can't see why anyone who loves to climb mountains ought to go to the war. Many of the Germans are great climbers, aren't they?

—Naturally.

—And they've parks like this one in Berlin, and in one of those parks there must be two people like us, talking like this right now, and one of them is going. Don't tell me it isn't true, because it is. And what difference in the world would it make if you stayed and he stayed, and none of us had to say good-bye?

—It's a lovely thought. But I don't believe it could ever happen—

—Things happen, Imogen counters, because people believe in them. One can't worry what the rest of the world does or thinks. All that matters is that you're here and I'm here, and we can do anything we like.

Ashley nods. Across the field the sun has vanished and the sky is turning purple. Imogen takes her hand back, remarking that it is nearly seven and she is meant to be in Mayfair for dinner. Ashley grins.

—I believe you won't make it to dinner.

Imogen turns her face away, trying to hide her smile.

—No, she says. I don't think I will.

SIGNS AND WONDERS

⤝═◉ ◉═⤞

After three days in London I still can't sleep straight through the night. All day I feel dead tired and all night I lie awake in my hotel room, my eyes open to the darkness, listening to the hum of the air conditioner. The English climber leaving a fortune to a woman he knew for one week. The summer house near Leksand refitted in the winter of 1916. And the single connecting piece, my grandmother, a woman I saw maybe three times in my life and only when I was very young.

Images linger on the edge of my memory. A visit to the seaside—it must have been California, but it doesn't feel like California. The old woman's slow walk, her thick ankles sinking into the sand with each step, my mother holding her arm. The wind tossing our hair. My grandmother's scent of musky perfume, her strange accent and stranger manner of speech. Some ancient sticky candies she put in my hand. A peculiar piece of advice she had given, now long forgotten; an embarrassment I'd suffered but never really understood.

The clock flashes 3:13 a.m. I throw back the sheets and get dressed. The doorman downstairs winks at me as he pulls open the door. He saw me around the same time last night.

—Still jet-lagged, sir?

The doorman wears a frock coat and necktie. A top hat is perched over his gray hair.

—I've got it pretty bad.

—Best to go for a walk, get yourself nice and tired.

I walk up Albemarle Street, zigzagging my way up to Marble Arch. On the way back I sit on a bench at the edge of Grosvenor Square and take my notebook from my jacket pocket. In large caps I write down two columns of research, ASHLEY and IMOGEN. Under these I make a list of subjects: *Great War. Everest Expedition. London. Sweden.* I draw arrows and connect the subjects to libraries. *Alpine Club. War Archive. Recheck British Library. Newspapers.* Most of these subjects lead to Ashley. I circle Imogen's name twice and connect it to *Charlotte.* Then I add *Eleanor.*

I put the notebook in my pocket and walk back to the hotel. Hopefully I can get some sleep now.

I start with Ashley in the morning. In the dim basement of the Alpine Club in Shoreditch the archivist lets me hold Hugh Price's ice axe, brought back from Everest in 1924. It is heavier than it looks. A well-balanced tool of wood and steel, its handle bears the double notches that Price carved to mark it as his own. I lift the axe to the light of the barred window. The steel head is engraved with the manufacturer's name: CHR SCHENK, GRINDELWALD.

—What about Walsingham's axe?

The archivist shrugs. —They never found it.

But this is only the beginning. I spend four straight days in archives from morning until closing time, allowing myself an hour break for lunch. I visit the reading rooms of the Imperial War Museum in Southwark; I page through the typewritten catalogs of the Royal Geographical Society on Kensington Gore, filing requests to see every surviving scrap of paper from the 1924 expedition. The librarian warns me that some documents might take days or weeks to be brought up from storage facilities, but I request them anyway. In hushed chambers I study yellowed letters and battered diaries, collecting stacks of memoirs as I flip through accounts of wars and climbs and expeditions. I learn of trenches and parapets and fire steps, of couloirs and moraines, of cwms and bergschrunds.

On Saturday I ride the Northern Line to the British Library's newspaper collection at Colindale. All morning I flip through tall red-bound volumes of musty newsprint, reviewing the press coverage of the expedition to make sure I haven't missed anything. Then I wheel through the endless microfilm collection, scanning carefully through June 1924. The same material appears again and again: headlines about the expedition's failure; vague accounts of Ashley's death; grainy reproductions of a snapshot taken at Everest base camp; the impersonal eulogy from the king. Only one article interests me, a small column of print that appeared seven weeks after Ashley's death.

EVEREST VICTIM

STORY OF A GRAND LAMA'S WARNING
(FROM OUR OWN CORRESPONDENT)
KALIMPONG, N. BENGAL

The death of Mr. Walsingham during his attempt to reach the summit of Mount Everest is stated here to have been foretold by the Abbot of Rongbuk, a High Lama with the physical deformity of immensely large ears, and who is regarded throughout the country as possessing second sight.

It is stated that he warned the porters when they left Rongbuk, near the expedition's base camp, that should they again attempt the ascent of Mount Everest disaster would follow.

He stated that the Spirit of the Mountain had up to that time been merciful, but should his solitude be again disturbed he would surely wreak his vengeance on the disturbers of his eternal peace.

Whether this statement had any effect on the morale of the coolies is not known, but it is a fact that after this warning cases occurred of porters making excuses to avoid going higher on the mountain.

I try to find more about the abbot of Rongbuk, but he doesn't appear in any other articles. So the next day I visit the British Film Institute on the South Bank to watch the official cinematic record of the Mount Everest expedition, directed by a man named J. B. L. Noel. I sit in front of a screen and pull headphones over my ears. The film begins with an unsteady placard, white letters flickering on the scratched black negative.

A story of adventurous explorers in a far-off land and their endeavour to reach the top of the world.

The clouds part to reveal a boundless range of mountains, the great peak hovering above them all. Then a telephoto image of the pyramidal summit, vignetted like a view through a telescope, the plume of wind and snow streaming past.

The film is silent, so I remove my headset. The second placard appears.

There is nowhere here any trace of life or man. It is a glimpse into a world that knows him not. Grand, solemn, unutterably lonely, the Rongbuk Glacier of Mount Everest reveals itself.

Pinnacles of ice appear, then the knife ridges of the mountain, the vapor pouring over windswept cornices from Nepal into Tibet. Tibetan villagers in soiled robes gawk at the camera from rough door frames. Sherpa porters walk past, freshly clad in windproof smocks and snow goggles. Finally the British, always shown from a distance: trekking in dense Sikkim jungles in short pants, swinging walking sticks; hiking in pairs on the bleak windswept Tibetan plain, among trains of laden yaks. Two climbers sit in the sun under pith helmets, their sketchbooks on their laps, squinting out portraits of villagers. A group of men take breakfast seated upon crates in the open air, behind them a dozen monks spinning prayer wheels in the wind. No one looks at the monks.

Into the heart of the pure blue ice, rare, cold, beautiful, lonely – into a fairyland of ice.

The glacier is pictured: a ponderous river of ice sailing down the mountainside. The party walks into a valley of ice, winding through a maze of frozen pinnacles, dwarfed by them, craning their necks to spy the summits. The British run mittened hands along crystal blue seracs, questioning their age or composition or provenance, or things even more unknowable. A climber snaps a huge icicle off a pinnacle and appropriates it for a walking stick, leaning on the glassy spire for uncertain support.

I search each frame for Ashley, but none of the figures is shown close up, so I click a button to fast-forward the footage.

Above the great mountain frowns upon us, angered that we should violate these pure sanctuaries that had never before suffered the foot of man.

The porters heft incredible loads on their backs; they scramble up rope ladders and pace over icy slopes. Ascending steep faces of slabbed limestone, the British bend gasping over their ice axes, straining to breathe in the rarified air. I fast-forward again. The image of the peak returns, the streamer blowing past, the clouds closing in.

Now could it be possible that something more than the physical had opposed us in this battle where human strength and western knowledge had broken and failed? Could it be possible we fought something beyond our knowledge?

The screen fades to black. I rewind the film, scanning backward and then forward. Suddenly I see the climbers and I hit the play button.

Eight men stand before the mess tent, sunburned faces with weathered half-beards, their mouths moving, their voices lost. The colonel stands at the center looking bemusedly at the camera. He is taller than the others but of equally lean build, his ice goggles perched over his hat brim. Beside him a handsome bareheaded man talks, hands stuffed in jacket pockets, leaning back to the colonel and laughing. This is Hugh

Price, the celebrated mountaineer. Behind Price a slim figure stands holding a pipe, someone's arm draped over him. I recognize the face from the newspapers. It is Ashley.

I set the machine to loop the ten seconds of footage. I lean up to the screen.

Ashley wears a tweed jacket with voluminous pockets, a long scarf wound around his neck. He is clean-shaven and looks younger than the other men, still boyish though his skin seems weathered from the Tibetan sun. His hand cradles the briar pipe, but he does not smoke it. He smiles faintly and looks away. He coughs. When Price speaks, Ashley's cough turns to laughter. For a half-second Ashley's eyes look into the camera and meet my own. The film loops again.

I eat dinner at an Indian restaurant on Drummond Street, thinking about Ashley the whole time. There was something in the film I didn't expect, something that seemed slightly off. I pay the bill and start back for the hotel, stopping in Euston Station to buy sleeping pills from a drugstore. As I walk out of the station I realize what had bothered me. For days I've been reading grueling accounts of the expedition—the altitude sickness, the weeks of terrifying blizzards, the climbers practically broken by the time they set up the higher camps. But in the film Ashley didn't look crazy or desperate. He looked happy. He stood in front of a camera with his friends and had no idea he'd be dead in a month.

—Or maybe he did know, I whisper.

The next morning I start with Imogen, running Web searches at an Internet café on Oxford Street. For hours I try her name in digital catalogs and genealogy websites. I find nothing. At the website of the Swedish National Archives I learn that most of their vital records haven't been digitized yet. For hundreds of years these records were the responsibility of the local parish clergyman, who recorded not only births and deaths but christenings, communion attendance and migrations into and out of the parish. They even kept a kind of census recording the inhabitants of a household, their ages and occupations. The Leksand church archive is held in Uppsala, an ecclesiastical and university town about fifty miles north of Stockholm. But even if I went to Sweden, there's no guarantee I'd find anything.

In the afternoon I visit the Tower of London, hoping that a break will help me think. The Tower is rainy and crowded with foreign tourists. I visit the armory and study the glimmering crown jewels: scepters and orbs and crowns on beds of blue French velvet, safeguarded behind thick glass, shimmering under the cross-rays of countless halogen bulbs. Standing beside a tour group, I hear an elderly American ask his guide what they are worth.

—They're priceless, of course, the guide answers.

—Someone, the American protests, must have some idea of the value.

The guide shakes his head. —They'll never be sold. They aren't insured, because no one will underwrite them. They can't be stolen.

The American ponders this.

—In that case, he concludes, they're worth nothing at all.

Night falls as I exit onto the riverbank beside Tower Bridge. Shapes swirl in the midnight water running between the stone piers of the bridge.

—*A glimpse into a world*, I whisper, *that knows him not.*

I think about Imogen on the walk home. If it's too hard to research her directly, the only way to find her is the way the lawyers did— through her sister. Because Eleanor was a painter, there's a better chance that her letters and documents survive, some of which could mention Imogen. I make a list of art libraries and archives in London. The National Art Library in the Victoria and Albert Museum seems to have the most extensive collection.

By 9:40 the next morning I'm standing on the museum's steps on Exhibition Road. I snap photos of the cratered facade, pockmarked by shrapnel during the Blitz. A security guard opens the door and directs me to the library on the third floor, where I get a reader's ticket and order my first round of books, mostly surveys of British modern art. Eleanor is mentioned only a few times in passing, but I follow the footnotes to painter's biographies and monographs on more specialized subjects: the Camden Town Group, the Omega Workshops. I call up all these books, but again Eleanor is mentioned only as an acquaintance of the painters Charles Ginner or Mark Gertler, a participant in group exhibitions at the Adelphi Gallery or Devereux Brothers. Twice she is referenced as the daughter of the sculptor and medallist Vivian Soames. There is no mention of Eleanor after the late 1920s, which makes me wonder if she stopped painting entirely.

I return to the reference computers to see if the library holds any of the catalogs from Eleanor's exhibitions. Several from the Adelphi Gallery are listed, but they all date from before 1925 and Eleanor's exhibition there was in 1927. "Devereux Brothers" gives no results at all, but in the appendix of one of my books it says that the 1929 "Sunday Club Exhibition" took place at their gallery with two of Eleanor's paintings: *Four March Hares* and *Odessa*. I show the entry to a librarian.

—Have you ever heard of the Devereux Brothers Gallery?

She squints at the name and frowns.

—Sounds familiar. I can look it up.

The librarian types into her computer.

—We haven't got anything on them here. But let's see. The Tate Archive has some material. Devereux Brothers Gallery, 158 New Bond Street. Two boxes, 1919 to 1936. Exhibition catalogs, personal letters, balance sheet, profit-and-loss accounts—

—What time do they close?

—At five, but normally you'd need an appointment. Let me try calling them.

The librarian persuades the archive to give me a three o'clock appointment. I ride the Underground to Pimlico and sprint along the river on Millbank to the museum, sweating in the sunlight. The clerk at the archive has the first box waiting for me: thick black ledgers of sales and accounting records, an assortment of thin exhibition catalogs bound in colored paper, shipping bills and lists. Although the gallery is called Devereux Brothers, the correspondence is all addressed to one man named

Roger Devereux. Most of the papers date from the 1920s. The inventory lists have occasional entries for Eleanor's paintings: *Night Scene (Black Dominion), Four March Hares, Kronborg Slot.*

I bring the box back to the enquiry desk and am given the second one. The label on the side says *Devereux, Roger: Correspondence 1911– 1927.* Inside are dozens of letters still in their envelopes, all slit neatly at the top. Most of the letters are in the same small, tight longhand, addressed to Devereux by a man named Coutts who seems to have managed the daily business of the gallery. The frequency of his letters to Devereux's address in Surrey suggests Devereux stayed away from London for weeks at a time.

I skim the pages, keeping an eye on the clock behind me. Eleanor's paintings are mentioned briefly in a letter about potential exhibitions in July 1919, and again in March 1921 among a list of sold works. Then I find a more puzzling note.

23 Mar 19

Dear Mr. Devereux,

I received your letter of the 19th inst. and have disposed of the study as directed. M. Broginart was terribly disappointed and offered to double his price for the canvas, until at last he was made to understand the situation. He enquired about the larger picture and is keen enough to buy the painting sight unseen, though he would not tender a figure and I expressed my grave doubts. Has Mrs. Grafton advised whether that painting shall ever be put out?

The other works in the shipment were the two portraits (The Housemistress, Dr. Lindberg) and Kronborg Slot. I received the inventory slips and prices for these works, so please confirm they are suitable for display and sale.

Yrs Faithfully,
Wm. Coutts

I read the letter three times. Then I take it to the desk and ask the archivist to make a photocopy. I hand him the box of letters.

—Could I have the first box again?

I go back to my table and take out the inventory ledger, flipping to the pages for 1919. It lists receipt of three "Grafton" paintings on March 14: *Kronborg Slot*, *Dr. Lindberg*, and *Nude Study*. The last one is crossed out. I turn the page and there are two more of Eleanor's paintings entered in July 1919: *Four March Hares* and *The Unvanquished*.

I lean back into my chair, looking up at the ceiling and trying to keep myself from smiling. I know I should stop, because I can't be sure about anything. But I keep smiling anyway. I look through the rest of the box, but it's hard to concentrate now and soon the archive begins to switch off its lights.

A warm rain is falling outside. I start off toward Victoria, stopping to call Prichard from a pay phone. His secretary tells me he's in a meeting, but when I get back to my hotel room the red light on my phone is blinking. I pick it up.

—Good evening, I'm calling from Twyning and Hooper. Is this Mr. Tristan Campbell?

—Yes.

—Please hold for James Prichard.

Sitting on the bed, I take my notebook and the photocopies from my bag. The red digits of the alarm clock read 6:17. Prichard must be working late.

—The prodigious Mr. Campbell. Don't tell me you've another theory.

I read Prichard the letter from Coutts and describe the ledger entries. It is a moment before he speaks.

—Is this all you've found so far?

—Yeah, but it's important. Don't you see—

—Yes, yes. Prichard sighs. You believe the picture was of Imogen.

—Exactly.

—Which is why it was destroyed.

—Right.

—And why would that be necessary?

—Because it showed her nude. Because she was pregnant. Or because it showed her in Sweden at all, right before Charlotte was born—

—Pure conjecture, Prichard counters. Very likely Eleanor wished it destroyed because it was only a preliminary study. It sounds as though it was shipped to London by accident. Perhaps she simply didn't like the picture.

—But someone wanted it. Why destroy a painting that already has a buyer?

—I can imagine any number of reasons. You don't know the subject of the destroyed painting. You're connecting it to this *Nude Study* by circumstantial evidence. What you really have is a theory, the two sisters in Sweden. You're looking for proof of that theory and so you find it, but the theory may be skewing your research, not to mention your conclusions. For instance, you say the letter is from 1919. But when was Charlotte born?

—In 1917, but I doubt there was much of an art market then. It makes sense that Eleanor wouldn't have tried to ship the paintings or sell them until after the war. Especially since they were up in Sweden.

—Possibly. But again, it's far too much conjecture. What you need are facts.

—I have plenty of facts—

I flip through my notebook, speaking quickly.

—I know they refitted the Swedish house in the winter of 1916, so that Eleanor could winter in a house that'd never been used in winter. I know Charlotte was born there. I know Eleanor painted something there that was shipped to London in February 1919, a few months after the war ended, and whatever was in the picture bothered her so much that it had to be destroyed at the gallery instead of being stored or sent back. I know there's a picture in the gallery ledger called *Nude Study* received in February 1919—

—It's all quite fascinating. But it's hardly evidence.

—It could lead me to evidence.

—To what?

—Birth records, for one thing. In Sweden they were all kept by the local parish, I've been reading about them. There ought to be an entry for Charlotte listing the names of her parents. It might say something different from the English records. The parish also kept annual registers of each household, and if the Leksand house is there, it'd say who was living there at the time. Imogen could be there. Has anyone looked at the Swedish records?

—There've been vital records searches at least three times, Prichard says. They were done internally by our staff. I don't know where they looked, but I'm told it was exhaustive. Of course, I know nothing of these parish registers. Do you intend to go to Sweden?

—It's a short flight over there. And it's the best lead I have.

Prichard sighs. —I won't dispute that. If you must go, I'd suggest sooner rather than later. You'll want to know as soon as you can if you're on track. And Mr. Campbell?

—Yeah.

—You're not looking for a painting. You're looking for evidence.

I hang up and walk downstairs. The concierge is still on duty and I ask if he can find me a cheap flight to Stockholm. He types into his computer.

—Tomorrow seems fairly booked, but the next day there's a Ryanair flight that's seventy pounds.

He grimaces. —But it leaves at six a.m. And Stansted's so far, you'd practically have to sleep in the airport—

—Can you do that?

The concierge looks up at me, hesitating.

—Some do. But I certainly wouldn't recommend it.

I show the concierge my credit card and walk away with a printout of my itinerary. Then I go into the business center and send an e-mail to the regional archive in Uppsala. I tell them I'm coming to their reading room on Thursday and I'd like to request materials in advance:

Leksand's birth records from 1906 to 1920 and two parish registers, 1910–1916 and 1917–1931.

I spend my last morning in London buying research books on Charing Cross Road: a fraying cloth-bound mountaineering history of Everest, a small paperback from the seventies titled *Daily Life in the Trenches, 1914–1918* and an enormous copy of *The Reckoning of Fortune: War on the Western Front.* Then I send e-mails to my father and stepbrother. I can't tell them about my research and I don't want to lie, so the messages end up short and vague. I send them anyway.

In the evening I go to the hotel to collect my bag. On my way out I try to give the doorman a five-pound note, but he won't accept the tip. We shake hands.

—Where are you off to?

—Sweden.

The doorman winks at me.

—Be careful, he says. Europe isn't like here. They've their own way of doing things.

It is past ten when I arrive at Stansted Airport. The last planes have departed and the next ones don't leave until morning. Sleeping travelers are strewn across the benches, their coats spread over them. On the terminal floor young backpackers doze on sheets of newspaper.

I brush my teeth in the public bathroom and fill my water bottle under the tap. On a sheltered spot beneath a check-in counter I spread my sleeping bag. I lie in the bag chewing squares of chocolate from the hotel. All night they continue security announcements every half hour.

19 August 1916

The Regent's Park

Marylebone, Central London

They walk out of the park onto Marylebone Road in the darkness. Most of the streetlamps are off for fear of air raids, a few with blue glass shades projecting murky light below. Beams of searchlights swarm across the sky, hunting zeppelins among the clouds and stars.

Ashley hails a motorcab and Imogen talks excitedly in the shadowed backseat, her mind arcing from one subject to another with giddy pleasure. She tells Ashley about a village in Brittany she wishes to live in; she describes an Autographic Kodak camera that her father gave her last month. She reads mainly in French and she likes the Symbolist poets best, Verlaine and De Gourmont and Corbière, but she has never seen anything so lovely in her life as Nijinsky onstage in *Le Sacre du Printemps*.

—They've interned him in Hungary now, can you believe it? A dancer in prison—

Imogen looks at Ashley. She smiles.

—You think I'm mad, don't you? But I don't mind.

The motorcab rounds the fountain at Piccadilly Circus, strange and gloomy with the lights darkened and the curtains drawn in all the windows, the rooftop billboards like huge blank slates. Ashley watches the silhouette of the Anteros statue at the center of the fountain, the nude archer loosing his arrow into the blackness. The taxi halts beside a maroon awning. Ashley pays the driver and holds the door open for Imogen, offering his hand. The girl regards him skeptically, then smiles and steps out, as if granting him this moment as an indulgence.

They are seated at a table in the café beside the mirrored wall, their bodies perching and sinking into gaudy stuffed chairs of scarlet velour. The fog of tobacco smoke is tremendous. A female waiter emerges from the haze to take their order, her paper collar soiled and yellowing, a starched napkin hung over the sleeve of her black jacket. She eyes them with weary indifference. Imogen orders a pair of brandies, winking at Ashley. He cranes his neck to look around the room.

—Rather jolly in its own way. Isn't it queer to see women waiters—

The waitress returns bearing two short-stemmed snifters on her tray. The brandy twirls in the glasses as she sets them on the tablecloth. Imogen leans across the table.

—I want you to tell me about your climbing. Once and for all.

—What do you want to know?

—Anything and everything. I've always been curious. We used to go to Switzerland when I was little, when we lived in Paris. I remember being terrified of the mountain guides. In the early morning they'd be waiting in front of the hotel for the guests. They'd never come in, they'd only stand outside smoking their pipes and talking in frightful dialect. I knew they lived high up, so I thought the mountains were a whole other country where ordinary people couldn't go, not without guides. And the places had such mysterious names. The Mer de Glace—it's near Mont Blanc, isn't it?

Ashley nods. —It's part of the same massif.

He lifts his napkin from the table, pulling off the silver ring and spreading the square of linen. He draws his fountain pen from his pocket and touches the nib twice on the linen to start the ink. This makes a pair of black dashes and from here Ashley begins to draw a crude map of the mountain range.

—This is the Mont Blanc massif, he says. Here's Mont Blanc itself, a little under sixteen thousand feet. Here's Chamonix Valley and the town. You probably stayed there. The whole range is less than twenty miles long. Perhaps ten across.

The pen's nib glides across the linen, Ashley pressing down to thicken the ridgeline where peaks connect.

—Here's Maudit, about fourteen thousand six hundred. Damned good climb up the southern face.

—You've climbed it?

Ashley nods. —Here's the Aiguille du Midi. So called because from Chamonix the sun hovers right above the needle of the peak at midday. Here's the Grandes Jorasses. Brilliant north face. Haven't climbed that. This is your Mer de Glace. Did you know it flows a hundred yards a year?

Imogen shakes her head. —Have you been on it?

—Once. It was very slick. We came down it at midnight without crampons. Rather unpleasant business.

—It must have been beautiful.

—I wasn't paying attention.

They order a second round from the waitress. Ashley takes another brandy, Imogen a crème de cassis.

—I'm surprised at you, she says. You speak as though you're only interested in the heights of the mountains, or their features. I imagined it was something different.

—Talking about it doesn't do any good. The best parts can't be explained.

—You might try. I'd like to understand.

Ashley frowns, capping his pen. He takes a silver case from his tunic pocket and lights a cigarette, setting the case on the table. Imogen takes a cigarette for herself and Ashley raises his eyebrows.

—You're going to smoke here?

She gives a coy nod in reply. Ashley lights her cigarette and stares down into the cut glass ashtray. He begins to speak, his words coming slowly and deliberately.

It is impossible to live without danger, Ashley explains. The danger is always there, the hazard of wasted lives, of decades bent over a desk, of squalid and lonely deaths in hospital beds. Fools turned their faces away from danger and pretended at immunity, but others went to the fountainhead of life.

—And what, Imogen wonders, is that?

Ashley taps his cigarette on the ashtray.

—I couldn't say. It's different for every man.

—Or woman. But what is it to you?

—There isn't a name for it, Ashley says. One could call it endeavor, or struggle, or give it a name, but then it only sounds silly. It's something one needs that isn't essential. Something one wants for no good reason at all. Not an animal desire. A desire that comes not from one's body, but from one's soul.

—But why do you want it?

—I can't explain it.

—You have been explaining it. Please go on.

Ashley looks at the tablecloth and shakes his head. He says that for one thing, lasting comfort becomes no comfort at all. All things in the world are perceptible only by contrast. For just as there is no heat without cold nor light without darkness, it is climbing that throws all of Ashley's life into sharp relief. It is climbing that makes one feel. It is the driving mountain cold that makes the fire in an alpine hut so delicious; it is the sore and cramped muscles that transform an ordinary hot bath into a sensory revelation; it is the hours of grueling ascent that make a supper of sardines and biscuits and jam so much better than a thousand dinners at the Criterion.

And it is impossible to live without hardship. The hardship of daily trifles, Ashley explains, ever accumulating and impossible to ignore, is so much meaner than pain or cold or fatigue. These annoyances make one weak and petty and shallow, just as greater struggles make one brave and wise.

—It's the little things that bring one down. Delayed trains and burnt puddings and drafty rooms. I was never so miserably cold on a mountain as I was in a drafty room. One can rise to dire occasions, but most of the time one worries about one's burnt pudding. It takes real struggle to see what life is. Then you realize you don't give two straws if your pudding's been burnt.

Imogen watches Ashley across the table. Her gaze is steady and unblinking, her hand turning the silver band around her wrist.

—Then you climb for what it does for your other life?

Ashley nods. —Sometimes. But not always.

For there is also the beauty. Ashley sweeps his cigarette across the room and says that to him all of human architecture is little but a screen, an elaborate facade of iron and glass erected to hide the majesties beyond. There is nothing in the untamed earth that is not beautiful. Of tamer beauties, Ashley swears that if one follows their streams up to the headwaters, the source of their fineness is very wild indeed. To walk the Mer de Glace at midnight is not only to be witness to the exquisite mystery of the natural world. It is to step away from the metropolis, from mankind's hall of mirrors, and to assume one's place among the wild.

—One doesn't see beautiful things in the mountains, Ashley says. One becomes them.

Imogen smiles. She draws a little from her cigarette.

—It was a wonderful speech. And I'm glad to have dug it out of you. But I wonder if it's another joke of yours. Do you really mean all this, or is it only what you think I wish to hear?

—You give me too much credit. I'm not so good a liar.

—I bet you're a very good liar, Imogen says. But I also think you're afraid to be serious, because somehow you are so very serious.

Ashley does not answer. He is looking at something beyond Imogen's shoulder. He closes his cigarette case and puts it back in his pocket, leaning across the table until he is very close to her.

—That couple across from us, he whispers. They've been watching us.

Imogen turns around discreetly. A few tables away, a man with a

Van Dyke beard is reclined deep into his chair. He wears a white dinner jacket and his bow tie hangs unknotted around his neck. The woman beside him is laughing, her hand draped over the man's lapel. The man's eyes meet Imogen's and he raises his glass in a salute. He rises and comes to their table, towing the woman in hand.

—I wonder, he addresses them, if you could settle a wager for my companion and me. We couldn't help but notice such a lovely pair of young people.

The man's voice is hoarse, his accent difficult to place.

—With pleasure, Ashley says.

The man fans his arm toward the giggling woman.

—My companion swears you are blood relations.

—Siblings, the woman adds, or at least first cousins. One can see it about the eyes.

The man shakes his head.

—But I say that you are lovers.

Ashley turns in awkward embarrassment, looking at Imogen, but she only laughs and takes a drink. Ashley puffs from his cigarette.

—You're both correct, he says. This is in fact my first cousin. And this very evening we've become engaged to be married.

The man raises his glass again in a salute. His drink is milky green and it swishes over the rim.

—I knew as much. I wish you joy.

The couple slinks back to their seats.

—What sort of people are these? Ashley wonders.

—Drunk people, Imogen says. I thought he was rather charming.

Imogen excuses herself to the powder room and Ashley lights another cigarette to pass the time. There is no band to watch here, nor any kind of entertainment. He glances back at the drunk couple. The woman is kissing the man's wrist and tugging at his bow tie. Ashley looks down at his wristwatch, flipping back the metal cover that protects the crystal. He had bought it yesterday and the salesman had said the hands were luminous, but in the half-lit room it is hard to tell.

Suddenly Imogen returns with a radiant smile, leaning toward him with her hands on her chair.

—I had a revelation in the washroom.

—Really?

—We'll go to the Alps. Switzerland, perhaps, because they're neutral. We'll hole up in a chalet in one of those steep valleys that hasn't any roads and is reachable only on foot. Surely there are such places?

Ashley feels a flush of warmth. He worries it will show on his face and he takes a drag of his cigarette.

—Certainly.

Imogen beams. —No one shall ever find us.

—That was the revelation?

—One of them.

—What was the other?

—I've lost my latchkey. I shan't be able to get inside my own house.

—Lost it?

Imogen pulls out her chair and sits down.

—Really, she remarks, it isn't so shocking as that. The wonder is that I didn't lose it sooner.

—Isn't anyone home?

She shakes her head. —That's the punch line. They all went down to Sussex today, even the housekeeper. She shan't return till morning.

They search among Imogen's possessions. Ashley scans the patterned carpet around the table, nearly bending to all fours. A few of the waitstaff assist in the search, circling the table without enthusiasm. They do not find the key.

—I might have lost it in the park, Imogen says.

Ashley laughs.

—You don't mean—we'd never find it there now.

—We might.

A GATHERING

⊷⟫ ⟪⊷

An airport security guard taps my shoulder to wake me. I sit up in my sleeping bag. It's 5:21 a.m. and the check-in line has snaked around my encampment.

I sleep through my whole flight and on the bus from Skavsta Airport into Stockholm central station. On the train to Uppsala I take out my printouts to review, but I spend the short ride looking out the window, wishing I could see more of Sweden.

The Uppsala Landsarkivet is in a tall brick building, a twenty-minute walk from the train station between the university's botanical gardens and hospital. The young woman at the reception looks up my appointment, addressing me in fluent English.

—Campbell, she says. Here it is. I'll bring the material into the reading room. Put your bag in the lockers and take anything you need in the clear carrier bags.

—Can I bring a camera?

—Yes, but please no flash.

A few minutes later the woman brings three volumes to my table along with a pair of cotton archival gloves. The books are all leather-bound, a few hundred pages per volume. The spines read *För-samlingsbok—LEKSANDS Församling.* I start with these registers, a kind of census recorded by the parish. The sisters would have been in Sweden during the winter of 1916–17, so I've ordered two volumes, 1910–1916 and 1917–1931. The sloped handwriting is sharp and fairly clear, but the books are still almost impossible to decipher. The names are entered in numbered horizontal rows, but there are eighteen vertical columns whose categories are all printed in tiny Swedish. In some cases a whole block of the names is crossed out and I can't figure out why. Finally I get the young woman to help me.

—What does this word *torp* mean?

—It's like a farm. The records are listed by area. So these people are all living in the same farm, you see? Here is the person's job, the birth date, the birth parish, the place they moved from—

The woman helps me for a few minutes, but another patron has a question and she moves on. I decide to ignore the columns. Unless I find the right family it makes no difference what they mean. I look through through the end of the 1910–1916 book and the beginning of the 1917 book. Nothing, unless the sisters' names and dates were entered completely wrong. There are several women with the name Charlotta or Eleanora— Gunborg Eleanora, Aldy Erika Charlotta, Anna Eleanora—but all these seem to be middle names, and in any case they are listed among households filled with completely unfamiliar names. There's no Imogen anywhere.

I go to the bathroom and splash water on my face, looking at myself in the mirror. It could still turn out all right. Maybe they weren't around when the parish was surveyed in 1917. Or maybe they just didn't show up to be counted. I go back into the reading room and start the other book, the ledger of birth records. *Födelse-och Dopbok för Leksands för-samling.* The entries run from 1906 to 1920. They're largely chronological and easier to follow than the parish registers. I scan down the names with my gloved finger.

April 20 Anders Johan. April 14 Tora Margareta. Maj 13 Lars Ove. Maj 17 Charlotte Vivian. Maj 30 Sven August.

I pull my finger back.

Maj 17 Charlotte Vivian. Fader: Charles Francis Grafton 87%/10 Moder: Eleanor Soames Andersson Grafton 91²¹/3

I turn away, shaking my head. But when I look back it's the same thing. I'd come nine hundred miles just to see this, the proof of how foolish I'd been. I take a photograph of the page and stare at it for a final moment. The entry has a few other columns with dashes or the number 1 in them, but I don't bother to figure out what they mean.

A few minutes later I walk out into the afternoon sun, heading back toward the train station. It was beyond stupid. I'd stacked guesses on top of guesses because I wanted to believe in them, because I wanted to believe I could find something other people couldn't. The answer was on that page.

Maybe it didn't matter how clever I was. Maybe there was nothing to find, because Eleanor was the mother, and even if she wasn't they'd all been careful enough not to leave a single piece of clear evidence behind, so that all the experts with all the time in the world wouldn't find anything. Much less an amateur with seven weeks. I walk quickly, overtaking people on the sidewalk as I pass the red facade of Uppsala castle, the tiered garden spilling down toward the city.

—But they'd never have put Imogen's name on anything to begin with, I whisper to myself. Even if she was the mother.

I was crazy to have believed otherwise. Prichard had warned me that the vital records had all been searched, but I'd ignored him and come here anyway. I'd been following one kind of evidence, indirect clues in letters, and I'd gone after another, the most obvious of all records. I was done with all that.

The spires of the town's cathedral project above the treetops ahead. I'm not in a hurry anymore, so I cut through a backstreet and enter the cathedral through the transept. It's dark and cool inside. Slowly I walk through the nave, craning my neck to look at the rib vault ceiling, the stained glass high overhead. I sit in a pew in front of a huge astronomical clock, carved of wood and painted in burgundy and royal blue. A sign explains the mechanism's function. The clock dates from 1424.

The timepiece has two dials. The upper dial displays the twenty-four Roman numerals of the hours, the orbits of the sun and moon swinging against the gilded letters. The perpetual calendar turns on the lower dial, running for a hundred years from 1923 to 2023, the religious holidays inscribed minutely in Latin, the twelve signs of the zodiac along the outer band. I watch the circling lion carved in gold relief; the sheep with spiraling horns; the pair of fish; the long-pincered crab. At the dial's center the figure of Saint Lawrence stands passive and eternal. The mechanism clicks on, reckoning away the centuries since its creation.

The clock strikes noon. The church's organ plays "In Dulce Jubilo." Between the dials, the carved figures of the magi and their servants parade around the seated virgin and child.

1916. Eighty-seven years since she walked into the Somme mist, taking all the answers with her. Six weeks until I lose the fortune. I leave and cross a bridge, walking across a town square and into the travel office of the train station. A young clerk waves me forward.

—Is there a train station in Leksand?

—Sorry?

I write *Leksand* on a piece of paper and push it across the counter. The clerk types in the info.

—If you make the next train, he says, you can get there at six fifty-three. Change at Borlänge.

The train takes me north through endless pine forests. At each stop the towns seem smaller and smaller. At Borlänge I go to a grocery near the station and buy a bag full of bread and cheese and fruit. I devour half the food on the next train, trying not to worry about where I'll sleep tonight.

When I get off at Leksand it's almost seven, but the sun is still bright near the horizon. Only one taxi is parked in front of the station. The driver is sleeping in his seat with the windows down, the radio blaring a talk program. I tap on the car door. The driver wakes and I pass him the map I photocopied in the British Library. Examining the sheet, he blinks wearily and says something in Swedish. I point to a spot circled on the page.

—Can you take me there?

The driver blinks again, speaking in English now.

—There's nothing there. It's a tiny island.

—Does a bridge go there?

He shakes his head. —Bridge to what? There's nothing there. What do you want to go there for?

—A vacation. Can you take me to the lake at least?

The driver shakes his head and mutters. He raises his seat back into position and starts the engine.

—Get in.

We drive for fifteen minutes through thick forests of spruce and birch, the radio still tuned to a call-in show. We turn onto a dirt road. Lakewater glitters in interstices between the slender birch trees. The road ends at the lake's muddy shoreline.

—This is it, the driver says. You want me to leave you here?

—Sure.

—It'll be dark soon. It won't be easy to get back.

—I know.

I pay the driver and lean my backpack against a tree. Across the water an orange sun hovers on the treetops. I study the lake, the water slinking in a white shimmer, the distant little island enveloped by trees. It'd be a long swim and I'm a poor swimmer.

I wander along the shoreline to a dense spruce grove where I find a pair of small boats covered with a plastic tarp. There are muddy tracks where the boats have been dragged into and out of the water. I touch the imprints. They are wet.

The sky darkens and I choose a campsite on a level patch of ground near the boats. I spread my sleeping bag here. If someone comes to take the boats, I'll see them and maybe get a ride to the island. I don't have a tent, but the sky above me is cloudless. I read *Daily Life in the Trenches* under the purple twilight until it's too dark to see.

The next morning I traverse the shore of the lake, hoping to find a way onto the island. The forest is dense in places and three times I'm forced into the lake to continue on, skipping across rocks or wading in the cool water up to my waist. I continue along the shore until finally I've made a full circuit of the lake.

Back at my campsite the sun is high overhead. I go over to the boats and lift the plastic tarp, uncovering an aluminum fishing boat with an outboard motor, beside it a small white dinghy about eight feet long. I flip the dingy over. The hull is lightweight plastic and it lifts easily. There are two aluminum oars inside lashed together with nylon cord. I pick up the oars, looking at the birch trees across the water.

—There's no choice.

I take hold of the bow and drag the dinghy down toward the lake. The trail is muddy and the boat slides smoothly. At the shoreline I pull off my shoes and toss them in the boat. I look around, suddenly feeling that someone is watching me, a spectator in the trees. I don't know who would be watching or why, but I'm anxious and the feeling is hard to shake. I get behind the stern and push the dinghy into the water, then I jump in. The boat bobs pleasantly from side to side as I fit the oars into the rowlocks. I pull one long stroke and glide forward. I scan the trees for other people. No one.

I row toward the north side of the island. It's hard work and after ten minutes my arms begin to ache. I take a break and row on, watching the glassy wake, the mirrored trees and sky in the water. When I turn around I can see a small wooden pier on the northern tip of the island, so I row the boat north along the shore, avoiding branches of the overgrown trees and shrubs that line the island.

Finally I approach the rough wooden pier. A boat is docked here, another aluminum fishing boat. I tie my dinghy to a post and follow a trail up through the trees, a steep climb through further groves of birch and spruce. As I climb the path I can hear talking and laughing ahead of me. Near the top of the hill the forest opens into a sloped clearing with two wooden houses, both stained the same deep shade of red with white window frames. A field of pristine grass separates the houses. The smaller house is perched higher than the other. It looks far older. At the edge of the clearing beside the larger house, a group of young people sit at a table, talking and laughing. They haven't seen me. I walk closer slowly.

The group is sipping from tall beer cans, their empty paper plates before them. The young man at the head of the table notices me and stares as the others go on talking. He stands. Now they are all looking at me. A girl in a comic cone-shaped paper hat gets up and says something in Swedish.

I shake my head. —I'm sorry, I only speak English. I'm looking for a house that used to belong to my family. They were named Soames-Andersson.

The Swedes keep staring. I look up at the yellow sun above the trees, feeling dizzy. I explain I've come to Sweden to research my family's history, and I know my relatives once had two buildings here, a summerhouse and a barn. In 1917 my grandmother was born in the summerhouse and the barn was being used as a painting studio.

The girl shakes her head.

—There's no barn. That other house is really old, but my family doesn't use it.

—Do you know when they bought this place?

She shrugs. —A long time ago. Maybe the fifties?

The girl studies me for a moment. She has long straight hair and wears round plastic eyeglasses.

—I've brought my friends up here for a party—

The girl's voice trails off. Her friends are all still looking at me. The young man says something to her in Swedish and she snaps at him. They talk for a moment longer, then the girl turns back to me.

—Have you eaten? There's more food in the house. Why don't you join us?

After a moment she remembers to smile.

Once I've sat at the table the party resumes its course. The young man in cut-off jean shorts introduces himself as Christian, explaining that they've all come here for a traditional late-summer crayfish party. He asks a few polite questions about my trip to Sweden, then goes into the house to look for food. He comes back with a plastic tub of potato salad, then puts a cold beer before me and pats me on the shoulder.

—There's your lunch. We'll start dinner soon anyway.

The girl with eyeglasses is named Karin. I'm introduced to the other three friends, two girls and another young man, but I'm too distracted to remember any of their names. They're all drinking heavily. Beside the table there is a cardboard box brimming with empty beer cans. Twice I ask if I can see the old house, but my request is deflected.

—It's a mess in there, Karin says. I don't even know where we keep the key, I'd have to call my uncle.

—Is there stuff inside?

Karin shrugs. —A lot of junk, tools and furniture. The house is so old we're not supposed to knock it down, but it's not practical to use it. My uncle says he's going to clean it out and restore it, but he never does.

Christian puts another beer in front of me.

—Have another one, Christian says. How'd you get here, anyway?

—I took the train from Uppsala.

—But how'd you get on the island?

—I slept on the beach last night. In the morning I found a boat on the shore and rowed it over.

Everyone laughs, considering this a joke.

—We should get started with cooking, Karin says. Tristan, will you stay for dinner?

Christian grins. —He only just rowed over.

As dusk falls we go into the newer house to cook, emptying bags of frozen crayfish into a boiling pot. Karin spreads a cloth over the table outside and I help one of the girls hang paper lanterns from the trees above. We sit and Karin makes a toast in Swedish, then we all drink aquavit, a golden Swedish liquor with a strong taste of caraway seed. Everyone devours dozens of crayfish, sucking the juice noisily from the tiny red shells. I eat only the salad and potatoes.

—You don't like crayfish? Karin asks.

—I'm vegetarian.

—Then have another beer, Christian says. There's your dinner.

We drink beer and vodka and more aquavit. At every toast the Swedes insist that we look one another in the eye. They talk in English at first, asking me questions about San Francisco and my Swedish relatives. But as the dinner goes on most of them switch back to Swedish. Karin is on the far side of the table and our eyes meet a few times, but she never speaks to me.

After dinner we walk down to a fire pit beside the shore. Christian and I light a bundle of newspaper under a teepee of spruce logs. We begin to drink the aquavit in earnest, for we've finished everything else. Someone staggers drunkenly into the woods. A second person sent to find him never returns. I throw more logs onto the fire and it grows larger and hotter until we all have to move a step back. Suddenly I realize it must be after midnight. That makes it August 28.

—It's my birthday, I say. I'm twenty-three.

The Swedes cheer and congratulate me. Christian gives me a bear hug and Karin gently scolds me for not telling her sooner. They sing to me in Swedish and we swig the aquavit in a toast. I throw more wood onto the fire, watching the smoke spiral up to the sky, the stars seeming to go in and out of focus. Twenty-three. I'd come here at least, and that was something. I break a branch in half and throw it onto the fire. Karin nudges me with her elbow.

—How's it feel, spending your birthday with a bunch of strangers?

—I don't mind. It's really beautiful up here.

She nods. —Sorry I was weird this morning, it just spooked me when you showed up—

—I'd be spooked too. It scared the hell out of me when I was coming up from the lake and I heard you guys. I wasn't expecting to find anyone here.

—What were you expecting?

I shake my head. —Nothing. I figured I'd come here, the house would be gone, and I could forget—

—The house, she gasps. I totally forgot.

Karin grabs the bottle of aquavit and we start up the hill. She takes her cell phone from her pocket and selects a number, holding it to her ear. She winks at me.

—My uncle.

As she talks on the phone in Swedish, we walk up to the new house and go into the kitchen. She kneels down and pulls out the lowest drawer, fishing out a jar of keys. She finishes talking and puts the phone back in her pocket.

—He wasn't even asleep, he watches TV all night. He said there used to be a few boxes from the old owners. Come on—

I follow her down the sloping field between the two houses, the stars bright above the trees. We reach the old house, its pine planks stained dark red, weathered by centuries of frigid winter and evening sun. Karin wiggles the key in the lock and pushes open the small wooden door.

—Happy birthday.

The inside is a mess. A dark mass of boxes and furniture stacked high, in some places nearly to the ceiling. We search for the light switch, but the wall is blocked by a huge table covered in boxes. I leave to get my headlamp from my bag, but when I return Karin has cleared a path to the light switch. She flips it on and off. Nothing happens.

—Maybe the bulb's out. Or the fuse.

I switch on my headlamp, directing the beam over plastic crates and stacked chairs. A chain saw, a pile of wooden oars and planks leaning against the wall.

Karin laughs.—Ever seen so much junk?

—Sure. My parents' garage used to look like this.

We take down a storage box and pull off the lid. A vacuum filter still in its dusty package. Cans of wood stain, boxes of white packing plaster. A thick catalog of SKF ball bearings. There's a knock behind us as Christian appears in the doorway, saying something to Karin in Swedish. She turns to me.

—We're going for a swim in the dark. Want to come with us?

—Maybe later. Is it all right if I look around here a little?

Karin shrugs. —Sure. Just let me know if you find anything. And don't make a mess—

—Birthday swim, Christian interrupts. Let's do it.

—I'll be down later.

They walk out leaving the door open behind them. I shine my headlamp over the crevices of the room. The ceiling and walls are all dark wood, the roofbeams hanging low. There's some kind of decorative textile hanging from the far wall, but it's covered in dust and I can't make out the subject. I pull another storage box from the table and look inside. Automobile repair manuals from the seventies. Yellowed composition books filled with longhand notes in Swedish. Brittle picture magazines. I stack the boxes behind me and start clearing a path to the staircase.

They cross the street and enter the park through a green wrought-iron gate. The grounds are pitch-black, only the searchlights weaving tracks among the clouds above.

—We're lucky there aren't sentries, Ashley says. If anyone sees us they'll take us for spies.

—They'll take us for what we are.

—Which is?

Imogen smiles but she does not answer. The sky mists dark rain upon their shoulders and they step in shadow through a curtain of hedges. Imogen trips on a root and tumbles, laughing as Ashley helps her to her feet. They come out onto a lawn and Imogen spreads her arms, trotting forward under a huge willow.

—Here it is. This is the tree.

—You're certain?

Imogen nods and points authoritatively.

—The French gardens were to our left, the houses to the right. You were asking whether I was properly English or not—

Ashley kneels on the damp grass, running his hands through the foliage.

—It isn't here. I don't see it.

They circle the tree, each following the other as they scan the grass, kneeling, their fingers groping among shadows. After a few circuits Imogen sighs.

—I suppose you were right. We shan't find it here.

Imogen lifts her face to the rain and puts her hands out to feel the gathering droplets. She crouches at the foot of the willow, testing the dampness of the earth.

—You'll get wet if you sit there, Ashley warns.

—I don't mind.

She sits down and leans back against the tree trunk. Ashley continues to inspect the grass, orbiting the tree with his eyes fixed upon the ground.

—Mr. Walsingham, Imogen calls. Ashley. Sit with me.

Ashley screws his face up to the sky. It is raining harder now, the droplets drumming a quick rhythm against the leaves.

—We'd as well wait it out here, she says.

—This tree won't keep us dry forever.

—We don't need forever. Sit down.

Ashley takes a seat beside her, leaning his swagger cane against the inside of his knee. He picks a few twigs from beneath his legs and tosses them away. He smiles.

—Did you really lose the key?

—Yes.

—Under this tree?

—I think so.

—Couldn't you find some other way to get in?

—I'd rather not.

—You'd get in trouble?

—I'm already in trouble, she says. I've neglected certain plans to-night. You make me terribly irresponsible.

The rain quickens. A few large drops sink between the leaves, landing cold on Ashley's neck. Imogen leans her head upon his shoulder, her fingers brushing the knot of his khaki necktie.

—But I've no regrets, she adds.

—Nor I.

Ashley puts his hand to her bare forearm. Her skin is damp and cool. He can feel the fine goose bumps on her arm. Imogen kisses the bottom of his chin and moves up toward his mouth, her lips skirting his.

—I knew you'd be at the concert, she whispers.

She takes his swagger cane and tosses it aside. Ashley brings her close and they kiss softly at first, then harder. Imogen pulls back and looks at him. She smiles, then takes his hand and lays her head upon his chest.

—I suppose you shall think me the sort of girl to kiss a man she scarcely knows.

—I expected so. For heaven's sake, why do you think I came—

—Ashley!

He laughs as Imogen elbows him. He runs his hand over her hair, smoothing it, spreading the raindrops into the glossy band above her face.

—You aren't any sort, he whispers. You're only yourself.

—Darling. You know I've never done anything like this. It's only that I felt we had to. There isn't time enough for you to take me on strolls once a week—

She looks up at him.

—You leave on Thursday?

—Yes.

She nods. —Five days.

Ashley strokes her neck, bringing her close until he can feel the warmth of her body through her wet dress. They kiss on and on with mad abandon, trying to satisfy something that will not be satisfied. Imogen leans back against him. Ashley wraps his arms around her shoulders.

—I've seen you before, he says suddenly. I didn't tell you, but I knew

it the moment I saw you at the lecture. It was in Snowdonia, the Gorphwysfa Hotel. The last Pen y Pass party before the war. You were with
a group motoring by—

Imogen springs up.

—You were there? she gasps. I'm sorry—

—We didn't meet. I only saw you. You play the piano, don't you?

—A bit. But how could you remember that? It was years ago.

—It's not the kind of thing one forgets.

Imogen laughs and puts her arms around his neck. She kisses him
on the cheek and tells him that this is wonderful news.

—It wasn't any accident that brought us here.

—With only five days?

—Five days, she repeats. We'll spend them all together.

—I'm meant to go to Berkshire tomorrow. I have to see my people
before I cross—

—I'll go with you.

—To Sutton Courtenay?

—Why not? I'll stay in a hotel nearby. In the evenings you'll say
you're visiting school chums and you'll sneak out to see me. You'll go out
your bedroom window and climb down a trellis. You do love to climb.

—You're so certain of this already?

—Already?

—It's been only a day.

Imogen lies back with her head on his chest. She looks up to the
canopy of leaves above, all of them humming in the rain.

—But we've known each other for years, she says.

—You didn't remember me.

Imogen plucks a wet blade of grass from the lawn and lifts it before
her eyes. She studies the blade, turning it in her hand.

—No, she says. But you remembered me.

THE CACHE

⚬

It is late. I know this from the brightness of the stars in the open door-way, and because the shouting and singing outside ended long ago. Ev-eryone must have gone to sleep by now.

I went through the boxes one by one, sifting through contents and stacking, moving chairs and garden tools and old appliances to clear a path. All the documents and mail here are addressed to the Sjöbergs, which must be Karin's family.

Finally I reach the staircase and I begin pulling out the boxes. Rusty old socket wrenches, tubes of grout, paintbrushes and scrap-ers. At the top of the steps there's a roll of fiberglass insulation and a heavy box full of hardcover books. I move the insulation and step over the box.

Moonlight pours through windows onto the warped floorboards of the hallway. As I walk I have the sensation of leaning sideways. The floorboards groan. My feet make tracks in the thick dust.

I enter the bedroom facing the woods. More boxes everywhere. I push them aside until I reach a short bed of ancient oak, the bedposts decorated with elaborate carvings. Against the opposite wall there is an antique writing desk stacked with old linens and bedspreads. I move the linens to the bed and go through the desk drawers. Paper clips; rolls of undeveloped film; rusted keys on a ring; steel sewing bobbins still wound with thread. In a bureau wedged below the desk there is a heavy case of stained walnut. I flip the brass latches. A butterfly collection under glass, the insects speared with pins and labeled in Latin and Swedish. *Danaus plexippus. Monarkfjäril.*

—The monarch butterfly, I whisper.

A paper tag is affixed inside the lid of the case. *Per Andersson. Svartmangatan 11, Uppsala.*

A shiver passes through me. I sit on the floor to take a breath and think. A few minutes later I cross the hall to the opposite bedroom. More boxes, a pair of twin beds covered in hand-knitted throws. No doubt once snow-white, the throws are grayed with decades of dust. Inside the boxes are folded linens and porcelain plates wrapped in brittle newspaper. I move the boxes and sit on one of the beds. Beside me is a red nightstand, its year of manufacture painted in florid numerals: *1663.* The nightstand has a large drawer. I pull on the handle, but it is stuck shut. After a few jerks it pulls open.

The drawer is filled with magazines. *The Athenaeum, Nouvelle Revue Française, The Egoist, The Burlington Magazine.* I check the dates. August 1915. *Julliet 1916.*

I pace around the two bedrooms, peering under the beds, throwing back curtains. The air is full of dust and it makes me sneeze. In the hall closet there are lapelled jackets, a long fur coat and several pairs of rubber boots. I reach for the tag on the coat and some of the fur comes off on my fingers. *Fourrures Weill. 4 Rue Ste Anne Paris.* I pull out all of the clothing and make a pile in the hallway. I'm making a lot of noise now and I think I hear footsteps on the staircase. I stop and listen, my breath heavy. No one comes in. I go back to the second bedroom and sit on the bed.

The sisters must have come here in December. I imagine them being rowed across the lake in the cold, a thick cloak wrapped around Imogen's shoulders as she watched the trees of the town grow smaller, the trees of the island grow larger and larger. There must have been snow everywhere, the ropes at the pier coated in ice. They would have walked up the twisting path to the house, someone carrying their suitcases, Eleanor in front and Imogen following slowly behind, about to see her home for the next six months. She had never seen it in snow before. Finally the red house would come into view through the trees, black smoke rising from the chimney, the caretaker coming out into the icy clearing and taking the bags from their hands.

I go back into the bedroom and look inside the boxes with the porcelain, unwrapping the newspaper to check the date. *Tirsdag aften den 6 Mars 1919*. I pull everything from the box, the plates and linens, a dark cardboard portfolio with cloth ties. Inside the portfolio are receipts in Swedish and English: railway tickets, hotel receipts, folded grocers' bills. The dates run from 1916 to 1919. One of the receipts is in French, the top printed *MOISSE—Toiles & Tableaux et Couleurs— Encadrements—28, Rue Pigalle*. There are columns for the order numbers, the *designation des articles* and the prices, but the handwriting is in a wild longhand that's hard to read. I make out *ocre jaune* among the list of items. Another line says *terre de Sienne*. It must be a receipt for oil paints. I refold it and put it in my pocket to look at later.

I open the other box on the bed. A small silver pitcher wrapped in cloth, a set of pewter apostle spoons in a wooden case. Beneath these is a parcel wrapped in brown paper, about the size of a shoe box. I shine my light at the address on the front. *C. F. Grafton, 58 Cartwright Gardens, London WC1, ENGLAND*. There are no stamps and the box isn't postmarked.

I tear off the paper. There is a tin inside, the lid stamped *Green's of Brighton: The House of Quality*. I take off the lid. A blue booklet is at the top, and beneath this two tightly fitted bundles of letters, each secured with twine. The booklet's cover reads *The Geographical Journal, Vol. XLVII No. 5, May 1916. The Astrolabe and Wireless. Notes on the Alto Rio Branco,*

North Amazonas. *The Position of Sir Ernest Shackleton's Expedition.* The booklet parts at the center to reveal a white notecard engraved *The Langham Hotel, Portland Place, London W.* The card is inscribed in brown ink.

24 Aug 1916

To my Darling –

That she will remember that I belong not to Flanders mud,
nor to His Majesty's Army, nor to God, nor yet even to myself, but
instead am held as surely & as easily as a loving girl holds a lover's
note. For you shall hold this, and I shall come back to you.

A.

I flip the card over and over. My hands are shaking. I untie one of the bundles of letters. The envelopes are of plain stock or YMCA stationery, the paper brown and brittle. A few green envelopes are marked ACTIVE SERVICE with printed instructions on the front. They are all addressed in blunt pencil.

Miss I. Soames-Andersson
Yarrow Cottage
Selsey
England

All of them have the same return address: *A.E. Walsingham, 2/Lt.,* *1 Batt. Royal Berkshire Regt.* I take the sheets from an envelope.

So we marched all night; if I tried to describe the cold or fatigue
I should fail. The men hadn't any consolation but to sing. And so
they sang – endlessly, to the tune of 'Auld Lang Syne': 'We're here
because we're here, because we're here, because we're here.'

It was terrible at first, then beautiful, and finally terrible again.
I shall not forget it.

I go to the next page and read to the end.

You are the source & measure of all good things; even in a pit
so wretched as this I know my happiness comes from you.

When we come back into the dug-out after 18 hours crawling
in frozen mud, and we have a cup of steaming tea & a tin of bully
beef, I know what pleasure there is comes from you.

When at midnight watch the shelling ceases suddenly, for no
more reason than it ever started, and the sky is incandescent with
streaming flares – then I see some signature of the divine and,
knowing there is no God, I know that signature is yours.

I did not need to see such cruelty as I have to know how I loved
you, nor to know how rare & fragile the time we shared was.

But I have learnt something. We have words for places of utter
bliss & utter agony; we call them heaven & hell, and place them in
some distant domain, far beyond death. But this is mistaken. These
are names we give to things that exist in this world and only here,
and I have seen them share the same field.

Imogen, I care nothing for future salvation, nor for the prizes
of this stumbling world. You were the wise one, wise to understand
what we were when I hardly knew myself; wiser still to weep when
I left, knowing the price we paid for my conceit. If this war tests
men as men have never been tested, I survive only through you.
And when we stand again together beneath the arch at All Saints, I
shall have the only salvation I desire.

Yours Ever,
Ashley

My hands are still shaking. Again I get the feeling that someone is watching me. I go to the window and pull back the dusty curtains, peering into the dark woods. There's no one outside. The sky is turning blue at the horizon.

I look through the rest of the boxes and check the closet again, but I don't find anything else. I carry the tin downstairs and go outside, standing in the shimmering field in my shirtsleeves. A warm breeze passes through the trees.

20 *August 1916*

Cavendish Square

Marylebone, Central London

Ashley and Imogen do not find the latchkey, not in Regent's Park or anywhere else. An hour after dawn they go to Imogen's house and Ashley watches from the sidewalk on Cavendish Square as Imogen taps the ground-floor window until the housekeeper opens the door. A few minutes later the light goes on and off in the second-story window. Then Ashley knows she is all right.

He boards the 9:38 from Paddington and tries to sleep. But with fewer trains running all the time, the carriage is crowded and stuffy, and when Ashley closes his eyes he can think only of Imogen, replaying scenes from the night before with a surge of pleasure at each fresh memory. He does not know whether he trusts or mistrusts her, whether he understands her or knows less about her than any woman he's ever spent an hour with, let alone a whole night. Had they really stayed out until dawn? And what had they said to each other in those smaller moments, the ones he was already forgetting? The train travels at half speed to save fuel and when Ashley reaches Didcot Station the only transport is an ancient hansom cab, the caped driver peering down from his sprung seat above the carriage.

—No motor taxis, sir, we haven't the petrol. But I can take you as you please.

Ashley grins, stepping in through the twin front doors of the cab. When he reaches his mother's house he pays the driver and claps the knocker on the door. He embraces his mother hurriedly.

—Awfully sorry, but I'm only dropping my bags. I'll be back this afternoon. I need to take the motor back into town. Is it starting?

—But Ashley, his mother protests, you've just arrived.

He kisses her on the cheek.

—I'm having luncheon with Richards. You remember him, don't you? Archaeologist chap from Magdalene. I shan't be long—

Ashley meets Imogen at noon at Abingdon Station with the borrowed motorcar. She steps off the train and grasps his hand, whispering into his ear.

—The slowest train I ever took. I've a present for you, darling.

Imogen opens the clasp on her handbag and rummages through its contents, but the bag is so packed that she finally has to sit on a bench to the sift through the mess. There are tattered political leaflets and leather pocketbooks, celluloid safety pins and railway timetables; a small glass bottle of perfume, a wooden birdcall. At last Imogen pulls out an iron key triumphantly. Ashley shakes his head.

—Don't tell me it's the one you lost.

She smiles, putting the key in his hand.

—You're right, I shan't tell.

—Is it the latchkey? What does it open?

—Ashley, I shan't tell. You'll have to find out, that's the whole point. I promise it's something terribly important. Have you eaten yet? I'm positively famished.

They check into the nearby hotel as Mr. and Mrs. Walsingham and as Ashley says these names, Imogen touches his hand and looks away. The clerk gives an inquiring smile.

—Newlyweds?

—Married yesterday, Ashley says. How did you know?

—You have that certain glow. I can tell it every time.

At lunch in the hotel restaurant their bodies vacillate between exhaustion and euphoria, Ashley constantly looking around the room for fear of being discovered in their ruse. This amuses Imogen.

—What does it matter what anyone thinks? In four days you'll be in France. Anyhow that clerk thinks we're married.

Ashley looks up from his soup.

—You looked unhappy when he said it.

—Unhappy isn't the word, Imogen says. It's just not how I want to think of us. Look at Ellie and Charles. It's a wonder to me how two perfectly fascinating people can become so dull once they've married—

—They don't seem dull to me.

—Because you didn't know them before. You should have seen Ellie three years ago, when she was still at the Slade, forever coming home with new ideas. New books, new fellows brought over for tea, the cleverest fellows you ever met. We spoke of getting rooms together, Ellie and I, where we'd have people over every day of the week. If only she'd waited a few years, I might have gotten out of Cavendish Square. But now it's hopeless, because Papa will never let me live on my own. And even if Ellie spends half her days with us, it's not the same, because she's not the same.

—What happened?

—Charles happened. Would you guess that when we met, I thought him the cleverest, the most fascinating of all the fellows? He'd just come down from Trinity and wouldn't talk anything but pure genius rot. We'd pour the tea and he'd start at once on the perversity of beauty, the masochism of God, the meaning of earthly love. He once quarreled with Papa for an hour over universal suffrage. Charles said that Ellie and I had it wrong, that it wasn't so much that women ought to have the vote, but that men oughtn't to have it, because only men made war and valued profit over people—

—Isn't he in the army?

—He is now. Of course he doesn't fight, he just follows some major around and takes notes. And I haven't the faintest idea what he believes anymore, because all Ellie and Charles talk about now is who was in the exhibition on Bond Street, or how much some fellow paid for his house in Clerkenwell. They don't want to talk about the important things anymore.

—You could ask.

Imogen sighs. —I know I ought to, but it's been so long that one can't simply knock on Ellie's door and ask, are you in really in love with Charles, or do you stay with him only because you have to? And are you really going to have children, because if you can't or won't, then stop moping about it, because anyone can see it's making you miserable—

—You can't blame all this on marriage.

—Can't I? They were never like that before. It's as if they're playing roles instead of acting the way they feel, only after a while they aren't roles anymore. Most people seem to regard a wife as half servant and half fool. I don't say that Charles or Ellie subscribe to that, but what people expect can change you in the end. One oughtn't give names to what two people are to one another. It only makes it harder to be one's self.

—And what are we to one another?

Imogen smiles, shaking her head and looking into her bowl.

—Darling. You know there isn't a word for it in any language.

—I might say there is.

Imogen looks up at Ashley. —Those are words other people give to other things. We're here because of how we feel, not because we have to be here. Nor because there's some name for this, strolling in Regent's Park with a fellow, then running away to Wiltshire—

—Berkshire.

Imogen smiles. —Berkshire. My point is that it's no good for two people to live together, never knowing whether they come home each night because they care for each other or because they're bound to be there.

—One has to sleep somewhere.

Imogen kicks his foot under the table.

—Be serious.

—I am serious, Ashley says. One can't do everything for the grand-est reasons. I expect sometimes people do share a bed simply because they're married. On other days they do it for all the right reasons. Besides, how could one share a life with someone if one never knew whether they'd be around the next moment?

Imogen sets her spoon down on the table and shrugs.

—We never know that anyway. Even if you and I were married, I might be struck dead by lightning. Or exploded by a bomb dropped from a zeppelin. Or you could come home one day and I'd be gone, in spite of all the promises I'd made to God and the law alike—

—You'd do that?

Imogen smiles. —Never. But neither would I marry.

After lunch they go up to their hotel room. They are alone now for the first time and they kiss wildly. Ashley remembers at once the taste of her mouth and her neck, how she felt in Regent's Park and how she feels now, the scent of her skin against his, her breath warming his cheek. They kiss on until their mouths are tired. Even then they still look at each other in plain wonder, lying clothed in their stocking feet on the bed, Ashley holding her in his arms. He feels mad with fatigue, and in this haze Imogen seems more impossible than ever, more beautiful and more loving than he can fathom. They wake and sleep and wake and sleep until it all seems nearly the same. At times Imogen kisses him as soon as she wakes, before her eyes have opened, as if it is the first in-stinct in her being, coming before breath even.

Now it is time for Ashley to return home. They get out of bed and he pulls on his tunic, cinching his belt and reknotting his necktie before the mirror. Imogen pulls aside one of the curtains and looks out the window.

—I can't stay here all day. I need fresh air. Could one hire a bicycle here? I could see the villages—

—There's nothing to see.

—I adore looking at nothing. You promise to return tonight?

—Nine o'clock at the latest.

—If you're a minute late, she teases, it'll be an hour to me.

Ashley kisses her again at the door for a long time and has to pull himself away. He shuts the door behind him and follows the long hallway to the stairs, trying to straighten his shoulders and walk like a soldier. His steps fall softly on the carpet. *Imogen Soames-Andersson*, he thinks, *who waits for me at nine o'clock*. The name alone makes him feel crazy.

Back at home Ashley half-dozes through supper with his mother and a wizened aunt. In the parlor afterward the aunt plays Elgar on the piano as Ashley falls dead asleep in an armchair, his glass of Madeira in hand. The glass tips and the dark Madeira soaks his jacket sleeve. Ashley wakes to his mother's shrieks. Drowsily he removes his jacket and pats it with a napkin. He excuses himself to bed.

In his bedroom Ashley changes into a suit of light flannel and steps out of the first-story window, on his shoulder an old climbing rucksack holding two bottles of champagne taken from the cellar. He feels ridiculous, but it only makes him smile. When he meets Imogen in the hotel lobby, he knows by her expression that she has some new secret to uncurtain.

—I've a surprise for tonight, she says. It's all planned out.

—All I planned for was two bottles of Mumm's.

—That's a start.

It is a warm night. They take the motorcar to the fields outside the village where as a boy Ashley had taken long walks alone. It feels strange to be there with anyone else, let alone with Imogen. They park the car and Ashley leads her along the familiar dirt paths, rough lanes made for horse carts, overgrown with weeds through the years. They sit in a dormant field on the driest patch of grass they can find. From the rucksack Ashley takes the champagne and a pair of teacups wrapped in a tablecloth from the kitchen. He had chosen teacups because he supposed they would be less fragile than champagne glasses, but the handle on one of them had broken anyway.

—Now you can't take it back, Imogen says. They'll deduce everything from the broken teacup.

—Even you?

—Especially me.

Ashley shakes his head.

—There isn't a man alive who could deduce you.

—Isn't there? You came to the concert, didn't you? You must have deduced something. Or felt something—

Ashley looks away in embarrassment, but Imogen smiles, running her hand through his hair.

—Darling. What color would you say your hair is?

—Reddish brown? Auburn?

—Nothing so prosaic. Let's say a dark Venetian blond. Like a Renaissance courtesan, but more sinister. Too beautiful for a young man—

She laughs. —My darling courtesan. Are you ready for the surprise?

—Certainly.

—Back to the motor, then. We're going to church.

A CLUE

I sleep on the floor of the new house on a pile of blankets and pillows, Christian snoring beside me late into the morning. As soon as I get up I go to my backpack in the hallway and take out the green tin. I pull off the lid and feel the stiff paper of the envelopes, the thin hard twine binding the bundles together.

In the dining room Karin is setting the table for breakfast, moving slowly as she sips from a cup of coffee.

—We're the only ones up, she says. And my head is killing me. How are you?

—Not too bad. I drank a lot of water before I went to bed.

—I should have done that. How late were you up? You never came to the lake—

—I found something. Let me show you.

I go to the hallway and come back with the tin of letters. Karin looks up at me, her eyes wide. She unties one of the bundles and leafs through the envelopes, shaking her head.

—Where'd you find this?

—Upstairs, in one of the boxes in the bedrooms.

Karin removes a sheet from its envelope.

—And in English, she murmurs. I had no idea there was stuff like this in there. I'll have to tell my uncle—

She studies the letter for a moment.

—This is from one of your relatives?

—I think so.

She shakes her head. —I'm sorry, but you can't take them, not now anyway. I have to show them to my family. My father will probably want to see them too.

—Do you mind if I copy them?

—Of course not. But there's no copy machine here.

—That's OK. I'll do it by hand.

As the others bask in the sun along the lakeshore, I sit at the dining table in the new house, slowly transcribing letter after letter. It's harder than I thought. Some of the letters are so difficult to read that I leave out whole lines. Others are so engrossing that I stop copying and set down my pen.

> I chose the shorter route, for it was dark now & I imagined we would be screened by a meager thicket to the east. We had gone 200 yards when the first shot came, then a second, amid cries of 'Sniper!' The men pulled Cpl. Locke to the shelter of a low hill. I found him spread out atop a dirty shallow puddle, his tunic pulled open as men worked feebly to stop the bleeding. He had been shot in the lungs.
>
> Locke tried to speak. He seemed desperate to tell us something, though we hushed him & begged him to be still, for each time he opened his lips, all that came was blood. The men still wonder what he wished to say. It's been days now & still they speculate endlessly, as though he'd been privy to some deep secret, if only because he could not share it.

I put the letter down and go outside, watching the wind pass through the trees above. Christian walks by with a large cooler.

—Are you all right?

—Yeah.

—You were staring all funny.

—Just a little hungover.

He grins. —Everybody is.

It takes me another hour to finish copying. The text fills thirty pages. My wrist is aching. I lay the letters out on the table to photograph them, two sheets at a time. I meter the exposures carefully, but I still bracket them anyway, taking identical shots with different settings to make sure I'll have clear pictures. On their own I don't think the letters have any useful evidence, but I can't be sure. Karin tells me to leave the tin on the kitchen table for her father.

Back in the old house I try to put everything the way it was, even the mess downstairs. It takes a long time to move the boxes and tools back to their old locations, and even then I'm only guessing. I leave a path to the staircase and go up one last time to check on everything.

In the upstairs bedroom the notecard from Ashley is sitting on the nightstand. I'd forgotten to replace it in the magazine where I found it. I hold the card in my hand for a moment, looking around the room.

—A bad idea, I whisper.

I slip the card inside my notebook and flip it shut.

We clean up the house and prepare to cross the lake, passing luggage and bags of leftover food into the boats. Christian and one of the girls are already drinking beer again. A garbage bag of empty cans falls into the water and I wade in to grab it, everyone laughing and calling. I go up to the house to get my backpack and change into dry pants.

When I put on my other pair of pants I notice something in the pocket. I pull out a sheet of thin yellow paper. It's the receipt from last night. In daylight the handwriting is easier to read.

MOISSE

TOILES & TABLEAUX ET COULEURS—ENCADREMENTS—

28, RUE PIGALLE

blanc d'argent

jaune de Naples

ocre jaune

terre de Sienne naturelle

vert cinabre

terre de Sienne brûlée

laque d'alizarine

rouge de Venise

bleu d'outremer

bleu de Prusse

noir d'ivoire

siccatif de Courtrai

There are two more colors I can't make out, another kind of *vert* and another kind of *bleu*. The bill is marked *Paris, le 11 décembre 1916* and made out to *H. Broginart, 18 rue de Penthièvre*. The name sounds familiar. I get my folder from my backpack and flip through the papers until I find the photocopy from the Tate Archive.

23 Mar 19

Dear Mr. Devereux,

I received your letter of the 19th inst. and have disposed of the study as directed. M. Broginart was terribly disappointed and offered to double his price for the canvas, until at last he was made to understand the situation. He enquired about the larger picture and is keen enough to buy the painting sight unseen, though he would not tender a figure and I expressed my grave

*doubts. Has Mrs. Grafton advised whether that painting shall
ever be put out?*

—What you know for sure, I whisper. That's all that counts.

I run my hands through my hair, rehearsing the details step by step. In the winter of 1916 Eleanor is living on this lake near Leksand. Imogen is almost certainly here too, because I found letters addressed to her in the old house. Around the same period, in December 1916, an art-supply dealer in Paris fills an order for paints made out to "M. Broginart" and the receipt ends up here. In May 1917 my grandmother Charlotte is born here. In March 1919, five months after the end of the war, at Eleanor's request a gallery employee in London destroys a painted study recently shipped from Sweden, in spite of the fact that Broginart wants to buy the study and a related larger painting. The same month a painting by Eleanor titled *Nude Study* is entered in the Devereux Brothers ledger, only to be crossed out.

She could have painted a million things here. She could have painted the trees or the sky, the red house or any damn thing that would be a waste of time for me to chase after. But why have it destroyed? What could be so bad that even after it had reached London it had to be destroyed at once?

—That doesn't make it Imogen.

I look at the receipt again. Broginart had bought Eleanor materials in Paris in 1916, so they must have had some kind of relationship to each other. She may have been painting something for him, or he may have been a collector of her work, which would explain why he wanted the study two years later. Or Broginart may simply have been a friend who bought the paints as a favor, because they were better than anything Eleanor could get in wartime Sweden. But what happened to the larger oil painting? Did Broginart ever get it, and if he did, what did it look like?

If Broginart was a serious collector his papers might have been saved. His collection could still be in Paris, or he might even have owned a gallery with surviving records of its own. His address is on the receipt and I know the exact dates I'm interested in, so I'd have a starting point. But Prichard would probably say it's a waste of time, because even if I found the painting and it was Imogen, even if it showed her pregnant—

A voice is calling from outside.

—Tristan? You'd better come down now, unless you want to swim back.

I gather my things and run down the hill, catching up with Karin. Everyone else is already in the boat. Christian hitches the dinghy onto the aluminum boat with a length of nylon rope. He pulls the starting cord on the outboard motor and the engine belches to life, sputtering black smoke. The boats glide forward.

The Swedes pass around cans of beer. Karin sits down beside me.

—Do you want a ride down to Stockholm?

—That'd be great.

Karin smiles. —It beats rowing. Did you copy all those letters?

—Yeah.

—What was in them?

I drag my hand in the cold lake. I shake my head.

—You'll have to read them. There's a lot of stuff in there, it's hard to explain.

—Are they good letters?

—Yeah. They're good letters.

Christian cuts the motor as we near the muddy lakefront. It's only noon, but it's a long drive back to Stockholm. I hope I can get a flight to Paris tonight.

20 August 1916

All Saints' Church

Sutton Courtenay, Berkshire

Beneath the night sky the churchyard is a mass of shadows. Imogen strides two paces before him though the ragged grass. Ashley's shoe clips something hard and he nearly falls. Imogen stifles a laugh.

—Haven't you been here before?

—We never came here, Ashley whispers. My mother had some aversion to the priest. I was baptized at Abingdon.

—Well, we've entered the graveyard. There's no fence on this side. Mind the tombstones—some of them are quite short.

Ashley takes a final swig from the champagne bottle and pitches it into a clump of bushes. He does not need any more. He has no idea how much Imogen has drunk; for her it makes no difference. He quickens his step to catch up and they walk single file through the maze of lichen-covered headstones. Imogen is unafraid and speaking louder now.

—I had a lovely tour of the villages. Did you know there are German prisoners working the fields on the other side of the river, past the abbey? I tried talking to them—

—Not in German, I hope.

—Naturally in German. They were from Saxony, awfully nice fellows. They told me they'd prefer a month of harvesting to an hour back in the trenches. Said they hadn't heard a women speak German in months. Of course, the guards overheard me and I spent a quarter of an hour convincing them I wasn't a foreign agent. Gave them the name of every monarch since the Conqueror, I expect. Then I walked down to the church. The old sexton was cutting the grass here and he told me all kinds of bosh about the church's history. He showed me something inside and I knew I had to show it to you.

As they approach the church Ashley sees the black mass of the nave, a square tower looming above.

—Are we meant to break in? I doubt they leave the door unlocked. And I don't fancy being cashiered before I reach France.

—The door will be open, she calls back.

—It will not.

They follow the perimeter of the church toward the front entrance. As she walks Imogen runs her fingers along the rough walls, feeling for the gaps between each stone. They reach the front portal, an arched wooden door set at the tower's base. Imogen puts her hand on the door's iron ring. She smiles at Ashley.

—Do you trust in me?

—In nothing else.

Imogen turns the ring and pushes the door. It swings open with a creak.

—After you, Lieutenant.

It is dark in the nave. Only a faint shimmer of starlight passes through the stained glass above. They walk abreast of each other toward the altar, but they do not touch. By accident Ashley's hand grazes hers and he reaches for her palm. She dashes away.

—I shan't kiss you in a church. I may not believe in God, but I still fear him.

—And what are we here for?

Imogen reaches the altar, taking the steps in one stride. She plucks a ceremonial candle and tosses it underhand toward him.

—Catch.

Ashley puts up his hands to receive the candle, but her aim is wildly off and it bounces on the floor. He retrieves the candle and Imogen walks back down the center aisle toward the entrance. On her way she lifts a chair and carries it with her.

—This way.

Ashley follows dutifully behind her, the candle in his hand. Imogen sets the chair before the front portal and steps onto it.

—Light the candle, please.

Ashley strikes a match and at once the darkness recedes before the yellow flame. He lights the candle and passes it to Imogen. She holds the flame close against the beam that frames the top of the portal, running her hand over the dark wood.

—Here it is.

Ashley squints, but he sees only a beam of gnarled wood.

—The sexton said this is a perfectly typical fourteenth-century church. But even a typical church has its bits of interest.

She steps off the chair.

—Your turn, she says. Stand up.

Ashley takes the candle and holds it up to the beam. He sees the carvings now, thrown into sharp relief by shadows cast under the flame. They are crosses. Carved long ago upon the seasoned oak, there are square Greek crosses and Latin crucifixes, some finely wrought, others hewn crudely against the grain.

—Crusaders, Ashley murmurs.

Imogen repeats to Ashley what the sexton told her in the afternoon. She says that hundreds of years ago crusaders stopped at this very spot before they sailed for Constantinople. They knelt and prayed here, she says, and they heard a priest tell them they would go to God if they fell.

They stood on a chair and carved the crosses before walking out of their last English church.

Ashley runs his hands along the indentations. Behind him Imogen draws a pocketknife from her bag and unfolds the blade. Ashley had not seen the knife until now.

—You're damned theatrical, he says. You shan't carve in that.

—It's for you, Ashley.

—You're joking.

Imogen shakes her head. —They were told they were Christ's own army and still they stopped to carve these crosses, so that they would return.

—You're mad. You shan't carve in that.

—I want you to do it. Don't you see, Ashley? It's because they didn't give a damn for God or heaven. They wished to see their wives and homes again. They wanted to drink and stay out all night as we have. That was why they carved. That they would come back.

—I can't do that.

—I will do it for you, Imogen says, if you will not.

She drags another chair across the stone floor and rests it beside his. Imogen steps on the chair and plunges the knife into the beam, and with both hands she hacks up and down against the grain.

—Imogen, Ashley pleads. For God's sake, it's historical—

—We are bloody history!

She jerks the knife back and forth across the wood to make the horizontal bar of the cross. For a moment Imogen pauses and there is only the quick panting of her breath. Ashley puts his hand on the thin ivory knife handle. They begin to carve together, slowly at first, then with real effort.

—You'll come back, she says. I can't have been given you only to lose you so quickly.

Ashley takes his hand off the knife. He looks at Imogen.

—The war can't last forever. They're making a big push, I could be home by spring. We'll go straight to the Valais and watch the snow melt down the mountains—

Imogen says nothing. She makes a few careful marks to finish the carving, fluting the ends of each cross. Then she lifts the candle closer to the beam to inspect her work. She blows the shavings from the carving and cleans the hollows with the blade.

Ashley grins. —You know, most of these fellows probably never came back.

Imogen refolds the pocketknife.

—It occurred to me. But you could be a better sport.

—Don't be cross. I was a good sport.

They step down and Ashley replaces the chairs. Imogen stands in the doorway holding the candle. She looks away from the flame, her expression clouded.

—By the way, Ashley asks, how did you know the door would be open? Was that destiny again?

Imogen blows out the candle.

—No, she says. I bribed the sexton.

THE PICTURE

✦══ ══✦

On their way back to Stockholm Karin and Christian drop me off at Arlanda Airport. I visit the ticket counter of several airlines, where I learn that the next flight to Paris costs nearly two hundred euros, far more than I ought to spend. Before I left California I transferred all of my savings into an account I could draw from in Europe; it added up to only $1,800 and I'll have to make it last. But the flight leaves soon and I can't waste time staying in Stockholm. I buy the ticket.

A few hours later I'm underground in the Paris métro, following dense crowds through tunnels of glazed white tile. Even after studying the system map for several minutes, I get on the wrong train at Opéra and don't realize my mistake for a few stops. I switch trains at Bonne Nouvelle and take a seat, trying to steady my hand as I write in my notebook, the train bumping on into the night.

QUESTIONS

1. Who is M. Broginart?
2. What was in the larger picture and what happened to it?

My hostel lies on a quiet street in the Fifteenth Arrondissement. The lobby is also the bar and it seems like half the guests are drinking here tonight. I check in with the bartender. He hands me the key to my bunkroom and a slick visitors' map of the city printed by Galeries Lafayette.

I sit on my bunk and unfold the map, my eyes following the sweep of the Seine around the city, the two islands in the center, the Left Bank where the boulevard Saint-Germain meets the boulevard Saint-Michel. All my life I've wanted to come to Paris. I think of the years of French classes, the suitcase full of yellowed Gallimard paperbacks in my father's garage. I fold up the map and go to the hostel's computer beside the bar.

For the next two hours I look up libraries and archives. By the end of the night I have seven places marked in ink on my map. The bartender winks at the girls sitting beside me.

—Look at this guy. Just got into town, he's already mapped out which bars he's hitting. Where are you going first?

—The Bibliothèque Nationale.

I start early the next morning, but Broginart is not an easy man to trace. There's nothing on him at the Bibliothèque Nationale: not in the catalogs or the digital library, nor in any of the dozens of books I call up on prominent Parisian collectors. At the Bibliothèque Sainte-Geneviève I spend hours under its soaring cast-iron columns, paging through gallery catalogs, reading the letters of painters and sculptors from the 1910s and 1920s. Broginart's name appears nowhere. I move on to the specialist libraries, the Bibliothèque Kandinsky at the Pompidou Center, the Médiathèque of the École des Beaux-Arts. After four days of research I know the names of the famous Paris galleries, the collectors who bought their paintings, the major salons and exhibitions. I know nothing about Broginart.

The nights go better than the days. At six o'clock each evening I leave the libraries and buy a bottle of wine or beer from the nearest grocery, walking the streets until I don't worry anymore, until I can't think about anything but the city itself.

Because I love everything in Paris. The enamel green color of the water fountains. The brown fold-up seats on the subway cars that the accordion players sit on, old men in fraying pin-striped suits who play to no one but me, the melody coming in and out as the train crosses the Seine at Austerlitz. The cups of *café allongé* I drink on the café terrace each morning, one euro and twenty cents.

My third night I'm in the Jardin du Luxembourg at dusk and a short man approaches me with a friendly smile. He tells me his name is Mohammed and he's a native of Casablanca. He wears a dirty sweater, blue jeans and white basketball shoes with no laces. We talk in French and English. Mohammed knows the best places to sleep on the riverbank and where to get the best couscous in Paris for three euros a plate, but only on Sundays.

—You will be the only British there, Mohammed says. But if you come with me, it's no problem.

—I'm American.

Mohammed nods sagely. —*Et qu'est-ce que tu fais à Paris?*

—*Je cherche un tableau de l'artiste Eleanor Grafton.* Let me know if you see it—

—You can go to Le Louvre, Mohammed says. There are thousands of paintings there. Tonight is Wednesday, it's open late. And it's always warm and dry inside.

I walk through the backstreets of Odéon to the Louvre. Everywhere in the museum I imagine Eleanor's painting, even though I don't know what it looks like. In the rows of gilded frames in the Denon wing, it's always at the end of the hallway, the last picture in the gallery. Because I see Imogen everywhere here. In the cold stare of the *Grande Odalisque*, or underground in the shadowed brickwork of the Medieval Louvre; in the gallery for the blind beneath the stairs where you're allowed to feel the statues, to recognize faces by the contours of their features, the hard lines of the nose and chin. Even the dark-haired girl standing before me in line at the museum café. She might look just like her, but I'd never know it.

The next day I follow a different track. At daybreak I ride the métro to visit 28 rue Pigalle, the address of the dealer Moisse where Broginart bought Eleanor's paints. The building now houses a small grocery store. I cross the boulevard de Clichy and wander around Montmartre, but all the artists have been gone for decades, replaced by hordes of summer tourists. I take the métro back to the Left Bank. At the Magasin Sennelier on the Quai Voltaire the clerk has never heard of Moisse, but he directs me to another shop on the rue Soufflot where the old man behind the counter squints at the receipt and frowns.

—Moisse. Very famous *couleurs.* They've been gone a long time.

—Were they good paints?

The man shrugs. —I never saw them. But they were supposed to be very good. Moisse started at the Maison Édouard, and they mixed the best colors in Paris. Manet used them, Caillebotte, everyone—

—Would they be worth buying from overseas?

—*Comment?*

—Were they good enough to order from another country?

—Of course. Once a painter has his colors, he doesn't want to use different ones.

I thank the man, walking out the door. The bell chimes behind me. Suddenly I turn around and walk back in.

—Have you heard of a collector named Broginart?

—*Qui?*

—Broginart.

The man shakes his head.

—*Non.*

I start west along the quai toward the Bibliothèque Nationale. It's a long walk but I need time to think. There must be a thread I still haven't followed, a piece of evidence that could unravel everything if I tugged hard enough. But which piece of evidence?

When I get to the library my research flits from topic to topic. I read about pigments and linseed oil, the grinding of colors and manufacture of tube paint in France; I flip through the catalog from the 1920 Salon des Indépendants. But I feel like I'm circling my goal instead of getting closer. So I study the catalogs of Paris museums and galleries, searching for collections of early twentieth-century paintings. Some of the smaller museums may not have listed their collections online. I call up a stack of catalogs and flip through the indices one by one. Then I see the name.

GRAFTON, *Eleanor* . . . 39

I turn to page 39. The entry is brief.

GRAFTON, Eleanor
    The Unvanquished (Étude de femme nue), vers 1917. Huile sur toile.
733 x 1000. *Don de Henri Broginart*

The front page of the catalog says *Musée Konarski: Catalogue sommaire des collections*. I skim the introduction. The museum is housed in the former home of Ludwik Konarski, a poet from Warsaw who migrated to Paris in 1909. Konarski befriended many painters at La Ruche, an artists' residence in the Passage de Dantzig where Konarski bought the paintings that would be the cornerstone of his collection.

The catalog doesn't list the museum's phone number, only its address: 54, *rue de Monceau 75008 Paris*. I copy it down and walk quickly out of the library, trying not to run.

The Musée Konarski lies on the one-way rue de Monceau south of the Parc Monceau, the small white building set back from the street by a courtyard with a locust tree. When I open the door the woman behind the front counter stands up in surprise.

—Monsieur, the museum closes in fifteen minutes.

I explain that I'm not here to visit the museum.

—I came to see if you have a painting I saw in your *Catalogue sommaire*. It's by an artist named Eleanor Grafton.

The woman frowns. —I don't know—

—It was donated by a collector named Broginart.

—Ah, Broginart. We have most of his collection. Let me look.

The woman sits down and I help her spell out Grafton letter by letter into her computer. She makes a few clicks with her mouse.

—*Étude de femme nue,* 1917. Yes, it's in our storage.

—It's not here?

The woman shakes her head.

—We have a small museum, but quite a large collection. Most of it
rarely gets displayed.

—Do you have a picture of it?

—*Bien sûr.* It must be in one of the books—

The woman looks through the books on the shelf behind her, making a clucking noise as she closes each volume. She goes into a back room
and comes out with a large black paperback in her hands, smiling triumphantly. She sets the dog-eared book in front of me, the pages already
parted to show the picture.

—*Voilà.*

The image is captioned:

Eleanor GRAFTON (1891–1969) Cat. 537
> *The Unvanquished (Étude de femme nue), vers 1917.*
> *Huile sur toile*
> H. 0.73; L. 1.
> Don de Henri Broginart

The painting is a series of geometric slabs, the flat plane of the picture broken into shards of varying color—cold grays and blues receding
into the background, warmer earth tones surging out. It takes me a moment to make out the subject. A woman standing with one leg forward, a
blue cloak draped over one shoulder, the rest of her nude body sculpted
in prisms of ochre and sienna. Her face is visible both straight ahead and
in profile, the bold line of her nose dividing the two perspectives.

But the face could be anyone. It is only an arrangement of brown and blue planes with a dark triangle where the cheek should be, and a few lines to suggest the brow and jaw and chin. The woman's hair is modeled in two shards of copper. In one hand she holds a yellow object, thin and narrow, but the form is so simple that it could be anything from a stick to a scepter. Below the picture there is a commentary in French.

A painting by the British artist Eleanor Grafton. Daughter of the sculptress Vivian Soames-Andersson, Grafton was trained at the Slade School of Art in London under the direction of Henry Tonks, and was known as a painter of competent—if unambitious—portraits and landscapes. Grafton was a slow convert to modernist experimentation; she mistrusted the abstract, machine-driven ethos of Futurism and Vorticism developing in prewar London. But in the years preceding 1914 Grafton repeatedly visited Paris and is known to have taken a deep interest in the works presented at the Salon de la Section d'Or, some of which approached Cubism or Orphism with a harmonious palette and classical proportions based on mathematical principles. The experiment was difficult for Grafton, who destroyed preparatory studies in 1914 and again in 1916 before completing this final work. Never entirely satisfied with the result, Grafton abandoned the Cubist method and never returned to it again.

I push the book back across the counter. The librarian looks at me.
—It's not the right painting?
—No. I mean, yes it is.
—Do you want a copy of the image?
The woman takes the book into a back room and comes back with a photocopy of the page. I thank her and put it in my bag, walking out of the museum without knowing where I'm going.

It couldn't have been simpler. The picture was started long before Imogen would have been pregnant and the studies were destroyed for the most ordinary reason of all. They weren't very good. Neither was the final picture. It'd been hard to find because it wasn't worth displaying. Maybe Broginart wanted the earlier study because it was better, or because he collected modern paintings and thought Eleanor's experiment might eventually pay off.

I'd been crazy to follow the painting. The letters in Sweden made me think I could find anything, but that had only been dumb luck. Then I'd tricked myself into believing I could solve everything with one piece of evidence. A painting. Of all the things in this world.

—You're out of your league, I whisper.

I turn right into the Parc Monceau, following a wide path toward a rotunda on the north side. It's time to admit I don't know what I'm doing. I'm going after a huge fortune and I'm acting like a freshman researching a term paper. Maybe I should have hired a lawyer or a probate researcher, even if it broke the confidentiality agreement, even if I risked forfeiting my claim. Prichard had told me not to share the trust's details with anyone, but in listening to him I'd chosen a stranger over my own friends and family. Today is September 3. In five weeks I stand to lose every cent and there's no one I can turn to.

There are two choices now. I can go back to London and start over. I could even hire someone there. Or I can follow the only evidence I've found—Ashley's letters—and go to northern France. Ashley last saw Imogen in the Somme, about a hundred miles northeast of here. The truth is I don't want to go back to London empty-handed. And I don't want to break the agreement when there's a chance I can find the evidence on my own.

I walk past the rotunda and down the stairs into the métro, riding line 2 to the Gare du Nord. At the SNCF counter I ask for a one-way ticket to Amiens. I lean into the counter's microphone and repeat the name of the city several times.

—Amiens, I say.

—Orléans?

—Amiens.

The woman lifts her eyebrows and hazards a guess.

—Rennes?

Eventually she understands me. I leave the counter with a ticket on tomorrow's one o'clock train. At an *alimentation générale* behind the station I buy a bottle of cheap red wine and uncork it on the sidewalk, pouring it into my water bottle. I've wasted a week in Paris. At least I have one night to myself.

23 August 1916

The Langham Hotel

Marylebone, Central London

They take their dinner in the hotel restaurant. It is the night before Ashley crosses and Imogen would have preferred to eat in private in their room. But Ashley wants to be among a crowd.

—We'll only have to go upstairs afterwards, he promises.

Most of the other diners are men in khaki or older couples in evening dress. When the waiter puts the menu before her, Imogen is astonished by the richness of the dishes.

—One would think there isn't a war on.

—Not for those who can pay.

—Darling, I don't want to eat us into the workhouse—

—You shan't. Not tonight, anyway.

They eat bowls of potent consommé. They have roast shoulder of mutton in a rich brown onion sauce, served with plates of wax beans and lady cabbage. Ashley remarks that the mutton is dry, and as soon as he says this he wishes he had not. Imogen does not seem to notice. She seems distracted throughout the meal and Ashley does not know if she is nervous or impatient or simply unhappy.

For dessert they have pineapple ice followed by a wedge of

Roquefort. Ashley portions the whole cheese with a golden knife, but in the end they do not finish the slices. Imogen asks the waiter if they can have the coffee brought to their room. The waiter bows in affirmation.

They take the elevator up the three stories, the uniformed operator eyeing them curiously, Imogen holding Ashley's arm as they ascend. They get out of the elevator and Ashley looks at her.

—Are you all right?

Imogen shakes her head.

—Let's forget it's the last night. Let's not even think of it. Can we do that?

—Of course. But is something wrong?

—Darling, we needn't talk about it. Let's simply be together.

They go inside the hotel room and Ashley begins to kiss her as soon as the door is closed. He kisses her neck as she takes off her hat and throws it on the floor. He says things to her he has never said before, things he did not know he would say.

—You're everything, Ashley whispers. You're more than everything. The things I never believed in.

They are standing beside the bed and she is kissing his face, holding him very tight, her arms firm and tense. Ashley's hand runs over the linen-covered buttons at the back of her dress. He touches her cheek but Imogen guides his hands back to the buttons. She is looking at him all the time. Ashley pulls the buttons through the fabric loops and the dress slips lower down her body.

—Darling, Imogen says. The curtains.

Ashley draws the curtains shut and flips the switch on the electric light. It is easier now in the dark. He takes off his tunic and necktie and they get in bed under the counterpane, Ashley pulling the sheets over their heads until they are close together in the blackness. Their hands are free now and Imogen takes off her lace chemise and silk hose. Ashley can feel her bare legs against his. There is a knock at the door.

—The coffee, Ashley gasps. I completely forgot.

Imogen laughs. She pulls the counterpane over her shoulders and dashes into the bathroom. Ashley switches the light back on and dresses hurriedly. He opens the door and the waiter walks in with the coffee service on a silver tray. Ashley tips him a few coins. Ashley's shirt collar is open and his necktie is balled up on the floor. The waiter salutes and closes the door behind him.

—Safe to come out now.

—Do you promise?

Ashley switches the light off.

—Safe as houses.

Imogen comes out and wraps the counterpane around him, her naked body pressed against him as she pulls him toward the bed. She is breathing fast now and she gasps a little as he kisses her neck and shoulders. He puts his hand to her face, trying to look into her eyes. It is very dark.

—Are you certain?

—Hush.

—It's what you want?

—Hush.

She reaches for him and draws him closer.

—I'm not so good as you, Imogen says. But I don't care.

The night stretches long before them and still it is not long enough. Hours pass and Ashley drifts toward slumber, but when he wakes holding her he sees Imogen's watchful eyes looking back at him.

—You don't want to sleep?

She shakes her head.

—I can sleep when you're gone. We've only a few hours left.

Ashley nods and sits up in the bed. He pulls the sheet over his bare chest. His mouth is dry and his head has a dull ache.

—I had a dream. Though I scarcely slept.

—What did you dream of?

—I'm not sure.

—Perhaps you dreamt of me, she teases.

He shakes his head. —I'd have known if I had.

Ashley grazes his fingers along her cheek.

—That will come later, he adds.

Imogen goes into the bathroom and when she comes back she is wearing a silk dressing kimono. She walks to the windows and pulls a long rope, gold-tasseled at the end. The curtains part in the middle and gradually draw open.

—It's dark, Ashley says. You won't be able to see anything.

—We can see the searchlights. That's something.

Imogen pours a cup of coffee from the china pot on the tray. She takes a sip and frowns slightly.

—It must be cold, Ashley says. We could ring for more—

—It's fine, darling. I like it cold.

Imogen cradles her saucer in one hand, holding the cup with the other. She looks out the arched windows toward Portland Place, the dim beacon of a single blue streetlamp among the darkness.

—Ashley. I've another of my fool questions.

—All right.

—Do you believe in what happens in dreams?

Ashley blinks wearily. He is watching her back, his eyes on the blue sash girdling her waist.

—You mean the events in dreams, he says. You're asking if they really happen.

Imogen nods. —If they happen somewhere. It needn't be here.

Ashley considers for a moment.

—I expect you want a better answer. But they're just dreams. I suppose our minds need something to work on in the night, so everything's let loose, fear and desire. We may dream about real people and places, but that doesn't make the dreams real.

—But this hardly seems real, Imogen says. It's only been a few days and here we are together.

—This isn't ordinary.

She smiles.

—No, she says. I suppose it isn't.

Imogen sets the empty cup and saucer on the tray and climbs into bed beside Ashley, staring up at the ceiling. She says that at times this world seems certain to her, but at other times the world of dreams seems equally certain, or even more certain, for dreams cast a shadow over this world, while the present world hardly figures in the world of the night.

Imogen sits up and asks which of the two domains is more human, for this world is cold and stark and banal, and here all is governed by exacting calculation, from the moment of our birth to the chemical causes of our death. She says that all of science and mathematics is but the feeble discovery of these ruthless mechanisms, and in this world all the affection or pathos one could ever summon would not shift a single physical atom. She says that it is an unholy world where human souls are decided through mean reckoning of the trajectories of bullets or the multiplication of diseased cells.

Ashley moves to touch Imogen, but she catches his hand and grasps it.

—We deserve more than that, she says.

It is the domain of dreams, Imogen continues, that is crafted on the scale of the human heart and constructed of the same materials, and for this reason feels warm and vivid and familiar even as it is strange. It is in the world of the night, she tells him, that we are at last set loose from the trivial and the crass, and left to seek what is truly worthy. Imogen says finally that in dreams neither distance nor even death can prevent the meeting of two hearts of sufficient will, and surely this is the way our world ought to have been fashioned, and if it was not so fashioned she wants no part in it.

—It isn't fair otherwise, she says. It just wouldn't be fair.

Ashley comes to Imogen and wraps his arms around her. He holds her tight, watching her eyelids sink slowly with fatigue. When her breathing becomes soft and regular, he sets a feather pillow beneath her head.

Clothed only in his underwear, Ashley goes to the desk and takes a white card from the drawer. He writes a few lines on the card and studies them. He frowns and tears the card up, droppings the pieces in the wastebasket. He writes another card and reviews it carefully. When he is satisfied he hides the card inside her bag where it is not easily seen.

Ashley goes to the window and begins drawing the curtains closed with the rope. Through the paneled glass he sees the sky lightening faintly at its edges. He wonders if dawn is truly breaking, or if he is only imagining the coming of this light. He wishes he had not seen it. The two curtains meet in the center and cinch shut. Ashley climbs back into bed. He looks at the sleeping girl beside him.

—You'd want me to wake you, he whispers. We ought not to sleep tonight.

He smoothes the dark band of hair on her forehead. She stirs slightly. Ashley lies down beside her and shuts his eyes.

MIREILLE

It's my last night in Paris and I want to see as much as I can. When I come up the métro stairs at Châtelet the sky above is blue and black, beneath this a chandelier of yellow streetlamps. I cross the Seine on the Pont d'Arcole, the water riding fast below, and I sit on a bench in front of Notre Dame. For half an hour I stare at the cathedral, snapping photos and sipping wine from my water bottle, imagining the laborers and masons and bishops that pulled Notre Dame from the dirt of the Île de la Cité. They knew what they were doing. Even if it took a hundred years, they got it right in the end.

I take the Petit Pont to the Left Bank and pass into the Latin Quarter, skirting the periphery of the Sorbonne, then I climb the hill to the Pantheon, mausoleum of dead French heroes. On a nearby side street I pass a bar that looks interesting. I walk on half a block, then I turn back and go inside. The walls are layered with posters blackened from years of smoke. I sit on a stool and order a *pression*. The bartender pulls a small glass of lager from the tap and flips a beer mat before me and sets the foaming beer down.

On the way to Paris I'd bought a tin of cigarillos from a duty-free store in the airport. I'd seen them in pictures and always wanted to try them. I take the tin from my shoulder bag and light a cigarillo, smoking it until my throat begins to ache. A girl stands beside me, leaning on the counter as she waits to be served. She asks if I can spare a cigarillo. I pass her one.

—I can give you a cigarette in return, she says in French.

The girl has cropped hair and light gray eyes and there is a white flower pinned to her blouse. I thank her and tell her I don't need a cigarette. We talk a little and when the girl learns I'm American she switches to English, which she speaks fluently with only a slight accent.

—That's a beautiful camera. Can I see it?

I look at the girl. She wears a wool skirt and ballet flats, dressed up as though she expected to go somewhere nicer than this grimy bar. She asks the bartender for a whisky and soda. I unsling the camera from my shoulder and hand it to her. She turns it slowly in her hands.

—Where did you get this?

—It was my dad's.

—He was kind to give it to you. You can't buy such things these days.

The girl looks through the camera's viewfinder toward the front door.

—How does it work? It's different from my camera.

—See the two images in there? You have to line them up. It's dark in here, you'd better open the aperture all the way. Probably won't come out anyway. Maybe if you prop your elbows on the bar. And hold your breath—

She points the lens at me and turns the barrel to focus, sucking in a breath.

—Don't move.

She pushes the shutter button gently. There is a faint click. The girl smiles and hands me back the camera.

—I don't think I did it right.

—That's OK. Half of my photos never turn out anyway.

—Are you in Paris to take pictures?

—No, I was doing research in some libraries. I got here on Sunday and I'm going to Amiens tomorrow—

The girl raises her eyebrows.

—Why would you go there?

—More research. Historical stuff about the Great War.

—That's funny, she says. I grew up near there.

The girl explains she is from Noyelles-en-Chaussée, a *commune* in the Somme *département* not far from Amiens. Her name is Mireille and her friend farther down the bar is named Claire. They are both in their first year of art school. When she hears her name Claire smiles at me from down the bar, making a circular wave as though polishing an un-seen window. Claire sits beside a studious-looking man in eyeglasses, the man speaking to her with intense concentration.

—A friend of hers? I ask.

Mireille leans in and smiles. —They just met.

—You're out to make new friends in Paris?

—Claire wants to make new friends, Mireille says. She says I'm staying in my apartment too much, like an old lady. So we got dressed up and went out.

The bartender comes around again and I order another beer.

—You speak French well, Mireille says.

—It should be better. I studied it all through college, but my gram-mar's still pretty bad.

—It was your subject?

—No. I studied history.

—American history?

—European.

—Really? Why Europe?

I shrug. —Look at this city. Miles of catacombs under the street. A palace full of stolen treasure from all over the world. Revolution after revolution until nobody can remember which is which. They'd just pull out the same cobblestones to make barricades in the same places. Even the monuments here are crazy. A Roman-style victory arch made for Napoleon that Prussians march under in 1871, the French again in 1919, then Hitler in '40, de Gaulle in '44—

Embarrassed, I take a sip of beer. Mireille lights her cigarillo.

—But isn't everywhere interesting? Where did you grow up?

—California.

—It must be very beautiful.

—It's perfect. Everything you could ever need.

—Are you joking?

—I don't know. Maybe I always liked things better that were far away.

Mireille looks toward the entrance. A group of people have come in and they are taking off their coats, glancing around the grotty interior as if surprised to find themselves here. Mireille turns back to me.

—You like things that are far away. But you're here now, so you won't like it for long.

—I'm leaving tomorrow, so I should be all right. But you said you're from the north. What brought you to Paris?

—That's a long story.

—I'll tell you my story if you tell me yours.

—Do you have a good story?

—It's not bad. But tell me yours first.

Mireille begins to roll a cigarette on the bar. She says that she moved to Paris three months ago from the south, where she had been living with her husband. She is twenty-three years old and she is divorced. Mireille sees that this surprises me and she laughs in embarrassment, looking down into her glass.

—I never tell people this. But you asked.

Three years ago Mireille and her boyfriend were at university in northeastern France. They were bored with college and wanted anything but the life they had. They ran off to the Mediterranean coast and got married. In the south they wrote fiction and lived mostly off welfare. Mireille learned seventeen different ways to cook a sack of potatoes and she hated them all. Their writing was published, but the marriage failed. This past summer Mireille had moved to Paris to begin an art degree.

—What made you get married?

Mireille shakes her head.

—I don't want to say. I knew it was stupid, I just didn't care. Maybe I thought that made it romantic. For now I just try to forgive myself for the last three years. And start over, pretending I'm eighteen again.

I watch Mireille as she talks about her art school. At times she seems shy or even embarrassed, looking away when I ask questions about her, but at other moments she seems comfortable, even playful. She makes a few good-natured jokes as if to test the waters. The way the bartender bounces his head in time with the music. The way I keep my camera slung over my shoulder even when I'm sitting down.

—Are you about to leave? It looks like you're ready to go—

—It's just safer this way.

Mireille lights her cigarette and begins to roll another one as she smokes.

—You seem like a careful person.

—I wish. If I were careful, I wouldn't have come to Paris at all.

—Why are you here? You never told me your story.

—You won't believe me.

—I'll believe you if it's true.

I tell Mireille about my week in Paris, about the libraries I visited and all the mistakes I made. Soon I'm telling her about the painting and the estate, and just as I realize I'm breaking the confidentiality agreement I also realize that I don't care. Because I can't see how telling a person with no connection to any of this could make any difference, and how Prichard could ever find out. And even if I am drunk, I'm tired of having no one to confide in, no one to tell about everything that's happened in the last three weeks. Mireille listens without interrupting. When I'm done she gives me the cigarette she has rolled.

She smiles. —It's not much, but it's all I have.

The bartender turns up the stereo very loud. He switches on the overhead lights.

—I think they're closing, Mireille says.

—Do you believe my story?

Mireille looks toward the door. She stands and puts on her coat.

—No, she says. But I liked it anyway. Come on, we'd better go outside.

We leave the bar and stand uncertainly in the narrow street, looking at our shoes, at the shiny paving stones below us. Finally Claire comes out, pulling on a bright red overcoat.

—What happened with your friend? Mireille asks.

—He was strange, Claire says. Very strange.

The métro is closed for the night, but Mireille invites us to her apartment in the Eleventh Arrondissement to have hot chocolate until the trains begin running again.

—Besides, she whispers, I have something I want to ask you.

—What's that?

Mireille puts a finger to her lips as Claire walks on ahead.

—*Attends*. Wait till we're alone.

The three of us follow the riverbank to the Pont Sully. We pass over the Seine and the Île Saint Louis, walking toward the place de la Bastille. I pull the plastic bottle from my bag and take a sip. Claire watches me.

—What's that?

—Wine. I can't afford to get drunk in bars.

Claire looks at my bottle dubiously. —So American.

—You don't want any?

The girls both take a drink. It's a long walk down the rue du

Faubourg Saint Antoine, the green street-sweeping machines rumbling past us into the darkness. Finally we reach Mireille's building on a backstreet off the boulevard Voltaire. Mireille types a code into a keypad and we walk through a foyer with a large mirrored panel and a door.

—Madame Fuentes's apartment, Mireille says. The concierge. I don't think she likes me, she never gives me my packages—

We go upstairs to Mireille's small studio apartment, furnished only with a desk and a foldout couch. Claire sits cross-legged on the carpet rolling a cigarette. In the closet-size kitchen Mireille warms milk on a two-ring electric burner and breaks squares of dark chocolate into a saucepan. She pours the steaming chocolate into mugs.

—When is your train to Amiens?

—One o'clock.

Mireille nods, pouring the third serving into a bowl.

—I don't have enough cups, she says. But I like drinking from a bowl.

We drink the chocolate sitting on the carpet. Claire changes the CD in the stereo and we talk about music for a while.

—I want to visit the States, Claire says. Have you been to New York?

—Once. I took the bus there last summer.

Mireille raises her eyebrows.

—From California? Isn't that far?

—It took a couple weeks each way. With a lot of stops.

—What was you favorite? Claire asks. New York?

—Not New York. Probably someplace in Montana. Or New Mexico. The middle of nowhere, that's my favorite.

Mireille smiles. —That's because you didn't grow up in the middle of nowhere. Where are you going to visit in Picardie?

—Everywhere I can. I want to see this battlefield near Eaucourt.

I have a photocopied map of the Somme battlefields in my shoulder bag and I show this to Mireille. She points out her town and a few nearby landmarks. Claire spreads out on the couch and shuts her eyes. Mireille goes to the kitchen and gets a small bottle of whisky, pouring a little for each of us. She smiles.

—Aren't you glad you came to Paris now?

I shake my head. —I just feel stupid. It's not just that I wasted time. It's the way I made the mistake. Looking for a picture because I liked the idea of it, because I thought I knew something about paintings.

I lie back on the carpet, resting my head against the side of the couch. I take a sip of whisky.

—All I need is one good piece of evidence, and I keep getting sidetracked. It's hard because when I was doing my senior thesis, every time I got sidetracked I found the best stuff. I was reading all these diaries and letters in French—

—You wrote about France?

—Sort of. I wrote on the International Brigades in the Spanish Civil War. But I got interested in the French and Belgians. There was one guy in Toulouse who was still alive, he'd been at the Siege of Madrid. I was supposed to interview him, but his daughter canceled three times. He was always too tired to talk. By the fourth time my paper was already done.

—So you never talked?

I shake my head. —I should've done it anyway.

—You should have. Maybe he could have told you something.

—Maybe.

—I don't mean something for your paper.

—I know.

There is a long pause. Mireille looks up at the clock. It is after six and the trains have started running again. I excuse myself to go, but Mireille says she will walk me to the métro. We leave Claire sleeping on the couch and start down the rue de Montreuil, the morning sky dim and murky. I put my hands in my pockets to keep warm.

—What was it you wanted to ask me?

Mireille shrugs. —It doesn't matter. Claire was always there, I didn't want her to hear—

—We can talk now.

—On the street?

We walk up to the green cast-iron entrance of the métro. I look at Mireille.

—It's your city. Take me somewhere. You must know a place.

24 August 1916

The Langham Hotel

Marylebone, Central London

The lovers stand beneath the portico. A porter sets Ashley's haversack on the space beside the motorcab driver's seat, cinching a canvas strap over it. Ashley passes a coin to the porter and waits behind Imogen as she takes her seat in the cab. He leans up to the glass, whispering to the driver.

—Victoria Station.

The driver pushes the red flag down on the meter. He touches his cap to the doorman and shifts the taxi into gear.

Ashley and Imogen do not speak. They are not sitting close to each other, the hem of the girl's skirt some distance from his woolen puttees. Ashley lowers his window and leans his head toward Regent Street, the morning air cold upon his face. He hopes the breeze will wake him. He watches a motor omnibus come into view, the passengers at the back clutching the brass handrail and stepping or jumping from the running boards as it slows. A uniformed female conductor climbs the staircase to the upper deck, calling out to the passengers.

—Gentlemen, please hold tight.

The huge placard beneath the conductor advertises Dewar's White Label. The omnibus disappears from view. Imogen crosses her arms.

—It's cold—

—I'll shut it, Ashley says.

—Keep it open.

Imogen's eyes are bloodshot. She puts her hand to Ashley's chest.

—Careful, he warns. You'll smudge the buttons. They're meant to gleam like a mirror.

—Let them throw you in jail.

—They'll throw me in the front line. Only as a private.

—You said the men last longer than the officers.

—So I've heard. But neither lasts forever.

Imogen shakes her head. —You needn't say such things.

Ashley's mouth tightens, but he says nothing. He unfolds his embarkation orders and rereads them. He replaces them in his pocket.

—I'm sorry, Imogen says. I don't feel well at all.

—It's no wonder. How much have we slept this week?

—Perhaps two nights in five.

—It's good practice for France.

The motorcab passes Hyde Park, rounding the Wellington Arch. Ashley resolves not to speak for the rest of the journey. It will be better that way. He will report to the RTO at the station and then they will say good-bye.

The station is teeming. Swarms of returning soldiers in tin hats emerge from the long troop trains, their greatcoats and haversacks caked with dirt, entrenching tools and shovels swaying from their bodies as they walk toward Victoria Street or queue for the free buffet, some of them already holding cups of tea and cakes or sandwiches. The soldiers bound for France are cleaner but equally burdened, brown paper parcels of foodstuffs or extra clothing dangling from their shoulder straps.

Ashley leads Imogen by the hand, pushing his way through the crowd until they are halfway down the train platform. They stop here, the traffic of soldiers streaming past the island of their two bodies. An idling locomotive periodically steams and screeches. Amid the chaos they can barely hear.

—Damned hard place to say good-bye, Ashley says.

—Then let's not say it.

—You know the things I would say to you. I've said them already. It was the best week of my life—

—Is that all it was?

Ashley shakes his head. He looks up at the dusty glass roof, the sunlight breaking in among the ironwork.

—I shouldn't have come onto the platform, Imogen says. I'd sworn I wouldn't do it.

—It doesn't matter. You'll have a letter from me before you miss me.

—I miss you already.

The conductor marches down the platform, blowing his whistle and calling for boarding. Ashley holds his rail ticket and his stamped orders in his hand.

—I ought to board.

Imogen unwraps the silk scarf around her neck. She folds it and puts it in his hands.

—I know you don't want to take it, she says, but I don't care. You don't believe I can protect you, but the protection doesn't come from me.

Ashley pushes the scarf back toward her.

—I'd lose it. It would be torn, or dirtied—

He closes Imogen's hands around the scarf.

—There's a note in your bag, he says. Read it when I've left.

They stand awkwardly apart. Imogen's face is turned away, her eyes on the puffing locomotive. Ashley knows he will regret not embracing her, but still he does not do it.

—Good-bye, he says.

Imogen turns to him, shaking her head in exasperation. Her voice breaks.

—You can't just stand there. You can't leave like this, when we've only just begun—

—Imogen.

—You ought not to go, she insists. You ought to choose me instead.

He kisses her on the cheek, but she only stands there woodenly as he touches her and backs away.

—I shan't say good-bye, she whispers.

Ashley steps onto the train and takes his place in the cramped compartment of an officers' carriage. He greets the other three officers, a pair of boyish second lieutenants and an RAMC captain reading the newspaper. Ashley sits down and his legs graze those of the captain. Gruffly the captain shuffles his newspaper. Ashley recrosses his legs, resisting the urge to look out the window. Finally he looks down to the platform, but he does not see her there.

Ashley hears a clatter a few compartments down. The RAMC captain lowers the corner of his newspaper to look.

—Madam, a voice barks. Madam, the train is departing.

Imogen comes into the compartment, the conductor trailing in the corridor behind her. Her eyes are wet. The scarf is in her hands.

—Take it, she says. Take it.

THE PLATFORM

⋅⊶⊷⋅

We climb the steps of Montmartre in the thick morning fog. I walk behind Mireille, gripping the handrail to keep up, following the back of her upturned coat collar. Mireille turns right onto a cobblestone street, then makes an abrupt left.

—Do you know where we're going?

—It's possible.

—But you're no Parisian.

—No.

We walk through winding streets and climb stone staircases, passing from the shadow of apartment buildings into a field on a hillside. The sky opens above us. Through a wire fence I see neat rows of plants and we walk along the fence until we reach the gate. Mireille tugs at the low doorknob.

—It's locked, she says.

—What's inside?

—A vineyard. The Montmartre vineyard. They have a festival once a year where you can drink the wine.

Her hand slips from the doorknob.

—It's bad wine anyway. Give me your camera, I'll take a picture of you. Then you'll have that at least.

I unsling my camera and hand it to her, standing awkwardly in front of the gate. Mireille laughs.

—Tristan, you have to smile. It wasn't such a bad night.

I laugh and Mireille snaps the picture. We start back down the hill toward the place des Abbesses.

—Do you need to sleep before your train?

I nod. —I should probably go back to the hostel.

—Of course. We're not too far from the métro—

Mireille looks down at the cobblestones, walking with her hands in her pockets. She looks up at me.

—I wanted to ask you. What you told me in the bar, about the lawyers in England and the inheritance. You weren't joking?

—No.

—And the English soldier and his lover. The letters you found in Sweden. It's all true?

—It's all true.

Mireille nods. —I wasn't sure if you were serious.

We walk for a few blocks in silence. Then Mireille says, —I hope you find what you're looking for in Picardie.

We reach the place des Abbesses. The square is empty, the sycamores shedding leaves in the breeze. A carousel is stored under its plastic covering. I'm thirsty from the night of drinking and I cup my hands under a cast-iron fountain, pulling out gulps of water that spill onto my shoes. As I drink Mireille wanders the square, pausing beside a trash can. She reaches into it and when she comes back she is holding a newspaper triumphantly, the pages still crisply folded. She hands it to me.

—*Un journal en anglais,* she says. It's yesterday's, but that's fine.

Mireille leads me under the gate into the métro, the glowing Art Nouveau letters above spelling *Abbesses.* We go down a long spiral staircase to a broad landing. From here the steps lead on each side to different platforms, one for trains bound for Porte de la Chapelle, one for Mairie d'Issy.

—I'm going the other way, Mireille says.

A faint smile comes over her face.

—Do you have something to write on?

She writes her phone number on the flyleaf of my notebook in red ink. Her elaborate cursive is hard to read.

—Is this number an eight? If I can't read this—

A train roars in below us. Mireille sighs and shakes her head. She looks at me, waiting for the rumbling to stop.

—What if we go to Picardie together? I was going to leave on Friday, but I can miss a few classes. Then you can stay with me at my grandfather's house, you won't have to go to a hostel.

I look at Mireille. She shuts my notebook and hands it back to me.

—I was thinking about it all night, she says. But I'd drunk a lot, so I didn't trust myself, and I knew if Claire heard she'd kill me. So I waited to tell you, but I'm sure now. We can take your train to Amiens, we just go a few more stops.

I write down the time of my train, then I tear off the page and hand it to Mireille.

—I'll meet you on the platform, she says.

I go down to the Mairie d'Issy platform and sit on a bench, opening my notebook to look at Mireille's handwriting on the flyleaf. I smile and shut my notebook. A current of warm air shifts through the station. I look up and see Mireille sitting on the bench across the tracks from me, her face turned to the empty tunnel. My train comes screeching in and I get on, checking my map to see where I change for line 8. I notice that the trains from Mireille's platform don't go toward her apartment, only toward northern Paris. To get home she should have gone one stop with me and changed at Pigalle. Unless she didn't want to ride with me.

I put the map back in my pocket. I'm not going to worry about it.

⬥

My dorm room at the hostel is locked up for cleaning, but the desk clerk lets me in to get my backpack. I sleep for a couple hours in the luggage room on a pile of old mattresses stacked in the corner.

I reach the Gare du Nord half an hour before my train. At a bakery inside the station I buy a pair of croissants and two paper cups of café au lait. I take the newspaper that Mireille gave me from my bag, the *International Herald Tribune*. The headlines all look familiar: the upcoming American elections; a state of emergency in the Gaza Strip; a suicide attack in Iraq.

I fold the newspaper under my elbow and look up at the station's enormous black signboard. The plastic letters flip from the center with blinding speed, spelling out the destinations letter by letter. To pass the time I try to guess at the cities as the letters arrive, but I'm usually wrong.

BRUXELLES-MIDI ROTTERDAM AMSTERDAM. LONDON WATER-LOO. LONGUEAU AMIENS ABBEVILLE ETAPLES BOULOGNE.

I walk to my train's platform, searching up and down its length. Mireille isn't here. It's three minutes until one. I jog along the platform peering into the train's windows until the conductor waves at me and blows his whistle. I board the train and pass down the aisles of each car. In the last second-class car I find Mireille sitting beside the window, her legs propped against the opposite seat, a sketchbook in her lap. She lifts her pencil and looks at me.

—You thought I wasn't coming.

I take the seat across from her, handing her the lukewarm cup of coffee and one of the croissants in its paper wrapper.

—That's so kind, she says. I guess this is breakfast time for us, isn't it? I'm sorry I was late, I almost missed the train.

—Didn't you get on in the wrong direction this morning?

Mireille smiles. —I told you I'm no Parisian. I felt drunk all morning, and I had to do a million things before leaving town. I went to see one of my professors about my project. When I told him I was going to Picardie we had an argument in front of the whole class. Tristan, I was almost crying, it was so embarrassing—

The train starts to move forward. Mireille closes her sketchbook.

—And that's not the worst part. After class he asked to see me in his office and he said, I know about your past, Mireille, I know you're different from the other students. But we have to treat you the same. You might be a good artist, but that doesn't matter, because you're immature, and you'll have to grow up to get anywhere in the world.

I stifle a laugh. Mireille looks at me.

—Do you think it's true?

—You're plenty mature. You're divorced, for one thing. And you know fifteen ways to cook a sack of potatoes—

—Seventeen.

Mireille smiles. The conductor is coming down the aisle checking tickets. I reach into my pocket.

—My ticket's only to Amiens. Do I need to buy an extension?

Mireille shrugs. —It's only a couple more stops, it might be the same price.

—We'll see. Want half this newspaper?

Mireille shakes her head. —The letters you told me about. Can I read them?

I get my notebook and flip it to Ashley's letters, handing it to her.

—Hopefully you can read my handwriting. Some of the letters are pretty grim, I don't know what you'll think—

—It's fine, she reassures me. I love old letters.

She drapes her coat over her legs and begins to read. I spread open the newspaper, but as the train pulls away from Paris I lose interest in the articles. Outside the window the city gives way to suburbs and finally farmland, fields and trees swept by a gentle wind. I study a set of gray thunderheads over the horizon, but I can't tell if they are getting closer or farther away. I fold up the newspaper and watch the scenery.

BOOK TWO

EMPRESS REDOUBT

I have made fellowships—
  Untold of happy lovers in old song.
  For love is not the binding of fair lips
  With the soft silk of eyes that look and long,

By Joy, whose ribbon slips,—
  But wound with war's hard wire whose stakes are strong;
  Bound with the bandage of the arm that drips;
  Knit in the welding of the rifle-thong.

—Wilfred Owen, "Apologia Pro Poemate Meo"

There are a thousand kinds of weapons here and Ashley has seen them all. When they are in a museum one day, he thinks, they will know how we went back to the Middle Ages. But Ashley had seen medieval weapons in the Tower of London and even the poorest had been finer and cleaner tools than some in this war.

Ashley lifts a whisky bottle from the dugout's crude shelf, no more than a plank hammered into the clay wall. He studies the bottle's label. Strathisla, a good single malt. He wonders where it has come from and why it is not yet empty. He pulls the cork out, letting the aroma drift up the bottle's neck. Peat and oak, a faint scent of honey. Ashley recorks the bottle and puts it back on the shelf.

The dugout is lit by a single candle set in an empty wine bottle on the table. Beside the table are a pair of upturned crates serving as stools. A few pictures have been tacked to the dugout walls, photographs of actresses torn from the illustrated papers. Ashley rinses his mouth with his canteen and takes his pistol from its leather holster, the oily black barrel still warm to the touch. He sets the pistol on the table, but he does not reload it.

Fully clothed, Ashley lies down on one of the makeshift bunks, two nets of chicken wire hung on a wooden frame. A muddy blanket lies beneath him. The bunk is short and his boots are propped upon the bed frame at the far end. He pulls an overcoat across his body and tries to sleep.

As a boy he had loved the Tower and best of all he had loved the weapons. He remembers when he was barely tall enough to see the hilts of the swords arrayed in long rows along the stone walls of the armory. He remembers the elegant Toledo rapiers, the massive German *Zweihänders*, the gilded French maces, the flails, the war hammers, the morning stars.

Then there was this war. The German patrols had favored knives from the beginning; the British had thought this crude, until they turned to cruder weapons of their own. On a night raid a knife was a clean and silent instrument. To have your throat slit was not the worst death.

The British favor clubs and there are dozens of kinds. There are coshes, wooden sticks loaded with a lead core; there are truncheons and blackjacks tied to leather lanyards. One could attach anything to a handle to give it heft: an emptied hand grenade, an enormous cog. The regimental carpenters fashioned such weapons, or wooden maces studded with iron nails, a weapon a farmer might have carried into the field in 1525. Centuries ago they had turned to maces because plate armor had become too hard to pierce.

And we have turned to maces, Ashley thinks, *because we fight like vermin in a gutter.*

There are brass knuckles, and knives with brass knuckles set into the handle, and knives with brass knuckles studded with spikes. Ashley has seen faces gored with such weapons and the result was very bad. There are also spades, trench shovels sharpened to a fine edge, and the Germans favor these. Ashley had seen one of his men cleaved by such a spade. He was a delicate private from Newbury, sixteen and covered in freckles and grime; he had lied about his age to the recruiting sergeant, but once the platoon had reached France he bragged openly about being born in the new century, claiming the round number was good fortune. The private was so innocent that the ceaseless swearing of his platoon had scandalized him and he had even complained to Ashley. A few weeks later a huge German cleaved the boy with a sharpened spade, the blade coming down on his shoulder and splitting his torso nearly to the belly button. The private had lived on for nearly an hour, blubbering on about nothing. One of the older men held his hand and waited for him for die.

For one raid the battalion had grafted meat cleavers onto the ends of broomsticks. Ashley had been astonished to see the men marching these weapons down the trench, the shafts perched smartly on their shoulders. They might as well have requisitioned arms from the Tower.

There are a thousand ways to die, Ashley knows, and some are better than others. To be honorably wounded is the best a brave man can hope for. Not even fools believe they will survive unscathed. To lose a limb is a small thing weighed against surviving the war.

There is artillery fire and there are dozens of kinds. There are shells and mortars and canisters with shrapnel balls that lodge into supple flesh. You can get shrapnel in the face, the groin, anywhere, or your legs or arms blown off, or all at once. You can have your guts shredded, your arms cradling steaming intestines as they writhe out into the mud.

There are the machine gun and the rifle, but one doesn't flinch at the sound of these, because they are felt before they are heard. This makes some men less anxious, but when Ashley is being shot at his whole body sings with terrible sensitivity, waiting for the searing lead slug. As deaths go, many hope for a bullet in the head, and when mothers or sisters or lovers write to you to ask how their man died, you tell them he died this way. They might believe you because they wish to.

There is the searing gas that blisters skin and turns eyes into vacant clouded orbs, all the while scouring your lungs into bleeding mush. You might take weeks to perish, mutely suffocating in bed.

There are the elemental ways to die—burying, drowning, burning.

A dugout can collapse under shelling and bury you alive, or drown you as it slowly fills with water. The two sometimes come in tandem, so that it is hard to tell which will prevail. Burning happens many ways, but the most feared is from a flamethrower. All the soldiers know how bad it is because the victims scream horribly and look worse afterward. The smell of burning skin and fat is sickening. Flamethrower operators are always killed with relish, even those who surrender.

There is the sucking mud that takes waders and guns and horses and love letters, and flailing men you leave behind under retreat, knowing they will never be dug out.

Cruelest of all are human hands and the weapons they wield. Hands that drive bayonets into seizing heart or flooding lungs; hands that smash your skull or slit your throat from ear to ear, hack muscle or crack bone as best they can. Before he reached France, Ashley had often traced the course of flesh, from loving conception to mother's swaddling arms, fed and bathed and kissed; instructed by teachers, treated by doctors, and caressed by lovers, until the day that men who had no cause to hate you tore you sinew from bloody sinew. It was absurd from any perspective. But since the Somme he thought no more of this.

On balance Ashley wishes to be shot in the head, the most prosaic of deaths. He fears a stomach wound most, or anything that takes hours of agony, stranded in some godforsaken shellhole. If he has to get a wound like that, he hopes to bleed and die fast enough, or be able and willing to use his revolver. But he is not sure he could do that, no matter his wounds, and it troubles him. Ashley worries about moaning in front of the men, for he has seen the toughest of officers whine like children. Terrifically wounded soldiers of any rank are a danger, for if they cry out within earshot of the trenches, brave men might go out for them and get themselves killed. The best thing is to quickly bleed to death, or if you can to bite down on something and wait for nightfall.

Three days ago the Berkshires had launched an attack in this sector, but the Germans repelled them with intense artillery and machine-gun fire. The Germans had rallied in a counterattack that had ended with desperate hand-to-hand fighting here at Resolve Trench. Since then there have been many wounded stranded in the shattered forest of no-man's-land, just beyond the British wire. By now most of these had died or been brought in, but there remained one wounded German who had been weeping and raving all the while. He was still alive. He lay less than twenty yards from the British front-line trench.

Ashley was the only man in the company who understood German. He had been listening to the wounded man for three days.

The German passed between periods of lucidity and great delirium. At times he seemed to be dictating a letter to his wife, telling her that he was ready to die. At times he addressed the British directly, describing his wounds in detail, describing the shellhole he lay in, saying that he was running out of water but could survive if only they would bring him in. He explained that he had no quarrel with the English, that they were all brothers in God's kingdom. Except for the word *Kameraden*, which the German repeated over and again, the British understood none of this.

The men nicknamed the wounded German "Kameraden." One of the oldest men in the platoon, a soft-spoken postman called Stewart, had actually gone over the top at night to bring in Kameraden, but the Germans had seen him in the moonlight and begun strafing him with machine-gun fire. Stewart crawled back to the trench without ever seeing Kameraden.

Against all expectations Kameraden lived on, moaning all the while. He quoted popular songs or nursery rhymes or folk ballads. But mostly he recited poetry. Kameraden knew prodigious amounts of poetry, and Ashley wondered if he was a schoolmaster or a professor or even a poet himself, though he doubted the last. The German quoted whole long epics he knew by heart, and even the denser men could tell these were poems from the rhythm of the words or the patterns of rhymes. Ashley recognized only a few: Goethe's "Mignons Gesang," some verses by Heinrich Heine. One morning at dawn stand-to, Ashley was astonished to hear what he believed to be a German translation of Byron's "She Walks in Beauty," but the man fell into weeping before it was completed.

Late last night as Ashley was on watch, Kameraden's moaning reached a fevered crescendo. The men sleeping on the trench floor complained of the noise. A few of them yelled at the German to shut up, but this brought out further cries of protest from the other Berkshires along the line.

—Wish the bugger would get it over with.

—Wish you'd get it over with. What if it was you out there, three days bleeding in the mud?

—I'd get it over with.

Ashley told the men to go back to sleep. He found Bradley, the platoon sergeant, and told him he was going into no-man's-land to see Kameraden.

—It's hopeless, sir. You can't save him. The Huns might see you—

—I know, Ashley said. But I can't stand it any longer.

Ashley pulled a pair of thick toeless stockings over his knees and elbows, then checked the cartridges in his revolver's cylinder. He traveled north along the trench to get closer to Kameraden, stepping over men sleeping in niches in the wall or wrapped in capes on the muddy trench floor. They groaned in half-sleep and rolled in the mud. Ashley trudged up to the forward sap nearest Kameraden, really only a fortified shell-hole holding a sentry and a few flares. The sentry jerked to the side when he saw Ashley, swiveling his rifle and then lowering it.

—Thought you was a German, sir. Can't hear nothing over that blubbering.

—Certainly not.

—You understand German, don't you sir? What's he moaning on about now?

—He wants us to kill him.

Ashley saw the outline of the sentry's helmet move from side to side as he shook his head. His face was sheathed in blackness.

—He never said that before, did he sir?

—No. I'm going over. Don't fire unless they open on me, and only then well to the left. Eleven o'clock at the farthest, do you hear? I shan't be far off.

Ashley rinsed his mouth from his canteen and spat into the mud. He stepped on the crude fire step, peering above the rim of the parapet. It was quiet and he guessed there was little wind, but the shattered trees had no leaves by which to judge.

Ashley climbed over the parapet. On elbows and knees he zig-zagged through the British wire into the morass of no-man's-land. His chin trailed in the mud. It took twenty minutes to go fifteen yards. The stench was rich and sweet, decaying corpses and chloride of lime. He ascended the rim of a huge shell crater and floundered over. Inside there was a mound of dead Highland soldiers in muddied kilts and kneesocks. Ashley rested here and studied the terrain. The German was still wailing away, his voice hoarse. The sound was coming from the right.

Ashley crawled farther until the sound was very close. He flopped into another large shellhole. He saw Kameraden's murky silhouette a few yards away, but Ashley was afraid the German might have a weapon, so he lay in silence waiting. After a few minutes a flare went up over no-man's-land and the scene was illuminated.

Kameraden was a plump corporal from a Jäger regiment, known as forest hunters and expert riflemen. He was on his back, his tunic soaked with black blood where shrapnel had perforated his chest. His eyes were open but his face was turned up to the sky, watching the flare sink through the darkness. He was holding a water bottle in one hand and clutching his wounds with the other.

Ashley crawled up beside Kameraden and spoke softly in German. At first the man barely seemed to notice, perhaps mistaking him for a hallucination. He breathed in a terrible sucking wheeze. Suddenly the German's head bolted and turned. He begged for water. He said his canteen was empty and he had already drunk all the water in the shellhole. Ashley took his water bottle from his waist and poured it onto Kameraden's cracked lips. The liquid ran over his face and stained beard. Kameraden gulped feverishly, muttering something indecipherable.

Ashley heaved the German onto his back and began carrying him toward the British line, crouching as low as he could. Kameraden whined in pain. He was very heavy. Ashley could feel the man's blood dripping down his neck into his shirt and it was hard to crouch with the weight of the body upon him. The mud sucked back at every step. Ashley lost his balance and dropped Kameraden. The German moaned as Ashley lifted him again. It took ten minutes just to get out of the crater.

A machine gun burst open on the German side. The British returned a few sharp rifle rounds, then a Lewis gun began rattling to Ashley's right. He would never get Kameraden all the way to Resolve Trench. He went on forward anyway, the German raving with the pain of movement. It took twenty minutes to reach the shellhole full of dead Highlanders. They went over the lip and Kameraden slipped from Ashley's grasp and rolled to the bottom. Ashley pulled Kameraden's face out of the mud and propped him up. The man was in delirium again. He was talking to his wife, the mud trickling down his face. Ashley cursed and drew his revolver.

He stepped back and tried to level his pistol at the German's bare head. He pulled the trigger but his hand was shaking. The bullet clipped the man's scalp, tearing off a chunk. He moaned and whimpered, raising his hands above his face as if the soft flesh of his palms were any protection. Ashley moved closer and fired again. The bullet tore through Kameraden's finger and went into his eye. There was much blood. Kameraden slumped over.

Ashley crouched in the shellhole and watched another flare go up. The German machine gun was traversing the horizon wildly. A few grenades went off in the distance. Ashley bent over the mud and vomited his supper. It had been biscuits and bully anyway, and he was damned sick of biscuits and bully. Ashley spat and drained his canteen with a long drink. He wiped his face on his tunic sleeve.

Ashley waited half an hour until the guns went quiet. He crawled slowly back to the forward sap and tumbled in beside the sentry.

⬥⬥⬥

In the dugout Ashley shifts onto his side in his bunk. He takes the letter from his tunic pocket. He knows the words by now, but it pleases him to see the handwriting, the arcing shapes on the page.

1 October 1916

Dearest –

> *I write from the pebbles of Selsey Beach. Without you London is an empty shell – I have only the Sussex Downs & the seashore to make me whole again. There is a sound here that is not the roar of the ocean, nor any signature of God's labour – they say it is the thud of guns in France, a hundred miles away – but the distance renders it soothing.*

> *Is it selfish to note that I've had no letters from you for three days? Probably the post is to blame, but if you haven't sent word, please do. My heart keeps vigil in two places – whatever piece of France you lay your head upon at night, and the patch of road between the Post Office and the house.*

> *I have assembled ¾ of the requested items – but I doubt there remains in all of England such a torch as you describe. The man at the Army & Navy Stores gave me second best, and you shall see the result yourself. I managed the wire-cutters, at least. I go back to London on Saturday to gather a last few surprises & I shall post the parcel then. Beside it every F & M hamper that ever was shall be emerald with envy.*

> *Ashley, I don't allow myself to miss you. For I am terribly wise & patient & every other fine thing – as you make me over again through your love. Nor do I wait for you – not wanting to count the hours & days we lose apart. The day you left I pulled the stem on my watch and put it in my jewel-box. The hands stand sentry at*

half-seven in the morning – the Universe, and I, your modest love,
slumber peaceful until your return.

Your Imogen

There is a voice at the dugout's entrance. Boot heels rap on the steps, descending as Ashley folds the letter away. Jeffries comes in, taking off his gas mask bag and tin hat and hanging them on a huge nail. Jeffries is B Company commander, at twenty-six the oldest officer in the company. His blond mustache is so fair as to be nearly invisible. The other officers joke that he is a German agent.

Jeffries sets his revolver on the table and calls to Ashley.

—Spymaster? You awake?

—I am now.

—Your eyes were open.

—I sleep with them open, Ashley says. I close them only when I'm awake.

Jeffries snorts derisively. —Got any rats today?

—They're about, but I've not been hunting. May have heard one a moment ago.

Jeffries eyes the muddy floor with faint interest. He sits down before the table on an upturned crate.

—Heard about you and Kameraden. Awfully decent of you to go over.

—Ought not to have.

Ashley tosses the overcoat from his body. He rises from the bunk.

—Three days, Ashley says, he's been moaning about his wife. Telling her how he'll kiss her, what presents he'll bring to her and the children. He spoke to us too, you know, telling us how he'd been to London once and saw Buckingham Palace. One night he even spoke to God. Think it was God, at any rate. Said he'd done his best, but he hadn't done enough. He swore he'd never killed a man, had only wounded a few.

—Is that so? I always thought he was reciting poetry—

—It was poetry, much of the time. Love poems. I think they were to his wife.

Jeffries nods. He takes out a leather tobacco pouch and a small meerschaum pipe. He packs the bowl and lights it with a long match.

—Then last night, Ashley continues, he starts begging for us to kill him. Says he knows one of us speaks German. One of us is a kind man who will come over and send him west. I felt he was speaking to me.

—The spymaster grown sentimental over the Hun? I don't believe it.

Ashley sits down at the table. He yawns and rubs his eyes.

—So I went over last night. Found him awake but done for. His guts a puddle of blood. He'd lived off the water in the shellhole for three days, though it was brimming with corpses. He could speak at first. I gave him a drink from my bottle. Then I tried to carry him. We didn't get far. I shot him in the next shellhole. Missed the first time, took off part of his head. It felt like pure bloody murder.

—Don't be absurd. Decent of you to go over at all.

—Possibly. Yet there was something else about it. At Crécy—

There is a faint shuffling on the other side of the table and both soldiers jump to their feet. On the dirt floor a rat licks a half-empty can of Maconochie that has been left as bait. Jeffries grabs his revolver from the table and fires twice. The shots from the large-caliber Webley ring loud in the dugout, the dirt geysering up as the bullets strike. The rat bolts along the wall into the darkness. Both men sit down.

—I say, those buggers are improving.

—Natural selection, I suppose, Ashley remarks. We killed the slow ones and only the quick ones are breeding now. We ought to stud them. We could race them at Epsom Downs.

—Why not over here, at Chantilly? After all, the Continental horses are otherwise engaged.

Ashley grins and sets his revolver on the table.

—Brilliant, Ashley agrees. They'd be our legacy to the French. Fitter rodents. Fleet of foot. The veritable flower of their race. We'll start the first studbook right here.

Jeffries takes a box of cartridges from a shelf. He releases a tab on his pistol and tilts the barrel down. The bullets in the revolver's cylinder extrude outward and Jefferies replaces the two spent cartridges with those from the box.

—Sorry, Jeffries says. That beast interrupted. You were saying—

—Crécy.

—Of course. The battle or the town?

—The battle.

—Hundred Years' War?

—That's right, Ashley says. Beginning of the end of knighthood proper, all that bosh. English longbows mowing down the flower of French chivalry.

Jeffries sets the pipe back in his mouth.

—Shame we can't re-create that.

Ashley grins. —Rather. But the part I was thinking of was after the battle. Ordinarily the victors would take the enemy knights prisoner and ransom them. But some of the French were too badly wounded for this. So the English sent out footmen to kill these wounded knights. This wasn't meant to happen.

—Only other swanks ought to have done it, Jeffries offers. Not peasants.

—Precisely. At any rate, I was thinking of how these footmen used daggers.

Ashley takes a bayonet from a shelf. He holds the blade before the candle on the table.

—The daggers were long—longer than this—and came to a fine point. The old *miséricorde*, the mercy giver. Plate armor was too hard to pierce, so you'd lift the wounded knight's arm and plunge the dagger through the armpit into the heart.

—And so the end of chivalry.

Ashley watches the reflection of the slinking candle flame on the blade.

—You see, I wrote an essay on this at Cambridge. At the time it struck me as rather unsporting.

—It's not so bad, Jeffries says. Sharp dagger to the heart. Quick at least.

Jeffries lifts the bottle of whisky from the shelf.

—Have a drink? Fine stuff. Bennett picked it up on leave.

—No thanks.

Jeffries shrugs. He pours some whisky into an enameled mug. Ashley is still looking at the bayonet.

—What do you think it feels like, Ashley asks, a dagger straight in there? If one's dying already—does it even hurt?

Jeffries shakes his head, but he does not answer. He takes a sip from the mug.

—First-rate whisky, Jeffries finally murmurs.

Ashley puts the bayonet back on the shelf and sits down. Jeffries strikes a match to relight his pipe.

—Shame about Kameraden. Bringing in wounded often turns out like that. But the men can get some sleep tonight. You kept your own skin, that's what counts.

—I suppose.

—Very decent of you to go over.

THE HOUSE

—Tristan, she whispers. Wake up, it's the next stop.

I open my eyes to the white light of the train car. Through the window I see autumnal trees, their yellow leaves carried off by a gust of wind. Picardie.

—The autumn has come early here, Mireille says. I heard it was cold all last week.

The conductor announces the stop over the scratchy loudspeaker, but we are still ten minutes away. I look at my notebook in Mireille's lap.

—Did you read the letters?

—All of them.

—What did you think?

She hands me back the notebook.

—*Elles sont belles*, she says. *Mais c'est une histoire triste.* I kept hoping things would work out for them, even though I knew they wouldn't. And the war—Tristan, it's all so dark. Of course it's interesting, but I couldn't read it for pleasure. I know you have to learn about this to get the money—

—It's not just about the money.

—But isn't that why you're here?

I look out the window at the flat brown fields.

—When I first heard about the money, all I thought about was where I could live and what I could do with it. But after I came to Europe and heard about these people, after I read their letters—

I shake my head. —It just makes me feel terrible to think about it. The money's dirty. The only reason it's still around is because of all the bad things that happened to them. I bet that's why Imogen never wanted it.

The white building of the station appears in the window. We take our bags from the luggage racks and sit back down. Mireille looks at her hands.

—I know you care about this story, she says. It's part of what I like about you. But you can't spend your life feeling sorry—

—I don't feel sorry for them. However badly things went for Ashley, I bet you anything he wouldn't have traded his life for mine. They knew what they cared about, both of them. Even if they lost it, at least they knew.

—You care about things. Last night you were talking about so many things. Paris and Notre Dame, the old man in Toulouse—

The train is pulling into the station. We go down the aisle and wait beside the sliding door. I adjust the straps on my backpack, looking out the window at the station house, a one-room brick building with its windows painted over in white enamel. I shake my head.

—That was before. Now all I do is go around looking for old papers. So what do I care about now? Dead people?

Mireille looks at me.

—They're not dead to you.

Mireille's friend waits for us in the station parking lot, a tall girl leaning against an old Peugeot hatchback wearing a pair of headphones. When she sees Mireille she runs up and embraces her.

—This is Hélène, Mireille says. She's lending us this beautiful car while we're here.

Hélène pulls off her headphones and we exchange awkward kisses on each cheek. She opens the hatch of the tiny Peugeot and I toss in our bags. As we drive off Mireille warns me that the house we are staying at has been in bad shape since her grandfather died twelve years ago.

—It'll be a little dirty, she says. But you like old things, don't you?

We drive to a supermarket in town to buy groceries for our stay. Mireille tells me to get anything I'll need. I wander the aisles with wide eyes, staring at the exotic wares labeled with words I've seen only in textbooks. Mireille laughs when she sees the cheese and bread in my corner of the cart.

—There's a kitchen there, she says. You don't have to eat like that.

—I like to keep things simple.

Mireille puts a blue can of *sel de mer* in the shopping cart. She looks at me.

—No one has lived there for years. You'll see.

We drive for half an hour through desolate farmland, chestnut-colored fields and shedding trees. I snap pictures with my camera as Hélène and Mireille talk quietly in the front seats. They seem to be having a disagreement about Mireille coming to Picardie early. They're talking in French and the conversation is hard to follow from the backseat.

We turn off the road and follow a long driveway to an old farmhouse, two stories tall and in great neglect. Ivy grows erratically up walls of chipped brick; copper gutters sag under the weight of dead leaves. A few of the windowpanes have long and curving cracks in the glass. We load the groceries into a wooden shed that links to the house.

—The refrigerator is broken, Mireille says. But it's cold enough in here.

I unpack vegetables and cheese onto an old workbench in the shed. We enter the house through a side door. In the kitchen we test the faucet and it burps brown water, then runs clean and clear.

Mireille shows me the large living room with its fireplace and a set of worn armchairs. The wooden floor is coated with antique grime and partly covered by a huge threadbare carpet, the fringed ends fraying to nothing. Hélène and I collect firewood outside and stack it beside the fireplace. Mireille takes me upstairs to the bedrooms.

—You can choose first, she says.

The rooms are all similar, so I choose one for its wallpaper: curling ivory flowers on a dark purple background. In the corners the paper is sliding off the walls. Beside the window there is a metal bed with creaky steel springs and a bare mattress. Mireille kneels before the fireplace and frowns.

—It's filled in, she says. But we can use the one downstairs.

She stands up and dusts off her pants.

—My grandfather never wanted to fix anything. My parents don't use the house, but they can't sell it for some reason, taxes or something. When we were at *lycée*, Hélène and I used to come here to drink, but I never had a reason to sleep here—

Mireille looks at me.

—Not until now, she adds. Do you have your sleeping bag?

I get my sleeping bag from my backpack. Mireille pulls it out of the stuff sack, fluffing the feathers in the air and spreading the bag gently over the mattress.

—*Et voilà*, she says. I know it's dirty, but I thought you might like it—

—It's perfect. Better than the Ritz.

Mireille smiles. —I'll go look for a pillow.

The misery begins long before the attack. The nights grow long and longer still, the days only a gray smoke of clouds and chilling rain. The rain begins in October and does not cease for three weeks. The soldiers can hardly remember the sun.

The ground becomes its own galaxy of wretchedness, a cesspool of failed ambition. Land that begins as green fields and neat villages is pulverized by explosive shells for days and weeks and months. All relics and histories of civilization sink back into the earth, pummeled into dirt or dust, divided and subdivided into finer particles and finally fused with icy rain into a single sucking gray morass, the binder and fixative of this chance apocalypse.

The mud is everything. It is contagious, the destiny and endpoint of all mankind. The mud coats and replaces all things until men no longer believe in anything else, until they can stare with wonder at any surface that has survived, clean and immaculate. The frontispiece of a King James Bible. A silk scarf, still faintly scented with perfume. If the soldiers take out these objects to admire, they will also become tainted, so they preserve them inside their tunics or haversacks as long as they can.

In the last week the cold snaps into frost, the tumbling rain and slush hardening to snowflakes drifting westward. A dry stinging wind. The pools in the shellholes crust with an inch of ice. One morning the men crawl out from their sleeping quarters, shelves in the trench wall curtained with a waterproof sheet, and when they look over the parapet toward the front line all is blanketed in white.

Ashley stands on a fire step sweeping no-man's-land with his collapsible periscope. At intervals he blows warm air onto his gloved hands, cupping them tightly. He wishes it would snow more, ten times more, until the pitiful ridge across no-man's-land gleamed as white as the Weisshorn. It must be a few hundred miles from here, but it feels like ten thousand.

Ashley shuts the periscope and comes down the stairs into company headquarters.

—Hunting season is over, Ashley says. If we couldn't get forward in the slop, we shan't get forward in this.

Jeffries shakes his head. —I wouldn't be certain. Brass hats will want to straighten the lines before we settle in for winter. And they'll want the Empress.

—Impossible.

—We're long past impossible.

Two days later they receive their orders to attack. The battalion is to travel by night to Patience Trench, arriving at the position well before dawn. From there they will attack the following morning. B Company will be in the second wave.

Their target is a German fortification called Empress Redoubt, a prehistoric burial mound rising dramatically from a bog of icy mud. The white chalk of the mound's summit has been shaped by months of shelling into a queer humanoid projection: to the staff officer who named the redoubt, it resembles the figure of the Empress of India in her youth. The enemy has fortified the mound into a maze of barbed wire and dugouts and tunnels and concrete pillboxes; the British general staff claims the redoubt is an essential artillery observation point that must be seized.

In truth it is useless to both armies. But it is the only landmark in an ocean of mud and the enemy holds it. The crumbling chalk and rusting wire of the redoubt look down upon the British every morning, upon subalterns inspecting troops at dawn stand-to, upon staff officers eyeing the position with field glasses. Since July the British have attacked the redoubt four times, failing each time at great cost.

The soldiers now believe the Empress to be German.

The evening before they go forward, Ashley asks his servant Mayhew to clean his revolver. Private Mayhew is a stocky man from Wiltshire who joined the army because he thought it would be easier than dairy farming. He lopes among the trenches in an odd shuffle, never looking another man in the eye when he can avoid it. But Private Mayhew wears the 1914 star. He fought at Mons and Loos, and the other soldiers say he has survived too many battles to ever be killed now. Ashley does not like Mayhew personally and finds him a poor servant, but Mayhew is a crack shot and an experienced soldier, and orderlies fight side by side with their officers. So Ashley keeps him on.

Mayhew takes the revolver from Ashley. He murmurs the name Patience Trench, giving a low whistle.

—Patience Trench, Mayhew repeats. Hoped I'd never see it, sir. Worst of the worst, they say. Chum of mine come out of there last week. Not any kind of trench, he said, just shellholes strung together. Nowhere to kip but in the mud—

Ashley smiles. —Look on the bright side, Mayhew. We shan't be there but a few hours.

The battalion begins its march shortly after supper, the sky well darkened in the November blackness. They travel by a sunken road flooded with icy water and dead horses. The road has been photographed by German airplanes and is printed on German trench maps of the sector in red ink. German artillery officers who have never laid eyes upon the road know it intimately, raining explosive shells on every curve and rise with pinpoint accuracy, night and day.

The road is a channel of misery and there is no other way forward.

Ashley marches at the front of his platoon, an electric torch in hand, the muck lapping at his knees. Small bergs of blue ice bob in the channel, the water pockmarked by the tumbling rain. The soldiers slog forward at a crawl. They are all heavily laden, carrying rifles and haversacks and shovels, the bodies draped with bandoliers and water bottles and bombs. Some of the men have added equipment on their shoulders: iron pickets, coils of barbed wire, drums of Lewis gun ammunition. They duck under sagging telephone wires that have been strung and restrung zigzag above the sunken road to hold taut. The men have no waders. Their feet are wet and painfully cold, but they suffer with little complaint. A few of them are singing.

—Could be worse, one man says.

—How's that?

—We could be going to Patience Trench.

The column arrives at a blockage in the road. A horse has fallen into a trap of mud, a deep crater filled with tacky gray sludge. The horse is sunk nearly up to its shoulders. The driver has unyoked the animal from its wagon and is coaxing it forward, but he cannot get it out of the mire. The horse brays and snorts, its shoulders thick with foaming sweat, its legs skittering hopelessly for footing. With every motion the horse sinks further down, with every suck of air.

—She'll never make it, Ashley tells the driver. You oughtn't let her suffer like that.

—He's a stallion, sir. A strong brute. He might get out yet—

—Bollocks.

Ashley watches the horse struggle, stirring up the mud with its forelegs only to collapse further down. A captain from the Durhams arrives from the other direction and halts his soldiers behind the wagon. He comes around the cart and Ashley salutes.

—That horse is drowning, the captain says. What's the holdup?

The captain does not wait for an answer. He draws his automatic pistol, approaches the channel of mud carefully and levels his pistol at the horse's head, aiming at the base of the brain, behind the eyes and below the ears. The captain fires. The horse jerks and its neck collapses. It goes on sinking with a soft gurgle, its eyeballs huge and grotesque, the fine musculature of its neck tense and rigid. The driver stands stupidly by the road, watching the dead animal. The captain orders Ashley's men to push the wagon to the side of the crater. It is impossible to move the horse.

—Just tread right on him, the captain instructs. That's right, on the withers, safest place to step.

They go on eastward. The men are no longer singing. The trench water gives way to thicker mud and their progress is slower. As they advance the shelling grows fiercer and several times they dive deep into the mud to seek cover. They come out dripping with sludge, several pounds heavier.

The column passes more stalled carts with dead horses still attached, mouths grinning in the darkness. Below the mud lie worse things, spongy or rigid forms that collapse under the men's boots and send up bubbles of foul gas. The soldiers follow only the man in front of them, too dumb and tired to think for themselves. The road disintegrates into a mess of shallow channels breaking off in different directions. The column goes in one direction, then another. The soldiers become lost in the night and the shells that fall upon them could be theirs or those of their enemy, for it makes no difference. A huge howitzer detonates at the rear of the column and two men are pulverized into a mess of blood and bone. One of the new recruits starts gathering the meager remains into a sandbag, but Ashley shakes his head, calling over the booming artillery.

—It's not safe here. We must keep moving—

They trudge on toward the flashes of the front line, making their way along another drowned road, the ground sinking until it is waist-deep and impassable. Jeffries comes back along the column to consult

Ashley, bearing his torch and a map in a waterproof case. The two officers go a few paces away so as not to be overheard. Ashley's boot slips into a hole and he tumbles into the mud. Jeffries pulls him up by the shoulders, stifling a laugh.

—We're at Ten Bells, Jeffries says. Must have passed our turning point under the shelling. I suppose A and C companies made the turn. We must come out of this road and traverse to the north. It shan't be easy, but it can hardly be fouler than this. How are your men?

—They know we're lost. We're always bloody lost.

Ashley leads his men up out of the sunken road. On hands and knees they scramble up the slope of mud, tossing rifles up and clawing at the gunk, sliding back down and squirming up until they flop over. They travel northeast across the refuse of old battlefields. The men march with their eyes half-open. They can no longer feel their feet. Some collapse and they are ordered forward, and when this fails they are cajoled and insulted and dragged back into the column. The soldiers drain their water bottles and even in the frost they sweat under seventy-pound loads until the sweat turns clammy and makes them shiver. Once an hour the officers halt to let the men rest, but later Jeffries worries that once halted the men will not start again, so there are no further breaks.

The sky goes from rain to icy rain. At three o'clock in the morning it begins to snow, the thick flakes silhouetted under the star shells flaring and sinking over no-man's-land in the distance. The column descends into a shallow basin of limbless trees and a few minutes later a barrage of shrapnel opens upon them, the metal pellets bursting and singing through the broken forest. Two of Lieutenant Bennett's men are killed and Ashley loses another, a lance corporal who is all but decapitated by a huge metal shard. The wounded are taken to the aid station and Ashley leads his men around a vast shell crater. At the far side of the crater Ashley sees a shadowy figure sunk up to his waist in mud. Ashley halts his men and calls out to the figure. It is difficult to hear over the crashing artillery.

—Just leave me be, sir, the man begs. Soon I'll be out of everyone's misery.

—Who are you?

—Evans, sir, C Company. Hit in the leg. Fell in here and they never saw me. I don't want to trouble no one. No point in bringing me out, only for me to die under the Empress. You can shoot me, sir—

—Rubbish.

It takes ten minutes to extract the man from the mud, and then he has to be half-carried by Ashley's men, dripping and exhausted. His leg wounds are slight, but he has lost his rifle and most of his equipment. He repeats over and again that he wishes he had drowned where he lay. Ashley tells him to shut up.

At dawn they reach the ruins of Patience Trench. The Berkshires relieve a ragged battalion of the Manchester Regiment identifiable only by their accents, their uniforms too caked with mud to reveal any insignia. The Manchesters begin to file out as soon as Ashley's platoon approaches. One of the Manchesters cadges a cigarette from Private Mayhew.

—Yous are after the Empress, aren't yous?

—Suppose we are, Mayhew says.

—Did you know, you can tell the weather by her?

—Is that so?

—Look up at her in the morning, and if she's there it's going to rain today.

—Very funny.

A second Manchester takes a drag from the cigarette and joins in the conversation.

—There's more to it than that. So long as she's looking down on you, you'll suffer more than you could believe. She belongs to the Huns. She's their good luck, and you won't believe the misery we've had under her. Last night we went out to cut the wire for you lot. We had two lads wounded and drowned in the mud, sucked into the ground. Let me tell you, you're better off never looking in her direction. If you look up at the chalk and see her face in it, your number's up. All them that drowned, they seen her face—

Mayhew shakes his head. —She won't be winking at me, chum.

The Manchester raises his hand in protest.

—Listen. I didn't say wink. You look at her, she looks right back. A pair of blue eyes. That's all it takes.

A captain from the Manchesters debriefs the B Company officers for the handover. The captain says the mud has gotten much worse over the past week. The dugouts have all flooded and there is no decent cover. A few days ago they lost a Lewis gun to the mud. The men nearly drowned trying to extract it. Last night the Manchesters opened a hole in the British wire in preparation for the attack, but even that simple task was torture.

—We're barely keeping our heads above water, the captain says, and now they've sent you in to attack.

—We'll manage, Jeffries says.

Ashley tries to guide his men into position for the attack tomorrow, but the ground bears little relation to the neat lines of his field map. He is looking for the second line of Patience Trench, a short lane called Patience Support from which his platoon will attack. But everything has been decimated by rain and shelling. In some places there are sandbags stacked a few feet high, in others only fortified shell craters linked by shallow flooded ditches. Patience Trench was held by the Germans until the July fighting and their dead are strewn everywhere. Among all the crevices hangs the same sweet rotting stench. The corpses are built into trench walls and parapets, their boot soles or black hands jutting out from the chalk.

In the grim half-light of dawn Ashley searches the shadowy ground with his torch, looking for a safe place to step. Bodies everywhere. A set of ivory teeth gaping from the dirt. It is impossible not to step on the corpses, so Ashley switches the torch off. In some places the trench is impassable, a well of bubbling silt, and the men have to climb onto the parados and dash under gunfire to their positions. Two men are hit in this way, one of them shot through the head and killed instantly. By late morning the four platoons of B Company have reached their positions. They will stay here until they attack the next morning.

Ashley spends the next hour inspecting the men for trench foot. He kneels before them holding a candle in a murky ditch as the men strip off their boots, struggling to wipe their feet with socks already black with mud. The best feet are merely caked with filth; the worst are red and swollen, dangerously close to gangrene. He orders the men to massage whale oil into their feet, watching them change into spare socks that will be soiled again in minutes. Ashley blows out the candle and hands it to Sergeant Bradley, whispering to himself as he walks back along the trench.

—*If I then, your Lord and Master, have washed your feet, ye also ought to wash one another's feet.*

In the afternoon Ashley studies the layout of the country using his pocket periscope from the Army & Navy Stores on Victoria Street. He scans the flat horizon, all white snow and gray morass, the occasional wisp of smoke or khaki figures dashing around the flanking positions. B Company will be the second line of attack, in close support of the first wave. Ashley's platoon is on the far right of the attack: Lieutenant Eaton commands the platoon to his left, beyond this the two other platoons of B Company under Lieutenant Hawkes and Lieutenant Bennett. Beyond no-man's-land the redoubt is conspicuous, a tower of chalk above a heap of snowy mud. Ashley watches it for some time before he can make out the figure of the Empress, but once he has seen her he can see nothing else. The figure remains faceless.

All day the men wallow in the mud, hungry and cold, waiting for the ration party to arrive. They have marched all night without water and there is nothing to drink here. Ashley sends a pair of men to scout for water in the vicinity, but they bring back only a sackful of canteens gathered from the German dead. Some of the men will not drink from these, saying it is bad luck, but when one of the canteens is found to be full of schnapps there is great jubilation.

Near dusk the ration party finally arrives. They have taken seven hours to carry their loads through the mud, their rifles slung on their shoulders, in each hand a petrol can full of water. Some of them carry sandbags full of biscuits and bully beef. There is no hot food. The water tastes of gasoline and the men have trouble drinking it even as they pinch their noses. Ashley mixes in a little whisky from his flask and gulps it down. The smell of bully beef makes him queasy, so he eats only a couple of biscuits and prepares to sleep a few hours. Zero hour for the attack is 06:00 tomorrow.

Ashley lies as the men lie, against the wet remains of a trench wall, his gas mask bag for a pillow. As he grows drowsy, he whispers a few words to her, indulgently.

—I could stand even worse. Anything for you. Imogen.

It thrills him to speak her name, but he feels embarrassed even though no one can hear him. It snows most of the night. Ashley is not fully awake, but he is shivering too much to sleep.

By four o'clock in the morning Ashley is wide-awake and feeling quite nauseated. He rises from the ground and walks a few yards toward a hole designated as a latrine, no more than a ditch dusted with quicklime. He urinates into the hole. Then he tries to vomit. Over the sleepless night his mind has become a wreck of nervous anxiety, and he imagines it might help to empty his stomach. Ashley bends over the ditch and the odor makes him gag, but nothing comes out. He straightens and stands there for a moment, the frigid breeze singing past his ears in the darkness. He wonders if this is how his last morning on earth begins. It is a useless question, he decides.

Soon afterward Ashley meets the other officers of B Company, the five men standing in the muck at a crossroads of crumbling trenches. They synchronize their watches and Jeffries says a few words about the attack. Everyone already knows the plan. Jeffries has brought an empty ammunition box and the officers fill it with addressed parcels for their wives or lovers, letters and mementos to be sent if they should be killed. Ashley drops in a short letter to Imogen, but he has no keep-sake to leave behind. Jeffries latches the box shut. They shake hands all around.

At a quarter to six the order goes down the line. Fix swords. The men each draw the long bayonet from the scabbard at their waist, set-ting them onto their rifles with a soft rustling of steel. They wait in the trench, many smoking cigarettes. Morning breaks colorless and bleak. It has stopped snowing and a thick mist curls over the ground.

At six o'clock the British batteries open all at once with a clank of shells jetting overhead, then thundering blows in the distance. The Ger-man lines on the horizon explode with color: bursts of red and yellow, geysers of dirt and smoke. The bombardment is short, a twenty-minute prelude to the attack. Ashley lights a cigarette to calm himself. Feigning cheerfulness, he walks among the men making trivial jokes, checking rifles and equipment. He eyes the sweep hand of his watch, forty ticks until the first wave goes over. The Germans send up signal flares in pink and green flashes. On both sides the machine guns rattle ferociously. Above the mist hovers the obscene white prow of the Empress.

Fifty yards ahead there is a low groan as the first wave clambers over the frontline parapet. Ashley watches them through his periscope: the men crawl up the mud and many are caught by a traversing machine gun as soon as they step over the top. The line wavers, men dropping their rifles and crumpling to the ground. A few stagger forward and disappear into the mist.

Ashley collapses the periscope and sets his whistle in his mouth. All around him the men look at Ashley expectantly, the whites of their eyes showing through the fog. It has begun to drizzle again. Ashley draws his pistol from its holster, the gun attached to a long lanyard around his neck. He eyes his watch, the sweep hand curving up toward twelve. It is time. He raises his arm and blows the whistle. Awkwardly he scrambles up the lip of the parapet, but he slides backward in the mud. He steps up again and waves the men forward, blowing his whistle in a burst of shrill notes. The line of men goes forward with a primordial bellow, their rifles leveled.

At once half the line is cut down as a machine gun opens on Ashley's left. It traverses at shoulder height and the taller men catch bullets in the neck, the shorter ones in the eyes. They crumple to the ground, spewing blood. Ashley urges the remaining men onward, expecting the machine gun to catch him at any second. The soldiers struggle to move quickly, sinking with each step over mud and ice and refuse. They waddle forward under heavy loads, shovels swinging on their packs as they walk over a set of planks strung across a long muddy ditch. They have reached the British front line.

Ashley urges his men forward, waving his arm. They step around the bodies of wounded and dead Durhams from the first wave. The gunfire is deafening. Farther on the ground is a latticework of mud and snow, icy in some places, sticky in others. Ashley has lost sight of all but a small party of his men, Sergeant Bradley and Mayhew and a few others. He cannot see far in the mist. He charges on, his eyes on a flashing machine gun ahead, but he stumbles on the rim of a shellhole and falls flat into the mud. A shrapnel shell bursts high overhead. Half-swimming, half-walking, his revolver lifted high, he limps out of the shellhole, dripping with mud. Mayhew follows close behind. They meet Sergeant Bradley and three men taking cover below a tiny ridge.

—Where are the rest of the men? Ashley demands.

—Don't know, sir, the sergeant says. Dead, I think. The machine gun caught most of them when we come out. Mr. Eaton and Mr. Hawkes was shot before we crossed our own lines. Haven't seen Mr. Jeffries or Mr. Bennett.

—C Company is to the north. If we get nearer the enemy wire, we can link up with them.

—We're closer to the Huns than we are to anyone else, sir. Only the six of us. We'll never make it—

—Nonsense. Let's go.

Ashley dashes forward before the others have time to consider. The soldiers follow. They stumble through glutinous mud, passing clusters of khaki and gray corpses floating in shell holes. Ashley fires his revolver stupidly in the direction of the flashing German machine gun. They reach the German wire. Slowly they zigzag between small openings cut by high-explosive shells. The machine gun to the north rattles off well to the left of them, the mist very thick. They approach the enemy parapet and Ashley makes a signal. Each man hurls a bomb into the trench. There is a thudding series of blows. The men jump over the parapet and stand on the neat planked floorboards of the German trench. It is empty.

—Bloody eerie, sir, Sergeant Bradley says.

—Careful, Ashley says. They could be anywhere—

They walk down the trench, Sergeant Bradley in front with his bayonet, Ashley behind with his pistol drawn, his other hand fingering the pin of a Mills bomb. They round the corner of a fire bay and turn another corner into a traverse. There is no one. Around another fire bay they find the entrance to a dugout, a wood frame with stairs descending into the darkness. Ashley begins to reload his revolver. He looks at the men.

—You will stay with the sergeant to consolidate the position. Mayhew will come down with me.

Mayhew looks at Ashley but says nothing. The men throw bombs down the staircase and wait for the concussion. A series of bangs, smoke and acrid fumes rising from the doorway. Ashley and Mayhew start down the staircase. The walls are lined in concrete and the ceiling is hung with electric bulbs at intervals, but the lights are off. They go down ten feet. The staircase goes on in the darkness. Ashley does not have his torch, so he strikes a match and holds it before him. He sees the steps under him, then farther below the ruined timber where one of their bombs exploded uselessly, scrapping the wooden steps. They walk carefully over the splintered wood, descending fifteen feet. Twenty.

They enter a room with a wooden floor. Mayhew pushes a metal lever attached to the wall, but the lights do not come on. Ashley finds a candle and lights it. The walls are papered and hung with pictures in wooden frames, colored lithographs of forests and churches. There are the remnants of a table, severed and splintered by the bombs. Broken china plates and shattered glasses. On one wall there is a bookcase filled with four neat rows of books, the spines stamped with gilded Gothic text. Ashley finds a trench map on one of the lower shelves and folds it into his tunic pocket. He walks into the far corner of the room, thrusting the candle before him. A large black shape—an upright piano, twisted ribbons of shrapnel embedded in the glossy wood. Mayhew fingers one of the ebony keys, shaking his head in disbelief.

—A bloody piano. And us living like rats just across the wire.

—Must be the battalion headquarters, Ashley says. What's through that door?

They go through the narrow corridor into a small kitchen, then an adjoining room with rows of bunks and shelves of supplies and foodstuffs. Mayhew finds a pair of dry socks and cries out in joy. He unties his boots and begins changing his socks. Ashley finds a square lantern-style electric torch and switches it on: a small yellow beam of light. At the end of the room there is another descending staircase. Ashley shines the torch down into the darkness. A rat dashes up the stairs and disappears into the shadows behind him. Mayhew double-knots his boots and stands up.

—Don't think we ought to go down there, sir.

—Naturally we ought to.

There is dull roar as a howitzer crashes above them, shaking the dugout. Clumps of dirt fall from the ceiling.

—Hope the men didn't catch that, Ashley says. Hell of a dugout. Quite deep.

Mayhew spits onto the floorboards, his thumb rubbing the bolt of his rifle.

—It's not the shells that worry me, sir. There's Huns about—

Ashley starts down the staircase, the torch hanging from one hand, his pistol in the other. Mayhew follows. There is a strong stench, the sickly bouquet growing as they descend. A rat squeals up the staircase between their feet, then another one, then a dozen, until they are treading on the rats. The staircase opens into another large chamber, this one dirt-floored. Sturdy rafters support the room and there are rows of iron bunks, shadowy figures upon them. A few of the shapes wheeze and reach toward the torchlight.

—*Kamerad! Kamerad!*

Ashley swivels, holding his pistol high.

—Mayhew, don't touch them—

—No intention, sir.

Ashley's torchlight darts around the room. The floor is a sea of obese rats scurrying back and forth, their fat pink tails sooted with grime. Empty tin cans and bottles. On the lower bunks, German corpses in their greatcoats, perhaps a week dead, faces blue or green, eyes sunken in black sockets. Some of the dead seem to move. Ashley approaches one of them, the chest throbbing under the greatcoat. Ashley comes closer. Maggots swarm from the neck and crevices of the coat, pulsing the body with a synchronized horror. Ashley jerks back, raising the torch. On the upper bunk a man is muttering in strange German, his head bound with a large bandage blackened with dried blood. He holds his hands over his eyes, blocking the light.

—What's he saying? Mayhew says.

—It's gibberish, Ashley says. He's not talking sense. They must have been wounded in the show last week. Probably they couldn't evacuate them since.

—It's awful, sir. I can't stand the smell—

—Go upstairs and tell the sergeant it's secure down here, then come directly down. I want to know if that howitzer caught them. And see if you can find any water.

Mayhew goes upstairs and Ashley passes along the row of bunks, shining his light. He is halted by a figure raising his hand in bed, beckoning to Ashley. The young man is beardless, his face jaundiced and sickly. His mouth is stained and his eyes are crusted. On the shoulder boards of his tunic there is the single diamond star of an *Oberleutnant*. He waves Ashley closer.

—*Herr Leutnant.*

Ashley squats beside the bunk and shines his torch at the officer's face. The German raises his hand to block the light.

—Too bright, he says in German. We have been in darkness all morning. They cut the electricity when they left. You speak German?

—*Ein Bisschen.* Are you the officer in charge here? What regiment are you—the second Marine-Infanterie?

—Let me see your face better, *Herr Leutnant,* you look familiar. Or perhaps you are a captain? There are very young captains now—

Ashley shines the torch on his own face and points it back at the German. The officer smiles faintly.

—I thought it was you, the German says. We met before, don't you remember? You were in Berlin before the war. We met at the old Café des Westens, you came with that other foreigner who would speak only French with us, she didn't like to talk German. *Vous parlez français, non?*

—Nonsense, I've never been to Berlin. Are you the officer in charge here?

—I think no one is in charge here, *Herr Leutnant.* Tell me, what happened to that girl? She wasn't really French, was she? But she had a camera, she took wonderful photographs. She may have forgotten you, but you can't forget her—

Ashley stands up, no longer listening. Private Mayhew clambers back down the stairs, the dark outline of his head peeking from the doorway.

—The howitzer missed them, sir. But there's no water.

Ashley finds a candle amid the refuse on the floor and gives it to the German officer, lighting it with a match from his pocket. He puts the matchbox in the German's hand. The officer smiles.

—Don't worry, *Kamerad.* They may be gone now, but they'll be back.

Ashley and Mayhew climb back to the surface. They find Sergeant Bradley and the men moving sandbags to reverse the defenses, blocking off traverses on each side to prevent flanking attacks. Ashley looks up at Empress Redoubt. It looms in the mist still a hundred yards beyond them, past the second line of German defenses. Sergeant Bradley takes Ashley aside.

—The Huns took their guns with them. We've done what we can, but if they come back in any number—

—The Border Regiment will be along in relief.

—They think we're dead, sir. If they were coming, they'd have come by now.

—They'll come all right.

The German counterattack begins ten minutes later. It starts with a fearsome bombardment of mixed high-explosive and shrapnel shells. The parados comes aflame with shock and light. A huge explosion rocks the nearest fire bay, surging flame and smoke down the trench. Ashley and the sergeant dash around the corner. They find Gregory already dead with much of his head missing, his mouth torn open to reveal a wreck of shattered teeth. Stewart is screaming as blood pours from an enormous gash in his stomach. The sergeant shoves a bandage into the wound, telling Stewart he will be all right, but the blood wells up over the bandage and the sergeant's hands. Stewart turns white and stops breathing. More shrapnel bursts overhead, wounding Private Reynolds badly in the arm. Ashley wraps the arm quickly, but Reynolds has to abandon his rifle, holding the lifeless right arm with his left hand, his face ashen, small cuts all over his neck.

Ashley hurries across into the traverse, looking over the parados with his periscope toward the German reserve lines. The machine guns have opened in orange flashes. He can make out a line of gray figures approaching at an arm's length apart, the column spanning a huge field of mud. Mayhew stands beside him on the fire step, rapidly firing his rifle.

—There's millions, Mayhew murmurs.

—Only a hundred or so, Ashley says.

He gives the order to retreat. The four men climb the ladder out of the trench and crawl between the openings in the German wire. They make westward for Patience Trench, a nest of wire and yellow flashing guns in the distance. With a sluggish jog they hobble through the mud, artillery raining upon them. A high-explosive shell bursts nearby in a hurricane of red flame. Ashley is tossed against the ground, his ears ringing as he spits mud and blood from his mouth. He must have bit his tongue. He sees the sergeant, the man's eyes wide in dazed horror, pulling himself forward by the arms through the muck, the stumps of his legs dragging on the ground, gushing crimson. Mayhew slings his rifle and grabs the sergeant's arm, pulling him forward. Ashley takes the other arm and they carry the bleeding sergeant to a shellhole, ducking under a heap of black clay. Mayhew is yelling at Ashley, but the ringing is very loud.

—What?

—Dead, sir. Sergeant's dead.

—Where's Reynolds?

—Gone, sir. We should take cover here, wait for nightfall.

Ashley cannot hear. He catches his breath and points toward Patience Trench. The two men rise and set off. They pass rusted heaps of wire, dud artillery shells planted in the mud. Mayhew points and says something Ashley cannot hear. They go left around an enormous crater, and then descend a short ridge. A trench is in the distance ahead, perhaps the British line. Another shell bursts above them. A rain of pellets. Then a second concussion, a third, mud and smoke and steel everywhere. Ashley falls to the ground, sucking for air. His ears are still ringing.

A VISIT

The trenches are the softest of hills now, waist-high mounds of grass threading minute valleys among the sleeping fields. I'm the only one here. I walk on new and shiny planks, ducktracks re-created on the old trench floor. A nylon rope is strung along the side for safety. A red plastic sign is staked in the dirt. PATIENCE TRENCH. DANGER: UNDETONATED EXPLOSIVES.

I hop over the rope and scale the mounds on all fours, my hands pulling at tufts of damp grass. No-man's-land. I find a hollow between the tallest of knolls. Lying back against the grass, I read from Ashley's letters in my notebook.

Who are these people we fight against? I never see their faces, except those of the dead.

The sun rises behind them as it sets behind us; theirs is the east & it belongs to them. We own the dawn, as breaking light draws their shadows against the horizon. They own the dusk. We are clad in khaki where they are grey. Their wire is stronger & thicker than ours, their rucksacks of queer dark cowhide, the fur still attached.

And yet they are men, no different from us, and when we prick
them they shall bleed, and have their just revenge. 'The villainy you
teach me, I will execute, and it shall go hard but I will better the
instruction.'

After an hour I come out of the trench, ducking under the rope and
walking to the parking lot. At two o'clock Mireille pulls the car up and
gets out.

—How was the coast? I ask.

—Really windy, so it was hard to draw. But the light was pretty. I
have my sketchbook, I thought I might draw something here.

We walk across a flat field to the cemetery, white headstones arrayed
in neat rows of ten. The grass is finely manicured and there are small
trees throughout the cemetery.

—Did all these people die around here?

—I think so.

Mireille walks on toward a stone monument on the far end of the
cemetery, her sketchbook under her arm. I stay behind reading the headstones.

5/2819 PRIVATE P. ECCLES
DURHAM LIGHT INFANTRY
5 NOVEMBER 1916 AGE 19
HE ANSWERED THE CALL

At the end of the cemetery I find Mireille inside the monument, a
tall cross surrounded by a circle of white stones.

—Tristan, I think this is also a grave—

—It can't be.

Mireille crouches in front of one of the white stones.

—But look at this. It's like a tombstone, but there's no name.

I walk closer to the stone. At the top it says A SOLDIER OF THE
GREAT WAR—ROYAL BERKSHIRE REGT. Beneath this is a large white

cross and the inscription KNOWN UNTO GOD. Dozens of these head-stones are arranged in a circle surrounding the cross. Mireille touches the stone, frowning.

—Why are they like this? Why don't they have their own graves like the others?

I look around the monument, but the only inscription is by the small entrance gate: EAUCOURT CEMETERY. Mireille is still looking at the headstone. She puts her hand to her face.

—Tristan, what's under here?

—I don't know. I read about some mass graves. Sometimes there were too many, they'd just put them all in a shellhole—

I walk around the base of the monument. A few of the stones have flowers or red paper remembrance poppies in front of them.

—But maybe it was a different place, I say. Maybe it wasn't Eau-court.

Mireille stands and looks at the fields around us. She picks up her sketchbook and starts walking back toward the car. I follow after her.

—Do you want to draw the cemetery?

—No, she says. Let's go home.

5 November 1916

Empress Redoubt

Somme, France

The shrapnel comes from a single 77-millimeter round manufactured by Friedrich Krupp AG at its gun works in Essen. The shell is fired from a Feldkanone 96 n.A. four kilometers behind the German front line, the gun operated by a crew of five men from the Neumärkisches Feld-artillerie-Regiment Nr. 54, all of whom are wet from the very inside of their underclothes, their skin dank and clammy. The men have cropped hair beneath their caps. They wear mustaches and the dirt and rain and sweat are strained by the hair of their upper lips.

Gefreiter Otto Bäcker pulls the firing lanyard on the Feldkanone and retreats for cover as the gun recoils and the shell flies westward. Crouching in the mud, Bäcker wonders how long it will be before the ration party arrives with lunch. He has eaten only a fistful of dark bread and salt herring since daybreak, and the herring has made him very thirsty.

The 6.8-kilogram artillery shell travels four kilometers across the German lines at supersonic speed, the faint singing whine of the shell cutting the air preceding the thudding report of the gun. The shell detonates above no-man's-land at a bursting height of three meters, spewing three hundred eleven-gram lead balls at low velocity. Ashley Walsingham is facing the detonating shell as he moves toward Patience Trench, advancing at full stride with his pistol drawn. He does not hear it coming.

One of the shrapnel balls pierces Ashley's throat two inches above his right clavicle, passing between his trachea and his esophagus and starting a substantial hemorrhage. At the same time Ashley's right thigh is perforated by four shrapnel balls, and though these wounds are not deep, vivid crimson blood begins to gather in pools atop his trouser leg, soaking the khaki fabric in growing blotches. He crumples to the ground, blood coursing from his mouth. The color of the blood seems to Ashley perversely bright. He loses consciousness almost immediately.

Private F. P. Mayhew is only a few yards behind Ashley, his head lowered as the shell explodes. A shrapnel pellet pings off the brim of Mayhew's steel helmet, sparing his face. Mayhew's right arm and shoulder are pocked by a few lead balls. He puts his hand to his shoulder, and though his fingers draw blood, the wounds seem superficial. There is little pain.

Mayhew kneels beside Ashley's body. Half of Ashley's face is black with sludge and blood is tumbling down his chin. Mayhew hoists Ashley onto his back, pulling an arm and a leg over each of his shoulders. He staggers fifty yards toward a meager shellhole, teetering with the unbalanced load. He can smell urine on Ashley's trousers and there is a wetness against his neck. When they reach the shellhole Mayhew lowers Ashley to the ground. He looks around. The hole is a shallow cauldron of exploding mud less than three feet deep, its outer borders growing vaguer with each subsequent blast. High-explosive shells whine overhead and crash nearby, machine-gun fire traversing the horizon at an indistinct distance.

Mayhew kneels before Ashley, feeling in the inner skirt of Ashley's tunic. The field dressing is stitched in. Mayhew cuts the threads with his pocketknife and severs the khaki cover of the dressing wrapper. There are two sterile pads inside, two roller bandages and a tiny glass ampoule of iodine. Mayhew slits open Ashley's trouser leg. He cracks the crown from the ampoule and sprinkles the fluid over Ashley's throat and leg wounds. A few golden drops in a sea of red. He presses the absorbent pads onto each wound, at which Ashley stirs a little in pain, though he does not wake. The dressings soak with blood immediately.

Mayhew lifts Ashley's head and winds the bandage around his throat, deftly spiraling, then reversing the spirals so the pressure will be uniform upon the pad. He cuts the bandage and secures the final wrap with a safety pin. He repeats the process on Ashley's upper thigh, then flops onto his stomach, taking a moment to think. Another shell bursts close, tossing a shovelful of debris over his back. He feels something hot on his leg, perhaps a small cut. His ears are ringing.

They are still some distance from the British line and they should wait here until nightfall. Mayhew supposes he ought to dress his own wound. His forearm is slick with blood. It has come down his cuff onto his wrist.

Two hours after nightfall Private Mayhew arrives at the regimental aid post carrying Ashley with the help of a soldier from the Durhams. The two men trudge forward with Ashley strung between their shoulders, his body slouched and lifeless. Often they have to stop to make way for soldiers and stretchers coming down the communication trench.

The two men prop Ashley against a sandbag at the tiny aid post. He slumps down like a rag doll, the crust of dark blood hardened on his chin. The other soldier goes off to find his regiment. The battalion medical officer glances at Ashley and shakes his head.

—I've no stretcher bearers left. They're out in the mud, God knows where. Has he a good pulse?

—I don't know, sir.

—What's his name? He's the one with the funny—

—Mr. Walsingham.

—That's right.

The medical officer squats beside Ashley and feels for his pulse at the neck.

—Who dressed these wounds?

—I did, sir.

The officer glances back at Mayhew. He directs an RAMC orderly toward Ashley while he moves on to another case, a captain who has lost most of his face to a high-explosive shell. The captain is somehow still living. He had once been a country solicitor in a village called Emmbrook, but now his face is gone and someone has pulled a rubber sheet over him. The medical officer lifts the sheet and looks under it. He lowers the sheet.

Mayhew watches the orderly tend to Ashley. The orderly unbuttons Ashley's tunic and pulls out his identity disk, a reddish circle of vulcanized asbestos fiber with a length of cord passed through the disk's eyelet and around Ashley's neck. The orderly fills out a paper tag containing Ashley's name, regiment and a description of his wounds. He ties the tag around Ashley's arm. The orderly looks up at Mayhew.

—What is it?

Mayhew does not answer. Someone has given him a water flask and he drains it and hands it back. Mayhew spits into the mud. He slings his rifle over his shoulder and walks away.

An hour before midnight the battalion colonel and his adjutant visit the aid station. Ashley has been spread out on a dirty stretcher beside the sandbags, his arms and legs akimbo. The captain with the missing face is laid beside him, the sheet still over his head. The colonel hovers over the captain and lifts the sheet. A glimmer of white teeth and eyeballs, the rest pinkish red. The colonel lowers the sheet. The two officers turn to Ashley's body, the chest distinctly rising and falling in labored breaths. The RAMC orderly is giving a corporal an injection in the leg against septic poisoning.

The colonel addresses the orderly.

—Why is Mr. Walsingham lying here? Are there no bearers to take him?

The corporal is occupied by his syringe and does not look toward the officers. He thinks they are asking about the faceless captain.

—There aren't nearly enough bearers, sir, the corporal says. Dr. Hall said he hasn't a chance of surviving the night. We've given him a great dose of morphia—

—He's still breathing.

—That may be, sir, but Dr. Hall gave him a great dose—

—Very well.

The adjutant draws a small notebook and pencil from his pocket. He adds the name Walsingham to his list.

At three in the morning Ashley is finally taken from the regimental aid post. He is not awake to see the four men lift him and carry him away. He is not awake to see that the faceless captain is no longer breathing.

Ashley revives only once in the night. He comes to as they are navigating a choked communication trench in the reserve lines. A wooden cart and a field gun have been swallowed by the mud, blocking the path. The stretcher bearers argue over whether to go left or right. One of the bearers holding the rear of the stretcher is a German prisoner and he becomes involved in the argument. The German is a senior NCO and he considers the English soldiers to be stupid.

—*Links*, the German says. *Links!*

—What's he saying?

—Fritz wants us to go left.

—Fuck him.

It is then that Ashley wakes with a fevered start, his throat and lungs drawing closed as though the strings of a corset are being pulled around his breath. He is suffocating.

Ashley's eyes come open. For a moment he does not breathe at all. He is seized, halted in one great spasm of airlessness. Above him it is cloudy and there is not even a star to look at, not even a bursting shell or flare, only a vast murky field of black. It seems a pointless end, hardly anything at all. Ashley gasps for air desperately and bubbles of frothing blood come to his mouth. He gurgles, a sound too soft to be heard.

The bearers go right. They hump along at a crawl, their legs knee-deep in the mud, their footing sinking. The stretcher sways from side to side. It is all they can do to keep it above the mire. Ashley sucks another breath, just barely. The stretcher lopes on, the two bearers in front muttering to each other.

—Stinks of piss, don't he? Bloody awful.

—There's worse smells out here. A little piss does wonders to a trench, cleans it better than Pears soap. I'd call it the eau de cologne of the Somme—

—Stinks of piss.

Five days later on the morning of November 10, 1916, Imogen Soames-Andersson descends the carpeted staircase at the house on Cavendish Square, taking certain of the steps two at a time. She is on her way to the Charing Cross Road to collect a volume of Laforgue's poetry that she ordered in a French bookshop a month ago. She had forgotten the book until this morning, when she realized suddenly and with pleasure that it must be in the shop awaiting her. Imogen is engaged to meet a friend at ten o'clock, but she supposes she can collect the book and still make it on time.

The parlormaid stops her in the hallway with a letter.

The letter is from Messrs. Twyning & Hooper, Solicitors. Imogen tears it open hastily, assuming it relates to some business of her father's.

Dear Madam,

> *I deeply regret to inform you that 2nd Lieut. A.E. Walsingham died from wounds received in action in France on 5 November, this news confirmed by a letter from Capt. W. Towse, adjutant of 1 Batt. Royal Berkshire Regt. I beg to offer you my sincere sympathy. It may be some slight consolation that Capt. Towse said 'Lieut. Walsingham was a very brave and gallant soldier and one of our best officers.'*

As Executor for Mr. Walsingham's estate I am instructed to notify you in the event of his death. Would it be possible for you to call upon our offices on Bedford Row? There are certain particulars relating to the estate that I should like to discuss in person.

If there is anything I can do for you, I remain at your service.

Yours faithfully,
P. L. Twyning

Imogen hardly makes a sound. Standing in the hallway, she reads the letter twice, then goes up into her bedroom, tearing the sheet into smaller and smaller scraps of paper. She throws the scraps into the fireplace, where they flare and burn out in tiny flashes.

Imogen climbs into bed and then crawls back out, pulling the pillows and counterpane and duvet off and throwing them to the floor, crying out and muffling her cries, for no one must ever know what a fool she was, what a fool he had been. She walks to the lavatory and splashes water on her face, pacing the corridor in a haze, the parlormaid watching her from the landing downstairs as Imogen wipes her face with her sleeve, crying and whispering to herself, making strange bargains with forces she does not even believe in. For it could so easily be a mistake. A solicitor's trick. A soldier with a similar name, a myopic clerk at the War Office—

Ten minutes later Imogen's mother comes into the room and finds her daughter curled up on a pile of bedding on the floor.

—My Lord. What's happened?

She takes Imogen by the shoulders, asking the question over and over. But Imogen will not even look at her.

On the same day Ashley Walsingham lies upon an iron-framed bed at No. 17 Stationary Hospital, Albert. He has been in the hospital for four days. Ashley has been awake very little of the time and only in dazed intervals. A searing pain travels up and down the length of his windpipe, as though the sinews of his throat are continually being torn apart. He cannot swallow and yet he feels the need to swallow, an expanding shape in his throat that will soon strangle him. But when his throat muscles tighten and he nears the point of swallowing, the pain is too great and he has to stop. So Ashley lies in silence.

The hospital has been appropriated from a great house on the edge of town, a mansion in the provincial style. It was converted to a hospital in June, shortly before the Somme offensive. Ashley's ward is in the long gallery, the largest room in the house. There is a high ceiling and ornate wood-paneled walls; a marble fireplace below a great mirror. The beds lie in neat rows, each patient swaddled in white sheets and bedspreads. The steel nightstands bear flowers in vases. Medical charts are clipped to the wall above each patient's head. Ashley cannot see his own chart.

A red-haired nurse notices that his eyes are open. Her peaked white cap hovers in and out of his field of vision. The nurse looks very young, but she speaks with assurance, leaning close to him.

—I know you can't speak, she says, and you oughtn't try. If you need something, write it here.

The girl puts a pencil and a small pad of paper in his hands. Ashley sees that she is not a nurse but a VAD, a kind of volunteer nurse's assistant. The girl wears a starched white apron with a paper collar, and beneath it a dark dress that comes nearly to her ankles. A bright red cross is centered on the bib of her apron. To Ashley she resembles the saintly Breton peasant women of Gauguin paintings. He closes his fingers around the pencil and writes slowly on the pad in shaky block capitals. POSTCARD.

He wakes again the following evening at dusk. Purplish light slants through the windows of the ward. The nurses' stacked heels rap upon the checkered marble floor. Ashley lifts his arms from beneath the sheet and flashes of pain pulse through his body. He keeps still to stop the pain, studying the blue flannel sleeves of his pajama jacket. Delicately he feels the wounds on his leg through the sheet. A series of erupting scabs along his right thigh, hardened and brittle. Already the wounds have nearly healed.

Ashley supposes he must not move his neck, so he holds his shoulders even while reaching out to the nightstand beside him. On the surface lie the pair of letters he keeps in his tunic breast pocket. Beside these is a brown field-service postcard and the stump of a red pencil. Gingerly and with great labor Ashley picks up the card and pencil. He crosses out sentences so that the desired message remains.

I am quite well.

I have been admitted into hospital.

> ~~*sick*~~   *and am going on well.*
> *wounded*   ~~*and hope to be discharged soon.*~~

~~*I am being sent down to the base.*~~

> ~~*letter dated*~~ _____
> ~~*I have received your*~~   ~~*telegram*~~ _____
> ~~*parcel*~~ _____

Letter follows at first opportunity.

I have received no letter from you

> *lately.*
> ~~*for a long time.*~~

Signature only.

Date

Ashley deliberates about the date for a moment before filling in the blank. The red-haired VAD sees him writing and comes to his bedside. She takes the postcard.

—To the return address on those letters?

She points to the pair of letters on the nightstand. Ashley picks up the pad of paper and writes slowly.

SAME ADDRESS. MORPHIA PLEASE.

The VAD shakes her head.

—I'll have to ask the doctor.

Three days later on November 13, the maid enters the front parlor of the Soames-Andersson house on Cavendish Square carrying the brown postcard. But the parlor is empty. The maid turns and is halfway up the stairs when Eleanor comes through the front door, in her arms a packet full of magazines she has brought for Imogen.

—Hello Lizzie. I just passed the postman. Is that the second post?

The maid holds the card uncertainly. Eleanor starts up the stairs toward her.

—What is it? You know well enough you oughtn't to be reading Papa's mail. Even if it is only a postcard—

Eleanor seizes the card and waves it in the air.

—If you keep it up, Eleanor teases, I shall have to read yours.

Then Eleanor recognizes the seal and the inscription FIELD SERVICE POSTCARD. She reads the card and walks upstairs to a window in the guest bedroom, watching the postman cross the street and go around the wrought-iron fence. Eleanor thinks for a moment, tapping her finger on the card. The bedroom had once been hers and they had altered nothing except the damask curtains. But somehow it seemed different.

Eleanor walks down the hallway past Imogen's room, a slit of light coming under the closed door, her sister probably in bed. Eleanor enters her mother's bedroom, closing the door behind her. Her mother is at her desk writing a letter. Eleanor sets the postcard in front of her.

—My God. Has Imogen seen this?

—No. It just arrived.

—Then let us go tell her.

Eleanor shakes her head, kneeling beside her mother.

—But look at the address. I know the look of his writing, I've seen it often enough. That's someone else's writing. He may have sent it before he died—

—But it's dated afterwards.

Eleanor takes her mother's hand.

—I hope it's true, Eleanor says. I do so hope it is. But imagine the effect on her if we say he is alive now and it turns out he isn't. It would all begin anew, only worse. She could hardly be more delicate than she is now. The slightest breeze could topple her.

—But to keep it from her—

—Only until we're certain.

She sighs, giving the card back to Eleanor.

—Shall you call his people then, or write to someone with the army?

—I shall do both.

On the evening of November 17 the Soames-Andersson daughters sit in the parlor awaiting dinner. The last rays of daylight project among the lace curtains, illuminating an overgrown fern potted in the window. Eleanor reclines on a purple divan reading back issues of *The Burlington Magazine*. Imogen is playing the piano. There is sheet music spread before her but she plays from memory, the piece slow and pensive, the notes tumbling forth at uneven cadences.

Eleanor glances up from the magazine, raising her voice above the music.

—Really. You're going to send us all over the edge.

Imogen does not answer. She continues playing as her sister pages through the magazine, Imogen's eyes on a stuffed pheasant diving from its wooden setting on the wall. Eleanor flings the magazine down and comes to the piano bench, putting a hand on her sister's shoulder. Imogen stops playing, her fingers still poised on the ivory keys.

—The doctor, Imogen whispers, agreed that I ought to play.

—Not this sort of thing. It's melancholy.

—I don't find it melancholy.

—Naturally you don't. But you must make certain efforts right now. Imogen plays on. Eleanor throws her hands up in the air.

—Imogen, if you don't want me here, I'm happy enough to go home. I want to help, but I can't see how listening to two hours of funeral marches—

There is a soft rapping on the door. The sisters turn to see the maid on the threshold. She has been polishing windows and is wearing her chamois work gloves. An envelope is in her hand.

—A telegram—

Eleanor plucks it from the maid's hand.

—For Miss Imogen, the maid continues.

Eleanor clutches the envelope uncertainly, but Imogen snatches it from her and tears it open, stepping away from her sister as she reads. Imogen looks at Eleanor and back at the telegram. Then she dashes up the stairs to her bedroom, Eleanor in pursuit, calling after her. Imogen locks the door behind her. She sinks into the chair beside the door without removing her eyes from the telegram. Eleanor is knocking on the door and calling Imogen's name. Imogen reads the message again.

17 NO 16

IMOGEN SOAMES ANDERSSON
18 CAVENDISH SQ LONDON W
WOUNDED BUT RECOVERING NUMBER 17 HOSPITAL ALBERT
IGNORE ALL INDICATIONS CONTRARY LETTER FOLLOWS
INDESTRUCTIBLY YOURS ASHLEY

A LESSON

⊷⫘ ⫘⊷

Mireille and I have never touched. Not in Paris, not in three days together in a remote house in the countryside; not a hug, not even a handshake. She smiles at me in the morning and never fails to say *bonne nuit* before we go to bed. She treats me with care and consideration, but often this seems formal, as if I'm a guest to her rather than a friend.

Mireille is never bored. When things turn slow, she picks up the pen and draws, or puts on her coat and goes for a walk without a moment's notice. When she leaves in the afternoon I stay at the dining table, studying a map I bought in Amiens and marking the locations mentioned in Ashley's letters: the hospital in Albert, the convalescent ward at Étaples. I take out my notebook.

Sept 6   Picardie

This is where it all went to pieces. But I can't figure out why.

Ashley was wounded Nov 5, 1916. Imogen must have come to the front sometime between then and Nov 24. After that, Ashley's letters are different—she has stopped replying.

What brought Imogen to Picardie in the middle of a war? Where did they meet? What caused the final break?

I look back at the map, staring at the web of roads and villages and hoping for some kind of revelation. Across the table are Mireille's pencils and spiral-bound sketchbook. I walk over and look down at the green cover. Then I flip it back.

The sketches are all captioned, mostly in English. *The City Is Sleeping*. A drawing of the rooftops of apartment buildings, probably in Paris, layers of chimneys stretching out to the horizon. I feel guilty, but too curious to stop. I turn the page. *Young and Fearless*. A drawing of what looks like Claire and another girl, seated in high-backed chairs, looking straight at the viewer. *Un Américain en France*. A sketch of me, sleeping on the train with my jacket rolled up against the window and a book in my lap.

I shut the sketchbook and grab my jacket, following a path that crosses a field behind the house. The trail is damp and spotted with puddles from the rain last night. At the end of the field I meet Mireille coming from the opposite direction. She looks surprised to see me.

—I thought you were reading, I didn't know you wanted to come—

—I didn't either.

Mireille smiles. She leads me on a one-lane footpath into the forest and we cross a narrow stream. I ask her what the beech trees are called in French and soon she is telling me the names of oak and sweet chestnut and maple trees, of the white flowers on the ground and the black birds flapping overhead, fleeting silhouettes against an iron sky.

—Ce sont de ardéidés, je crois. Comment dit-on en anglais?

—I don't know. They looked pretty big. Were they crows?

She laughs and shakes her head. —They weren't crows.

—Don't laugh at me. I didn't grow up near a forest. I never learned the names of these things.

—Well, Mireille says. You're learning them now.

After that Mireille never leaves the house without inviting me. There is no television here, no computer and no books except those we brought with us. So we talk the rest of the day into the night, in the house and on the trails that wind throughout the forest. Our conversation alternates between French and English. Mireille loves her language and she lends me that appreciation, reminding me of the days when I was infatuated with its thick exotic sounds. We both want to practice the foreign language, but when the words come quickly we revert to our native tongues, especially if we are arguing a point.

We talk about war and Mireille tells me about her grandfather who became a *résistant* at the age of seventeen, killing Germans when he was only a child himself. We talk about death and Mireille says she isn't afraid to die, that she is curious to see any world other than this one. But I say she will be scared enough when the time comes.

—You can be scared for both of us, Mireille teases. You worry enough for two people.

—I know. Maybe you should take your share.

We go on talking all through dinner, and though I mean to work on a new research plan, I never do. Mireille uncorks a bottle of wine and pours it into a pair of empty jars. I ask her why she decided to go to art school.

—If I study design, she says, I can get some kind of job later. I'm getting older, I need to find some kind of career—

—I didn't know you were so practical.

Mireille looks down into her wine. —Of course there's more than that. To create things that are beautiful, I think it's important. Even to make something ugly, as long as it's true. After the last few years—it's the thing I can still believe in.

—What did you believe in before?

—A mistake. Thinking you could fix anything if you cared enough about it. That may be true for art. But not for people.

She looks up at me.

—Anyway, you know what I'm talking about. You take pictures, it's the same thing—

I shake my head. —I'm not making anything special. Usually I barely look at my pictures after I print them.

—Then why do it?

—I just like taking pictures. When you carry a camera, it's a different way of seeing things. You notice more, you have to look for details.

—What about the pictures you took of me and Claire in front of the Seine? Did you take those just to notice more?

—No. I took them because I'm a tourist.

Mireille smiles. —Come on, let's sit outside.

I pick up the bottle of wine and Mireille gets a couple of wool blankets from the living room. We sit on the back steps. The night is cold but the stars hang bright above the treetops in the yard.

—You know when I first met you, Tristan, I didn't know what to think. Maybe I still don't.

Mireille lights a cigarette. I see the silhouette of her face turn away and then back to me.

—On the train here, everything you told me about the northern railway and the Rothschilds. How do you know that?

—I don't know. I read some books about railroads.

—And in Amiens, Mireille adds, you knew about the Hortillon-nages even though you've never been there before. Or at the cathedral, all the statues in the doorway and your story about the head of Jean le Baptiste. How did you know all that?

—I took a class on it. Plenty of people know that stuff—

—Not like that. They might tell you one or two things, but most people wouldn't know enough to talk for hours, because they're not that interested. Tristan, you don't look in the mirror before you leave the house, but you spend ten minutes worrying about what to carry in your bag. You keep changing your mind, taking out your jacket and putting it back in. And you're so strange about money. You'd rather walk an hour than pay two euros for the bus, but when I ask you about this inheritance, you don't want to talk about the money.

—It just makes me feel weird.

—I believe you. But anyone but you, it'd be the only thing they'd think about. I know it must be hard for you, all this pressure, and I want to help. But I don't really know you. I don't know anything about your real life—

—Then ask.

Mireille taps her cigarette against the steps. She looks at me.

—What happened to your mother?

—She died three years ago.

—From what?

—Colon cancer.

There is a long pause. Then Mireille says, —I'm sorry.

We sit in silence. Mireille pours more wine into the jars.

—Is that why the money bothers you? Because it comes through your mother?

—Maybe.

I take a sip of wine, flipping up the collar of my jacket.

—The way she lived, it wouldn't have made much difference to her. But I think part of me really wants it.

—That's normal. Why should it bother you?

—It's just money. There are better things to care about. What else do you want to know?

Mireille hesitates. —Do you have a girlfriend in California?

—No.

She takes a drag from her cigarette. A car passes on the road and she turns to follow its headlights.

—How did you know those letters would be in Sweden?

—Dumb luck. I was looking for something else, but I found them instead.

—You don't think it's strange?

—Of course I think it's strange.

Mireille nods, drinking the last of her wine. I rub my hands together under my blanket.

—It's freezing out here.

—We can go inside.

We stand up, gathering the jars and the empty bottle. Mireille turns back to me.

—One more question. Do you really believe in all this? The lawyers, the money, the English couple?

—You've asked me that before.

—Do you believe in it or not?

—I do.

Mireille pulls the door open for me, the yellow light pouring out from the living room.

—I just wanted to be sure.

We are setting the table for breakfast. Mireille puts down two cups of coffee and begins to butter a long tartine of baguette. I stir milk into my coffee, shaking my head.

—She came all the way to France to see him. And whatever happened, whatever she told him was so bad it broke them up—

Mireille puts the bread on the table.

—Maybe it was what he told her.

—Maybe. But I bet it's the key. I just don't know how to get at it. I could go to every place the Berkshires went to, but there's probably no point. I'm not allowed to ask anyone for help—

—You could ask the lawyers.

—They'll just tell me to come back to England.

—Maybe they won't. Or maybe you should talk to your family. The lawyers will never find out. Why don't you call your father?

I shake my head.

—He'd just tell me to hire somebody.

Mireille sits across from me.

—Your stepbrother then. Why don't you talk to him?

—He's a scientist, he'd think the way I was doing this was crazy—

—What kind of scientist?

—Bioinformatics, he's doing a PhD. I know what he'd say, I don't even need to ask.

—What would he say?

I shrug. —Don't trust people you don't know. Especially not lawyers who promise you money.

—And what about the English couple?

—Adam thinks history's pointless—

—So what would he say?

We start eating breakfast, chewing the bread and taking sips of coffee in silence. I look up at Mireille.

—Don't worry about things that've already happened. They're not your problem. Don't worry about money that doesn't belong to you and probably won't make your life any better. Don't think everything in Europe's better, because you always liked Europe and it's messing with your head. Don't trust French girls you met in a bar.

Mireille smiles. —That's good advice.

She cuts a pear and puts a few slices on my plate. I lift my cup and set it down again, shaking my head.

—Last year I was trying to decide if I should to move to LA after graduation. I talked to Adam about it for a couple hours. In the end all he said was that I always ask for advice so I can worry about it. Then I go and do the thing I was going to do anyway, because knowing it's a bad idea never stopped me.

—It never stops anyone.

—You think staying here is a bad idea?

Mireille shrugs. —You have to follow your instincts. If you think the evidence is around here, maybe it is. But you can't expect it to fall in your lap. That may have worked before, but it won't always work.

—Then what should I do?

We clear the table and Mireille fills the sink with hot water. She turns to me, holding the sponge in her hand.

—*C'est facile.* You decide what you're looking for. Then you'll find it.

19 November 1916

No. 17 Stationary Hospital Albert

Somme, France

It is the hour in the garden each day that makes life tolerable. There are no flowers, of course, for the planters are all empty, their contents long ago carted away and stored, whether for winter or for the whole duration of the war. But there is grass. There is a whole lawn of unkempt green grass, whitecapped with hoarfrost in the mornings when Ashley's slippered feet crunch upon the field, or thawed and damp in the afternoon gloom under ominous skies. But Ashley seldom looks at the sky. It aches to raise his chin too high.

The doctors say Ashley's recovery has been swift, but to him it feels interminable. A day confined to bed is an eternity. He gets through the nights only by his imagination. At eight o'clock each night, when the lights are switched off and the curtains drawn in the long gallery, Ashley shuts his eyes dutifully. Two hours later he is staring at the carved flowers in the coffered ceiling and following the stony ridgeline at dusk, the long descent down into valleys and pasture, Price asking for a drink from a herder who loans his wineskin, the wine cold and tasting of rawhide. They say they aren't hungry, but the herder feeds them polenta from an iron pot and they sleep in a vast chalet with the herders and their black cattle, Price curled under a railway rug, Ashley watching the stars through the open doorway. Somehow Ashley likes ordinary memories best. They seem the easiest to go back to. Other nights he might remember the needle point of the Aiguille du Dru, or the crystal water of the Seelisbergsee he dived under, kicking and sinking into the cold blue heart of the lake. All the while Ashley lies perfectly still in bed. If he shifts his head on the pillow, the pain will make him wince.

When he was admitted to the hospital Ashley could not raise his head two inches, nor utter a word, nor even swallow a sip of water. But by his second week he can speak in a hoarse whisper and is well enough to be wheeled into the garden for the ten minutes it does not rain that Sunday. The red-haired VAD puts Ashley under heavy woolen blankets, two over his lap and one pulled up to his chin. When they reach the garden doors the sky begins misting, but the VAD knows how badly Ashley wishes to be outside. She puts two fingers to her lips and smiles.

—I won't tell if you won't tell.

She props open the doors and pushes Ashley out in the wheelchair. The air dazzles him, brisk and fresh. The VAD wheels him into the paltry shelter of a leafless wych elm and they wait for the weather to break. Ten minutes later the sky begins to shed an icy rain.

—And I thought English weather was rubbish, the VAD says.

Soon Ashley is among the fittest men in the hospital. The doctors say a scar will remain on the interior of his trachea, but this does not seem to affect him negatively. One of the surgeons remarks that Ashley is a man of extraordinary regenerative power. Ashley supposes this means they will return him to the front sooner than he expected.

His voice has changed and this is obvious even to Ashley. It remains slightly hoarse and he speaks more softly out of a protective instinct, and in a tone he seldom used before. All his life Ashley never thought of his voice, never considered how it grew and matured with him since boyhood, how the pitch and timbre told others that it was Ashley who was speaking to them, in words tender or vengeful. He realizes what it means only when it is gone.

—My old voice, Ashley asks the doctor. I shan't get it back?

—I doubt it.

Ashley looks out the window. The doctor frowns, writing something on Ashley's chart.

—You sound perfectly well and manly. You ought to take pride in your wounds, honorably acquired. A man who has held His Majesty's commission in battle—he ought to sound different thereafter. For he is a different man. It's rather fitting, isn't it?

—Certainly.

He thinks of Imogen always. Over and over he replays the slim newsreel that is his memory of her, a set of gestures or sensations derived from less than a week together. He can remember the places well, how they felt—the field in Sutton Courtenay where she lay upon his chest, her body warm, the cool neck of the champagne bottle against his leg. But Ashley cannot picture her face. He knows what Imogen looks like, of course, as well as anyone can call back a face they have last seen two months ago. The photograph she sent him suffices for this, bent slightly but otherwise preserved by a waxed envelope inside his tunic. The picture is on his nightstand now.

But Ashley wants more than this photograph, a fixed image impossible to translate into a lover of flesh and spirit. He wants to remember how she had looked in particular moments, to bring back her scent and the sound of her voice, the feel of her voile skirt between his fingers. He wants to see her face in Regent's Park, where they kissed in the darkness and his gaze went always beyond her shoulder. He wants to see her eyes the last time he saw her at Victoria, when all he can remember are her wet hands, clasping and unclasping in futile shapes.

She must have had a terrible time in the confusion of these last weeks. Three days ago Ashley received a letter from Eleanor in response to his postcard, and although Ashley quickly telegrammed Imogen in reply, he received no answer. It all seemed very peculiar, and in weaker moments Ashley wondered if her affections had wavered or expired altogether with the news of his death. There could be many reasons for Imogen's silence and Ashley wasted hours considering and dismissing them in turn. Finally he began a letter explaining everything—the battle, his wounds, the colonel's mistake—but it took him several attempts to write anything coherent. He sent the letter yesterday. He has only to wait now, and to keep himself from speculating.

In truth he knows so little of her. He had fallen for Imogen so quickly that there had not been time to decide what he truly thought of her, as if it mattered. He'd had no choice. Ashley had felt powerless to resist her magnetism, her peculiar beauty, her pervasive sense of certainty about everything. That certainty had spread to Ashley too, until he believed in their destiny as much as she did.

Still it feels strange to know so few facts about one's lover. For Imogen had spoken always in abstractions, talking of beliefs or sentiments and sending any questions back toward Ashley. He can describe her habits or her interests, but when the other officers in the ward look at her photograph and ask the most basic questions, Ashley falters. She mentioned reading English at Somerville next year if she passed the exams. Was it true? Ashley never quite grasped why she hadn't passed the first time, for she certainly seems clever enough. She had lived abroad, he knows that. She plays the piano. She had printed a few poems in little magazines. Ashley has not seen these poems, and though Imogen mentioned people like Mallarmé or Debussy with great familiarity, he would not be able to describe her preferences in any detail. He is not even certain whether she is nineteen or twenty, but when the other fellows ask, he always says nineteen to be consistent.

So long as she cared for him, none of this mattered. In the first week

Ashley had eagerly watched the VAD distribute letters, his eyes following the envelopes and parcels as she handed them out from the mail cart, some of the men grinning, others not even turning to look, their faces swathed in white bandages. The post was usually distributed in the afternoon, but the VAD knew Ashley was eager for a letter and it seemed to him that she deliberately gave out the mail while he slept, for he often woke from naps to find the young lieutenant next to him reading a letter, his lips moving swiftly and silently.

By the second week Ashley ignored the distribution. He slept in the afternoons when he could, and if he heard the porcelain casters of the mail cart rolling down the hallway, he turned in bed and shut his eyes.

At the end of the fortnight he finally gets his answer. The weather is clear in the morning and Ashley paces the garden in weaving formations, making figure eights among the shrubs and flower beds. He still limps slightly, favoring his right leg. When he returns to his ward there is a letter on his nightstand. There is no address or stamp on the cover, only his name in the familiar script.

My Darling —

I stand at the reception of your hospital, but they will not allow me in. Only terminal cases are allowed visitors here & they say you are quite well. You cannot imagine how happy this makes me. They say you are being discharged tomorrow, but they will not say where.

Do not be alarmed by my visit — all shall be explained when we meet. I am perfectly well & staying with a M. Louchard, on the eastern edge of Laviéville. Have not been here long — took only a day to find you in this mess.

Is it possible for you to meet me out of hospital tomorrow? Immediately on the eastbound road out of Laviéville you will see a yellow house beside a small copse, the only house in the vicinity. I

stay in the cottage at the back, but you may call on M. Louchard
first to let him know you have come.
If you cannot come, send word at least.

Your own true
Imogen

Ashley lies motionless in bed the rest of the afternoon. In the evening when the VAD comes to change the dressing on his leg, she does not give her usual cheerful greeting. She pulls back the sheet and looks gravely at his leg, staring at the cotton bandage as though she had never seen it before. She begins unwinding the bandage and speaks in a whisper, not lifting her eyes.

—Your wife was here this morning. You've read the note?

—Yes.

—I didn't see her. The doctor told me about it. She made a terrible row. She seemed to think you were at death's door. Why on earth is she here?

—I don't know.

—They had to send her away. We can't accept visitors, you know. But you ought to have enough time to see her after you're discharged tomorrow. Is she really your wife?

Ashley hesitates.

—Never mind, the VAD says. I don't want to know.

The next morning Ashley receives orders to board a military train at 20:20 for Amiens and to proceed by a second train to No. 6 Convalescent Depot, Étaples. He decides to ignore these orders. He has been given two days to go sixty miles on ancient French trains that move at walking speed and halt every half hour. He is sure that if he can find his own transport he can see Imogen and still arrive at the depot early.

Ashley wishes to say good-bye to the VAD and thank her, but she is not on his ward that morning. He changes from the soft hospital clothes into his stiff khaki uniform. At once he feels different in the heavy tunic and breeches and riding boots. He pulls on his raincoat, the dried blood scraped off but the gabardine stained and shredded in one patch where the shrapnel had struck his leg. Ashley takes a final walk around the hospital. He sees the VAD at the far end of a roped-off corridor where the nurses have their canteen. She is with another nurse but she looks his way and it is a moment before she smiles at him. Perhaps she did recognize him in uniform. The VAD seems almost to wave as she turns into the canteen, the white straps of the apron on her back crossed in a large X.

Ashley is discharged from the hospital and it is afternoon by the time he walks into the town center. At a private garage he buys a V-twin Royal Enfield that some enterprising mechanic has stolen or salvaged from the army, then repaired and repainted in flat black. Ashley haggles for five minutes, then pays double what the motorcycle is worth. The garage owner calls the teenage apprentice into the yard to demonstrate the motorcycle's engine. The apprentice has spent weeks learning the secrets of the English machine. He seems regretful to part with it.

—Monsieur has ridden this machine before?

—A similar one.

—*Le mécanisme est très facile.* It runs beautifully. I will show you how to start it.

The apprentice moves quickly in his soiled coveralls. He opens the shutoff valve on the fuel tank, pushes the spark advance lever on the left grip, sets the choke and pulls the throttle lever on the right grip. He pulls the compression lever with his left hand, puts his foot on the starter and kicks hard. The engine coughs, hesitates, then roars awake with a cloud of smoke, settling into a throbbing idle.

The apprentice grins, wiping his hands on his coveralls.

—Now Monsieur will try?

Ashley nods and squints up at the sky. It will be dark in an hour.

THE CIPHER

Long after Mireille has gone to bed, I sit sleepless before the living room fire, studying Ashley's letters in my notebook. The wood burns down to a heap of dwindling embers, radiant slivers of red and orange. I push my armchair closer to keep warm. The sunset was hours ago, but dawn seems little closer. I read on.

There are footfalls behind me on the staircase. Mireille stands in the door frame with a blanket wrapped around her shoulders, blinking wide eyes at me as if unconvinced of my presence at this hour. We are meant to rise early to go to Étaples and I'm embarrassed to still be awake.

—I thought you went to bed.

Mireille drags the other armchair toward the fire and sits down.

—If you're doing something secret, she says, you don't have to tell me—

—It's no secret.

I hand her my copy of *Daily Life in the Trenches*, the passage already marked with a scrap of paper.

—I found this after you went to bed.

Among the mundane duties of the infantry subaltern was the censoring of soldiers' letters, the responsibility of the day's orderly officer. In their letters home, front-line soldiers were forbidden from revealing their location, but some used codes to communicate their whereabouts to loved ones. In one common code, the soldier would agree upon a 'trigger word' with his wife. When the soldier's wife read the trigger, she would note the second letter of each following line and thus learn the location of the soldier.

Mireille looks at me. —This code is in the letters?

—Not exactly.

I give Mireille my notebook and she turns the pages slowly, noticing the word I have circled several times.

—Mistletoe, she reads. What does it mean?

—It's a plant you kiss under at Christmas. I don't know what it's called in French—

—*Le gui*, she says. Why did he use that word?

—I don't know. But it's a trigger word, you can see for yourself. He did it a little differently from how they describe it. He used the first letter of each sentence.

Mireille looks down at the notebook and after the word *mistletoe* appears, she writes out the first letter of each following sentence onto a sheet of paper. When she is finished we both look at the word on the sheet: *SOMME*.

—It's incredible, she says. How did you find this?

—*Mistletoe* isn't a common word, so I noticed the second or third time it showed up in the letters. Then I read about the code. I tried it the way they described it, and it didn't work, but then I saw *Somme*. It's pretty obvious, once you see it.

Mireille flips the pages of the notebook and begins to decode the next location.

—Don't bother, I tell her. I already know them all—

—I want to do it myself.

Beneath *SOMME* she spells out *COURCELETTE*.

—That's a village, she says. It's near Albert.

—I know.

—Is there another one?

I nod. —It's the last letter in the notebook. The one after she came to the Somme.

19 Dec 1916

My Darling Imogen,

Four days ago I left the convalescent depot & rejoined the battalion. I was pleased enough to go, for the idleness of that depot had begun to feel more sinful than the trenches. And I have rejoined the battalion at the perfect moment—they have just come into the rear for rest.

It is a luxurious respite. I am billeted with a family called Lefèvre, in the upstairs bedroom of a large house – my own four-poster bed and feather duvet, opulence beyond imagination. There is a girl of eleven here, unusually clever, who is keen to learn English. I give her lessons in what spare moments I have. I have tried to teach her the meaning of poetry – the Sphinx you encountered as a girl – but its charms are yet foreign to her, even in her native tongue. Still I persist, that one day she may know the sounds of Shelley half so intimately as the Vickers gun.

Like the neighboring country, the house itself is grim. It lies along the periphery where town gives way to farmland, but there is an old water tower in the Romanesque style, and in spring I suppose the fields might be picturesque. At least I shall be here to see the farm in its gayer moments, the rafters draping Mistletoe – for we stay here through Christmas, they say.

Can I hope for anything in the New Year, the ever-receding mirage of the war's end? Any peace without you would be worse than futile. Let the others celebrate Yule and turn their faces from the carnage we have wrought together. Of all my sins this year, those against you seem the mildest, and still they cost me dearly. This life without you is beyond senseless — a mad lieutenant among a lunatic army, separated from the only thing I care for, the one thing that keeps me good & true & loving. The thing I lost to keep the thing I hated. Even a madman knew it was a poor trade, but what would you have me do? Reason could take me only so far. In the deep of night I dream you have come back for me, to meet again at that cottage, but this time we give each other everything. Even that which isn't ours to give.

I reveal all secrets to you — but only so well as I may.

Imogen, I never meant to ask the impossible of you. When I left England I hadn't any notion what it meant to care for someone, nor to have someone care for me; nor to wait for something that cannot wait, nor risk the thing we ought never to risk. For what does a man do when all the world pulls him east, with only his instinct tugging west? You know the answer to that & always have. But it's never been so simple for me.

I don't offer any excuses, not even the obvious excuse that I have seen & done things here that have left me a stranger even to myself. You needn't forgive me or accept my choices. Only write to me anyway, that I shall have the slightest reason to greet the dawn tomorrow.

> *Yours as ever,*
> *Ashley*

Mireille has copied the third message onto the sheet: CALOTTERIE.

—La Calotterie, she says. It's near the coast, beside the dunes. Not so far away.

—Can you take me there? I want to find the house where he stayed.

—It's not such a small place, there will be more than one house—

—He said there's a Romanesque water tower on the farm. There can't be many of those. And we have the name of the family. Lefèvre.

Mireille shakes her head.

—That was eighty years ago. They will have moved. Or knocked the house down. And what would we do, even if we found this family?

—We'd talk to them. Ashley stayed there for a long time. He was friends with the family, they might know something—

Mireille sighs and hands me back the notebook. She goes to the fire and throws on a fresh log, prodding at it with the iron rod. For a moment there is only the hissing of the wet wood over the coals.

—You can't change the past. Learning about it doesn't mean you can change it.

—I know.

Mireille leans the rod against the fireplace, telling me that she'll speak in French now to be sure of her words. Her voice sounds different in her own language, and though she speaks softly her words are confident and without hesitation.

Mireille says she believes that to be more interested in people because they lived long ago or because they suffered greatly is a mistake. She tells me that people still suffer greatly now, and that in any case one must not admire suffering or loss, because life is brief and time spent dwelling on things that have already passed is surely wasted. She says that even love can sometimes be a mistake, and that perhaps this vanished love of Ashley and Imogen's had been a wasted one. She asks if a person could truly love someone they had not seen for so long, and for whom they had so little reason to harbor such wild affection.

—*Pendant des années*, she says. *Pas la moindre raison.*

Sometimes it is hard to tell the difference between love and longing, Mireille says, but they are not at all the same thing, and while one is worth very much, the other is always wasted. I follow Mireille's gaze into the fire. In the windows behind us the sky is lightening a dim pale blue to the east.

—The past or the future will never be there with you, she says. You'll only ever have what you have right now. Not any more or any less. *Ni plus ni moins.*

I get up from my chair and stand beside Mireille, both of us very close to the fire. The heat pulses against my legs. I put my hand on her shoulder, but she looks straight into the fire. We stand like this for some time. Then she turns and holds me by the shoulders. She touches my hand and her fingers brush my wrist.

—So delicate, she whispers. Your wrists are probably smaller than mine.

I watch Mireille but her face is turned away.

—Tristan, why did you come to Picardie?

—You know why. To look for proof—

—*Mais oui.* Of course that's why you're here. And what will you do after this?

I hesitate. —I don't know.

—Sooner or later you'll have to go somewhere else.

I shake my head, looking at Mireille, but I don't know what to tell her. I put my hand to her face but she turns away.

—I'll drive you to La Calotterie in the morning, she whispers.

—*Merci*—

—*Mais écoute-moi.*

Mireille turns back to me, her face very close.

—I'm not just something you found while looking for something else.

She kisses me lightly on the forehead, then picks up the sheet of paper with the names of the villages. She throws it into the fire. The paper catches on the embers, flaring into a brilliant yellow that casts light on her face as she backs away. I ask Mireille why she burned the paper, but she only shakes her head, walking toward the stairs.

—The name of the village is La Calotterie, she says. You would never forget that, would you?

22 November 1916

Laviéville

Somme, France

Ashley reaches Laviéville late in the afternoon. He circles the outskirts of the town twice on the motorcycle before he sees the building, a two-story yellow farmhouse partly obscured by a row of beech trees along the road. He turns the motorcycle into the gravel yard before the house. Louchard has heard the engine and he comes out into the yard holding his cap between his palms. Ashley turns the motor off, swinging the motorcycle back onto its kickstand. Louchard jerks his chin toward Ashley.

—*Vous êtes l'officier anglais?*

—*Oui.*

—*Vous êtes venu rendre visite à la mademoiselle?*

—*Oui.*

Louchard pulls his cap on and Ashley follows him to the back of the house. They walk through what was once a vegetable garden, now cratered by shellholes, stepping around dried and rotting tomato vines until they approach a small cottage set in a beech grove. Louchard points to the cottage, motioning for Ashley to go on ahead.

—*Elle est là.*

Louchard walks back to the house and Ashley goes to the cottage door. The curtains are drawn in the window. He hesitates for a moment, then knocks twice, not very loud. The door opens and she comes to him in a flash, her body pressed against his. He feels the softness of her cheek, the long sweep of neck, her scent of jasmine perfume. Her face is still pressed against his shoulder.

—Ashley.

—You're a fool, he says. You're mad.

He tries to pull her back to see her, but she holds fast.

—I can't believe it, she says, it's too much to look at you. Your voice sounds different—

—It is different.

She draws back and looks at him, her mouth pursed tight. Her fingers run over the delicate crease of his scar.

—Darling. Your neck—

—It's all right, Ashley says. It's all right.

He kisses her cheek and pulls her close. They kiss madly for long minutes, but when Ashley's hand moves across her body, she grasps it and he can see the hesitation in her eyes.

—Ashley. Only wait a moment.

They sit at a small table on a pair of straw-seated wooden chairs. Columns of light pass through the linen curtains onto the table and a black iron stove. The rest is shadows. Ashley unbuttons the front of this tunic.

—Why have you come? I don't even know how you managed it.

—It's not so hard. If you say you've a dying husband in hospital, they'll let you come this far. But I couldn't get inside your hospital, because they knew you weren't dying. Can you promise me something?

—No.

—It's an easy promise to keep. I ask only that you listen to all I have to say before speaking. It's important that I tell it in its entirety.

Ashley shakes his head.

—They've shelled here before. They're expecting a Hun push any day now—

—It doesn't matter. Will you listen now?

—It's madness.

—Please, Ashley. Please listen.

Imogen takes his hand and begins to speak. Her words sound prepared and Ashley does not interrupt her.

—Even now I hardly believe you're alive. I got the letter from your solicitor on a Friday. I didn't get your telegram until the next Friday. For one week I lived in the certainty that you were gone, for all time. One week.

Imogen pulls back her hand. She looks at Ashley.

—You can't know what that was to me. I was too ruined even to grieve. The first few days I wouldn't believe it was true. Finally I believed in it and nothing else. I blamed everything for your death. The war. Their army. Ours. I wouldn't go out for fear of seeing someone in uniform. I hated myself for having let you go. I knew I hadn't tried hard enough to keep you.

She shakes her head, looking at the floor.

—And I blamed you for giving up our life for this war. For leaving me alone in this world. It was our fate to be together and you had thwarted that.

Imogen begins to turn the bracelet around her wrist.

—I nearly tore the paper from the walls. They kept Ellie with me always, she even slept beside me. I stopped speaking. I thought my whole being was gone, that it had been taken with you, that my mind and body were no longer my own.

Ashley loosens the knot of his tie without looking away from her. Imogen shakes her head again, her voice rueful.

—Ashley, you could not know what misery it was. How I envied you, not to live apart from all you cared for, for all decades to come.

—I sent you a postcard. Why did it take so long—

—They kept it from me. They didn't believe it, that's why Ellie wrote to you. I didn't know you were alive until I saw the telegram. As soon as I saw it I knew I had to see you, because everything's changed, darling.

Imogen puts her hand to Ashley's cheek.

—I'm with child. Our child.

Ashley stares at her, his eyes wide, his mouth opening slightly. Finally he says, —You're certain?

—Yes. Certain enough to come here.

Ashley looks at the candle on the table. He touches Imogen's shoulder.

—It's all right. It's earlier than we may have liked, but we'll make do. You know how I think of you. I'd have asked you in London, if I'd thought you'd have me—

—Please don't ask me.

—Why?

—Because you'll think I'm refusing you, when it isn't that at all. Let me tell you something. When we were at the café in Piccadilly, and you were talking about the mountains and drawing on that napkin—I wanted to listen to you. But all I could think was that I knew with perfect certainty that we were made for one another, you and I, Ashley. Perhaps you felt as I did, and it made you wish for certain things for us, and it made me wish for other things, but that doesn't mean they're any less.

—What does it matter—

—Let me finish, darling. In that café, I thought of us having a child together. I thought of being with you every day for years, of what it would mean to have even one week together in a house, with no one to trouble us. I knew we were as lovely together as anything paired in this world. And as soon as I knew it, I knew it always. It's never left me, not even when I thought you were dead. But I can't go through another month like this.

—I don't understand. You've come to France only to refuse me? Only to say—

—That I prize you, Imogen says, a thousand times more than myself. So I have come to say what cannot be put in a letter—

She puts her hand to his face, cradling his mouth so that he cannot speak.

—You can't go back to the front, Ashley. You musn't. Not now.

—Don't be absurd.

Imogen shakes her head violently. —It's absurd to go back. Can't you see that? We've a child and I won't have it grow up without a father, simply because I was too weak to say what I thought, and you were too blind to see—

—I'm not blind.

She throws her hands in the air.

—You aren't? Look around you, Ashley. What's happened to all the fellows from your OTC? Why are half the girls in Mayfair wearing black, looking as though they were struck by lightning? Because all of England is lying to themselves, saying they'll be the ones to make it, or that their husbands will survive. And I did it too, Ashley, but after this month I can't do it any longer. A year ago I wanted to save everyone, the Germans and the English, the French and the Austrians. Now I can't bear to look at a newspaper. And do you know why?

—That isn't the point—

—Because I know how selfish I am, for if you should have to kill a hundred men to survive, I'd want you to do it. It's a dreadful thing to admit, but it's true. Ashley, I've given up on principle. The war will go on and on until everyone's dead, and I can't save them all. But I can try to save the things that matter.

—I know what I'm doing. I've been careful out there.

Imogen stands up, pushing her palm against her forehead.

—Ashley, she gasps, you were nearly killed. What more can it take to convince you? Will you not believe me until you're dead on the ground? You're the reasonable one, so tell me why it's reasonable to suppose that if one in ten lieutenants survive this war, you'll be the one.

—I've lasted this long for a reason.

—Lasted, she repeats. Listen to yourself. It's only been three months. Look at the awful scar on your neck, you can't even speak as you used to. You've given them enough, must you give everything?

—It's not my choice whether—

Imogen comes back to him, taking his hand and looking him in the eye.

—It is, darling, it is. That's what I've come to tell you. I daresay you hate the war more than I ever could, but you won't admit anything, because you're blind to it. You're inside the machine and you can't see that there's any way out, that a man can do anything but go on and die.

—Have you any idea what you're talking about? Even if I wanted to leave, it would be impossible.

—Nothing's impossible. There must be a way out, we need only find it. It means your life, Ashley. I've already left England, I don't care if I ever go back. We could plan something and wait for the right moment—

Ashley shakes his head, his voice louder.

—Are you mad? You're speaking of desertion.

—I'm speaking of saving your life. If you won't leave, get transferred somewhere, away from the front. Get sent to a training camp, to any damned place where I'd know you were safe and I could sleep again. All the men you worry will look down on you will be long dead by then. What does it matter what anyone thinks if we have each other?

Ashley pulls off his necktie and puts it in his pocket. He stands up.

—You're living in a fantasy. You imagine I can walk away from my men as if this were the Boy Scouts. You imagine we can simply forget about your people and my people, and have a child without ever getting married. They've a name for such children, Imogen, and they aren't invited to the embassy ball.

Imogen backs toward the door, her face coloring as she feels for the doorknob behind her.

—I can't listen to this.

She walks out of the cottage, the door swinging shut behind her. The candle's flame is sucked out. Ashley stays at the table in the blackness, watching the smoke curl from the smoldering wick. He goes out the door.

→▷ ◁←

Imogen stands in the beech grove beyond the cottage, the gray daylight now beginning to fail. It has stopped raining but the trees are shedding huge drops of water. Ashley walks up to her, but she does not turn around.

—Who knows about the child?

—A doctor in Kensington.

—Anyone else?

—Ellie. That's all.

Ashley looks down at the wet leaves.

—For God's sake Imogen, be sensible and take me as I am, even if all this is less than perfect. Tell me you're not afraid to spend your life with me, as I'm not—

—I'm not afraid.

—Then marry me.

Imogen turns and touches his shoulder, her fingers running over the golden Bath Star stitched onto his epaulet. She bites her lip.

—Darling. I can't. Least of all when I hardly know if I'll ever see you again. You have to get away—

Ashley shakes his head, looking at her and speaking gently.

—I can't leave the army. Even if you are with child. It simply isn't possible.

—It must be possible. It's our only chance.

—I wouldn't go even if it were possible. Imogen, I've led men to their deaths. Men who went willingly because I pushed them forward. Men with families of their own—

—Getting killed won't bring them back.

—It won't. But I've a duty—

—You haven't a duty to me? Or our child?

—I do.

—Then which is more important?

—I have to see this through.

Imogen's voice breaks. She shakes her head, her eyes shining.

—But you'll never see it through. Can't you understand that? And I can't spend another week waking three times in the night, knowing you'll be cold and dead before I'd even get a message. Ashley if you go back, I'll never see you again, I know it. I've seen it in nightmares a dozen times, where I look for you, but you haven't even a grave to mark—

—You're only frightened, Ashley interrupts. You're frightened and so you imagine things, but that doesn't make them true. We're all scared sometimes. But I'm an officer. I can't abandon my men because it's dangerous.

—You're a man. You're a man with one life to live and you'll lose it. Have them send you somewhere safe, anywhere but the front. You've been wounded, get the doctors to say you're unfit for active service. I know you could do it, other men have—

—I can't do that. I shan't.

—You won't do it for me? For our child, Ashley?

—I can't.

Imogen throws her arms in the air.

—And you expect me just to wait? To stay up each night, carrying your child, knowing you might never see it, because you weren't willing—

—I can't leave the army.

—Then I can't wait for you.

Imogen swallows hard. She looks at Ashley, her eyes large and wet, her cheeks flushed as she turns her face slightly from side to side, her mouth open without any words. No one speaks. Still looking at Ashley, Imogen turns and goes back to the cottage. Ashley does not follow her.

There is the taste of iron in his mouth and he spits into the ground, but the taste does not go away. He stands under the dripping trees for a few minutes. Then he goes back to the cottage door and knocks, but the lock is drawn and she does not answer. He puts his ear to the door and he thinks he hears her weeping, but the rain has started again and it is hard to tell. The sky has turned from slate to black. In Louchard's farmhouse there is a lantern lit, a figure watching in the window.

—Imogen, he pleads. Open the door.

There is no answer. Ashley kicks at the door and curses. Still no answer. He walks back through the garden to the driveway and tries to start the motorcycle, the figure still watching him through the window. Ashley goes through the cycle of steps—spark, choke, throttle, compression, starter—but he cannot start the engine. On the fourth try he finally brings the motorcycle to life. He lets the engine idle, waiting to see if she will come out when she hears the noise. Nothing happens.

Ashley puts the motorcycle in gear. He begins riding to the north.

The bombardment begins eighteen minutes later.

At eight o'clock last night, as the red-haired VAD flipped the row of switches that controlled the electric lights in Ashley's hospital ward, several miles to the east a German dispatch runner waded down a communication trench flooded with blue-gray sludge. The runner made his way westward until he found the dugout entrance, a crooked door frame signposted with a plank nailed into the clay trench wall. He wiped the mud from the plank and read the sign under the fluttering light of a descending flare. He let out a gasp of relief.

The runner went down the slick dugout steps and handed a sealed envelope to an artillery officer at his supper. The envelope was damp and tore open easily. Inside there was a card bearing typed orders from division headquarters, the card spotted with something dark. The officer glanced up at the dispatch runner. Deferentially the runner averted his gaze from the card. The officer grunted. He signed for the orders on the wet envelope and handed it back to the runner.

The artillery went to work within the hour. As Ashley turned in bed in his last night in the hospital, across the line men in field-gray uniforms whipped horse and mule teams to a start, jerking wheeled guns from their resting places and dragging them through tracts of sinking mud. The enemy faces were hidden beneath steel helmets or the long cowls of waterproof capes, mouths and chins lit only by erratic flares or the sparks of an incoming shell. It was damp and freezing.

The artillery trawled on through acres of sludge. The wheels of guns and wagons stuck. The spokes and axles were gummed and coated with mud, the undercarriages dragging and catching on the black morass. The enemy cursed and raised dumb horsewhips in the darkness, flailing for any bestial hide to punish. They pushed on through traps of sucking clay, whipping their animals onward, shifting the cannons one inch at a time.

At last the guns reached their appointed places, slightly after the appointed hour. The artillery officer sent two words of explanation to his superiors: *Widrige Umstände.* Adverse conditions.

When the bombardment begins Ashley is riding north on the road to Louvencourt. He does not have a map with him and he has become lost in the backroads above Laviéville, the roads all the same in the darkness. Then the shelling starts. At first Ashley hears the faint singing of whiz-bangs, then the barrage opens into a pounding rhythm, a whole thudding sky.

Ashley pulls the front brake lever and pushes the rear brake pedal, the tires skidding over the slick ground as the motorcycle squirms to a halt. He wipes his goggles and looks at the horizon to the east. In the direction of Thiepval, white flashes are breaking across the clouds, beneath these the arcing red and orange sparks of high-explosive shells. The silhouettes of trees and buildings seemed to waver and crumble under fire.

Ashley turns the motorcycle in the mud and starts back toward the cottage.

He is riding fast now. Above the throttling engine there is the crash of approaching German five-nines, singing faintly in the air and cracking like thunder close by. He swipes the water from the lenses of his goggles, his fingers clumsy in their gloves. The road climbs uphill and he pumps a lever to feed the engine more oil. In the distance a Very light soars and bursts above the trees; under the flare's white brilliance, a group of figures is silhouetted on the road ahead. Ashley eases off the throttle.

He reaches the group of retreating civilians, a few families in wagons and on foot. They must have been warned before the bombardment started. Ashley coasts past the drenched civilians, then he opens the throttle again, engaging second gear. He knows it is foolish to ride this fast. Even in the daytime he isn't much of a motorcyclist, and now it is very wet and there is little visibility.

The road bends and rises until Ashley reaches Laviéville, the familiar town square with the small church and the white stone building of the *mairie*. Riding slowly and squinting into the rain, Ashley circles back to Louchard's yellow farmhouse. He parks the motorcycle before Imogen's cottage and throws open the door, shining his torch inside. It is empty. The girl's portmanteau is gone, only a tangle of disturbed sheets on the bed.

Ashley goes to the farmhouse door and knocks. There is no answer. He pounds on the door, yelling for Louchard, but he knows the man is gone. He swings the motorcycle off the kickstand and turns onto the main road to Amiens, traveling westward now. He approaches a pair of French gendarmes smoking cigarettes in the rain. They watch him pass without expression. Farther up there are more civilians going westward, a longer convoy that stretches into the distance. Ashley reaches a blockage in the road. He stops the motorcycle behind the crowd.

The civilians are gathered around a toppled wagon with a broken axle, its load dumped into the thick mud. An armoire reclines half-submerged in the morass, a few of its drawers open as if to collect the brimming rainwater. A fat gendarme is barking at a pair of civilians. Ashley pushes the motorcycle through the forest along the side of the road. He remounts and rides on.

A mile farther Ashley reaches another ragged convoy of civilians, Louchard near the front driving a wagon with a pair of mismatched horses. Ashley slows the motorcycle and calls to Louchard, who pulls his wagon to the side of the road and steps down, standing in the mud with his horsewhip in hand, the rainwater dripping off his cap. Ashley asks him where the girl has gone. Louchard shrugs.

—*Je ne sais pas.* She left right after you did.

—Where did she go? Which road did she take?

Louchard squints at Ashley through the rain. He repeats that the girl left this afternoon, but he does not know where she went. Ashley pulls a roll of francs from his pocket and shows it to Louchard.

—*Dites-moi.*

Louchard spits into the mud. He shakes his head ruefully and asks what reason the girl would have to tell him her destination. Ashley throws the money at Louchard's feet and shines the torch in his eyes, the air now thick with icy sleet. Along the road a crowd has gathered to watch. A shell explodes at some distance and they all crouch to the earth. Ashley rises, drawing his revolver.

—*Vous êtes fou,* Louchard says. You're mad.

Ashley swings the torch across the dripping faces of the crowd and they look away as the light strikes them. The bills at Louchard's feet sink into the mud. Someone in the crowd curses the Englishman. Ashley backs away toward the motorcycle. He holsters his revolver and starts the engine on the second attempt, the crowd watching him in silence.

Ashley threads the motorcycle through the crowd and rides on toward the west.

THE CROSS

⟻⟺⟼

It rains the whole drive to La Calotterie. Mireille drives as I try to guide us by an old Michelin map from the glove box. We see the water tower as we approach the village, a circle of Romanesque arches in brick with a basin at the top. It lies on a treeless brown field on the far side of town. Mireille navigates to it by sight, zigzagging on paved and gravel roads until we find the fenced-in plot of land that borders the tower. We follow a dirt driveway up to the house and see the name glued in metal letters onto the mailbox: DESMARAIS.

Mireille looks at me.

—You still want to go?

—I don't know. It can't hurt to ask.

We park in front of the two-story stone farmhouse. I ask Mireille if she will do the talking. As we get out of the car, the front door of the house swings open and an elderly man looks at us. He wears a checked shirt and his pants are clasped high above a sagging paunch by a leather belt. Behind him a television blares from the living room, something about cigarette price increases in France.

—*Bonjour,* Mireille says. *Êtes-vous Monsieur Desmarais?*

The old man regards us suspiciously through pale and watery eyes. He admits that he is Monsieur Desmarais. Mireille tells him our names, touching my arm as she explains that my great-grandfather was an English soldier who was billeted near here with a family called Lefèvre during *la Grande Guerre*. Desmarais studies us further. He inches forward and looks at the iron sky above our shoulders, at the dirty Peugeot in the driveway.

—*Bien*, he says. Come inside before you get wet.

Desmarais takes our coats in his beefy hands and sets them on wooden hangers. He hooks the hangers on a curtain rod above the radiator in the living room, then he sits down in an armchair. We sit on a sofa wholly encased in yellowing plastic that adheres to our clothes and makes strange noises as we shift uncomfortably in our seats. Desmarais switches off the television.

—I live alone, he says in French. I don't go shopping often. So I have nothing to offer you to drink.

Mireille tells him that we are fine as we are. Desmarais asks Mireille where she is from and they talk a little about Picardie. He asks Mireille if I'm English and I tell him I'm American. The old man nods.

—I knew Americans. In '44. But you have not come to talk about that.

Desmarais glances at Mireille. He looks back at me.

—I was born in 1926. So I never met the Englishman.

—The Englishman?

—He stayed here with my mother's family. The Lefèvres. My father's name was Desmarais—

The old man has a strong northern accent and I understand him only with difficulty. He explains that many English soldiers stayed with his mother's family during the war, but only one officer. His mother was a young girl then and the officer helped her with her lessons.

—The Englishman had been wounded, Desmarais says. Do you know where?

—*La gorge*. And in the leg.

Desmarais touches his throat.

—*Oui, la gorge.* My mother said he spoke very softly. I never heard about the leg.

—It's incredible, Mireille says, that your family remembered him this long.

Desmarais shakes his head and says that it is only natural that his family remembers the Englishman. He tells us that this whole village hated the English, for to be occupied by them was only one step above having *les Boches* here. He says the English were low people who drank too much and caused trouble.

—They knew they were going to die. And for this piece of land?

The old man gestures toward the bleak landscape outside and says that it must be a hard thing to fight for a country that is not your own. But he says that this Englishman was different, for he was an officer and he spoke French. Desmarais holds the proof of these things. The old man goes into the next room. He is gone for some time, and when he returns he has a box upholstered in burgundy fabric. He opens it on the coffee table.

—Some of my mother's jewelry.

He looks up at us and grins, revealing a set of crooked yellow teeth.

—Nothing valuable. That was all sold.

Desmarais pulls a small drawer in the jewelry box. He takes out a silver cross and hands it to me. The cross is square, its four arms adorned with the imperial crown, the royal cypher of George V set in the center. The medal doesn't have its ribbon.

—What is it? Mireille asks.

—A war medal, I say. The Military Cross.

Desmarais says that it is because of this medal that his mother remembered the Englishman. For all her life the cross was hung over the mirror of her dresser. The old man stands abruptly.

—I just remembered, he says. My niece gave me a box of tea. I can make you tea.

Mireille tells him we don't need a drink, but Desmarais insists and finally Mireille offers to make tea herself. Desmarais tells her where to find it and Mireille goes into the kitchen. The old man leans toward me with a conspiratorial whisper.

—I suppose you have come to ask about *la malle*.

—*La malle?*

Desmarais raises his eyebrows. Was it not for *la malle* that I had come here? I shake my head and explain that I don't know the meaning of the word. A *malle* is a case for traveling, Desmarais explains, and when he was a child one would take *une malle* on a voyage on an ocean liner. When the English officer left this house he left behind a small *malle*. Later the Englishman wrote and said he would come to collect it. For this reason, Desmarais tells me, the family had kept *la malle* for many years and though the Englishman never came, Desmarais had now kept it too long to dispose of it.

—My niece wants me to get rid of everything in the attic. But one can't simply throw these things away. When a man grows old he wants to keep what's left, even if it isn't useful.

Desmarais winks at me.

—Of course, a young man like you won't understand. But wait until you get older—

—I believe you now.

The old man smiles with polite disbelief. I ask him what is inside *la malle*, but he only shrugs.

—A bunch of burned papers. You can see for yourself.

I follow Desmarais up a set of carpeted stairs to the second story, the old man gripping the rail as he climbs the steps one at a time. He asks me to fetch a step stool from the bedroom, then instructs me to stand on the stool and push up a square door in the ceiling. I push the panel and it swings open on its hinges. There is a short iron ladder that pulls down.

—*Faites attention*, Desmarais warns. There may be rats up there. I think *la malle* is next to my fishing things, on the side with the window.

I climb the ladder into the attic. The roof drops steeply on each side, the space lit by a single window that projects a shaft of light across the room, exposing the odd remnants of a long and varied life. Stacks of cardboard boxes and piles of old electronics. A few rusty fans, a rack of old coats. Everything is dusty but arranged in good order. A pair of old bamboo fishing rods is leaned against the sloping ceiling. Beneath a stack of tackle boxes I uncover a small brown trunk, my fingers carving tracks on its dusty surface. The trunk is about two feet wide and a foot deep, perhaps intended to carry boots or hats. It is crafted of leather and fitted with brass hardware. Three initials are stenciled onto the front: AEW.

The latch at the center is unlocked. I unbuckle the two brittle leather straps and pull back the lid.

Ash and half-burned paper, the canvas lining blanketed with powdery soot. A few cloth-bound books: *Scrambles in the Alps*, *The Spirit of Man: An Anthology*. The spines creak and snap as I flip their pages. I take a breath.

Beside the books there is a bundle of charred envelopes. Some are blackened on the corners, others all but burned. *2nd Lieut. A.E. Walsingham, 1 Batt. Royal Berkshire Regt., B.E.F., France.* Ashes flake off my fingers as I open the envelope and unfold the sheet inside. The letter is written in a peculiar blue-black script: long and florid capitals, frequent dashes of varying length, elaborate ampersands. It is dated October 17, a few weeks before Ashley was wounded.

Dearest –

Eleanor & I went to the London Library today. I picked a tall stack of volumes, but sitting down to them, found myself asleep before ten pages were read. I dreamt of wondrous things – the stave church at Urnes I told you of, but the famous portals were yet uncarved, so you drew out your knife & we shaped them together – you carving one creature & I the other, their bodies linked fast. You lopped off a piece of the portal as a Souvenir for me, and told me to guard it well, for we were now as joined as two souls could be. Then the carillon tolled, for it was time for us to enter the church, but when you put your hand on the door – I awoke.

So I bade good-bye to Eleanor & strolled along the Embankment. Surely, I thought, even this most English of rivers flows to the sea & then towards you. On the pavement I watched a tramp draw, in chalk, the most exquisite replica of a Delacroix, only to be washed away by a rain that began to fall. Having no shilling, I gave him a ring from my own finger as recompense. He at first refused it, but I explained the ring had been an unwelcome gift, and I was richer without.

Of your question – of an Engagement – you already hold me by far more tender strings, and they are no less binding. Can you love me so much – Without – for just so long? For ten times so long? We shall not speak of wills, even gold or silver. Without you all should become lead, and would be no gift to me. I would lose more than any widow ever had. They lost husbands – I would lose my morning star, not yet risen.

Of Promises – the greatest I can fathom – I give myself to you, not in the tired rites of civilization, but through my own Design – as if love had never been before, and so I made it just for you.

Imogen

I try to refold the sheet, but my hands are shaky and it breaks at the crease. I put the letters back in the trunk and carry it down the ladder. The old man nods approvingly.

—You should take it.

—But you've kept it all this time.

I open the lid to show the contents, but the old man dismisses this with a sweep of his hand. He tells me he has enough old papers of his own without the need for old papers in a foreign language.

—When I'm gone my niece will just throw it out.

Desmarais descends the staircase at a crawl. I swing the attic door shut and bring the trunk downstairs, setting it on the living room carpet. The old man lowers himself into his armchair and switches on the television with a remote control.

—The news will be on soon, he remarks.

Mireille comes in carrying a tray with three mugs of tea.

—It took forever to light the stove—

Mireille looks at the trunk. She looks back at me. Her mouth is open.

—*Tu as trouvé quelque chose?*

Desmarais grins. —He did. And now we will drink tea, just like the English.

The journey back from France was dreadful. After the quarrel with Ashley, Imogen left the cottage at Laviéville and spent a terrible night confined to a hotel east of Amiens, watching the train of refugees flow past on the muddy road. She had not eaten since breakfast and all the restaurants were closed, so she sent the elderly porter out to search for food. He came back half an hour later dripping wet with only a small round *pain de campagne* gripped under his overcoat. It was wet and flecked with dirt. Imogen tipped the porter and chewed the loaf greedily in bed, listening to the rumble of guns in the darkness.

She spent the second night at a dirty hotel in Boulogne waiting for a ferry the next morning, stir-crazy but also fearful of leaving her room. She drew a bath but the hot water went out halfway through and she sat paralyzed in the lukewarm tub, too weak to move, too cold to stay, wondering if Ashley had been harmed in the bombardment, wondering what reason she had to return to England at all. She put her hand to her stomach under the water and decided the swelling had started after all. But a moment later she changed her mind.

Imogen dunked her head under the bath. She listened to the

humming silence of the water against her eardrums, the soft ping of her bracelet on the enamel tub as she pictured continents they might escape to: sun-bleached fields with horizons twice as wide as they had ever known. She stayed in the bath until her teeth began to chatter.

Imogen boards the ferry in the morning. The sky is gray and blustery, the sea in the Channel very rough, the few passengers on deck searching the choppy waves for signs of U-boats. The only other woman is a stout nurse in the khaki uniform of the nursing yeomanry. She leans against the rail beside a life preserver, scanning the ocean with a set of field glasses. She invites Imogen to have a look. Imogen obliges, but she sees only the same dark water, the same white froth magnified to ten times the size. It makes her dizzy.

The woman lowers her voice. The mast and the cables of the ship's derrick sway high above her cap.

—Heard about the *Britannic?*

—Pardon?

—Sunk yesterday in the Mediterranean. Along with God knows how many souls. Imagine, there could be a U-boat under us at this very moment, or a mine—

Imogen thanks the woman and hands back the field glasses, continuing along the promenade deck toward the stern. The nausea has come back and she does not know if it is the ship or the child or Ashley or everything put together. She goes to the ship's doctor, but he is too busy attending wounded soldiers to see her. A sympathetic nurse gives Imogen a bottle of patent medicine for seasickness. It tastes of bitter herbs and alcohol and syrupy mint, and Imogen goes back on deck feeling worse than ever, the horizon pitching and rolling, the air thick with cold spray, black smoke pouring from the twin funnels above her. She grasps the railing and watches the swells break against the ship's hull.

It had all gone wrong. For weeks she had fretted away long nights in stark terror of Ashley's death, picturing how it might come to him in a bullet or a bomb, wondering if she would feel the smallest tremor in the ground, a rustling in the grass. But when the catastrophe finally arrived there had been no tremor, no warning, because in going to France she had somehow mangled the one thing she was trying to save. And he had mangled it too.

For it hadn't only been Ashley in danger, Imogen suddenly realizes. They could all be brought under the waves of chance, their whole being submerged in an instant. It could happen to anyone on land or sea: the gold-braided naval officers on the navigation bridge, the ladies at tea in Mayfair and Belgravia, the art students sketching the Velázquez at the National Gallery. Even the frock-coated gentlemen in gray suede gloves walking through the solid doors in Whitehall that were never locked, the War Office and the Admiralty from which the whole empire was directed—they were all weaker than they knew, so much weaker. For nothing was certain, least of all the things one counted on to survive.

Imogen takes the bottle of medicine from her coat pocket and throws it over the rail, watching it flip end over end until it is lost in the gray.

It seems hours before the ship reaches Folkestone. Imogen boards the connecting train and at dusk the conductor enters her compartment to draw the air-raid blinds. The electric light is too murky to read by and she does not know they are in London until the conductor opens the compartment door.

—Madam, it's the terminus. Charing Cross Station.

She takes a taxi to Cavendish Square and enters the house, creeping up the carpeted stairs to her bedroom. She throws her dress on the floor and pulls off the silk combination she has been wearing for three days. She had left her spare in Laviéville. Her bed seems alien with its Turkish counterpane and soft bolster. She is nearly asleep when she hears her door open in the darkness. Imogen turns her back to the door, pulling the covers tight around her shoulders. The door closes again.

In the morning they are waiting for her in the parlor: her father leaning beside the mantel clock with the smoldering stub of a cigar in hand;

her mother looking pallid on the divan, her hands in her lap; Eleanor perched on the piano bench, her legs crossed tightly at the knee. Her father clears his throat.

—Imogen. It's time we spoke.

Imogen glances at her sister, but Eleanor turns her face to the window. Imogen looks at her father.

—I was at Beatrice's in Surrey, didn't Ellie tell you? I meant to come back yesterday, but the trains got muddled by the zeppelin—

Her father taps his cigar on an ashtray on the mantel.

—She told us, her father says. And we've more pressing matters to discuss.

He comes quickly to the point. He impresses upon Imogen that the decision is not simply hers to make, that the ignominy of the existence she intends would not only be hers but scrupulously allotted to all four of them, even to the more distant relatives of the Andersson or Soames families.

—You imagine you're simply deciding for yourself. But what you do affects all of us.

Imogen crumples into a chair. She has not bathed since her return and her hair and skin smell of salt water. Her father continues his discourse, outlining the consequences of an illegitimate child, the hardship it would incur on Imogen and the child and the family at large. To this speech Imogen's mother adds meager words of agreement. Her father begins to question her.

—You say this fellow won't marry you?

Imogen puts her hands to her face. She can feel the nausea coming back.

—I don't want to marry.

—But what are his intentions?

—It doesn't matter what he intends. It's my life—

—Imogen, will he or will he not?

Imogen looks at her father. Her voice is hard.

—He will not.

—Can he pay anything?

She glares at him, too angry to speak, her fingers clutching the bracelet on her wrist. Her father is unperturbed.

—You don't care for money now. But you will in time.

—He can pay, Eleanor whispers. He gets thousands and thousands per year, so Charles heard. They say his uncle was frightfully rich and left him nearly everything.

Imogen's head turns with a start. She has never heard of Ashley's money before and she is on the point of questioning Eleanor when her mother begins talking in an oddly calm voice, her words evidently well rehearsed.

—Darling, what I say may sound cruel to you at first. But Papa and I have put a great deal of thought into this, and I promise you it's the best thing for everyone. Most of all for you—

Imogen has trouble listening, but she absorbs the dim outline of their plan. Eleanor will announce she is expecting a child; Imogen will write to Ashley to say she has miscarried; the two sisters will go to Sweden, ostensibly to escape a winter of rationing and bombing raids for the comforts of a neutral country; the sisters will live in the seclusion of a rural home, the secret of Imogen's pregnancy closely guarded; Imogen will deliver the child with the assistance of a hired live-in nurse; Eleanor will return to England with the child and raise it as her own. The plan would neatly solve every problem, for Imogen and the family would emerge with their reputations unscathed, the child would grow up without stigma, and Eleanor would gain the child Charles and she had so far failed to produce.

Imogen is horrified. She stands and curses them all, most of all her sister.

—Mind your own bloody lives! This is my life and my child—

—Darling, calm down—

Eleanor stands up and touches Imogen on the shoulder, but Imogen pulls away.

—I can't believe you told them. Why did you tell them? Why?

—You can't do this on your own.

—I am doing this on my own.

Her father stubs out his cigar.

—And how do you intend to finance yourself? Or the child for that matter? Filling shells at Woolwich twelve hours a day, one day off every fortnight? Imogen, you're nineteen years old and you haven't the faintest notion what it means to pull your own weight in this world. You've never done it and pray God you never shall.

No one speaks. Eleanor sits down and looks out the window. Imogen's mother comes to Imogen and takes her hand, practically kneeling before her daughter.

—You must think of us, Imogen. Think of what they would say. Think of Papa's position, you'll see he's only trying to protect us. For heaven's sake, think of your child. Don't you wish it to be happy, to have every chance in life as you've had?

Imogen shakes her head. —Does every girl in England have a family that makes decisions for her? And takes her own child from her?

Her father scoffs. He takes another cigar from a box on the mantel, but he is too agitated to light it.

—You're the child, he retorts, otherwise we shouldn't be having this conversation at all. Imogen, we're not here to beg for your consent. I won't see this family's reputation compromised on account of your girlish fancies. If you won't entertain your mother's ideas you shall have to entertain mine, and I daresay they'll please you even less. When I think of the thoroughly decent fellows you've ignored only to turn to this scoundrel, it makes my blood boil—

—What do you know of him?

—I know what he did to you.

—And you think I'm naïve. What makes you imagine I didn't do it to him?

They stare at her in frank amazement, Imogen staring back, looking at her family as if she had never seen them before in her life. Her father, his forehead slightly flushed, muttering to himself as he cuts the end of the cigar with a pair of silver clippers and strikes a match; her mother, grasping Imogen's hand and talking softly about dire consequences Imogen is too young to understand—her father's delicate position, the blockade and U-boats, no coal in Sweden save for what the Germans give, now the Russian problem too—not to mention the scandal of the last envoy's niece in Paris, which had not been half so delicate, and not in wartime; and Eleanor, worst of all Eleanor whom Imogen now hates as she has never hated anyone, Eleanor who still will not look her sister in the eye, her face turned to the window as she smoothes the folds of her skirt.

—It follows you all your life, Imogen's mother whispers. You're too young to know what that means, but I've known women who twenty years later can't enter a room without imagining they're being spoken of—

Imogen is not listening. She swallows and says some stupid, hateful thing to all of them, hardly aware of her words, then dashes into the hallway, grabbing her handbag and pulling her umbrella so violently from the basket that it topples, spilling the umbrellas and walking sticks and Grandfather's silver-headed cane. She leaves them all on the ground and runs out, slamming the door behind her and crossing the square before anyone can follow.

She does not know where she is going. The sky is drizzling as Imogen turns west on Oxford Street, the shops and sidewalks, the motor drays and omnibuses appearing and dissolving as her mind runs in frantic circles. She thinks back to Eleanor two weeks ago, when Imogen had told her she was pregnant and Eleanor had fallen silent, then taken her hand and said it would be all right. She remembers the last night with Ashley at the Langham Hotel, the lights turned off and the curtains drawn, Ashley kissing her bare shoulder and saying it was all right no matter what happened to him in France, that to truly love one person was the most anyone could ask of life, even if it lasted only for a week—

Don't say such things, Imogen had told him. *Never say them, Ashley.*

The rain quickens as Imogen crosses Vere Street, the newsboys running for shelter into the doorway of Marshall & Snelgrove. But Imogen is already soaked, the cold water running down her neck into the collar of her frock. She walks all the way through Hyde Park into Knightsbridge until a white-haired man on the Brompton Road sees her crying on the sidewalk. He raises his umbrella to shelter her from the downpour.

—I beg your pardon, but madam, you're soaked to the bone. You'll catch pneumonia. Can't I help you in any way?

It takes Imogen five minutes to persuade him to leave her be, fabricating some tale about how she has always walked in the rain without an umbrella, ever since she was a young girl, and she does not at all mind being wet. The man shakes his head, watching her in the rain.

—Madam, we've all lost something in this war. But we must carry on as best we can.

Imogen walks back through Hyde Park Corner carrying the man's umbrella. She goes into a *bureau de change* in Piccadilly and changes the rest of her francs for sterling, but she spent so much on the journey to France that she has only one pound, six shillings left. At the post office on Regent Street she writes two different telegrams to Ashley, tearing up each of them in frustration. He is too far away and there seems nothing she can say that will change anything. She walks down the street to a branch of the Westminster Bank, but none of tellers will let her draw from her father's account, even if she has the checkbook, and when they go to fetch the manager she decides to walk out rather than be humiliated further.

You mustn't despair. You mustn't think at all. Only keep going.

Imogen walks to the Alpine Club on Savile Row. The office is closed, but the club porter answers the door and Imogen asks for the London address of her cousin Hugh Price. The porter shakes his head. He says that Mr. Price does not reside in London, and in any case he is on active service in France.

—Miss, I believe you're chattering. Won't you come inside to warm up?

—You're very kind, but actually I'm in quite a hurry—

It is growing dark now and Imogen walks faster to try to stop her shivering. She must get into dry clothes. She goes to three hotels but they are far too expensive, for Imogen knows her money will have to last, and the last clerk says he cannot recommend a cheap hotel for a young lady. Finally she goes to the YWCA on Baker Street and pays two shillings for a membership card and a bed in a frigid room furnished only with a small table and a Bible. The light is off and someone is snoring in the other bed. Imogen hangs up her wet coat and frock and pulls the papery sheets over her, still wearing her damp cotton crinoline. The blanket is scratchy and it smells of mothballs. She reads the poster on the wall by the moonlight.

TO THE YOUNG WOMEN OF LONDON

Is your 'Best Boy' wearing khaki? If not, don't YOU THINK he should be?

If he does not think that you and your country are worth fighting for – do you think he is WORTHY of you?

If your young man neglects his duty to King and Country, the time may come when he will NEGLECT YOU.

Think it over – then ask him to JOIN THE ARMY TO-DAY

She has a violent urge to tear down the poster, but it is hung over the other woman's bed and Imogen feels too weak to get up. She turns her back to the poster and curls her legs, drawing the sheets and blanket tightly around her. Imogen sleeps fitfully for a few hours. She cries sometimes and hates herself for crying, thinking of the girls who must have wept in this room, angry that she should be one of them; she pities herself for having no one to turn to, then grows angrier still that she should need anyone. At eleven o'clock the girl in the other bed rises and dresses in the dark, pulling on coveralls and a cap. The girl goes out without a word. Imogen stays in bed.

By five o'clock she is frantic with insomnia and she tries counting backward from a hundred to fall asleep, first in English, then in French and German and Swedish, but she counts too fast and soon her heart is racing. Imogen tosses back the covers and dresses hurriedly, her clothes as wet as ever. She walks down Baker Street in the pale morning, forming words in her mouth without any breath.

You're hopeless. You couldn't last a single night, without even a child to care for.

Soon she is talking to Ashley and the child itself, saying foolish and extravagant things, swearing that she loves the child more than herself, that she is certain it will grow to be pure goodness, as brave and virtuous as its father. The sky is brighter with each block she passes and by Cavendish Square the sun is warming the sidewalk. Imogen has been gone for twenty hours and walked eight miles. Her legs are sore and there is a chafing sensation in her left shoe that she supposes is a blister; she is tired, hungry and dirty, and she feels angry with everyone in the world, most of all herself for doing the one thing she had sworn against. She climbs the stairs and turns the key in the lock.

The house is quiet. Imogen catches her reflection in the hallway mirror: an unruly thatch of bobbed hair, deep and dark circles under her eyes. She goes downstairs into the kitchen. Her mother is standing with the cook before the gas range, a large wooden spoon in her hand. Imogen's voice is sharp.

—If we're going, I wish to go at once. I can't stand to be in London any longer.

The cook looks away into the pot. Her mother opens her mouth to answer, but Imogen walks out of the kitchen.

THE RECKONING

⊶⇒ ⇐⊷

I have Imogen's letters now. Every night I doubt that I found them and every morning I pull out the trunk from under my bed and flip back the lid, opening the envelopes and touching the sheets of brittle paper. I feel sure that I'm getting closer to something, if only I'll recognize it when I see it. Because the signs are everywhere, I just don't know what they mean.

At the Internet café in the village I write Prichard an e-mail explaining the letters. There's no phone at the house but I send Mireille's cell phone number in case he needs to call me.

We spend the night at a farmhouse several miles away with Mireille's friends, nine of us dining at a long table on simple food and prodigious quantities of wine. Afterward they talk in French by the fire; half listening, I stare at the flames and spell out the letters in my notebook, S-O-M-M-E, as if one code were the answer to them all. At midnight Mireille stands up before the fireplace, her shadow long before her.

—*On y va*, she calls. Let's all go for a walk.

Outside there is no moon but plentiful stars, the galaxy streaked white above our heads. We follow a gravel path through the dense forest. After twenty minutes we reach a great wooden cross in the middle of the path, set high on a stone plinth without ornamentation or inscription. I realize this is our destination. As they drink the others become more jubilant. Some lean against the pedestal and swallow wine in huge gulps. Others sing and shout into the dark trees. I ask each of them in turn about the cross.

—What is it for? Who put it here?

They all look at me and smile, but if they know the answer they will not tell me.

On the way back to the house I walk far behind the group, swigging wine straight from the bottle and thinking about the letters. All seventeen are postmarked from England, along with one note written at the front desk of the hospital in Albert. But there is nothing after that. None of the letters mention her pregnancy, nor do they give any hint about what might have happened to her later.

—Maybe there was another one, I whisper. Maybe he burned the important one.

On the path ahead someone has separated from the group and is standing in the road, turned to me in the darkness. It is Hélène.

—*Bonsoir*. How are you? You're quiet tonight—

—I'm fine. Just trying to figure some things out.

Hélène nods, lighting a cigarette as we continue down the path. I offer the bottle of wine and she takes a sip.

—I heard you met Mireille in a bar. Who spoke first?

I smile, shaking my head in embarrassment. Hélène laughs.

—I knew it must be her. Where are you from in the States?

—California.

Hélène repeats the word, puffing from her cigarette.

—California. Mireille and I said we were going to run away there when we were seventeen. To Los Angeles. For me it was a joke, but she probably would have done it.

Hélène looks at me.

—We've been friends a long time, Mireille and I. Has she told you much about her past?

—A little.

Hélène walks forward, her eyes on the ground.

—Did she tell you she only got divorced six months ago?

—She didn't say when.

—You must have wondered why you're staying at that dirty old place, with her family so close by—

—They live nearby?

Hélène looks up at me. —From the cross back there, if you keep walking to the other side of the forest, you'll be at their house in ten minutes.

—She never told me they were here.

—Well, they know you're here. Mireille needed me to get the keys to that house, so she had to explain. They're worried she's going to get in trouble again. She had so many problems with her marriage. Finally she's back in school and doing well, then suddenly she comes to Picardie early, for no reason—

Hélène smiles at me.

—For some reason. Listen, I don't know what's going on between you two, and maybe you don't either. Maybe Mireille doesn't. But she's fragile, even if she won't say so. She isn't ready to be spending a lot of time with a stranger, but she won't listen to me, so I'm asking you something simple. Be careful with her. You might have to be patient, but with Mireille, once she cares about something—

Hélène throws her cigarette onto the path. She shakes her head.

—It's the best thing about her. And also the worst.

When we get back to the house the others are already spreading out on couches and pulling blankets over themselves. The young farmer who owns the house looks at me and grins.

—There aren't enough beds. Who wants to sleep outside?

Mireille and I sleep in the open air under a vast metal roof, lying on haystacks piled in neat squares, each a story tall. We lie four stories up, each bale our own queen bed. I can hear Mireille on the bale beside me, breathing softly as she turns on her side.

—Are you warm enough? she asks.

—I'm fine.

—You can have one of my blankets—

—No, I'm warm.

A cold wind passes over us, whipping the dry leaves on the ground below. I fall asleep and wake only when I hear Mireille's voice again.

—Tristan. What do you think of Picardie?

—I'm glad I came.

—So am I.

I draw the strings of my sleeping bag hood tight, watching my breath curl into wisps of steam.

Morning breaks with a dark purple sky. Mireille is already sitting up with the blankets wrapped around her, watching the horizon for the rising sun.

—Should we get going? Nobody else will be up for hours. I wanted to clean the house today—

We drive back to the house and spend the rest of the morning sweeping out floors caked with layers of dirt. Mireille goes upstairs to sweep the bedrooms, but a few minutes later she runs down the steps carrying a wooden box. She smiles triumphantly.

—My grandfather's chess set. Do you want to play?

We open the chessboard, sitting cross-legged beside the fire to keep warm. The wooden pieces are all carved and painted by hand. Both of the queens are missing, so we substitute one-euro coins. Mireille lifts one of the coins and frowns.

—They're so ugly. The francs were much prettier. I don't know who designed this junk.

—Probably the Germans.

She smiles. —We can't blame them for everything. It isn't fair.

Mireille chooses the white pieces. I watch her set up the board quickly.

—I saw Hélène talking to you last night.

Mireille lifts up one of her knights and frowns, setting it back down. She moves her king pawn forward to start the game.

I hesitate. —She said you're not ready to be spending time with me.

—Of course I'm not ready, Mireille sighs. You know before I met you on Friday, Claire and I went out to dinner. All I could talk about was how happy I was to be alone. I know it doesn't seem like much, to have this tiny apartment, to be starting school again. But even if it's small, it's my own life—

I move my king pawn forward. Mireille shakes her head.

—It just took so long to learn how to be alone. And I know I'm forgetting it now.

Mireille moves her queen pawn forward, but I move my pawn diagonally and take her piece.

—Then Hélène was right.

—No.

Mireille shakes her head, moving her queen's bishop pawn forward one space. I take that one and soon we are making moves quickly, but I sense I'm not playing against her, only reacting to what she is doing. Mireille looks up at me.

—Hélène thinks I'm not ready for anything, except to draw pictures and hide in my apartment all winter. But that's not life. Because even if I was ready to meet you, were you ready to meet me? Were you ready to meet the lawyers or go on this search? Nothing ever comes at the right time, and we're never ready for anything. But either we make excuses or—

—Or what?

She smiles, moving her bishop in line to attack my king. —*Échec.*

After a few more minutes Mireille has won the game. She tries to hide her pleasure, but it is obvious.

—That was *le gambit danois.*

—You never told me you're good at chess.

Mireille shrugs. —I'm not bad, but I'm not good either. When we lived in the south, I had an old chess book and I learned a little. I like the names for the moves. In chess there is a name for everything.

We set the board for a second game and each move our queen pawn forward. I bring up my bishop pawn and Mireille moves her pawn diagonally, capturing mine. She smiles.

—*Le gambit dame, accepté.*

We are halfway through our game when Mireille's cell phone rings. She looks at the number on the display and shrugs.

—*Je ne connais pas*—

Mireille answers the phone. She says a few polite phrases in French and offers the handset to me.

—*C'est l'avocat anglais.* And his French is better than yours.

I lift the phone to my ear.

—James Prichard here. Apologize to your friend for my appalling French, I'm afraid it's long out of practice. I wonder if you have a moment? I've some news.

—Of course.

—In London I believe I mentioned to you the many privacy clauses in the Walsingham trust. You may recall that such clauses precluded us from giving you certain details of the estate, particularly figures with regard to its value.

Mireille is watching me across the chessboard. She smiles and taps her rook against one of the black spaces.

—I felt concerned, Prichard continues, that without any such figures, you might be—insufficiently moved—so to speak, in pursuing your claim. Frankly, it struck me as unfair that you should have no idea what it is you stand to gain. So I called a meeting of the trustees and we've agreed to release certain details of the assets. Pursuant, of course, to the confidentiality agreement you already signed. You understand that all this remains strictly confidential. I presume you still don't have e-mail access where you are?

—Not at the house—

—No matter, I can give you the figures over the telephone. You're alone now and no one else can hear me on the line?

I stand up and walk into the kitchen.

—Yes. I mean, no one can hear.

—Excellent. I should explain that for legal reasons it's simpler not to divulge the value of the trust's UK assets. But I thought it sufficient to release to you the contents of a certain 'Offshore Portfolio C.' This portfolio includes some former assets of Mr. Risley, who you recall was Mr. Walsingham's great-uncle and the originator of the estate. The portfolio holds principally bonds and tangible assets, some of these rather exotic. Mr. Risley required that it be held in certain proportions of foreign 'treasury stock,' precious metals and the like. These assets were kept overseas for tax purposes. Are you ready for the list?

—Yes.

—First are holdings in various foreign bonds. The purchase of these bonds is generally renewed with the maturation of other bonds, though the denominations vary considerably. At present—Swiss government bonds, due to mature in 2011: 32,452,950 Swiss francs. Japanese government revenue bonds, due to mature in 2012: 874 million yen. German thirty-year bonds, to be cashed in 2016: 43 million deutsche marks—why ever do they still write it in marks? Ah, here it is: 22,356,390 euros.

Prichard clears his throat. —There follows certain tangible assets. Gold bullion, in one-kilogram bars, PAMP Suisse, Credit Suisse: 462 kilos. United Kingdom gold sovereigns, principally Edward VII mintings, 1903 to 1909: 2,358 coins. Platinum bullion, PAMP Suisse: 3,825 troy ounces. A set of uncut diamonds purchased from DeBeers in 1905, at present insured for 6.3 million Swiss francs. Do I still have you?

I sit on a chair beside the kitchen table, half listening to Prichard. One of the chair legs is short and the seat rocks from side to side.

—Yes.

—There's a bit of real estate. A villa outside Porto-Vecchio in southern Corsica, appraised at five and a half million euros. An olive farm with attached houses in Sant Llorenç des Cardassar, on the eastern bit of Majorca. Valued at approximately eleven million euros. Incidentally, that place is medieval, I've heard, and quite grand. But I've never been. It's being run as a hotel at present—

—Majorca?

—I suppose Mr. Risley was fond of the Mediterranean. There's also a small estate in Nyanza province, Kenya, but the title is disputed and there's been no end to the headaches. In any case, it's been removed from the portfolio. Now comes the bottom line. The aggregate value of these assets fluctuates a great deal, naturally. At the last valuation in January, Portfolio C was at 122,046,468 Swiss francs, 32 centimes, to be precise. Shall I convert that into euros, pounds sterling, or U.S. dollars for you?

—No. That's all right.

—Naturally, any value attached to this portfolio is approximate to say the least. Should a beneficiary emerge, there would be significant tax, legal and administrative expenses upon distribution of such assets. These would detract from its value to some extent, though of course there are other assets to the estate. Have you any questions?

—I don't think so.

—You take everything in stride, don't you? Not to bat an eyelash at a hundred million Swiss francs, it says something of your character. Where exactly are you in France?

—In Picardie. About forty miles northwest of Amiens, near the coast.

—Have you found anything substantive?

—Those letters I wrote you about. I think the child was what split them up—

—Mr. Campbell, Prichard interrupts, I read the extracts you sent from those letters, and while they may support your theory, it remains conjecture. What we need is direct evidence. It's the tenth of September and you must keep your eye on the calendar. A month may seem to you a good deal of time, but I don't want you to panic when the deadline really looms. Have you a plan of investigation?

—I've just been following the evidence. I know everything up until 1916, when Imogen came here. But I can't figure out what happened after that.

—Is that relevant? Finding more evidence of Miss Soames-Andersson won't necessarily lead you to evidence of your grandmother's maternity.

—It's the best lead I've got.

—It may be, but you could be on the wrong trail entirely. Unless you find a new plan of attack, I'd advise you to return to London to resume your research from square one. Remember, all you need is one piece of paper. The right one. It need only prove Imogen Soames-Andersson is the mother of Charlotte Grafton. Everything else is immaterial.

We say good-bye. I give Mireille her phone back and sit down. She looks up from the chessboard at me.

—I've beaten you. I know every move you could make and I can beat them all. So we don't need to play anymore.

—Let's play anyway.

Mireille shrugs. —If you want. Why did your lawyer call you?

—He's not my lawyer. He works for someone, but not for me.

—*Oui, je comprends.* But what did he say?

—If I don't find something soon, I should go back to London.

Mireille frowns. —Is that all he said?

I pick up one of my pawns and move it forward two spaces. I look at Mireille across the chessboard.

—I'll be rich if I get the estate.

—But you already knew that—

Mireille lifts her rook in her hand. The polished ebony glints in the firelight.

—*Échec et mat.*

19 December 1916

La Calotterie

Pas-de-Calais, France

The officers have the evening off. They sit huddled around a brazier in the disused barn that has served as company headquarters for the past week. In an hour they will take their dinner at an estaminet in the neighboring village. For now they wait.

Ashley is reading a book, a blanket snug around his shoulders. Jeffries plays a game of piquet with Bennett, each man dipping the cards toward the glowing brazier to read the suits and ranks in murky light.

A lieutenant named Ismay comes in, muddied and icy up to the waist of his greatcoat, his shift with the last working party completed. Ismay has recently been transferred from the Second Battalion. He is a tall man with dark hair and different-colored eyes—one brown and one light green—and the effect seems sinister to Ashley, as though Ismay is always gazing slightly beyond him. Ismay yawns and wraps a blanket around himself, dragging a chair up beside Ashley. Ismay begins shelling a sack of peanuts and props his boots on the brazier, the ice melting and sizzling on the iron.

—You'll ruin your boots that way, Ashley says.

—Only going to warm them up a bit.

Ashley tries to keep reading. It is too noisy to concentrate, but it is too cold to sit any distance from the fire. He reads the sentence again.

> Every night, do you understand, I see my comrades of the Matterhorn slipping on their backs, their arms outstretched, one after the other, in perfect order at equal distances – Croz the guide, first, then Hadow, then Hudson, and lastly Douglas.

Jeffries and Bennett finish their card game and the officers discuss rumors of the battalion's next destination. Ashley shuts his book. He draws the blanket around his neck until only his eyes are visible, his knees tapping at each other in the cold. Bennett wonders whether the battalion has any chance of being transferred out of France.

—They say the adjutant mentioned Palestine—

—Rumor, Ashley interjects. Worthless rumor.

—You're just not a man of faith. You never were.

Jeffries takes the last of the peanuts from Ismay and throws the sack in the brazier. He jerks his chin toward Ashley.

—The spymaster believes in the Kaiser's pistol.

—That's true, Ashley says. That's no rumor.

—I've heard nothing of the Kaiser's pistol, Bennett says.

—That's because it isn't a rumor, Ashley says. The truth hardly spreads.

Ashley leans back in his chair and smiles. He explains that the German emperor, like all men who make war, has always preferred the trappings of war to the risky endeavor itself. The Kaiser loves uniforms, Ashley says, and wore one in civil life long before the present conflict. Accompanying this uniform is a fine leather holster, and in this holster is a silver-plated Chamelot-Delvigne revolver that the emperor carries with him always. The pistol's ivory handle is engraved with the letter *V* and a crown, for the weapon was a gift from the Kaiser's grandmother and fellow sovereign.

—Victoria, Ismay murmurs. Rum story.

—It's no story, Ashley says. It's true.

—Why not get another revolver?

—Maybe he liked the old lady, Bennett offers.

—It's more than that, Ashley says. He keeps it for a reason, even if he doesn't know the reason.

Laughing, Jeffries shakes his head.

—What's the reason?

—To remember who the enemy is, Ashley says.

—And who is that?

Ashley smiles again, but he does not answer. The officers get up and begin to dress for dinner. Bennett runs a comb through his hair, suddenly turning to Ashley.

—Do you think he's fired the pistol at an Englishman?

—Only at English venison, I'd wager. He has other fellows for that business.

The night is windless but freezing. The estaminet stands in the center of a half-ruined village, across the street from a *boucherie* leveled nearly to its foundations. But the little estaminet, with its chipped marble tables, iron stove and tuneless piano, is yet untouched. The madame opens the door, her white hair gathered in an elaborate bun atop her head. Frantically she waves them in from the cold.

—*Bonsoir*, she calls sonorously. *Entrez, messieurs, entrez!*

The dining room is empty, so the officers take their pick of a round table beside the stove. The madame takes their greatcoats as she barks instructions to a pair of serving girls. The English are to be given both claret and chardonnay, to choose from as they please. The madame regrets she is without champagne. One girl brings out the wine as the other puts a new log in the stove. Jeffries tells the madame they will take whatever she has in the kitchen, the best food she can offer.

—*On prend le Bordeaux, je crois*, Jeffries says.

A blond girl uncorks the wine and fills each glass. Jeffries raises his.

—To sweethearts and wives.

The others raise their glasses and reply in chorus.

—May they never meet.

The claret is very dry and at first Ashley drinks little. The madame brings out onion soup and the officers spoon it up with gusto. They talk of military decorations, of the paucity of medals awarded by certain regiments. Ismay calls for a second bottle of claret before the first is empty. Jeffries mentions the Victoria Cross and Ismay scoffs.

—No fairer than a penny arcade. A chap can go on slaying Huns and rescuing wounded all day, but if there isn't an officer about to witness it, he'll go home empty-handed. As if the word of fifty privates weren't worth that of a single lieutenant.

The madame sets down a plate of lobster mayonnaise, each portion cupped in a lettuce leaf.

—If we took private soldiers' evidence, Jefferies remarks, we'd be issuing VCs with the rum ration.

—It's all bosh, Ismay retorts. Take the spymaster here.

The officers all look at Ashley. Ismay picks up a lettuce leaf and devours it in one bite, wiping his mouth.

—Heard about that business at the Empress, Ismay says. Very game. You might have got a VC for that, but you couldn't hold the trench. Which wasn't your fault, naturally, but it meant you were lucky to get decorated at all. You'd think the army would know by now that bravery hasn't a damned thing in common with success. But they don't.

Ashley says nothing. The madame brings in four bowls of *blanquette de veau*, a stew of veal shoulder with carrots and onions, the white sauce glistening with butter and cream. The officers eat contentedly in silence, Ismay draining his glass of claret.

After they finish the stew the blond girl brings out a wheel of ripe Camembert on an ancient serving tray. As Ashley slices the cheese, Ismay makes crude jokes to the girl. The brunette pours more wine and Ashley talks with her about the geography of the surrounding country. Ismay overhears them and interrupts.

—*Le jeune lieutenant est très brave*, Ismay insists. *Très brave.* He took a Boche trench with only a few men. Hundreds of men had tried to take this trench—

Ashley grimaces, but the girl looks at him with interest.

—*C'est vrai?*

—*Non*, Ashley says. The Germans thought there were more men than me, so they retreated. That was all. They came back later.

Ismay protests that the young lieutenant is in fact *très brave*. He directs his glass toward Ashley's tunic, speaking French with a strong English accent.

—Do you see that purple-and-white ribbon? It's the English Croix de Guerre.

The girl begins to say something, but the madame comes out with a box of Upmann coronas. Each man takes a cigar. A bottle of brandy appears and Ismay apologizes to the girls as they light the cigars and pour out the brandy.

—We're all married men, Ismay says. We're only joking around.

The blonde smiles, but the brunette eyes the group of young men intently, the bottle in her hand. She shakes her head.

—*C'est pas vrai.*

—We're all bachelors then, Ismay says. So much the better. Pity for married men to be killed in action.

—You're not all bachelors, the brunette says, looking at Ashley. He is married. Or engaged. One can see it clearly.

—Do you imagine any woman would marry him? Ismay protests. Even an Englishwoman?

Everyone laughs. The cigars are finished and the madame tallies the bill on a small chalkboard and sets it on the table. Ismay leans forward to read the bill and knocks his wineglass over, the claret saturating the tablecloth. He complains loudly in English.

—Highway robbery. Seventeen francs a bottle for that brandy? Double what it cost last year. And watered down to boot.

The madame clears the table and folds away the soaked tablecloth. She peers inquiringly at the officers.

—*Il y a une problème?*

Assuring her that all is well, Jeffries collects money from the officers and counts it out before the madame. As the others walk out of the estaminet, Ashley sets a pair of gold ten-franc pieces on the little zinc bar in the corner. His eyes scan the dusty bottles on the mirrored rack. He asks the madame for a bottle of brandy to take with them. He studies the rack further and frowns.

—*Non, je prends l'Armagnac.* The one on the top, the Boingnères. And could you uncork it?

—*Bien sûr,* the madame says, drawing the cork skillfully with an old wine key. Ashley takes the bottle and plunges the cork back in with the heel of his palm. He tells the madame to keep the change. The girls stand by the entrance ceremoniously, the brunette propping the door open with her back. Ashley wishes them a good night. He looks away from them as he walks out.

Descending the estaminet's frozen steps, Ismay stumbles and nearly falls, only caught by Bennett at the last moment. Ashley hands Jeffries the Armagnac bottle.

—From the foothills of the Pyrenees. Wasted on you philistines.

Jeffries admires the bottle in his hands. Trying to read its label by the moonlight, he nearly drops the Armagnac.

—Good fellow. And a wise man. You can't take it with you.

Ashley grins. —Rather. Only we haven't any snifters.

Jeffries uncorks the Armagnac and passes it around. It is fifteen minutes' walk to their billets in La Calotterie. The road is dark and empty, the void around them punctuated by phosphorescent flashes, Very lights tumbling down the eastern sky. Ismay whistles the melody of "Any Time's Kissing Time." From here the artillery is an elemental rumble in the lowest register.

The officers trudge a dirt path through fallow beet fields. They stumble and drag their feet, treading in puddles and splattering mud onto their puttees. Ismay passes the bottle to Ashley and puts his arm over his shoulder. He tells Ashley that he isn't after him, not about the Empress or anything else. He knows Ashley is a damned fine officer, probably the gamest in the battalion. He has heard about the business with Ashley's girl. Ismay's eyes are bright as he talks. His nose is red from the cold and a shock of dark hair spills from his cap onto his forehead.

—We shan't be here forever, Ismay says. We'll be back in the mincer in a fortnight, and it won't matter what we've said here unless we tell the truth. It's no use—mincing words, so to speak.

Jeffries stops his singing long enough to grab the bottle back. It is already half-empty.

—For the Lord's sake, Jeffries says, leave the poor spymaster alone. The last thing he needs is your counsel.

—Keep singing, Ismay said. We're only discussing Marlowe's *Faustus*. Spymaster's a literary chap, like myself.

Jeffries walks on ahead with Bennett. Ismay turns back to Ashley, his breath thick with wine and brandy.

—Now hear me out. I was in the same spot as you. Of course, you're thinking it's never the same. But I was engaged to a lovely girl. Known her since we were children. Wrote nearly every day for four months. Then I got a letter while I was at Loos, telling me she'd gone off with some worthless character. I did as you did, but not so well. Night patrols, as many as they'd let me. I didn't take any trenches, but I was out of my mind and I suppose I wanted to get myself killed. And for what? Let me have a gasper.

Ashley takes his silver case from his pocket, removing a cigarette for both of them.

—If I'd kept that up, Ismay continues, I'd be rotting in Delville Wood for a girl who wouldn't have come to my funeral, nor hardly thought of me again. When did you come to France?

—August.

—And you've been in some ghastly shows, haven't you? But you've survived. Surely there's a reason for that. You can't have made it through all that only to be ended by some girl. Remember, Walsingham, whoever she is, she's only some girl. Remember that.

—I'll try.

—You ought to go back to that estaminet and see that brunette. I saw how you looked at her.

Ashley shakes his head and draws from his cigarette.

—Perhaps I'm only tired of looking at you fellows.

—Perhaps. Look here, I'm only trying to be decent. You'll do as you like. But if I'd had my way, I'd be dead on account of someone I wouldn't cross the road to see today. That's the last I'll say of it.

Ismay takes his arm from Ashley's shoulder.

—Walsingham, what did you do before the war?

—I was at Cambridge.

—Naturally you were. But what did you really do? I'd like to know what counts for a fellow like the spymaster.

—You mean what used to count—

—And will again one day. Foxhunting, perhaps? Snooker? Are you one of those fellows who goes round the world looking at geese through field glasses—

—I liked to climb mountains.

—For sport?

—There's no other reason.

Ismay shakes his head.

—Climbing mountains for sport, he repeats. Sounds dangerous.

—Not compared to France.

—No, Ismay agrees, nothing quite compares to France. But how does it work? You rope on to another fellow and go up something tall and icy?

—More or less.

—And if he falls?

—He'd better not fall.

—But if he does?

—Really, I'd prefer he didn't.

Ismay grins. —Walsingham, you may be a damned strange fellow, but I admire you. You're cut from your own cloth, no one else's. You certainly know how to suffer fools gladly.

—It was a fine speech.

Ismay nods appreciatively.

—Tell me something, he says. When you took that Hun trench. What's it like, being the first man to step in there? I've imagined it so many times—

Ashley tosses his cigarette into the darkness, but he says nothing.

Ismay grins. —You ought to go and see that brunette.

The others have stopped singing. Jeffries stands in the rutted road, waiting for Ashley and Ismay to catch up. He regards Ashley with a queer expression.

—Where's your hat?

Ashley runs his hand over the empty air above his head.

—Bollocks. Left it there. I'd better go back.

—Forget it, Jeffries says. There's a spare around, I'm sure. You can send someone in the morning for it.

—Or he can go there himself, Ismay says.

—Or he can go there himself. Now where the deuce is Bennett?

Guessing that Bennett has gone ahead, the officers stagger along toward La Calotterie, calling out for him. Bennett never appears. Ismay is particularly irritated, for Bennett had been holding the Armagnac.

When they reach the edge of La Calotterie, Ismay can barely stand. Ashley and Jeffries drag him on their shoulders toward Ismay's billet, a second-story bedroom in a farmhouse whose timbered walls seem to meet at grotesque angles. They dump Ismay onto the yard before the house. He lies in the frosted dirt, squirming and ranting.

—I've only one question for you fellows. Have you an able-bodied groom, chauffeur, gardener or gamekeeper serving you who should be serving your king and country?

—Enough, Jeffries says.

—Have you a man digging your garden who should be digging trenches?

—Hush—

Ismay rises from the mud. He squints theatrically at them.

—I ask you gentlemen, have you a man preserving your game who should be helping to preserve your country?

Ashley takes Ismay by the shoulder.

—I'll see him up. We needn't both run the gauntlet.

The old woman of the house holds a candle as Ashley pulls Ismay up the stairs, his tall boots shedding clumps of black ice onto the carpet. The woman begins her usual tirade against the English, but she has a thick Picardie accent and Ashley understands few of the insults. Ismay bellows back at the woman.

—Madame, I can only reply with my own query. Have you a man serving at your table who should be serving a gun?

The old woman's eyes narrow in contempt. She pulls the bedroom door open and Ashley drops Ismay on his bed. The woman lights an oil lamp and manages a few words of complaint, gesturing at the sheets now coated with frozen dirt. Ashley promises to have the sheets cleaned himself, but this fails to placate her and she stomps off to her bedroom cursing. Ashley tugs Ismay's boots off and pulls the sheets over him, his greatcoat still on.

—Spymaster, Ismay mutters. Dear old spymaster—

Ashley sinks into a chair, taking a moment to consider things. The room swims with vertigoed motion. If only he could think. This is a puzzle he can solve. But what exactly is the problem? Ashley notices Ismay fanning his hand wildly, motioning for Ashley to come closer, muttering something indecipherable. Ashley goes to the bed.

—We'll come out in the end, Ismay slurs, won't we?

—Pardon?

—We'll beat them. Even you must admit it.

Ashley shakes his head. —I don't know, Ismay.

—My name is Edward.

—I don't know, Edward.

Ismay rises from the bed. He grips Ashley's arm forcefully.

—I shan't go back. I'm not so stupid as to go back, do you hear? Nothing could make me go. Let them shoot me.

—Calm yourself—

—You think I'm afraid to die? You think I can't die so well as any man?

—Quiet, Edward. Easy now.

—I shan't go back. Do you hear?

Ismay tosses the sheets back and gasps. Ashley worries that Ismay may vomit, so he brings the basin over to the bed, holding it at his waist. Someone bangs on the floor below them, appealing for silence. Ashley curses and drops the basin on the floor.

—We'll beat them all right, he promises.

—We'll beat them, Ismay repeats. But first they'll fucking ruin us—

Ismay pushes his face into the pillow, then rises feverishly toward Ashley, his eyes huge.

—You think we'll come out of this?

—Certainly.

—You bloody liar.

THE MESSAGE

Mireille and I stop at an Internet café a few miles from the house. We check our e-mail at a pair of aging computers beside a humming refrigerator stocked with soft drinks. The keyboards are sticky with grime.

There's a new message in my in-box, but I don't recognize the sender's name. I scroll down to the bottom of the message: *Gregory Bailey, Information Officer: Archives, Royal Geographical Society.* I read the e-mail again and call to Mireille. She leans over to my monitor to look.

—What does it mean?

—They found the telegrams.

I explain that in 1924 the Mount Everest Committee kept copies of all telegrams sent through the expedition to its members. I'd requested them in London, but it had taken weeks for the archive to pull them from storage and scan them. I click through images of old telegraph forms, yellow and pink slips with cryptic messages in purple type, transcribed and carbon-copied, marked by pencils and rubber stamps. I stop at one of the messages.

2 AP 24
IMOGEN SOAMES ANDERSSON HOTTINGUER ET CIE 38 RUE
DE PROVENCE PARIS
PLEASE CABLE ADDRESS HAVE WRITTEN POSTE RESTANTE
BERLIN GPO RETURN ENGLAND AUGUST YOURS EVER
ASHLEY

Mireille shakes her head in disbelief.

—They were in contact. But what does it mean?

—Hold on—

I run a search for "Hottinguer et Cie" and learn that Banque Hottinguer was a private bank established in Paris in 1786. Then I log on to an online encyclopedia and check the entry for *poste restante*.

Poste Restante (French, trans. "post which remains") is a service where the post office holds mail until the recipient calls for it. It is a common destination for mail for people who are visiting a particular location and have no need, or no way, of having mail delivered directly to their place of residence at that time.

Mireille looks at me.

—So she wasn't in Paris?

—I don't think so. That's just where her bank was. It seems like she was in Berlin—

—But how did she get the telegram if she wasn't in Paris?

—It must have gotten forwarded by her bank. Lots of people used to do it when they traveled, I've seen it in archives. People could just wire your bank and you'd let the bank know which hotel you were staying at.

—I don't understand. The message doesn't tell you anything—

—It does. I just have to think about it.

We stare at the telegram on the screen. I think of Ashley in 1924, sending the message from a hill station in India or the remote Tibetan plateau. I think of Imogen in Berlin the same year, and I wonder why she would be there and why Ashley would be writing to her. I turn to Mireille.

—He was on an expedition. He was on the other side of the world and he wanted to send her a letter.

Mireille shakes her head. I touch her shoulder.

—Just listen. He didn't have her address, but he knew what her bank was, and I guess he knew she was in Berlin. So he wrote her poste restante to the Berlin general post office, then sent her this telegram telling her to collect the letter.

I make a printout of the scan. Mireille goes to the cash register and pays the clerk.

—Let's go outside, she says.

We stand outside the café, at the crossroads of this deserted hamlet where no cars drive by and most of the businesses are shuttered. Mireille draws tobacco from a paper pouch and taps it into a neat line on a leaf of rolling paper. She looks at me.

—*Tu veux aller à Berlin?*

—I think I have to go.

—But this telegram, Mireille insists, has nothing to do with your grandmother's birth. Chasing it won't get you any closer to the money. You have no idea how long she was in Berlin—

Mireille tucks the cigarette into her pocket.

—Or if she was there at all, she adds. Maybe he was guessing. Maybe she never even got the telegram.

We walk past a *boulangerie*, its rusted steel shutters drawn shut. A stiff wind blows along the street and Mireille zips her coat up to the neck.

—You wouldn't even have an address to look for there.

—No.

—But you'll go anyway.

—I know it seems crazy. But every time I've tried to be logical and look at records or archives, it hasn't worked. And when I just go after something, like when I went to Leksand, or when I came up here with you, I've found things. It's just like Prichard told me, there isn't anything in normal records, so the only thing that works—

Mireille walks on past our car, shaking her head.

—Works, she repeats. You've learned a few things. But you haven't found anything that will get you the money. Do you think you're better off than before all this began? You're nervous all the time, worrying about something you can't control, something that already happened. You're spending all your savings on this crazy search, and now you want to go to Berlin. Where would you even look there?

—I don't know. The post office.

Mireille lifts her hand in the air.

—I don't understand you. I don't understand what you're after. You say you don't care about the money, but you'll go anywhere to chase this story. Why not Amsterdam while you're at it, why not Bruxelles or Genève? You're just guessing, you can't keep this up forever. How much money do you have left?

—Enough to get there.

—*Et après?* What do you think you're going to find over there? A hundred million Swiss francs? Even you aren't that crazy. You think this is going to have an answer at the end—

—There has to be some ending.

—There doesn't. *Même si*—

Mireille breaks off in frustration, shaking her head. She looks down the empty street.

—Even if there's an ending to all this, maybe it's lost. Maybe there's a reason it ought to stay lost. And even if you're lucky enough to find an ending, it might not be the ending you wish for.

—I've been lucky. I found the letters. I found you.

—And I'm asking you not to go to Berlin. Stay here and we can go back to Paris next week.

I stand in the street, not knowing what to say. Mireille stops before the window of a small *mercerie*, her back to me as she stares at the bundles of black and cream-colored lace.

—Just give me a month, I say. Then it'll all be over.

She shakes her head and walks on ahead of me. I follow after her.

—It's not because I care so much about you, she says. You're no one. You don't understand what's going on around you, or what any of it means. But what bothers me is that every amazing thing that happens to you, you'll just get on a train and go somewhere else, where you expect another amazing thing to happen.

—I don't expect that.

—You expect that, she continues, but that's not life. *C'est un conte.* A fairy tale. Forget about the lawyers and the money. They're never going to give you anything. And forget about these dead people and their story, it's probably not even true. What about our story? What were the chances that we would meet, that you would choose that bar in Paris, for no reason at all, and that I would take the seat beside you? Isn't that enough? Or are you only going to care about it in ten years or a hundred years, when I'm gone and you can't do anything about it?

—I didn't know you felt that way—

I reach for her shoulder, but she walks on a step ahead.

—I don't feel that way, she counters. But even if I did, you'd still go to Berlin.

—I'll be back. I'll come right back here when I'm done.

Mireille stops in the street and turns to me. Her face is streaked black with running mascara. She wipes her face with her sleeve, her chin raised high.

—No, she says. I'm sure you won't.

30 December 1916

Lake Ejen

Dalarna, Sweden

Eleanor always woke first. Dawn came late here, a dim haze of white in a world already carpeted in deep snow. And Eleanor rose instinctively at the first inching of day, as if her body were trained to extract the maximum of light from the grim Nordic winter.

The problem was not that Imogen slept late. It was that she stayed in bed. The days were short and bleak, and when her sister did not rise until noon it left her less than three hours' paltry daylight. Such gloom would sap anyone's spirit. So in the morning Eleanor would cross the hallway to find Imogen lying with her eyes already open in a vacant stare, her face turned toward the slim gray band of light slipping between the baize curtains. Eleanor would part the curtains; Imogen would continue looking where she had been looking, her gaze now passing through the squares of leaded windowpanes.

—Darling, Eleanor would say. You ought to just open the curtains yourself.

Then Eleanor would lean over her sister and kiss her lightly upon the forehead.

It was not only Leksand that was wholly alien to Imogen. It was her own life. It seemed a sentence levied for some private crime: an entire winter in a rough cabin at the northern extremity of civilization, quarantined from all society save her sister and an elderly Swedish housekeeper. Not that Imogen was bothered by the house, the snow, the isolation. She had often dreamed of such a life. What troubled her was how she had come to it.

No matter how often Imogen retraced the course of events that brought her here, she could never detect the aberration she sought, the mistake that had condemned her to this calamity—an existence that was ghastly chiefly because it could not be redirected. She could not go back. But if only she knew her error, she might find the thread that had been pulled to unravel her; perhaps then she could use that knowledge to repair everything. Imogen recalled an article she had read about the ingenious antivenin of Brazilian physicians, proof against the bites of pit vipers or adders: cures deposited in corked vials in a laboratory, crafted arcanely from poisonous venom. Where was the vial for her own condition, the cure that would swoop her back to six weeks ago, offer her a chance to replay the scene where a few missteps had derailed everything?

Still the unreality of Leksand bloomed on for Imogen, thriving as she refused the coming of each new day, lengthening as the icicles draped off the shingled roof. This was her life now, and yet she would not have it—the low sloping pineboard ceiling; Eleanor donning overboots and mackintosh downstairs to light the fire in the barn, as Mrs. Hasslo filled the kettle from a great pitcher; the bilious drifts of snow gathering and gathering around the house, obscuring the lush grass that was all Imogen remembered from the summer visits of her youth.

For Eleanor it was different. She had consolations for her hardships. There was the merit she found in her own sacrifice, for Eleanor was a generous person and it pleased her to sacrifice for the sister she had always protected. And when all of Europe was suffering so conspicuously, Eleanor wished to take her small share of the burden: six months sequestered in the social wilderness of a Scandinavian winter, then the charge of a child that was not her own.

To Eleanor the child seemed equal parts burden and gift. For though she had long wanted a child of her own, the likelihood of that had grown dimmer with each passing season, the physicians' advice more grasping and feeble. With his instinctive practicality Charles had accepted at once the idea of Imogen's child, dashing off a series of letters from Palestine with long and reasoned arguments, sensing in the plan the nearest resolution to two years of frustration. But perhaps he had accepted it too easily, for Eleanor remained unconvinced. She knew it was unnatural and she could not forget that. There was a sense of wrong that went beyond Imogen's reluctance, beyond the pageantry of lies they had fed to Charles's family about the pregnancy.

Eleanor had lost something she would never get back—her own child, the formless presence that had seemed real so often that she had never been able to give up on it, no matter what the doctors said. Only now had she released that presence. And though Eleanor's intellect understood it had not been a trade, to her heart it seemed an unholy bargain, a sin she felt in a thousand nerves, in a hundred subtle instances every day. She felt it as she watched and tried not to watch Imogen's body changing and swelling; she felt it as she imagined and fought against imagining the forming child that would look like Imogen or like Ashley, perhaps even a bit like her, but never Charles. At times this uneasiness was more than she could bear and she prayed the taint would not survive the child's birth, not stay with it over the years. But she could not be sure.

All this drove Eleanor to her final consolation—her work. She had always longed to take a creative retreat in the country, but like her sister she tended to distraction, toward the metropolis with its constant diversions of luncheons and exhibitions and lectures. There were no distractions here. The sisters shared the society only of Mrs. Hasslo, the housekeeper, and Dr. Lindberg, the village physician. The nurse would not arrive from England until the end of January. Occasionally Eleanor saw the grocer, but he was a taciturn man and Eleanor was too embarrassed by her crude Swedish to make much conversation. Eleanor had visited relatives in Stockholm exactly once since they had come to Sweden, and she had done this only to preempt any of them coming up to Leksand and discovering Imogen's condition. Not that anyone wished to come.

So chiefly Eleanor painted, working all morning in the old barn she had turned into a studio. Before the sisters' arrival, a wood-burning stove had been installed in the barn under Mrs. Hasslo's direction, and a large easel ordered up from Stockholm had awaited Eleanor in its packing case. Every day now she painted through the frigid morning with two shawls wrapped around her and a thick blanket spotted with varicolored oil paint. Even with the stove burning continuously it was impossible to warm the entire barn.

Eleanor had brought from London a few canvases that had been troubling her, but so far she had not worked on these, for she was flush with fresh subjects. Since arriving in Leksand, Eleanor had painted two views of the cottage whose blood-red hue so intrigued her; an ironic portrait of Mrs. Hasslo as a peasant woman; a series of sketches detailing Imogen's transformation into motherhood, a subject that captivated Eleanor, who had never been able to imagine her sister with child. For weeks Imogen had refused to pose nude, until one afternoon she had come into the studio and begun undressing without a word. Eleanor must have fed fifty logs into the stove that day, until the rafters above were thick with curling smoke, but still Imogen shivered in her sitting pose, balling her fingers, her skin seeming to acquire a faint bluish pallor that crescendoed in her verglas eyes. In hours of posing Imogen never complained. The resulting drawings were mesmerizing, magnetic in their peculiar charms: a pregnant girl with arms and legs crossed tightly, uneasy in her own skin, her guarded face awaiting this descending miracle or catastrophe. Eleanor prized these as she had never prized any sketches, if only because she knew she must destroy them one day. But she had not destroyed them yet.

→≡● ●≡←

On this morning Eleanor lingers in Imogen's room a moment longer, noticing the tiny drifts of dust collected in the porous woodgrain along the floor. She drags an inquiring finger into a crevice. It comes up gray. She will clean it this afternoon.

Eleanor pours a glass of water from a pitcher and sets it on Imogen's nightstand; they have ordered a bed table from Stockholm, but it has not come yet. Imogen stirs in bed.

—Why on earth, Imogen murmurs, must you rise so early?

—I don't know. I suppose we're bred to live up here.

—Half-bred.

—And you've the wrong half, Eleanor teases. Are you feeling poorly?

Imogen turns her head, but she does not answer. Eleanor kisses her sister's forehead and descends the stairs with heavy steps, her tactful method of waking Mrs. Hasslo, who otherwise might drowse on until nine. Imogen stuffs another pillow beneath her head. Under the sheets she rests her hands upon her stomach, as she often does now, sizing with cupped fingers the swelling that always feels larger than its appearance to the naked eye.

She should never have come to Sweden, Imogen reflects. She should have done anything but this. She might have married Ashley and kept the child for herself; she might have followed him rather than her family. It would have meant sacrificing her pride and having a different life than she had imagined, but in doing so she would have kept the two things that mattered most, Ashley and her child, at least as long as Ashley lived.

But Imogen could not have stood this. The days and weeks of waiting had grown intolerable even before Ashley was wounded, and the news of his death had ground her nerves to nothing. By the time she boarded the ferry to France, Imogen was in a state of constant dread even though she knew he was safely in a hospital. And soon Ashley would go back to the front. Imogen could not bear the thought of it, not one more week of that boundless terror, let alone months or years. The child would only make things worse, for Imogen remained convinced that it would grow up without a father. She had given Ashley a choice and he had chosen the war.

But had they truly made choices, or had they only given in to forces they felt too weak to resist? Imogen remembers the night at the YWCA, walking back to Cavendish Square and telling her mother she would go to Sweden. In doing this she had chosen, or believed she had chosen, the child's happiness above her own. She had done the right thing. And yet it did not feel right at all. For it was at that moment, Imogen now recognizes, that she had surrendered control of her life and left others to pilot the vessel, or let it be guided entirely by the chance swelling of the waves.

Imogen sits up in bed and sips from the glass of water on the nightstand. She senses the letters within the drawer, the newest of them only ten days old. Imogen had conspired with the parlormaid to forward the letters in packets with her other correspondence. If Eleanor suspects anything, she never speaks of it.

Imogen finds the letters dreadful. Ashley had written to her from the convalescent hospital at Étaples, then from his billet at La Calotterie. He spares nothing in recounting every sinew of his devotion to her. Occasionally he talks of his responsibility to his men, but he never mentions their quarrel. Even now he writes every few days, though he has had no word from her since they parted in the Somme five weeks ago.

For God's sake answer me, darling, he writes. *Send me a sign of rejection, even, that I shall know you are well and have decided against me.*

Ashley inquires not only of her, but of the growth of their child; he claims he will be the most loving of fathers, that he will do everything he can for Imogen and for their family. He asks nothing of her save a second chance.

You ask so much, she thinks. *You haven't any idea what you ask for.*

⬤⬤⬤

It begins to snow in the night. Mrs. Hasslo cooks pea soup for dinner, but there is no pork in it, for there was no meat of any kind when she went to the grocer yesterday, only the same canned herring that both sisters now flatly refuse. The three women eat in silence. Suddenly Mrs. Hasslo remarks that the lake seems frozen hard. Imogen spoons more mustard into her soup, looking up at Eleanor.

—What are *skridskor?*

—Ice skates. She means we could ice-skate soon—

—Not I.

Imogen takes a bite of a hard rye cracker. Mrs. Hasslo asks if they want pancakes for dessert, for she has plenty of flour and Imogen must eat more for the child's sake, even if she isn't feeling well. Imogen smiles apologetically and says perhaps they should have pancakes tomorrow.

Mrs. Hasslo clears the table and goes to bed. Imogen fetches her crochet hook and the blue afghan she has been working on for weeks. Twice already she has sent Mrs. Hasslo into town to order more yarn, but rationing in Sweden is growing stricter every day and when the yarn arrived yesterday its color was different from the original, more navy than indigo, and not quite as thick. Imogen went on using it anyway.

Eleanor picks up a broom and begins to sweep. She glances at the afghan and smiles.

—It's coming along quite nicely. One doesn't mind the color difference. In fact I rather like it. It's treble-stitched?

Imogen does not look up from her crochet hook.

—Double treble.

—By the time you finish, it'll keep an elephant or two warm. Or possibly a dreadnought. Imagine all those gallant Swedish merchant captains dodging U-boats to bring you indigo yarn.

—Better cargo than bombs.

Eleanor yawns.—Indeed. Darling, I'm off to bed, I'm simply exhausted. Perhaps you ought to come upstairs as well. You could use the rest—

Imogen looks at Eleanor. The bone crochet hook is fixed motionless in her hand.

—You mean the baby could use it.

—You need it too.

—But it's not me you're concerned about. You only care about the child.

—Of course I care about you. Only sometimes you're so cross with me, I don't know what to do—

—It's simple. Let me out of here.

Eleanor stops sweeping. She swallows, looking at the floor.

—Imogen, you can't change your mind now. It's too late.

They begin to bicker, the arguments running along circular tracks. Imogen tries to keep crocheting as they talk, but she grows more agitated and soon Eleanor puts away the broom and sits at the table, resigned to the quarrel. For on this night Imogen seems unusually animated, more angry and more wistful and more desperate than before. Around midnight she throws the afghan on the floor, swearing that she cannot stand the confinement of the house any longer.

—You can't keep me here. Nothing can keep me here.

—Darling—

—This isn't my life. And I'd rather die than live someone else's life. Is that what you want?

—Imogen—

—Did you know I haven't written to him? Of course you know. And do you know why I haven't?

—Please, Imogen. Calm down.

—Because I'm not going to lie to him. If you want a child, have your own damned child, it's not my fault if you can't. I'm leaving here. I'll go back to him and you shan't ever see me again. And you'll never see the baby.

Eleanor turns away and begins wiping the table with a cloth. Suddenly she swivels back toward Imogen.

—So you wish to change your mind now, and you blame me for

your troubles. But what put you in this position? You imagine it was me?

—It wasn't my idea.

—But it was your decisions that brought you here. Imogen, what's become of your life? After all, you're supposed to be the gifted one. Papa used to brag about it to Mr. Wallenberg and the other fellows, Imogen who learnt Greek so well in nine months that the tutor returned his check and said she needed a more advanced teacher. Imogen who had only to read a poem or hear a sonata to know it by heart—

—Stop it.

—It's true enough. But what I want to know is, if you're the gifted one, why am I painting all day in that bloody barn while you do nothing but stare at the ceiling or knit a bloody afghan? Is that your great dream for your life—to be twice as clever as everyone, then throw it all away to be melancholy, and raise a melancholy child? As if you could manage even that. Imogen, it isn't my fault if you walk out of your exams and spend a useless year in London. It isn't my fault if we're having a row at one in the morning. And it isn't my fault if we're in Sweden because you couldn't stand to wait for Ashley—

—Don't you dare.

—Am I wrong? Two months ago you told me Ashley wished to marry. It seemed to amuse you as rather quaint. But now that you're expecting, you tell Papa he won't marry. And yet he seems to send whole mailbags of letters.

Imogen gasps. —You read them?

—I don't need to. It's already clear enough to me why we're here. Because you couldn't stand to do what every grown woman in England does every day, and simply support the man she loves.

—Support him to certain death?

—He's a soldier, Imogen. He was a soldier when you met him, you simply ignored that as long as you could. When you finally realized what that meant, you decided you'd scorn everyone and raise a child on your own. Only when Papa tells you it's impossible and proposes Sweden instead, you'll go along with it for so long. You'll sit quietly while we tell the Graftons and half of London that I'm expecting. You'll say nothing while Charles and I move heaven and earth to prepare for a child, to prepare this house, and you'll come all the way here without so much as a word. But once we get to Sweden—once you know it's too late for us to turn back—now you say you can't do it, for if someone expects something from you, you can't bear to give it to them—

—I never chose this. Papa forced it on me.

—Because you'd turned away from ordinary choices. You wanted only the impossible. Can't you see that? If all the world wants one thing, you shall have to have the other, if only for that reason. If Ashley loves you, that's fine with you, because he's only in England for a week, and after that you'll write every day and say all kinds of things to him, so that he thinks of you the whole time he's in France. You'll sleep with him right away—

—Stop it.

—You did, didn't you? But you couldn't stand beside him, because it was too hard.

—You don't understand. I only wanted to save him, for the two of us to make our own way.

Eleanor scoffs. —I understand more than you know. Didn't I read the same books as you, years before you took them from my shelf? Do you imagine that Charles wished to be in the army, or that I wanted him away in Palestine? I didn't. But part of growing older is caring about other people enough to accept their responsibilities. Even when things are not quite perfect. Especially then. It's fine to have high ideas about the world, but Imogen, you find fault with everything. Ashley couldn't satisfy you, and Papa drives you mad, and now I can't please you. And I don't deny this has become a trap for us both, but hating each other won't bring us out of it. You think it's no good if you can't do it all yourself, but there are limits—

—It's my life. I can't give it over to other people.

—You can. You must, to some degree. A woman can't live only for herself. They may say she can, but she can't. Not even a man can do it and have much of a happy life, but a woman even less.

—How do you know? How long did you live for yourself, before giving in to the first decent man who proposed?

Eleanor narrows her eyes at Imogen.

—You're a child. An utter child about to have a child of her own, and it makes me fearful. You haven't a clue what you speak of, or I couldn't forgive you for it. You imagine you're cleverer than all of us, and perhaps so, but I think you're only more stubborn.

Imogen shakes her head.

—Then tell me what to do. If you're so clever, tell me what I can do, what will fix it all and make everyone happy.

—For God's sake, that's exactly the point. You'll have to give up something. You can't please everyone, but you want to please no one. Choose your family, or choose Ashley, or even choose your own bloody self over everyone, as you wanted all along. But don't change your mind every hour. And don't blame your troubles on me.

Imogen looks into the door of the stove. They have not put a fresh log on for hours and they sit in the cold with their arms crossed. Suddenly Imogen stands.

—Then I've made my choice. I'm leaving.

She goes upstairs and packs the large Gladstone, tossing in skirts and tunics at random. Eleanor comes into the bedroom, pleading for her to stop, saying Imogen will wake Mrs. Hasslo and if this goes much longer the housekeeper is certain to give notice.

—Let her give notice, Imogen says. You won't need her when I'm gone.

Imogen pulls on her overcoat, tugging fur-topped boots onto her feet with difficulty, Eleanor watching and wishing to help yet feeling that she must not help. Imogen dashes down the steps and out the front door, hatless with her coat buttoned halfway to her neck.

It is frighteningly cold. In the darkness Imogen stumbles down the twisting path to the pier, trying to follow a faint set of footprints covered with fresh snow. Eleanor shuffles a few paces behind, buttoning her own coat, a candle in her hand.

—Come inside, we'll freeze out here. Think of the baby, you might be damaging—

—All you care for is the bloody baby.

—You're hysterical. We must go back—

—I'll never go back in there. Never.

Imogen staggers through the powdery shadows. She veers from the path by accident, stepping in heaps of soft snow that come to her knees. Eleanor grasps at her sister's shoulders but Imogen pulls away and goes on downhill, zigzagging through the trees, the Gladstone swinging in her hand. She falls down twice and her back is covered in snow as she nears the lakeshore, hobbling among the stones.

Imogen finally reaches the pier. She runs down its length until she stands on the final rickety plank, the vast frozen lake spread before her. It looks as empty as anything she has ever seen, obscene in its bare white solitude. Eleanor catches up and tries to pull her own fur hat over Imogen's head, but Imogen struggles away. Eleanor's candle goes out. Their faces are in darkness.

—Just let me go. I can't do it. I know I said I could, but I can't. We're allowed some mistakes, aren't we? Our lives can't end because of one mistake—

—I'm not keeping you here.

—There's no one else.

—Then go on. Run away from here, see if it solves everything. I shan't stop you.

Imogen is shivering. Her coat is still unbuttoned at the neck but she holds the collar together with her bare hands. She has forgotten her gloves and her hands are shaking.

—I don't want to live without him.

Eleanor watches her sister shivering before the lake. Finally she pulls her hat on Imogen and puts her arm around her. Slowly they begin to climb the path back to the house.

—I can't live without him, Ellie. I thought I could, but I can't—

—I know. Hush, darling. I know.

THE BEARING

—Can you hear it? Mireille whispers. It's the train.

Her voice is so low that I barely catch it. We stand ten feet apart on the station platform under an iron-gray sky, both of us looking down the tracks. No one else is here. The wind whips our hair and lifts the refuse of departed travelers, empty paper cups and plastic wrappers writhing and coasting along the platform. Down the road at the railway crossing, the ruby lights blink in turn as the striped barrier lurches down.

I swing on my backpack. Mireille reaches into her bag and hands me a parcel wrapped in brown paper.

—*Un petit cadeau*, she says. *Ça ne coûte rien.*

—I didn't get you anything.

Mireille smiles. —I know. How many times do you change trains?

—Three. It was the cheapest way. Lille, Brussels and Düsseldorf.

—We don't make it easy for you to get there.

The train appears now, a distant point on the tracks ahead. The loudspeaker chimes twice and a recorded voice announces the arrival.

—Mireille, listen. I'm sorry I'm leaving like this. I'll call you from Berlin—

—*Au revoir.*

She touches my hand and starts off down the platform. I run after her, but before I reach her she stops and turns to me.

—Everyone said you were using me for a place to stay. They told me not to get too close to you, because sooner or later you'd just go. But I didn't listen to them. Was I wrong? Were you just using me?

—Of course not—

—How do I know that?

—Because I'll come back.

Mireille shakes her head.

—Tristan, I want to believe that. But I don't even know if you do.

For a moment we only look at each other. I run my hand over my face, wondering if I should get on the train. Mireille comes closer and touches my shoulder, forcing a smile.

—I hope you find what you're looking for.

She turns and walks off down the platform. The conductor is waving at me and calling for boarding, so I get on the train and take a seat beside the window. I unfold my tray table and set the parcel down.

As the train pulls away from the station, I tear away the brown paper to find a square metal case, dented and rusted, small but with a solid heft. It opens on hinges, revealing a brass disk in its fitted leather setting. I snap open the disk's cover. An antiqued white face indicating the four cardinal directions, with every degree of variation demarcated on the ivory dial. A compass. There is an engraving on the reverse: *Cruchon & Emons London 1917.*

There is handwriting on the scraps of brown paper. I piece together the fragments on my tray table to read the message. It is in French and it takes me a moment to understand it.

Dear Tristan,

    I found this in an antique shop in Abbeville. The dealer swore it was English, from the war, pulled out of a field by some farmer. I don't believe it, and I don't think it works. But if anyone could find out, it would be you.

Mireille

I put the scraps in a plastic bag, hiding them deep in the lining of my backpack against the packframe. It's over now and there's nothing I can do. Unless I forget about Berlin and get off at the next stop.

—You can't do it, I whisper. Not now.

The train is gathering speed. Through the window I see the other cars curving ahead as the tracks gradually change direction. I look down at the compass. The instrument has been disturbed from too much movement, the needle swinging wildly in every direction. I hold the compass level and watch the dial. Slowly the needle swings to fifty degrees, north by northeast. The compass still works.

2 January 1917

La Calotterie

Pas-de-Calais, France

Private Mayhew knocks twice on the door and enters the bedroom. Ashley lies in bed, the feather duvet drawn tight against his chin. His eyes are open. He is looking at the ceiling.

—Morning, sir, Mayhew says. Six o'clock.

Mayhew lights the fireplace and stokes the flames until he is confident the fire is sufficient. He puts a pitcher of steaming water on the dresser and prepares a bowl of shaving cream, foaming the lather in a porcelain bowl with a horsehair brush. He brings in Ashley's uniform on a pair of hangers, the tunic's brass buttons freshly polished. Since Ashley's injury Mayhew has been a better servant, and Ashley does not know if this is because Mayhew respects him more now, or simply because the battalion has been at rest these two weeks.

—Anything else, sir?

—No, that's fine.

Ashley takes *Le Journal d'Amiens* from the nightstand and pages through it for a few minutes, intermittently glancing at the gray morning outside. He wishes he could finish the newspaper, but he wants to shave while the water is still hot.

He rises from bed and props the newspaper against the mirror on the dresser. He swings the blade of the razor from its black celluloid handle, swirling it in the pitcher until the metal is warm to the touch. Ashley wets his face and brushes on the lather, then draws the blade carefully across his cheek, pausing at times to consider the newspaper's headlines.

He rinses off and looks into the mirror, studying the scar on his neck, a raised lump of pink and white tissue. Somehow it surprises him that scars are not carved in relief on one's skin, but stand out above the surface. Ashley rubs the blemish as if he could buff it smooth. He dries his face and hangs the towel around his neck, tossing the newspaper in the fire and calling to Mayhew.

—Has the lorry arrived?

—Any moment, sir.

Ashley points to the valisse by the door.

—That can go down.

Mayhew hauls the valisse downstairs. Ashley takes the brass poker beside the fireplace and prods at the logs, the newspaper already obliterated. He is thinking of the small trunk behind him at the foot of the bed, but he does not look at it.

Suddenly he turns and opens the trunk, removing a large cigar box inside. He looks at the box for a moment. Then he throws it into the fire. As the box burns away its contents are gradually revealed and now he sees the neatly bundled letters, the flowing blue-black script.

Ashley thrusts his hand in the fire and pulls out the bundle, smothering the flames with the towel. Smoke and ash hang wispy in the air. His singed hand throbs with pain. Ashley drops the half-burned letters into the trunk and examines the back of his hand. Most of the fine hairs have burned away.

Kneeling at the fire again, Ashley prods the logs with the poker, watching the remaining scraps of paper and cardboard incinerate. Then he sees the glittering silver cross, the purple-and-white ribbon flaring up. He lets the fabric burn away until only the cross remains. Ashley plucks the medal from the fire with iron tongs and drops it in the basin of water. The cross sizzles and sinks down. When it has cooled he puts it in his breast pocket.

Ashley dresses carefully. After he has put on his boots he feels sturdier, more soldierly. Mayhew clatters in again.

—Anything else, sir? Shall I take that small one?

—It's empty, leave it here. I'll meet you down at the lorry.

—Sir.

Ashley looks at the small trunk, the charred letters inside. He latches it shut and walks downstairs.

In the dining room breakfast has been set upon the table: a plate of boiled eggs, a long piece of buttered bread, a bowl of café au lait with the saucer placed on top to keep it warm. Ashley walks through the kitchen and the front parlor. All the rooms are empty. He goes back upstairs to the young girl's room. Beside her bed there is a small walnut commode covered with a crocheted doily. He takes the metal cross from his pocket and sets it on the white lace. He walks out downstairs and shuts the front door behind him.

A truck waits on the dirt path, the engine sputtering puffs of smoke into the crystal air. Mayhew and the driver sit on the bumper, sharing a cigarette as they talk in low voices. There is a lawn before the house, but in this winter it is only scraps of frozen grass and dirt. Ashley gets into the lorry, taking his place on the bench seat beside Mayhew and the driver. The driver shifts the lorry into gear and they pass the water tower, turning onto the main road. Ashley scratches his chin. He may have nicked himself shaving. He turns to Mayhew, offering a cigarette.

—Mayhew, you remember the Empress, don't you? That ghastly show in November—

—Of course, sir.

—You know they gave me the MC for that. God knows why. Made the show look less of a balls-up, I suppose. But I wanted to say. You saved my skin, Mayhew. I put you in for every medal in the mint, but nothing came through.

—That's all right, sir. Didn't expect nothing.

Ashley nods, passing Mayhew his lighter. —Another thing. You remember that Hun dugout, there was a sick officer in one of the bunks. I spoke to him for a bit. What I wanted to ask—do you remember what he looked like? Oddest thing. The other day I realized I may have met that fellow before, years ago—

—There weren't no officer down there, sir. They were all dead, except the crazy ones. But there weren't no officer.

Ashley looks at Mayhew, unsure if he is joking. But Mayhew's expression is solemn.

—There was an officer, Ashley insists. He was from the Second Marine-Infanterie, I distinctly remember.

—I beg your pardon, sir, we didn't talk to no one. We went down there, and they were all dead, so we come back up.

—Mayhew, I distinctly remember—

Ashley does not finish his sentence. He looks out the window at the snowy fields, a few houses with chimneys sending up faint wisps of smoke. If Mayhew does not wish to talk about it, so be it.

8 January 1916

Lake Ejen

Dalarna, Sweden

The light slants across the pine board ceiling. It must be afternoon by now. Minutes or hours pass, the same as ever, Imogen glancing at the envelope on the desk, then studying the woodgrain above her. She opens the novels and thin poetry volumes stacked beside the bed, gazing passively beyond tidy arrays of paragraphs and stanzas, then closes the books in turn.

At last she tosses the quilt from her body. She dresses warmly: a silk and wool combination, cashmere hose under her heaviest skirt, a Shetland vest and a knitted jersey. Imogen picks up the letter from the desk, already written and addressed, the envelope still unsealed with only the single sheet inside. She holds it for a moment, then carries it downstairs. When Eleanor sees Imogen's clothing, her surprise is obvious.

—You're going out?

—I thought I'd take a short walk. You don't approve?

—Not at all, Eleanor replies. It's a splendid idea, I'm only surprised, it's been days since—

Imogen sets the envelope on the table and Eleanor's eyes widen. Imogen's voice is flat.

—Mrs. Hasslo needn't make a special trip. Whenever she goes to town. It isn't sealed, you can read it and seal it yourself.

Eleanor shakes her head vigorously.

—I wouldn't dream—

—Read it, Imogen interrupts, then seal it. I'm going out now.

—Shall I come along?

—If you don't mind, I'd prefer to go alone.

—Certainly. Only don't wander too far—

—Just into the trees.

Eleanor forces a smile. She fetches Imogen's cloak and wraps her sister's neck in a muffler, tugging a fur hat low over her brow.

—It's too much, Imogen protests, pushing the hat up. I'm dreadfully hot already.

—It's arctic out there. And remember, if you go so far that I can't see you from the house, I shall come after you.

Imogen creaks open the door. She steps from the stifling heat through the doorway, a tentative foot onto the ice-clumped doormat. At once her senses are overcome by the wonder of the outside world. The movement of the bracing air, its scent of pine and wood smoke from the chimney; the luminosity of the snowy surface, the light glinting from every crystal of every snowflake. What sublime richness to everything.

Imogen walks slowly toward the forest, the band of trees surrounding the clearing on all sides. How long ago had they razed this field to erect these houses—three hundred years? She tries to picture the appearance of such people, but the results are comic, peasants in mock-Renaissance garb, brawny woodsmen with handcarved pipes. Imogen's boots sink down. The snow dusts the hem of her skirt.

Frederick if a boy, Imogen thinks. *Charlotte if a girl.*

Since the quarrel it had been quieter in the house. The sisters had not exactly reconciled. They had simply stopped talking about anything of consequence. They might discuss the weather or the food, Eleanor's painting or Imogen's afghan, any subject except the one that truly mattered. For eight days Eleanor had said nothing about the child, and though Imogen seemed tranquil enough, Eleanor had no way of knowing whether her sister had resigned herself to the plan or was simply plotting an escape. Only yesterday had it finally come into the open. They had been in the kitchen preparing vegetables for dinner while Mrs. Hasslo cleaned the bedrooms upstairs.

—Did you see the post? Eleanor had said. Mother sent you something. Can you believe I got three letters from Charles all at once, after a week with nothing? He's been out and back to Sinai again with the major, but of course he can't say much about it. He did have some ideas about the names—

Imogen was peeling turnips with a paring knife, intending to mash them with butter and cream in the Swedish fashion. At once Eleanor realized her mistake, but it was already too late. Imogen looked at her sister.

—Names?

—For the baby. They were just ideas—

—Which names?

Eleanor hesitated. —If you really want to know, I wonder what you think of Frederick for a boy, or Charlotte for a girl. They're ordinary names, of course, but Charles says ordinary—

It was then that Imogen cut her index finger on the blade, drawing a thin stream of crimson blood that dripped over the turnips and the cutting board. Afterward there had been a quarrel. But Imogen's real passion seemed to have evaporated, for as they argued she felt herself rehearsing a role she no longer believed in. In the end Eleanor simply came to the point.

—Imogen, she pleaded, just tell me what you're going to do.

Imogen said nothing. But as Eleanor looked at her sister across the dining table she knew the truth at once, for resignation was so unlike Imogen that she wore it very peculiarly. The sisters ate dinner in silence. Eleanor had not mentioned the child since.

Imogen pauses halfway down the field. She takes off her gloves, bending at her knees to pick up a handful of snow. It is fresh snow, light and dry against her fingertips. She packs it into a tight snowball, adding more powder until it is dense and solid, no larger than a cricket ball. She throws the snowball toward the trees and watches it sail through the air until she loses sight of it among a field of white. Imogen walks on.

Naturally Eleanor was right to choose the names, to have them chosen already. Imogen recognized this. For what would the child know of its true parents, of their tangle of embrace and loss? Nothing at all. The child would grow up in the carefully ordered bohemia of Charles and Eleanor's home, the study with its fashionable books on the shelves, the sitting room furnished with the right chairs or textiles from the Omega Workshops, and all reckless imagination relegated to the tidy painting studio upstairs.

It would be nothing like the home that Ashley and Imogen might have shared, the chaos of Imogen's clutter—parasols and baskets covering half the surfaces; bouquets of wilting flowers gathered from city parks; tables drowning in leaflets on women's suffrage or vegetarianism or Fabianism, inscribed in ink with some chance thought Imogen had wished to record. The furnishings themselves would all be Ashley's things, for she had none of her own. Framed photographs of Alpine peaks, Imogen supposed, or odd pairings of books, the Negretti & Zambra catalog on the shelf beside ten disintegrating volumes of *The Thousand and One Nights* held together with twine. She had pictured it often, and perhaps Ashley had too, but they had never had the pleasure of picturing of it together.

—Ashley, she whispers.

He was, perhaps, not at all extraordinary. Nor was he the lover she had imagined her whole long girlhood. Could one even call him a romantic? Imogen doubts it. His passion was concealed beneath so many layers of opaque humor and roguishness that it was often impossible to detect. As a lover Ashley seemed too hesitant to Imogen, almost timid, until the point at which he forced himself to make the most foolhardy leaps. It was only this strange resolve that made Ashley extraordinary, but

Imogen believed that however devoted he was to her, he had now given himself to the war at least as much, in a bargain he had made long before he could have any notion of its cost. Perhaps Ashley regretted this choice, but the bond felt too strong for Imogen to sever, for she sensed Ashley had lost something he could not get back—not so simple as the skin on his neck or the sound of his old voice, but something finer and dearer, a loss Imogen could probably never understand. There were countless men who returned to England unrecognizable to those who had loved them, but Imogen had never believed Ashley would become one of those men, just as she could not imagine herself under a dark veil, wearing a necklace of dull black beads. Those were for other women, the women who adhered to the rules. Imogen had thought that none of those rules applied to them, but now she feared that all of them did, for she finally accepted that Ashley was only a man and she was only a woman, and all the things they meant to each other could not protect them.

And yet their love had been different. Together they had been more than their discrete selves, and the force and strength of that attraction had lent them something mythical, a week so ardent and vivid that they alone were privy to the world's secret marvels. The colors and shapes, the sounds and scents of London and Sutton Courtenay, the hotel, the train station—it had all been sculpted by the gravity of their attraction, distorted as rays cast through a prism. Or had the prism only focused things, made her see them as they were, for one singular moment? Imogen cannot say. She knows only that it eclipsed all she had known before or ever would know.

If only she had recognized this at the time—how she wishes she could have loved him even more. How she could have savored that perfect interlude, that shimmering gem of one week among the slag-heap of decades that would be her life. But that was youth, she thought, and that was love. It was blindness that made it so. She will not meet that blaze again, not with Ashley or anyone else, nor will she waste her life searching for its sequel. There was no sequel. That was what made it extraordinary. That intensity of feeling was locked in her past now, the same as her first teetering steps or first immersion in the dazzling ocean. If she looks for anything in her future, she will have to look for something else.

Imogen reaches the trees now, taking a seat on a toppled pine and crossing her legs at the ankles. She rests her hands lightly upon her stomach. She has only five months to go, and then it will all be over. She must take solace in that, at least: it will be over then.

She had tried to write him a proper letter. There had been leaves of foolscap everywhere to prove it, and though Eleanor said nothing, she must have seen those sheets with his name on the first page, also the later ones where Imogen omitted the name, resolving to add it only when the letter was completed. But the letters were never completed, no matter how long they went. Imogen found it impossible to explain the condition she was in, impossible to reconcile what she wished to say with the fact of their separation.

She could say that to live life her own way was all she knew how to do, and it was unfair to demand that Ashley act any differently, whatever the consequences. She could explain that she was not surrendering any longer, that she had finally chosen her path and in five months she would be accountable only to herself, for she understood now that she could not bear the terrible responsibility of other people's happiness.

But Imogen could not send those sheets. To Ashley it would all be whitewash and she knew it. She had burned the pages this morning.

They shall not meet again. That is the lone fact and there is nothing to say about it. It is beastly. Imogen refuses to parley with that fact, nor explain it, nor soften it or render some pitiful apology. She had tried to do all those things and failed, and the proof of these efforts were the ashes in the fireplace, the letters of grand intent and great affection that would have kindled Ashley's every hope, only to collapse on the final page to the world as it was. The world distilled to the three sentences she had given Eleanor.

My Ashley –

I've lost the child. I'm going away and I cannot see you again.
I'm so very sorry.

> *I remain – your loving*
> *Imogen*

It is all he will hear from her. It is still a lie, but less of a lie than anything else she can say. Imogen shudders to think of this, but she reminds herself that the letter is not the cruelty, its consequences are. Once she had accepted those consequences, it had not been fair to hide them from Ashley, for he had asked for an honest reply and this is the best she can give.

Still it hurt so much to think of Ashley reading the letter. It hurt enough that she had not written it for six days, even when the words were clear in her head, even when she knew she could not go back to him. The lie about the child is worst of all, but what is cruel to Ashley is the only decent thing for Eleanor and Charles, who could hardly be expected to raise a child whose parentage might one day be questioned. And perhaps they needed an ending to this, all of them, even Ashley, even Imogen herself. If they are to move forward, they must know they cannot go back.

But what will come of all this? After the child is born the sisters will return to England. Eleanor will take the child and raise it as her own; Imogen will slip into the fog and shadow of London, the vivid chapter of her life already behind her. And Ashley—could he possibly survive the war? Might she have been wrong to think he had no chance, that only she could save him? Perhaps that had only been arrogance, the conceit that she could see things that he could not. Perhaps in leaving him she had only condemned herself to scanning the casualty lists in the newspaper every morning, never knowing if he lived or died until she saw him by chance across the room at a Mayfair party, or crossing Russell Square with another woman. No, Imogen cannot have that. Better to begin anew, to live among strange faces that would neither know nor judge her.

Imogen drags her finger in the snow and makes a few tentative shapes. A circle. Half the curve of a heart. She finds her hand dragged by a light but inexorable gravity, perhaps her own, and it draws across the crystals to mark her own initials, then the tall letter *A*. Imogen stops here, embarrassed by this childish gesture, even among the solitude of trees and snow. As a girl she had often drawn shapes in the sand of Sussex beaches, and now she considers how that sand felt similar and yet was different, resting for years upon the same shore rather than disappearing with the first thaw of spring. But surely ice melted into streams and waterfalls will return again as snow, the very same droplets? She hardly knows. It frustrates her, for Imogen had expected that by this age she would understand so much more than she does.

She glances back toward the house, but she has come far enough that the forest obscures all. It is very cold here. Could it be so cold in France? It is not so far north as here, Imogen considers, but it must feel so much colder, shivering in clammy garments at dawn stand-to, sleeping rough each night upon the frozen ground. How little she understands of all this. She is weeping now and perhaps a little feverish.

—I shan't ever change, she whispers, reveling in the completeness of this lie.

Imogen draws her boot across the snow, smoothing away all her marks. *I shan't grow older or love you any less*, she thinks. *I shan't love another or ever disappoint you, and we shall never be parted, not for one moment, from this world to the next.*

A figure is coming through the trees. Eleanor in a long cloak, bearing a mug of something steaming. She draws beside Imogen and hands her the tea.

—You've had your walk, Eleanor says. Now for God's sake darling, come inside before you freeze.

BOOK THREE

—∙⇌ ⇋∙—

NORTH COL

Exploration is the physical expression of the Intellectual Passion. And I tell you, if you have the desire for knowledge and the power to give it physical expression, go out and explore. If you are a brave man you will do nothing: if you are fearful you may do much, for none but cowards have need to prove their bravery.

—Apsley Cherry-Garrard,
The Worst Journey in the World

22 February 1924

Russell Square

Bloomsbury, Central London

Ashley comes out of the Underground station and buys the evening newspaper from a hawker, folding it under his arm and continuing eastward. It is six o'clock and all the city is traveling homeward, hordes in dark suits swarming the pavement and tube entrances. Ashley rounds the corner onto Lamb's Conduit Street. He arrives at the public house half an hour early.

It is a charming pub. There are large frosted windows facing the street, and beneath these a wall of green porcelain tile. Ashley enters the saloon bar and orders a pint of bitter, watching the barman's hands pump the ebony lever in three smooth strokes, the swoosh of foaming ale into the tulip glass. The barman's face is hidden behind a screen of paneled glass hung at eye level above the whole length of the saloon bar, blocking the view of the poorer classes in the public bar opposite. All the panels in the screen are shut.

Ashley brings his glass to a small round table. He takes a sip of beer, his first taste of English ale in five years. He imagined that it would make him remember something, but it does not. The flavor is at once familiar and unremarkable. At the first drink, it is as if he had never been away.

It is over now. Ashley had trained hard and whether the training was sufficient or not, it is over. The expedition leaves on Friday. Ashley will face the Himalaya as he is, stronger certainly than he has ever been, though whether he is equal to the mountain he cannot say. There had been no rubric to judge this, so he had simply trained as much as he could bear.

It had begun in the summer, before he had even known for certain that he would be accepted on the expedition. He had heard conflicting rumors from the start, but it was fine enough to be back in the Alps again, away from the aimless asceticism of his Arabian wanderings, returned to solid granite where he thought only of the rockface before him. And Ashley was good at it and he liked it. It had not been like the wretched coffee plantation in Kenya, which he had been good at and hated, or like Arabia, which he had liked at times but had never been good at. At twenty-nine Ashley had been climbing for thirteen years and was probably at the peak of his powers. This last season in the Alps had proven it. It had been grueling but also dazzling, and it had ended in August with the news of his place on the expedition: a telegram waiting for him on the front desk of the Hotel du Mont-Collon, Ashley tearing open the envelope, his face coloring as he laughed and passed the message to the desk clerk, fumbling in giddy French to translate its significance.

—*Je vais monter*, Ashley had explained, *le plus haut montagne du monde*.

And when at last the clerk was made to understand, all he could say, all anyone could say were the same two words.—*Bon courage*.

That telegram, twelve words taped onto a slip of paper, had changed everything. At first Ashley intended to winter in the Alps, training on snow until the expedition sailed in February. He stayed at an auberge outside Les Haudères and began to condition himself in earnest, climbing the mountain paths at daybreak, hewing and hauling timber for a fortnight until his hands blistered over and the innkeeper said there was no room left to store the logs. But with the first snow of autumn, Ashley found himself longing for the one place he had thought was behind him—England.

Ashley had not set foot in England since 1919. It was only now, encircled by snowy peaks in every direction, that he began to wish for a fantastical version of his homeland, a sleepy kingdom draped in rain and foliage. He longed for the sea, for the wreaths of fog that swathed the coast, for the curtains of water rolling up and down the shoreline. And he knew he did not need to train for Everest. The other climbers had told him the mountain was a question of force rather than finesse, a problem of sheer endurance.

Within a week Ashley was in London. He took a temporary flat near Coram's Fields and wandered among the places he had once known, feeling himself a ghost returned to dwell with the living. In the evenings he skipped rope in his flat on a Moroccan rug beside the desk, the raindrops pattering the window and soaking the pavement outside. He made tentative steps toward polite society: meetings at the Alpine Club; a show in the West End; drinks at the Café Royal. He prepared for a barrage of questions about the past few years. Where had he gone and what had he been doing? What were his plans for the future? And yet, as it happened, the whole city seemed hardly to have noticed his absence.

—The spymaster himself, they said, clapping him upon the shoulder. Haven't seen you about lately. Where have you been lurking?

It seemed unfair to Ashley that the city could go on so forgetfully without him, so forgetful of all the people it had lost. He knew this sentiment was absurd, but he could not help it. The lawns of Regent's Park looked no different than they had in 1916, and yet they could not feel more different. At once Ashley recalled all the bitterness from five years before: that they should go on serving pineapple ices at Gunter's; that magazines should print reverential pictures of the wedding of Lady Diana Manners; that *Chu Chin Chow* should attract huge crowds at

His Majesty's Theatre—while Jeffries and Ismay and Bradley and a million others lay in bone-heaps beneath the mud of France, their rotting corpses wrapped in rubberized sheets. In 1919 stonemasons all over Europe were amassing fortunes from the obelisks they erected in every village square, and Ashley supposed that the more obelisks they erected and the more hymns they sang, the faster they transformed the dead into the faceless mass they were fast becoming.

For nothing had obliterated Ismay so much as merging him with the Glorious Dead—a man whose chief quality had been resistance to all such cant, a vulgar and brave creature whom Ashley had never understood. Only later had it come to Ashley, in flashes while riding in a motorcar on the edge of the Nefud Desert, the driver chanting a cyclic tune in Arabic; or in a mountain hut in the Bernese Oberland, tossing the cover of his eiderdown and lying sleepless upon the wooden bunk. Ashley would think he had forgotten Ismay's face and then it would come to him all at once—the cocked smile, the unfocused gaze with one green eye and the other brown, Ismay swigging rum from a battered pewter mug as they stood in a vestibule watching the snow fall over the army camp.

Spymaster, do you know what makes us different from them?

No.

The difference is we're going to survive this war. And do you know why?

No.

Because we're too damned hopeless. It's a crime to kick a man when he's down, and even if God is dead he shan't allow it. We're not soldiers, you and I. This isn't how it ends for us.

Ashley had made little of this at the time, but he understood it more with every passing year. How much Ismay had feared death, so much more than the others, perhaps because he had seen enough of life to know what it was worth. And how deeply Ismay had pitied Ashley, and seen him for what he was, even as Ashley had been blind to it himself. And how all of them—Ismay and Jeffries and all the young officers in France—had been mere children, pantomiming roles in a production whose significance they hardly grasped, pushing on through an irreversible game of courage and death, puffing their chests or raving in waking or sleeping nightmares, but never once speaking earnestly to one another.

Only Ismay had been different, and Ashley could not say why, not even today. They had scarcely known each other, and yet lately Ashley found himself thinking of Ismay more and more, posing questions to him and apologizing for the mildest transgression—a military necktie borrowed and never returned. Or the day Ismay had left the camp, the day the pipes had frozen and burst and Ashley had not come to say good-bye. He never saw Ismay again.

It was these sentiments that had soured London in 1919, and the sourness was still there five years later, in spite of everything Ashley had done in between. What friends he had in the city seemed to find Ashley strange and distant. They did not understand his life and he did not understand theirs, and it could not have been the war, for they had all been in the war together.

Ashley left London the next week. He went to Sutton Courtenay and saw his mother, aged dramatically in the past five years, mellowed but also grown very frail. She left the house only on Sundays now, the housekeeper warned Ashley, and only if the weather was mild. That first night at dinner Ashley told his mother what he had done abroad, sometimes the truth and sometimes pure fantasy, saying always what he thought she wished to hear, for he could not have told her the whole truth even if he had been able to articulate it. Ashley spoke of Everest, carefully avoiding any suggestion that the mountain was dangerous. His mother received all this charitably.

—You've done wonderful things, she said. It's being a soldier that made you so strong.

The next day Ashley rowed his single scull on the Thames, starting in the afternoon and rowing on until he was alone in the blackness, not even seeing the oars dipping into the water. Only the swish of his stroke, the starlight above, the lantern of a passing barge swinging on its lonely prow.

He stayed a fortnight at Sutton Courtenay, and the more distant he felt from his own country and his own people, the more important his training became. He had become stateless, no longer an Englishman, hardly an expert on Africa or Arabia or any foreign land. The only thing he was good at was climbing, and it also seemed the only thing he could control.

Ashley bought an Austin Seven saloon and drove to Snowdonia, staying in small inns and double-timing the same paths where he had first learned of mountains. He walked all the daylight hours and sometimes longer, finding that he could overcome fatigue simply by going on, that he could recuperate even while moving. He developed special techniques for breathing that he intended to use at altitude, drawing rhythmic and nourishing breaths that kept pace with his steps. He craved any and every advantage. He wished to know the secret strengths of wild creatures, the raw musculature of animals he had seen in his travels through field glasses or silhouetted in the moonlight beside a glassy mere: the Swiss ibex, the fringe-eared oryx, the Arabian gazelle.

At the new year Ashley drove south and took a cottage on the Pembrokeshire coast. He spent dawn and dusk in fevered sprints along the shore, striding on sand and water and glimmering sea foam, racing the seagulls spiraling above him. He would lift his head as he dashed in ever-longer strides, the birds above wheeling and diving, then soaring with one flap of their wings ten yards beyond him, always just beyond, Ashley chasing with deeper gasping breaths until he had to stop, wheezing, a thousand yards down the strand. He sucked in the air. The cold waves broke over his shins, the gulls floating above him.

Ashley would race anything. He raced the sailboats half a league offshore; he raced the breeze and his own shadow. He raced against Price and Somervell and all of the strongest climbers in Europe, chasing them in a dead heat up some imagined alpine ridge, or picturing with fury how Price would overtake him on Everest's North Col, were he to betray an inch of slackness. Later Ashley decided none of these men was fast enough, so he sprinted against Paavo Nurmi or Eric Liddell, or any runner he heard accounts of on the wireless.

But most of all he would run for the idea of her, or the agony it drove him to, for pride and pain were equally ruthless horsemen. He raced against imagined rivals for her affection, faceless specters always faster than he, tall and lean athletes supple of limb and muscle. These Ashley could beat only through sheer force of will, for he knew his will was stronger even as his body was weaker, and on his better days Ashley let himself triumph. For he wanted her more than they did. He wanted the mountain nearly as much.

—So it is you.

Price taps Ashley on the shoulder and pulls out the opposite chair. He hangs his attaché case from a hook beneath the table.

—Sorry I'm late, Price adds. Had another row with Hinks.

—What about?

—Money, as usual. The man imagines I can use all the same kit from two years ago, and risk my neck with it. What are you having? Bitter?

Price goes to the bar and returns with two glasses of ale.

—It's strange to see you in England, Ashley. You do look well. Where are you staying?

—I've taken some rooms just around the corner.

—Then you're finally settling here?

—No. Ashley smiles. Not quite.

—Too much to hope, I suppose. How was Wales? I heard about your training. You've grown serious in your old age. Is it true you hired a coach? Farrar told me—

—It's not true, Ashley interrupts. But I'm fitter than ever.

—Grand. You'll need everything you've got.

—I know.

Price claps Ashley on the back.

—I say, it is good to see you in Blighty. How's it been treating you?

—Not bad. Feel a bit out of sorts.

—That's to be expected. You've been away a long time. But the committee's certainly confident about you. In fact, this year's climbing party is leagues ahead of the last show. All the old fools agree Everest's a sure bet this time.

—What do you think?

Price hesitates. He takes a long draft of beer.

—You know, I was hoping they wouldn't let me go. The syndicate, the committee, I wished for any damned thing that would get in the way of going back.

—You could have refused.

—I could have, Price admits. But Everest is not so easy to give up, once she's taken hold of you.

Price frowns, scratching the woodgrain of the table with his fingernail. He looks up at Ashley.

—You must see the mountain for yourself. Then you'll understand. The Himalaya are not the Alps. It isn't as if Everest is Mont Blanc, only thirteen thousand feet taller. That's what chaps like Hinks will never understand. We shan't be starting off from a comfortable hotel, fat as schoolchildren with pink cheeks. The march across Tibet is horrid. Half of us will be poorly by the time we reach the base camp. And the altitude. It's impossible to say precisely how ill one will be, but it's generally somewhere between nausea and death. Finally the climbing. The colonel has one notion of how we ought to get up, I've another. We're meant to work it out as we cross the plateau. But neither of us really knows what's at the top.

Price pauses, his face clouded with misgiving.

—I'm telling you things you already know.

—I know enough to be scared.

Price raises his eyebrows. —Scared? You're scared? Half the reason the committee didn't want you last time was they thought you'd lead your party into some catastrophe. They say you're too fearless to have any judgment—

—I know what they say, Ashley breaks in. But I'm scared anyway. As you say, it's not the Alps, I've never been there. No matter how much

I read about Everest or the Himalaya, it's all a great mystery to me. It's not only the height. Everything's different up there. The way the glaciers run—

—You'll work it out. You've always had the instinct for it.

—There's something else, Ashley adds. I've been having dreams about the mountain.

Price waves his hand dismissively.

—Everyone has those dreams.

—Perhaps they do. Only tell me something, Hugh. I know why I'm going, but why are you? Why go back if you don't want to? Why go back if it's so ghastly?

Price takes another drink. He shrugs.

—Wait until you've been there. Then you'll know.

They have a second round of beer, then Price says he must be going. The two men shake hands on the pavement. When Price's taxi has left, Ashley goes back into the saloon and orders a double measure of Vat 69. Although the barman cannot see Ashley's face, he has recognized his voice or clothing, for as he pours the whisky he says, —Couldn't stay away, sir?

—I suppose not.

Ashley unfolds his newspaper on the bar. As the barman sets the drink before him, Ashley pushes a panel in the screen above the bar; a square is opened and Ashley looks the barman in the eye. He is an older man, bald with a bushy gray mustache and a stout red neck. The barman's collar has been unfastened, his necktie loosened.

—You know, Ashley says, tonight was the first I'd been to a public house in five years.

—Then I'd say you're entitled to make up for lost time.

The barman is polishing glasses with a white cloth. Through the open square Ashley glimpses the customers in the public bar, men in flat caps or bareheaded, their backs turned to him. There is a woman's voice coming from the other end, but Ashley cannot see her face. He turns the page of his newspaper, noticing an article in a boxed column.

POST FROM THE PEAK OF EVEREST
HOW TO RECEIVE LETTERS FROM
THE SUMMITSPECIAL STAMPS

An avalanche of an entirely new character threatens members of the Mount Everest Expedition which leaves England next Friday. They have a beautiful stamp of special design printed, and I am authorized to announce that anyone desiring to possess one from the top of Mount Everest may do so for a couple of pennies. The postal avalanche has already begun. Capt J.B.L. Noel, the special photographer of the expedition, gives the following details of the plan –

Ashley taps the newspaper triumphantly, pushing it toward the barman with an impish smile.

—Let me ask you something. Have you heard of these expeditions to Mount Everest in the Himalaya?

—Of course. They're all over the papers.

—Then it might interest you to know the fellow who was sitting with me a moment ago was Hugh Price, the alpinist. The best in England, in fact. He's the one who found a route up Everest, and he's climbing leader for the next expedition.

—Price, the barman repeats. Was he the one who got all them porters killed last time?

—There was an avalanche, yes. Some of the porters were swept away—

—They didn't climb the mountain neither, did they?

—No.

—If you ask me, it sounds a fool's errand. Climbing a mountain just to say you done it. Is he going to try again?

—He is. The expedition leaves next Friday.

The barman shrugs. —To each his own.

—Indeed.

Ashley reads the rest of the article, a promotional piece for the expedition photographer's feature film of Mount Everest, to be screened on the party's triumphant return to England. Ashley orders another double whisky and the barman pushes it across the bar.

—You're going too, aren't you, sir? You're going to climb the mountain.

—That's right. How did you know?

—I guessed it when you first spoke of it. I saw your picture in the paper too, I believe. I recognized the look of you. Very serious. And you not being in a public house all these years.

—Of course. Are you the landlord here?

—Had it eleven years.

Ashley nods and takes a drink of whisky. Absently he watches the barman polishing glasses. Ashley reaches into his coat and takes out his pocketbook.

—My name's Walsingham. My rooms are just around the corner, on Lansdowne Terrace.

Ashley counts out five ten-pound banknotes. He sets the bills on the bar.

—Look for me in the papers, Ashley continues, because I'm going to climb Mount Everest. And when I get back to London, the first thing I'm going to do is come into this pub and use this money to buy champagne for everyone who happens to be in here. On both sides of this screen. Have you any champagne?

—No sir.

—Well, no matter, I'll buy anyone whatever they like. But if I don't climb the mountain, I'll be back to reclaim this money as a consolation prize. You lose nothing either way. How does that strike you?

—Very generous, sir.

Ashley pushes the notes across the bar. He shakes hands with the publican.

—One more thing. If I don't come back at all—and you'll hear if I don't—you're to take this money and buy everyone in the public bar drinks for the whole night, the same night you hear I'm dead. Remember, all the drinks until the money's gone.

The publican hesitates, perhaps finding something distasteful in this last agreement. But in the end Ashley persuades him.

When Ashley leaves the pub he is teetering only slightly. He pauses with his heels perched on the curb, testing his balance, his eyes searching for the moon above. Long trails of clouds coast across the night sky.

Ashley gropes through his coat pockets. He has left behind his wallet somewhere—in the club at luncheon perhaps, or on the counter at the bank, or on the bar of the public house. No, here it is. The wallet in hand, Ashley crosses Guilford Street and turns onto Lansdowne Terrace. With some difficulty he unlocks his front door, climbing the stairs two at a time. He sinks into a deep armchair in the corner of the sitting room, not his own chair, for the flat had come ready furnished. There is an electric lamp beside him with a mica shade, but Ashley does not switch it on.

I don't need the light, he thinks. *I can do without it all the long night.*

The arc light flares outside the uncurtained window, a corona of brilliant white sufficient for Ashley to read his folded newspaper. But the articles fail to hold his attention. He is anything but tired. He could take a book from the bedroom, but he knows it would not divert him. Ashley thinks of his fifty pounds, drawn out today at a counter in Cannon Street, the banknotes now tucked in the pocket of the bullnecked publican. He will return to the bank tomorrow to draw more cash. He will have a different clerk, or if he has the same clerk, no one would know he had squandered the last sum on a silly wager with a publican.

Ashley throws the newspaper onto the floor. He thinks of the five years he has been gone from England. The interval was nothing now that he had returned and it would have been the same had he been gone a decade. So too with the training. Now that it was over its hardships seemed nearly fictitious, save for the lean sinews of his build, the way he hardly drew a heavy breath from any kind of exertion.

Ashley thinks of his body as it is now, alone in the armchair in the darkened room looking onto Coram's Fields, his trunk and valises still unpacked in the corner. The wager: fifty pounds. And something else, the reason he had been gone five years. The reason he set himself against any trial he felt unequal to. Ashley dares not consider it too directly, for like a solar eclipse viewed through smoked glasses, it is only by gazing with an oblique perspective that he can preserve his sight.

It can't only be her, he thinks. *It must have been part of me before we ever met.*

But if it is not only her, it is somehow still twinned with the memory of her, for there was no other force that could lend him such resilience. And yet the lunacy of it all. Staking your whole being on a frivolous dare, imagining you could master the Dent d'Hérens or the Rub' al Khali or Mount Everest, when you were but a child before them, escaping only by their fickle mercy. Accomplishing nothing save some indulgent acrobatics of the ego. *Climbing a mountain just to say you done it.* Ashley strains to remember how it had been different in the early years, when he had loved simply to be among wild places, without the need to compete against them. Had the war changed this? That was too facile, for he had always loved to win, and yet this obsession with conquest seemed to have come after the war—not even conquest but only the prevention of failure, anything but a surrender to the superior forces that enveloped him.

It is a great mistake, Ashley knows. But if he does not go on—if he loses nerve or his courage falters—he will be unable to stand himself. He fears that most of all, more than death even. It was like the desert had been, at first only the question of what he was after, the notion of a city lost among the sands, awaiting him. Then later, once he knew he would never find that spectral city, only the question of himself—of what he could endure without giving in, of what it meant to persevere over a trifle. Imogen is no trifle. But it was even madder with her, the months of futile searching after the war, pleading for answers from her family and friends when he knew they would never tell him anything, when he doubted they knew anything themselves. By the time Ashley left for Kenya he had given this up, for it made him sick to look for her when he knew she did not want to be found.

Ashley remembers the first night he spent with Imogen, after they looked for the key in Regent's Park. They walked across the whole West End until the sky turned sapphire over the rooftops on Haymarket and Imogen put her arm through Ashley's. In the dark window of a tobacconist he caught their reflection, Imogen walking very close to him and clasping his arm tightly. A boy came up the street on a bicycle loaded with newspapers, staring for long seconds as he rode past, and for the first time in his life Ashley felt what it was to be seen with the woman he loved. He had thought he would know that feeling for the rest of his life. But it had not even lasted a week.

What sets Ashley apart? What is the reason he will not settle to writing poetry and trimming his rosebushes in Berkshire, or taking lamb chops for luncheon every day at a club on Pall Mall? Is it strength or only stubbornness, only foolish pride that keeps him so? Whatever it is, it had dangled contentment always at arm's length, while he supposes Imogen achieved happiness for herself long ago, without the need to risk her life to feel alive, nor to know who she is. And who would Ashley be without his love for her, without this reckless ardor that made him dare and waver and dare again?

Ashley switches on the lamp and opens a book of Nepali phrases. He will study these until he falls asleep. It will all be clear soon enough.

THE MANAGER

⇥ ⇤

It's ten in the evening in Düsseldorf when I board the night train to Berlin. I've been on trains for five hours now and I won't reach Berlin until morning.

There are five other bunks in my sleeper and it's hot and stuffy inside. After a few hours in bed I can't sleep anymore, so I walk to the dining compartment. The snack bar is shuttered, but there's a coffee machine and I stay up until dawn drinking *Milchkaffee* from small plastic cups, thinking about Berlin and Everest and Ashley's telegram. I pull out my notebook and pen.

Sept 14   City Night Line, Düsseldorf–Berlin.

In April 1924 Imogen was in Berlin. Or at least Ashley thought she was. But why was she there? How much contact did she have with Ashley, or with Eleanor and Charlotte?

I'd better find something in Berlin.

It's still dark when the train pulls into the station. The sign reads BERLIN HAUPTBAHNHOF. I step through the doors and look up at the soaring glass roof, the white face of the platform clock. Four twenty-eight in the morning. I eat breakfast in the deserted food court, then I ride the S-Bahn to a hostel in Mitte, the central district of Berlin. The day is cold and clear. After a week in rural France, Berlin seems vast and sprawling: the women watering flowerboxes on high balconies, the street signs painted in bold sans-serif type, the sunrise glinting from the soaring orb of the television tower.

The girl at the youth hostel lets me into my room to drop off my bag and take a shower. I ride the U-Bahn to the main post office on Joachimstaler Straße, leaning against the glass door as I wait for it to open. At eight o'clock an employee in a blue dress shirt and striped tie unlocks the door and waves me in. I ask apologetically if anyone speaks English. I'm passed between several employees, told again and again that my question falls under the jurisdiction of someone else, or that I'll need to make an appointment with another office. Finally I'm told to wait for a manager.

Minutes later the gray-haired manager shuffles to the counter. He has the same uniform as the other workers, but he wears suspenders and his shirt is badly wrinkled. He does not look pleased to see me.

—Impossible, he says in English. You cannot claim another person's poste restante.

—I don't want to claim it. I just want to know how long poste restante is usually kept.

—Two weeks for German mail. One month for international mail.

—What happens if it's not collected?

—It is returned to sender.

—If there's no return address?

—Then it is undeliverable mail. It is destroyed.

—There are no exceptions to this?

The manager grimaces. —I doubt it. Maybe if you tell me what you need I can try to help you.

I wipe my hand over my face and try to explain my case as reasonably as possible. The manager listens to my story without expression. He opens a door behind the counter and beckons me in.

—Come to my office. I want to speak to you.

I follow him through a labyrinth of low-ceilinged hallways to his office, a windowless room overflowing with mounds of curling paper. He sits down behind a steel desk and asks me to have a seat.

—I work on cases of missing mail having value. And I also work with the post museum. So you are very lucky to have found me.

The manager assumes an expression of immense gravity. He says he is taking the time to explain these matters to me because I am a foreigner and he knows things are different in my own country. In Europe public institutions have an important role in society, he tells me, and the postal service is no exception, for in Germany public service is a respectable occupation and not merely a final asylum for the lazy and incompetent. He allows that I am only a visitor in this country, but a visitor in any foreign country must respect its customs, and in this country it is very rude to obstruct the business of an important public institution on account of my own private whim.

It is because I seem an intelligent and reasonable young man, the manager continues, that I ought to know better than to waste the time of himself and his employees. Common sense alone should have dictated the answer to my question; it did not require the molesting of one postal employee, let alone five agents and a manager, to determine that unclaimed poste restante was not kept for eighty years. He finishes by explaining that in this country such institutions as this one are required to be transparent, and for this reason he will now listen to whatever queries I might have.

—But I didn't make up the story. It's all true.

The manager smiles. He takes a form off a filing rack and places it before me. He apologizes that they don't have this form in English, directing me to the blanks on the page.

—Here you write the sender's name. Here the name of the receiver. Here you write *poste restante*. Here you write your name, address, e-mail and telephone number. You sign here.

The manager hands me a ballpoint pen and leans back in his chair, explaining that in order for public institutions to be fair there must be regularity in the disposal of their services. It is for this reason, he says, that both legitimate inquiries and those of doubtful value must be impartially processed. It is not the civil servant's role to pass judgment. He urges me to fill out this form, for although he may have reservations about my inquiry, he will make certain that every effort is made to fulfill it.

I fill out the form and hand it back to the manager. He looks at it and smiles darkly.

—Tristan Campbell, he reads. But Tristan, where is your Isolde?

He puts the form in another rack on his desk and swivels his chair back to his computer. I leave the office without saying good-bye.

27 February 1924

Theobald's Road

Bloomsbury, Central London

Ashley carries an umbrella in his right hand, but in spite of the rain he does not open it. He walks quickly, the pavement slick beneath his leather-soled shoes.

He sees a figure ahead of him sitting against a building and he moves to cross the street, waiting on the curb for a motorcar to pass. Suddenly Ashley turns and walks up to the crippled man. His crutches are leaned against the wall and one of his legs is amputated below the knee, the trouser leg folded and speared with a large safety pin. Beside him is a tin full of matchboxes for sale.

Ashley feels in his coat pocket for a coin. His finger touches the folded sheet of the telegram and it gives him a surge of pleasure.

—Where were you wounded?

The man cocks his hat back with his thumb to look at Ashley, but the rain comes at his face.

—Ypres. Bleeding hole called Château Wood.

Ashley finds a half-crown in his other pocket and sets it in the man's palm. He turns onto Bedford Row, the water rushing in the gutter beside him. *The duckboards,* he thinks. *The planks of wood, the stilts strung over the muddy torrents of Château Wood.* Ashley stifles this thought, but he feels it more in the stifling so he lets it loose again.

He walks along the row of brick town houses, entering the white-columned doorway at number 18. The front office bustles with hushed activity: rows of clerks copying sheets of foolscap, a young woman clattering away at a typewriter. A bald man in a bow tie and waistcoat hovers over one of the clerks. His eyebrows spring up when he sees Ashley.

—Mr. Walsingham. Good morning. Mr. Twyning is expecting you—

One of the clerks takes Ashley's mackintosh and hat and umbrella. Ashley follows the bald man up a flight of stairs. They pass a padded telephone box on the landing and enter Twyning's office, a half-lit chamber with damask wallpaper and tall mahogany bookcases. Papers are cluttered everywhere, books and ledgers stacked in piles on the floor and mantelpiece.

Twyning rises from his desk to shake Ashley's hand. He wears a three-piece suit and a neat mustache. His hair is parted with shining pomade.

—Sit down, sit down. We've been at sixes and sevens since Monday, but I daresay we've succeeded. I've reviewed the papers and they look first-rate, given the complexities. Mr. Hotchkin, have the copies and originals brought up, if you please.

Ashley sits down on a buttoned leather chair. Twyning clears a space at the center of his desk, shifting a stack of papers to a pile behind him. He shakes his head.

—I must say, Ashley, I thought we had an understanding. God knows I've tried not to pester you while you were away. But it doesn't follow that I should manage things in utter ignorance of your aims, only for you to turn up at the last moment demanding wild changes. When do you go?

—Friday. We've the Wayfarers Club dinner in Liverpool tomorrow, then we sail the next morning.

Twyning sighs. —Look here, it's your money to do with as you like.

But it's my job to make these arrangements work perfectly, and no matter how we arrange this, it's bound to look suspect by reason of the timing. That makes it vulnerable to lawsuit. What do your people say about this?

—I haven't told them.

—And you don't intend to?

—No.

Twyning raps his pen on his blotter. He shakes his head.

—This may surprise you Ashley, but I didn't get into this line to be the architect of the twentieth century's Jarndyce and Jarndyce. Is the expedition really so dangerous? I'd no idea you entertained the notion of not returning.

—None of the climbers have been killed on the last two expeditions. Some porters have been. I thought you were all for keeping the papers up-to-date.

Twyning flashes a smile. —I shan't argue with that. To give her a reasonable legacy, fine. When you put her in years ago, I uttered not a word of protest. But to do as you have now—it raises legal and moral issues, if I may say so.

—Moral issues?

A clerk comes in carrying a black metal deed box painted G. RISLEY on the front. Twyning takes the folders from the box and unties their ribbons, arranging the papers on his desk. He glances up at Ashley.

—Do you imagine this is what he intended for the estate? Tossed outside the family within a generation?

—I don't know what he intended. I suppose he'd be surprised. What are the legal issues?

Twyning throws an empty folder onto his desk.

—Drastic changes before an event such as you're undertaking—your testamentary capacity could be challenged. It's made doubly worse by your choice of beneficiary. One could argue you weren't mentally sound—

—Who would argue? My mother?

—She could.

—She will not.

—It would be a terrible mess if she did.

Twyning walks to the window, his hands clasped behind his back.

—Not to mention the issue we haven't discussed. Why in God's name leave money to a missing person? Even supposing she is alive, it seems exceedingly unlikely she shall ever collect it.

—She's alive.

Twyning looks at Ashley. —You know that for a fact? If so, you must tell me. Otherwise, frankly it smacks of delusion, which is itself a legal issue. Indeed, if you know anything with regard to her whereabouts—

—I know nothing. But I don't believe she's dead.

—If we can't find her, Twyning insists, it makes no difference whether she's alive or not.

—Can't you put it in trust?

—We can. It's all been drawn up. But it's complicated. It requires a good deal of paperwork. And even if it's never contested in court, the administration of the trust will siphon money from the estate so long as it goes on. Which is fine by me. But I doubt your people will be happy about it.

—They've enough money.

—And she doesn't? If she's alive?

Ashley looks at Twyning. —Thank you for the legal advice. It is perfectly sound and I understand it. Now may I please sign the papers?

Twyning shakes his head. —I simply don't understand this eleventh-hour rush. Why couldn't you have told me sooner? Why yesterday?

—It struck me I ought to get my affairs in order.

—For Heaven's sake Ashley, you can't be serious. If she's turned up to ask you to do this—

—She hasn't.

—Or if she has turned up at all, you must tell me.

—She hasn't.

—And if she hasn't and she's alive, you'll excuse me but she's probably got a castle of her own. And has no need for yours.

—May I sign the papers or not?

Twyning sits in the chair beside Ashley. He turns the documents around to face them.

—I shall explain to you what we've done and how the trust works. But let me repeat that when you sign these pages, you create a knot that's not easily untangled. One shudders to think of the myriad—

—I understand.

Twyning sighs. —You know this is a mistake.

—Perhaps.

—You wish to do it anyway.

—That's right.

Twyning describes the purpose of each document. When he has finished he calls in two young clerks to witness the execution of the will and the trust. Ashley takes Twyning's pen and begins to sign them quickly, one page after another, the witnesses watching over his shoulder.

—Without a moment's hesitation, Twyning murmurs.

Ashley continues to turn the sheets and sign them.

—Do they often hesitate?

—On occasion, Twyning says, when making drastic changes. In a case like yours, I couldn't say. It's without precedent.

The witnesses countersign the signature pages. They shake Ashley's hand and wish him luck on the expedition, then they go out. Ashley stands up before Twyning, grinning to himself.

—Nothing is without precedent. Have those fellows take a look in all those books of yours, I'd wager someone has done exactly as I have. Aren't you chaps meant to do that sort of thing?

—When we're given the time.

Twyning pages through the signed documents, setting aside the duplicates. Ashley looks around the room with a faint smile, admiring the silver inkstand on Twyning's desk, the perpetual calendar by the window. *Tuesday 26 February*. Ashley walks to the calendar, turning the brass knobs to *Wednesday* and *27*.

—Busy morning?

Twyning sighs, shaking his head. He taps Ashley's copies into a neat stack and puts them in a blue solicitor's envelope.

—Not even a moment for a cup of tea. Not with clients like you.

He shakes Ashley's hand, offering the envelope.

—Send a postcard from Bombay. It's Bombay you're sailing to, isn't it? And cable if you change your mind about all this. We can set things back in order quickly.

—I shan't change my mind.

—And look after yourself, Twyning says, ignoring Ashley's remark. I don't like this business of eleventh-hour changes. It's not the right spirit. When do you return?

—August.

—Call here as soon as you can. We'll see how you feel about this then. And best of luck. I saw your picture in *The Times*. They say you may be the one to finally crack Everest.

Ashley shrugs. —There are eight climbers on the expedition. We'll be lucky if two of us reach the top, and I've no Himalayan experience at all. Three of the fellows are damned fit and have been there before—

—So it won't be you?

Ashley only smiles. The two men shake hands again. Ashley leaves the office and hails another motorcab from the sidewalk.

—Jermyn Street, please. To Fagg Brothers, the bootmakers. I don't know the number.

Ashley takes a seat in the enclosed compartment behind the driver. He flips his watch open, wondering if they will be able to refit the boots and get them to Darjeeling before he arrives. Then he realizes that he has forgotten to bring the boots.

—Driver, he says through the window. Rather, we'll have to stop by Lansdowne Terrace first. Number nine.

—Sir.

Ashley stretches in his seat, yawning contentedly. He takes the telegram from his pocket and unfolds it. It is only the third time he has looked at it today.

25 FE 24
AE WALSINGHAM MOUNT EVEREST EXPEDITION OBTERRAS
LONDON
DEAREST ASHLEY TAKE NO RISKS YOU ARE PRECIOUS
BEYOND RECORD I PROTECT YOU WITHOUT END IMOGEN

POSTE RESTANTE

⚬

Four days later I'm back at the Joachimstaler Straße post office asking for a clerk who speaks English. I lean on the counter watching the patrons wait in line with parcels in their arms. The same manager lopes to the counter and nods at me gruffly. He waits for me to speak first.

—I got an e-mail from the post office. But it was all in German.

—What did you expect? You are in Germany.

The manager leads me back to his office and tells me to sit. He walks down the hallway and returns with an archival box of blue cardboard. He sets the box atop the stacks of paper cluttering his desk.

—Look inside.

I remove the lid from the box and look at the five envelopes inside.

—They were in the philatelic archive, he says. I suppose even eighty years ago someone knew we don't often get poste restante from expeditions.

The manager leans back in his chair and watches me. Then he adds, —They are the property of the archive now. Even if the addressee came to collect them she would probably be refused.

—I don't want to collect them. I just want to read them.

The manager stands up and shakes his head.

—I don't have the authority. It's a matter of privacy. You can make a request with the archive—

The manager narrows his eyes at me.

—How long are you staying in Berlin?

—I don't know. A few days.

The manager nods, taking a steel ruler from a cup on his desk and tapping it against his hand.

—Someone has opened the envelopes, maybe a worker in the archive. But I doubt if anyone has read these letters. Probably no one will read them. They will go back to the same shelf where they have been sitting for fifty years. Then they will sit there for fifty more years—

He looks up at me.

—You say you are related to the addressee? Your family name is not the same.

—I'm related to the addressee and the sender.

—Do you have any proof?

I rummage through my bag, taking Ashley's inscribed card from my notebook and handing it to the manager. He puts on a pair of reading glasses and examines the card. His eyeglasses are bent and one of the hinges has been mended with electrical tape. The manager opens the archival box and removes a letter from its envelope to compare the hand-writing. Then he takes a glass loupe from his desk drawer and examines the card. He murmurs something in German, putting the loupe back on his desk.

—It's not typical, he says.

The manager looks at me and asks me where I'm from. We talk about California and the manager says he has visited San Francisco several times for philatelic conferences. He asks questions about my family and my university studies, watching me closely as I talk.

The manager grasps his steel ruler and swivels in his chair. He slaps the end of the ruler into his palm.

—How did you know these letters were in the archive? They're not in the public catalog.

—I didn't know.

—Then why did you come here?

—I knew the letters had been sent here and I doubted they'd been collected. So I figured I might as well ask. But I never thought anybody would have saved them.

The manager shakes his head, tossing the ruler on his desk.

—I would not think so either. Your grandfather sent them?

—My great-grandfather. Ashley Edmund Walsingham.

—Who is the woman the letters are addressed to?

—Imogen Soames-Andersson.

I hesitate. Then I add, —My great-grandmother.

—She was traveling in Berlin? Or living here?

—I don't know.

—Why did she not collect the letters?

—I don't know. Maybe I'd know if I read them.

The manager watches me across his desk. There is a long silence. He opens a drawer in a filing cabinet and hands me a pair of thin cotton gloves. He nods at the archival box.

—Wear the gloves, he says. There is a copying machine in the next room. Do not use the feeder, do not bend the pages. Put them in the envelopes when you are done. The correct envelopes.

The photocopied letters in my shoulder bag, I ride the U-Bahn back to my hostel at Rosenthaler Platz. My dorm room hovers several stories above the intersection of three busy streets. A group of Canadian back-packers greets me as I enter.

—Are you going out?

—Out?

—It's Friday night. You aren't going out?

The Canadians change clothes and set out for the evening. I undress and climb into the narrow shower stall. I open the tap and let the water grow hotter and hotter, filling the bathroom with dense steam until I can barely see. Wrapped in a towel, I lie damp and dripping on my bunk for a long time. The room is warm, much warmer than the house in Picardie. Mireille must be back in Paris by now. She could be on her way to the same bar where we met two weeks ago.

I get out of my bunk and get dressed. On the opposite corner of Rosenthaler Platz there is a two-story café that is open late into the night. I order a coffee at the counter and climb the stairs, sitting down at a small wooden table. I spread out the five photocopied letters in chronological order, then set my notebook and pen beside the copies. The pages have Ashley's familiar script in thick pencil, the letterhead printed MOUNT EVEREST EXPEDITION.

I pour sugar into my coffee from a glass dispenser, whisking a spoon in the dark foam. The spoon rings faintly on the china.

⊷≡◯ ◯≡⊷

Pedong

28 Mar 1924

My dear Imogen,

    I hardly knew what to think when I got your telegram. It was right before I sailed & it nearly smashed my mind to pieces; I went through my last days in London & Liverpool in a fog. I thought about you the long weeks at sea, and tore up half a dozen letters, wondering all the while whether I ought to write or not. In the end I knew you hadn't asked me to write, and so I would not.

    But with you, I never could control my feelings.

    This letter goes Poste Restante to the Berlin GPO and I cable you saying so; you shall collect it if you wish to, and I shall hope that eases my mind. In these spare moments near dusk, the other men take out pen & paper to write to wives & lovers; you are neither to me, but I write to you now anyway, too far away from civilization to give a straw what is proper. To me you are all that is proper.

From Bombay I travelled by train across the plains of India with two of the other climbers, Price & Somervell. The heat & dust were overwhelming, the train carriage a place of sweltering sleeplessness and ravenous mosquitoes, where I passed in & out of strange reveries and walked the corridors by night. The sole consolation was swinging open the carriage door and standing in the doorframe holding the rail, feeling the night breeze and watching the stars over the horizon, the woodfires burning in lonely huts below.

We came up to Darjeeling by the narrow-gauge railway, twisting through dense tropical forest, the track crawling to one direction & then the other. I craned my neck out of the window to watch the little blue steam-engine chug along. So steep was the climb that they stationed a man above the engine to throw gravel over the tracks for traction. Noel, the expedition's photographer, sat on the top of the carriage running his cine camera, ducking flat at times to avoid branches and vines thicker than alpine rope.

At Darjeeling we stayed at the Mount Everest Hotel. There I packed & weighed & repacked my kit. There I wrote you another letter that went into the wastebasket. There I donned evening dress for the last time and we went to dine with the Governor's wife.

We set off from Darjeeling in motors for the first few miles – wonderfully steep driving – then we began our march, a hot breeze carrying us down the hill, the air perfume-scented & bearing huge mountain butterflies. We chased after them with nets for Hingston's collection: he is our medical officer & a keen naturalist.

We all have ponies for riding, but when we can Price & I break ahead on foot, for the sake of quiet & solitude. Often in those moments my thoughts turn to you – how you would love to ramble here, how you would admire the scenery & the strange, kind people, the queer overgrown plants, the crystal sky. But I see it only through a glass darkly. For even in steaming jungles I think of the windswept plateau beyond, and high above the snow-covered ranges, one peak the most brutal & majestic of all. Imogen, I'm not ready to see the mountain. She could never be all I've imagined, and if she is we haven't a chance. And yet I want to see her so badly, searching the horizon for snow mountains at the crest of every pass, even though I know we are weeks away.

I write in comfort on a solid table in a dak bungalow. We shall not enjoy such luxury for long; I save the weightier words for then, for if I finish now this goes with the next mail-runner. You can write to me thus:

The Mount Everest Expedition
C/O British Trade Agent
Yatung, Tibet

Though I shall not expect it.
We return to England in August. Am I mad enough to hope your telegram marks the start of something new? I am so mad. As we were once so mad together.

Yours Ever,
Ashley

→≡ ◦≡→

Yatung
2 Apr 1924

My dear Imogen,

We've crossed the frontier into Tibet at last. From Kapup I climbed the whole 3,000 ft to the Jelep La on foot to test my wind.

*It was hard going, the pass snowblown & rocky, but even in a
gale it gave me some satisfaction to walk from Sikkim into Tibet,
standing higher than the summit of most Alpine peaks. I felt fit &
hadn't even a headache to trouble me. But am I fit enough? Can
any man be fit enough?*

*We shall know soon enough. For don't believe what you see
in the papers — we do not climb the mountain, we lay siege to her.
Against Everest we field an army of hundreds: for a leader, our
General Bruce, who commands the expedition, for officers, the nine
of us Britishers. For NCOs, the loyal Gurkhas; for soldiers, the
sixty porters and Sherpas, freshly clad in English underwear &
gabardine pyjama suits; lastly the mercenary army of 200 villagers
we enlist to take us as far as the base camp.*

*The stores for the assault, collected from the ends of the earth,
ride before us each day on the back of an endless train of mules.
Wooden cases of tinned food: Hunter's Hams, Heinz Spaghetti,
every vegetable that can be tinned and some that ought not to
be; Maggi soups, Horlick's powder; legions of biscuits. Also rarer
delicacies: crystal ginger; tinned quail with truffles; foie gras au
Lyonnais; four doz. bottles of Montebello's 1915. For the General
knows we march on our stomachs. Then our armaments: the
sinister oxygen apparatus, with its look of Victorian plumbing; the
sharpened crampons, steel stakes & pitons; the Swiss ice axes, coils
of flaxen rope; rolled Whymper & Meade tents, boxed Primus
stoves & Unna cookers; the countless silver oxygen cylinders, the
colour-coded canisters of petrol & paraffin.*

*The absurdity of it — the best that man can produce, pitted
against a tower of rock millions of years old. And we shall hardly
look like men at all, for you would laugh to see my costume for the
heights. Heavy boots with Alpine nails, underclothes of Shetland
wool & Japan silk; Norwegian stockings, woollen jersey and
mittens, Jäger trousers, soft Kashmir puttees, a suit of windproof
gabardine. Then a fur-lined leather motorcycle helmet, a six-foot*

muffler; snow-goggles of Crooke's green glass. Not to mention that inhuman breathing apparatus. One could say it isn't fair for the mountain, that it isn't sporting and it isn't alpinism.

And yet she might so easily beat us. This is the signature of her majesty.

Last night at dinner the expedition photographer Noel told a fantastic tale, evidently true, of how the highest lamas in Tibet are discovered after they have been reincarnated. After the lama has died the high monks use several methods to search for the new incarnation. They may dream of the lama, or some aspect of him; of a location where he may be found; they may note the direction the smoke travels from the previous lama's funeral pyre & search accordingly; they may seek a guiding vision at a certain holy lake in central Tibet. Following these omens, they look for a youth born near the time of the previous lama's death.

Once they have found a candidate, one of the tests is laying out the personal effects of the old lama amongst a selection of similar decoys. So they put out four sets of prayer-beads, one of which was the old lama's; or three walking sticks, or five fountain pens. The rightful heir always selects his predecessor's possessions.

Somehow this made me think of you. Perhaps the sense of the ordained wedded to the grandest caprice. To scatter the lama each time among the remote ranges of Tibet, only to find him anew every generation – that is to trust in something.

So I trust in the faithful Tibetan mail-runner – or is he faithless? – that he shall safeguard this letter so improbably across those savage peaks, evading flood & bandits & every manner of temptation, that these pages reach Darjeeling and, in time, Berlin. And then – shall this ever reach you? O Imogen, you would always have believed so.

You cannot imagine how I miss you.

Yours Ever,
Ashley

☞ ☜

Ts-tsang

8 Apr 1924

My Imogen,

 *I write from the packed dirt floor of a roofless temple, only
the firmament & a white-hot moon hanging over us for a ceiling.
Somervell & I left Phari a day behind the party; we came upon
this convent of Buddhist nuns and stopped for the night. We
cannot speak a word to them, nor they to us, yet their hospitality is
immense – they treat us like wayward sons.*

 *Beside me snores Somervell, a kind & agreeable fellow who is
a physician as well as an accomplished climber. We are flanked on
all sides by prayer wheels, a few of them spinning loose in the wind.
From the altar a dried-up billy goat gawks down at us, the victim of
some long-forgotten sacrifice. It is very cold.*

 *Two days ago at Dothak we saw a frozen waterfall, an elegant
sliver of a river arrested in movement. We halted at Phari to re-
organize. The town is set at 14,000 ft beneath a great peak 10,000
ft higher. It is never warm & never without wind. All the old hands
claimed Phari is the filthiest place on earth. It is.*

 *Rubbish runs through the street up to one's knees. Crossing these
rivers of flowing waste, it could be Ypres again, but for the laughing
children & barking muddied dogs. They say the people go from cradle
to grave without a single bathe; I saw a mother lovingly coat a naked
little girl with yak butter, as proof against the merciless wind & sun
& snow. Evidently Phari is the highest inhabited place in the world.
The summer is too short for crops to ripen, so the people live off mean
food and eat it raw: dried mutton, barley flour, tea mixed with rancid
yak butter. And yet they smile sympathetically at us, knowing enough
to pity us & our strange quest.*

General Bruce was forced back by recurring Malaria; our physician Hingston shall accompany him to Darjeeling and rejoin the expedition, and we are optimistic the General shall recover. Colonel Norton, a good fellow & an able climber, takes over as expedition leader. Still it is a blow to lose the General, and hardly the best of omens on a journey dependent upon the labour of superstitious hill people.

It is whispered that evil portents have followed this expedition since its departure: the Bhotia boy who witnessed errant stars in the mid-day sky, then flashes of sunlight upon the evening sky; the band of vultures who pursue us relentlessly across Tibet, hovering beside the camp in spite of the volleys of stones we throw at them; the strange fantastical dreams we have all been having. Hingston attributes the dreams to the effect of thin air upon the sleeping brain. But the porters see the dreams as visions of the past & future alike.

Most fancifully, our interpreter confided to me that Price's eyes were as dark as any Asiatic's when he first came to Everest in '21, and that they changed colour to blue after the ghastly avalanche in '22. Of course this is pure fantasy, and yet I had to admit I could not remember Hugh having blue eyes when I first knew him. I could not remember his eyes at all. The porters earnestly believe that Price is marked for death within the month, and that if he were to cup his ears he would not hear the usual whirling sound that marks us as earthly creatures, but only the terrific silence of the dead. I have not relayed this news to Hugh.

As the landscape grows monumental, all my feelings expand in proportion. One cannot describe how lonely this place is when one is feeling stricken. We are meant to go to the summit – one peak amongst dozens here – for King, country & Empire; to advance knowledge; for human progress; to further our reputations as climbers & as Englishmen.

In truth each man climbs for his own reasons: the Colonel,

from a sense of duty & honour, and a notion of England that
should not have survived Victoria, let alone Passchendaele;
Somervell, for the love of mountains & their scientific riddles,
forever unanswered; Mills, for good sportsmanship & the sheer
joy of it, as if climbing Everest were no different than rowing the
college Eight; and Price, most elusive of all, who climbs not because
he wishes to but because he must, as he alone is privy to the
mountain's deep secret.

But why should I climb? All my interest in posterity, or
winning glory for my country, was long ago buried at Empress
Redoubt. Nor can I argue for the advancement of knowledge – for
I cannot see how Everest demands more study than any other scrap
of the unknown territory around us. I cannot even plead a love
of alpinism, for there is no climbing to be had yet: here we trek &
suffer, trek & freeze, and the limit of our progress is not our skill
with rock & rope, but our capacity to endure.

So we march through knee-deep snow, in blizzards and under
a brutal Himalayan sun. The camaraderie of the party, their fine
spirit & the endless toil of everyone make me pray we take Everest.
But for my own sake? Most days I'm still the peak-bagger & want
the summit beyond anything. When I'm low I don't give a straw
for it, thinking all conquest & records are human folly, and that
what I wish for can't be found on any summit.

But I deceive myself. This isn't about Everest or any mountain.
And some rare & precious part of me surely survived the Somme,
to bring me here intact, vulnerable as I am. All my dreams die
hard, but those of you are utterly imperishable.

> Yours Ever,
> Ashley

⟡

Chobuk
26 Apr 1924

My dear Imogen,

I've seen it now – I had to write to you straight away.

Last night we stayed at Pang La below the high pass. We struck camp in darkness this morning & had not gone far before Hugh took me ahead of the party, at double pace & then nearly running until we crested the pass, dizzy & gasping on its summit.

It was a spectacular vision: layer upon layer of dark barren hills, then the jagged teeth of the Himalaya towering above – Makalu & Lhotse & Cho Oyu – all seeming to bend towards a pink sky, the sunrise dazzling their western flanks. One peak reigned above all, cruel & enchanting, a hurricane of vapour streaming over her summit. It was Everest, as exquisite as the tiger's fang & as tempting as black oblivion, for she stood miles tall & still I felt I was looking into an abyss. She seemed the remnant of some other world, a place elemental & unforgiving that left behind this mountain, to prove us trifles before the wild & howling universe.

I waited for Hugh to speak, but he only took out the field-glasses & we scanned the upper mountain for what seemed hours, searching for flattish places to pitch our high camp, imagining obstacles amongst specks of rock 35 miles distant. We shall soon get a better view – we are three days' march from our base camp, and the sight of Everest puffed new life into our tired party, though already the wind pushed much of it back out.

We are camped amongst the willows of Chobuk monastery. The tent wall is wet against my head & I halt frequently to grease my face from a little pot that stays beside me all night. For the Tibetan plain has broken my skin raw, which was never made for such a hostile climate. All the other Sahibs have grown beards against the wind, but my attempt was pitiable & I gave it up.

On a bench outside, Mills wrenches away at the oxygen kit by hurricane lamp. Over in the mess tent, Price & the Colonel debate the plans & personnel for the summit assault. There shall be two parties of two climbers each, one with the oxygen, one without— for it's a beastly load at those heights, and there isn't a fellow here who wouldn't prefer to summit without. If only we knew that was possible. I should like to be in the natural party, but it's likely I won't make a climbing party at all & will be kept in support.

A runner is departing with the despatches, so I end here. The post caught us at Shegar and though I truly didn't expect anything, still I stood beside the mailbag like a boy, remembering a parcel that came to me one day at Le Sars, a place wetter than here, but no more hospitable. I felt then – I feel now – beyond the pale, on the far side of every river and boundary that divides civilization from emptiness. But I had you; I had the parcel in my hands, a long walk back to our cellars in the rain, where there would be no dry clothes & never any time to sleep. It didn't matter. I was young and we were together.

The post goes out now –

> Yours Ever,
> Ashley

➤═○ ○═➤

> Rongbuk Base Camp
> 29 Apr 1924

Imogen –

We arrived at Rongbuk today. I began a meek letter describing our journey, but I've just burned it. For I'm cold & exhausted & there isn't any time for half-truths – the post goes out tomorrow.

*How I miss spring in this wasteland of grey moraine & ice;
how I miss true earnest spring of primroses & grape hyacinths
& long English grass. When I return, I shall know I have at last
earned such luxury.*

*For seven years I tried not to look at your photograph, nor
your handwriting, nor any trinket that could bring you to mind. It
wasn't any use. For even here I can picture you reading this, how
you recline holding these sheets, the string of beads around your
neck, everything.*

*It's no good sending letters Poste Restante to someone who
surely has a fine postbox of her own; but even if one knew the
address, one never knows whose fortunate hands reach into
that box. My own hands have only the fortune of touching
the mountain, a cruel mistress who leaves them red & sore &
cracked – but isn't suffering the true proof of love? Quod Erat
Demonstrandum.*

*It isn't. I'm proud to say I'm finally cured of all such foolish
ideas & don't allow myself to suffer for anything. Past my tent flap
is the Rongbuk Valley & I take her as she is; so I hope to take the
East Glacier & the North Col, and so I take you too.*

*Imogen, I made mistakes. I squandered the very things I ought
to have protected, and I expect no absolution, for in this world men
admire one's vices, but scorn true virtue & call it weakness. I broke
faith with everything, save for you, and still I lost you anyway.
Have I lost you for ever? The ceaseless wind whips back an answer.
But I don't listen. I trust only in the steadiness of own my heart –
too mad or ardent to be anything but*

> *yours – Everlastingly –*
> *Ashley*

THE BROKEN CITY

✦⇒ ⇐✦

I put the letters back in the plastic folder, looking out the tall windows of the café. I don't want to read them again.

Crossing Rosenthaler Platz, I go into a convenience store and study a pair of glass-front refrigerators displaying dozens of German beers sold by the bottle. I choose a squat brown one with an illustration of Saint Augustine. The sky outside hangs purple in the west. I set off into the street, climbing the gentle grade of Weinbergsweg toward Prenzlauer Berg.

Ashley didn't know a thing about her, I think. *Just like me.*

I guide myself with a battered tourist map and a vague desire to go eastward. At Zionskirchplatz I find a church with a towering steeple, the door unlocked, the inside deserted and in disrepair. I sit in a pew for half an hour, staring at the faded paint on the walls and pillars of the choir: borders and patterns of byzantine complexity, brushed on meticulously by long-dead artisans and now faded to almost nothing.

On Karl-Marx-Allee, grand boulevard of the former East Berlin, I walk on a sidewalk fifty feet broad, the Stalinist apartment blocks running east to the horizon. I buy a bottle of herbal bitters from an outdoor

fast-food counter and follow the boulevard to the old city gate of Frank-
furter Tor.

It's no good writing letters to people who never read them, I think. *And
a stranger reading them eighty years later doesn't make it any better.*

I follow Warschauer Straße south to the Spree, where I snap photos
along the last long stretch of the Berlin Wall, twelve-foot-high concrete blanketed with flaking graffiti. The huge mural above me reads
TOTALDEMOKRATIE. Gaps in the wall reveal entrances to vast riverside
nightclubs, the patrons spilling onto the sidewalk. Young people on foot
and on bicycle throng past me, drinks in hand, and I wonder where they
could be going at this hour. I check my watch. A little past three in the
morning.

Keeping some distance back, I follow a group around a vast train
station, then among side streets in a deserted industrial district. The
road ends in a turnaround where a line of cream-colored Mercedes taxis
wait for fares. Between a pair of chain-link fences, a dirt path leads to a
huge building of crumbling gray stone. Light and music pulse from its
tall windows. I file into the long line.

An hour passes before I reach the doormen. A pair of girls ahead of
me is turned away, then a large group of well-dressed students is refused.
The head bouncer sits on a stool beside the entrance, eyeing me with
dim curiosity. He has a dark beard and one side of his face is covered in
barbed-wire tattoos. I raise one finger to show I've come alone. He waves
me in.

I pay the entrance fee and check my jacket and camera, passing
through rooms of indistinct size and shape, vast caverns terminating
in blackness or colored only by spinning electric lights. Everywhere is
packed with sweaty dancers. The bass is driving. Thumping air pushes
at my lungs and shakes my stomach. I climb staircases and find other
rooms, secret crevices with embracing bodies barely distinguishable
from the walls or ceiling. I buy a beer from one of the bars and gulp it
down. No one else is drinking.

Soon I need to use the toilet. On the second story I find a bathroom line that is much shorter than the others, but there are only two toilets at the end. The line barely moves. I wait in agony, counting the people ahead of me. Nine. Seven. Six. The walls begin to turn. I fix my eyes on a green exit light at the end of the corridor to slow the spinning. A fashionably dressed girl trots up along the side of the line. Voices behind me heckle the girl for cutting. The girl notices I'm alone and stops beside me. She takes my hand, speaking to me in English.

—Let me stay. I really have to go.

I let the girl wait beside me. For a moment she keeps my hand in hers. She wears an oversize black sweater over electric blue tights. Her reddish bangs hang down to her eyes.

—Thank you so much, she whispers.

The girl asks where I'm from. I try to steady my gaze and concentrate on her words. She has an accent I can't place. I notice a silver brooch pinned to her sweater.

—That's Celtic, isn't it?

The girl looks at me, cupping the brooch in her fingers. It is a weaving of silver strands depicting a dragon and a pair of snakes, their bodies locked in struggle. I lean in to look closer.

—Christ. I've seen that before.

—Were you in Iceland?

I stare at the brooch. There was something similar in my grandmother's jewelry box in the garage, but I can't remember exactly what it looked like.

—It's a Viking style from Iceland, the girls says. It's some kind of battle. The dragon is good and the snakes are evil—

The girl frowns. She puts a cigarette in her mouth and lifts the brooch toward her eyes, reappraising the warring creatures.

—Or is it, she wonders, the other way around?

One of the restroom doors opens. The girl thanks me and dashes inside. Soon the other bathroom is free and I go in. As I lock the door and walk by the mirror, a shudder pulses through me and I turn away instinctively. I look back into the mirror. Something looks unfamiliar, some part of my face doesn't seem right. I lean on the sink and breathe in slowly, staring at my reflection. Are my eyes shaped differently now? Or is it the corners of my mouth, or the crown of my forehead? The fear begins to overwhelm me. I turn away.

—It must be the drinking, I whisper.

A few minutes later I come out of the bathroom, but the Icelandic girl is gone. I walk through all the dance floors looking for her. A few times I think I catch her silhouette under a strobe light, but when I come closer it's always someone else.

An hour later I leave the club, staggering out into the painful light of dawn. A long line of people is still waiting to go inside. I scan the crowd's faces for the girl, but she isn't here, so I ride the U-Bahn back to the hostel, rocked to sleep by the swaying train. A man shakes me awake holding an ID card before my eyes. A ticket inspector. I flash my ticket, skipping off the train at Rosenthaler Platz as the doors close.

The desk clerk at the hostel is asleep on the counter. I set a euro coin before his slumped head and sit at one of the lobby computers. I write an e-mail to my stepbrother.

> *Hi Adam—*
>
> *Europe is impressive. I don't know how much longer I'll be gone. Tell Dad I've been industriously researching UK grad schools. He'll be disappointed. If you told him it's 7 AM in Berlin and I've been out all night, he'd probably be happier.*
>
> *I have a favor to ask. It's a little strange, but trust me, it's important. I need you to find a brooch in my grandmother's jewelry box. It's in the garage, in one of those cardboard boxes on the top shelf. I don't know which box, but it's labeled and should be near the top of the stack, since I looked through it last month. The jewelry box is green. Look for a silver brooch—it's supposed to be a dragon and snakes, but it basically looks like a bunch of woven strands.*

Can you mail the brooch to me as soon as you can? I'll be eternally grateful. Send it to this address, the fastest delivery you can get, I'll pay you back:

Circus Hostel
Weinbergsweg 1A
10119 Berlin
Germany

Thanks a million. When I'm back I'll have some stories to tell.
Tristan

P.S. Don't tell anyone about the brooch.

30 April 1924

Mount Everest Base Camp, 18,190 feet

Rongbuk Valley, Tibet

He stands in a maze of wooden crates scattered among the stones. The expedition arrived at the base camp yesterday. Along the valley the wind blows viciously, flurries of snow churning the darkening sky. The crates surround Ashley, their lids breached, their contents open to the snow. He gives instructions to a pair of porters in bad Hindustani, his hoarse voice barely above a whisper. The porters nod in incomprehension. Ashley lifts his head to the swirling sky and tightens the muffler around his neck.

The steep valley walls crumble to a floor of colorless pebbles and dirt. The expedition's tents lie huddled beside a frozen lake, a moraine heap above lending meager shelter from the wind. On clearer days the mountain's pyramid might loom in the sky, but for now the blizzard obscures all.

Ashley runs along a column of yaks, a screwdriver in his mittened palm, scanning the cases roped onto the animals. He calls at a Tibetan handler to halt a yak. The handler pats the animal and unropes the case onto the rocks. Ashley unscrews the lid and lifts a tin up to the dusk light. *HARRIS'S SAUSAGES ARE THE BEST.* He sorts the tins into other labeled crates, each of varied size so that they all hold forty pounds when correctly packed. Camp I, Camp II, Camp III, Camp IV. Ginger nut biscuits. Beef tongue. He screws the finished crates shut and paces among the emptied cases, squinting in the fading light. He ought to get his electric torch.

—Walsingham. Time for dinner.

Price approaches, a candle lantern swinging in his mitten. Ashley clears his throat and barks a reply.

—Something celebratory? Cheese omelette à la Rongbuk?

—No, Price says, Kami is under strict instructions. It's the menu the general planned. Four courses and the champagne.

Ashley and Price cross the valley toward the mess tent, its four oil lamps glowing in the distance. They pass Mills, the young climber pounding a wooden stake with a huge stone. A porter holds the stake upright in the gale, his eyes fixed on his vulnerable fingers as he grips the wood. Mills waves at the two men.

—Come along, Price calls.

—Be right there.

They walk on. Beyond the curtain of blowing snow the army of hired local peasants prepares for the night. There are no tents for them. Some stack rocks to build shelters; others lie blanketless amid the snow, their thick woolen coats drawn tight over their chests. A few peasants struggle to relight a pile of yak dung in the wind. The dung is smoking, but no flame will come.

Price pauses to give instruction to a Gurkha corporal erecting a Whymper tent. Ashley waits beside them, stamping his feet to keep warm. They are only at the base camp and they are already wearing every stitch of their climbing kit.

A few minutes later they reach the mess tent. It is little warmer inside, but at least there is no wind. Most of the nine men are already seated at the table, each in his own camp chair. The folding table is without a cloth, the condiment bottles arranged neatly at the center. The colonel sits at the head of the table; Price and Ashley take their seats nearby. Price spreads his napkin over his lap and looks at the colonel.

—We need to have another powwow about the stores.

—After dinner, the colonel says. Let's keep our appetites while we can.

Price nods. His camp chair is so low that only his head is above the level of the table. The brim of his hat hangs down over his face, save for where it is held up by a large safety pin covered in candlewax.

—What's the first course?

—The quails, in *pâté de fois gras*. Also sardines and hard-boiled egg.

—The deployment of the quails at last, Ashley wheezes.

—Dear Lord, Somervell says. You sound like death himself.

—Air here isn't quite up to Switzerland, Ashley remarks. Might be the dryness. Or the dust. Or the cold. Hard to say, really.

Price looks at his bare plate.

—I don't suppose we've had menus printed?

—They're coming by yak train from Lhasa, Somervell says. They'll be here in forty days.

Mills clatters in, shaking the snow from his broad shoulders as he takes the last camp chair. A pair of Sherpas serving as mess waiters bring in the sardines, lifting portions onto each plate with a large spoon.

—I doubt a menu has ever been printed here, Noel remarks. They've only two printing presses in the entire country. With each page carved by hand out of wooden blocks.

—Two presses, Ashley says, and all those holy books in the monasteries? They must be busy.

—Those books are all they print, Noel says. It's said they have no written history for the last thousand years.

The colonel waves at one of the Sherpas and says something in Nepali, then addresses the table in English.

—I say, let's start with the fizz. You fellows have all earned it.

The Sherpa gives each man an aluminum mug painstakingly deiced over a spirit lamp. He fetches a green magnum bottle of champagne and uncorks it and wraps it in a dusty napkin. The Sherpa circles the table, rationing the wine carefully among the mugs. Ashley spears a sardine with his fork.

—No history at all?

—None has been found, Noel says. Those libraries have nothing but lamastic texts. One set of scriptures is a hundred volumes, a thousand pages per volume. Goes on the back of a dozen yaks. They've no time for anything else.

—Historyless, Ashley murmurs. That strikes me as jolly.

The colonel shakes his head.

—Jolly? I don't see that living in ignorance of the past is jolly. Surely it condemns one to repeat mistakes.

—Strikes me as jolly, Price says.

—You two are only trying to get my blood up, the colonel says. For God's sake, Price, you're a teacher. Who has the quail?

—They've got two presses, Ashley says. So they can print only so much. They take religion over history. Seems sound to me.

—You're an atheist, Price remarks.

There is much laugher.

—Soon to be a lamaist, Ashley says. I mean only that between wisdom and knowledge, one must choose wisdom.

Somervell lifts a piece of egg dubiously on the end of his fork.

—You're presuming those books have wisdom. I presumed this egg was hard-boiled. It isn't.

—We must send Kami to the Cordon Bleu, Ashley says. Let us start a subscription now.

—It's the roarer cooker, Mills says. It takes about a case of paraffin to get a boil. And up here it's a ten-minute egg.

The Sherpas circle with the third course. Tibetan mutton cutlets and tinned green peas warmed over a Primus burner. The colonel begins to prod Noel for anecdotes of his famous travels.

—That business about you in Tibet before the war, the colonel says. Let's have the whole story.

Noel sips his champagne with practiced relish.

—It was back in '13. I was in disguise.

He grins, putting a cube of cutlet into his mouth. He speaks in clipped sentences, directing his fork for emphasis.

—As a Mohammedan Indian, he continues. No Europeans being allowed in at the time, of course. Got within forty miles of Everest. Tibetan patrol caught up with us. Some chap fired a matchlock at me. Imagine, a matchlock. Frightful noise. Don't know where the shot went, but it sounded like bloody armageddon. Must have been plenty of powder in there.

—You were the first foreigner to get near Everest? Mills asks.

Noel shakes his head. —The pundits got here first.

Noel smiles and leans back into his camp chair. He explains that fifty years ago the government of British India wished to survey the Tibetan territory to the north, but the country was hostile and Europeans were strictly forbidden from entering the kingdom. So the government trained Indians to survey Tibet disguised as pilgrims. The surveyors were called *pundits*, a Hindi word for a learned man, and they were schooled in special surveying techniques so that no observer would recognize their labors. They entered Tibet at great peril, crossing remote and snow-blown passes at high altitude. The pundits counted distances in paces and recorded them by turning prayer wheels or spinning rosary beads; they learned to walk a mile in precisely two thousand paces, and on some journeys they walked two thousand miles.

—How many steps would that be? Noel wonders.

Price does not look up from his food. —Four million.

—With every step counted, Noel says. They hid compasses in amulets. Put boiling-point thermometers in walking sticks. Surveyed by evening stars, by sextant. At night they wrote all the figures down and rolled the paper inside those prayer wheels. Some were captured and tortured or killed, poor devils. Who's pinched the sauce bottle?

The bottle is passed down the table and Noel douses his cutlet in brown sauce.

—There was one chap called Kinthup, he continues. Very game fellow. Sent to find out if the Tsanpo in Tibet was in fact the same river as the Brahmaputra. Damned big river, but no one knew where it started in the Himalaya. Kinthup was meant to get deep into the forest and cut blocks of wood in certain shapes, then send them sailing down the Tsanpo. Fifty logs a day. Survey captain in India had another chap watching downriver for the blocks for years.

—Exciting work, Ashley remarks, if one can get it.

Noel grins. —But the blocks never appeared. This fellow Kinthup had been taken prisoner in Tibet and sold a slave. Took him four years to get free. As soon as he escaped he went straight into the forest, cut the blocks and sent them downriver.

—Bravo, the colonel says. That's the Indian soldier for you. Faithful to the core.

Noel swallows a bite. —Trouble was that no one was watching by then. Survey captain had gone back to England.

At the far end of the table, someone delivers the punch line to a bawdy joke and there is gleeful laughter. Ashley bends over his plate toward Noel.

—Was it the same river?

—Of course. Of course it was.

Noel takes a sip of champagne and shakes his head.

—It's a strange country. Have you heard of Everest's white lion? The Tibetans believe that a white lion lives on the summit of the mountain. The lion's milk is supposed to be a panacea. Cures all problems physical and spiritual. No one's ever gotten the milk. Except the Dalai Lama, of course. With his supernatural powers.

Price looks up from his plate. —The lion. When we first came in '21, they thought we were climbing the mountain for her milk—

—Not far off, Somervell says.

—If it's a question of divine right, Ashley remarks, perhaps our king should have a go.

The colonel frowns. —That's different. We don't ascribe magical powers to the king.

—Well, Price says, he's the head lama of the Church of England. That's something magical.

Noel shakes his head, squinting theatrically at Ashley.

—Now Walsingham, are you a brainy fellow like Price? Or are you the decent sort? I've seen you trading books with him. That's the road to sin.

—I'm probably indecent.

—He's thoroughly decent, Price counters. Did you ever bump into him under the blue lamp at Amiens? I'll wager you didn't. Though I say, Walsingham's French is topping. Plows through Rabelais faster than you read *News of the World*. He may have learnt it from those mademoiselles.

—The blue lamp at Amiens, Noel repeats. Rum place, may have seen him there. Saw the Prince of Wales there once, smoking a cigar. Looked like him, anyway. They ought to have opened a Berlitz school in those brothels. Come to think of it, Price, all those damned French books in the camp library are yours. But we know you're pure as the driven snow.

Ashley waves his hand in dismissal.

—Irrelevant. The *poules* all spoke English enough.

The table erupts. —Hear, hear! Noel bellows.

—I only chatted with them, Ashley says. Some were actually rather fascinating—

—But the white lion, Price insists. It isn't rot. These folk beliefs are based on real things. It could be the snow leopard, for instance.

—Possibly, the colonel admits. Some are seen very high. They go after the bharal, and we've seen those up here. Have you heard of the snow leopard, Walsingham? Very rare. Only one white man's ever laid eyes on them.

—Did he get the milk? Ashley asks.

There is riotous laughter, Noel roaring and wiping the tears from his eyes. Ashley's laughter breaks into a wheezing cough.

—I suppose up there, Ashley adds, it would be ice cream.

Noel stands officiously and raises his mug.

—To the white lion of the snows, Noel toasts. May we find her and bring forth her dairy.

The British raise their mugs and drink. Only Price does not join in, staring blankly at the table. Ashley whispers in Price's ear.

—You're not after the lion?

Price smiles. His face is a patchwork of shadows under the swinging oil lamps.

—Not even in jest. May she remain a mystery.

Price raises his mug and drinks.

—Then you're in favor of mysteries, Ashley says.

—It's the summit we want, Price shrugs. We ought not ask for too much.

THE JEWELER

⊷⊐ ⊏⊶

One morning as I pass the hostel's front desk, the clerk summons me
with a wave.

—Your package finally came.

He puts a FedEx envelope on the counter. I sit on a couch in the
lobby and pull the envelope's zipper, shaking out the contents. The
brooch drops onto my lap along with a folded sheet of notebook paper.

Dear Tris,

> *Now you're the best-dressed man in Europe. Hope you'll still
> come back anyway.*
>
> *Adam*

I turn the brooch in my hands, running my fingers along the
tarnished silver strands of the dragon's body. The metal is worn and
scratched, but otherwise the brooch resembles the one I saw in the
nightclub. There is a small inscription in the silver on the reverse: CVG,
the letters followed by a strange circular symbol.

I'd first seen the brooch when I searched the garage before traveling to London. Or had I seen it before? I think back to the seaside with my grandmother and I try to picture the brooch there, the twisted dragons glinting in the afternoon sun. But I can't be sure.

I log on to the Internet on one of the lobby computers, searching for a specialist in Scandinavian jewelry who might be able to identify the brooch. I run searches using every term I can think of, but the only dealers I find are outside Germany. It's already September 24 and I can't waste time sending the brooch away. I run more searches with the term *Berlin* and I find the website of a jewelry designer whose name sounds Scandinavian. Among a section called "Replicas" I scroll through images of Viking jewelry.

The brooch is there. The plaited bodies of the warring creatures, the curled dragon's head singing in exertion. It's the same brooch but the style is different, the strands thicker, the dragon more realistically defined. The caption advertises *Brosche im Urnes-Stil, Sterling Silber*. I click on the CONTACT button. The address is Kunsthaus Tacheles, Oranienburger Straße 54–56a, a short walk from the hostel.

I grab my bag and dash south across the intersection.

The building is immense, five stories tall and the length of an entire city block. I check the address several times, but it's the right number. The half-ruined facade is covered in graffiti; vast craters gape amid the ornate moldings and the sculpted figures high above, their heads and limbs pried off the stone.

The foyer is littered with beer bottles and cigarette stubs. I climb a grimy staircase to the second floor, a maze of hallways with closed doors. A young man walks past dragging a smashed television on a rickety dolly. I ask him for directions to the jeweler's studio. He answers in an Australian accent.

—Go to the third floor and make a right. Walk straight to the end.

I follow his instructions to a hallway of glazed white brick, everything coated in graffiti. The corridor ends in a sturdy metal door, the arch above painted in huge black capitals: HIER SIND SIE SICHER. It looks like the entrance to an abandoned bomb shelter. A business card is taped to the door.

L. KRARUP—SCHMUCKDESIGN

The door is cracked open, but I knock anyway. A woman's voice beckons me in.

The studio is cavernous. A series of worktables are pushed against one wall; against the other wall, an aging desktop computer and an assortment of wooden library card catalogs. Tools are everywhere. A rack of hammers in ascending sizes; tongs and files and pliers hanging on a pegboard; a table with soldering irons; a forging anvil, an electric polishing wheel.

The jeweler swivels around toward me. She speaks in German and then in English.

—Can I help you?

She has short gray hair and wears a canvas work apron over her dress, gold spectacles hanging from a chain around her neck. She is eating from a plastic take-out container with a pair of chopsticks.

—Excuse me. A late lunch today—

I tell her I'm trying to identify a piece of my grandmother's jewelry. The jeweler regards me with mild curiosity, wiping her hands on her apron. I hand her the brooch from my bag. She examines it for a moment and looks up at me.

—Your grandmother gave you this? Where are you from?

—California.

The jeweler frowns.

—But your grandmother wasn't from California—

—No. She was English. Part Swedish, really.

The jeweler sits down at her workbench. She switches on a bright halogen lamp, looking at the brooch under a swiveling magnifying glass. Her English is accented but fluent and clear.

—Generally, you would say it's in the Urnes style. There are a few late-Viking Urnes brooches that survive. This is a modern copy of one of them. But not so recent—

The jeweler flips over the brooch. She makes a little sucking sound through her teeth.

—An inscription. Do you know these letters?

—My grandmother's initials. I don't know what the symbol is.

The jeweler goes to a bookcase, pulling a huge paperback from the shelf and paging through it slowly. She murmurs something and hands the book to me. It is a glossy auction catalog in some Scandinavian language. On the page there is a photograph of a brooch identical to my own. The jeweler smiles triumphantly.

—I knew I'd seen that symbol before.

The jeweler thinks the brooch is the work of Ísleifur Sæmundsson, an Icelandic silversmith who worked in the early twentieth century. The symbol engraved after my grandmother's initials is his signature. Ísleifur's work is quite rare, the jeweler says, and she has never seen his pieces outside of a few museums in Scandinavia. She peers over my shoulder as I look at the catalog.

—It's in Danish. Do you want me to translate?

The jeweler takes back the catalog and puts her reading glasses on. She translates haltingly, considering her words as she goes. I take notes as quickly as I can.

—Urnes-style brooch by Ísleifur Sæmundsson. Made in—or around—1928. Based on original found on abandoned farm of Tröllaskógur, Iceland, thought to be eleventh century. The Tröllaskógur brooch is told to have belonged to one of the heroines in *Njáls Saga*. Ísleifur was a talented silversmith who revived the Urnes style in the 1920s. He made jewelry inspired by medieval originals. Few examples of his work survive. A fine example valued at nine thousand kronor.

The jeweler smiles.

—It's a beautiful brooch. And rare. It's probably quite valuable.

—Does the engraving mean it was commissioned in Iceland?

The jeweler sighs. She puts the brooch under the magnifying glass again.

—The initials could be Ísleifur's work. They're well done, they match his signature—

She turns and looks at me.

—But you can't be sure. Any good silversmith could do it.

—Then someone could have bought it from outside Iceland? And had it engraved locally?

The jeweler frowns. —I'm no expert. But I don't think this Ísleifur was so famous then. And Iceland was very far away. I doubt he sold his work in other countries.

—Then someone must have bought the brooch in Iceland.

The jeweler takes off her glasses and shrugs.

—Probably. But why does it matter? You're not going to sell the brooch, are you?

—No.

She nods. —You'll give it to someone one day. But not for money.

I thank the jeweler and ask her if I can give her anything for her help.

—Do you mind if I take a few photos of the brooch? For reference. It helps my work.

The jeweler puts the brooch under her lamp and takes a few photographs with a digital camera. She turns the brooch in her hand for a final moment and looks at me. Then she hands it back. I sling my bag over my shoulder.

—Can I ask you something? What's the story behind this building? It's so damaged.

The jeweler smiles. —I didn't get to Berlin until '87, but I know some of the story.

She tells me that when the building was erected a hundred years ago, it was one of the largest shopping arcades in Europe, running the whole length of Friedrichstraße to Oranienburger Straße. It had an ornate ribbed dome and a system of pneumatic tubes that whisked messages in capsules. Later the building became a department store, then a showroom of modern appliances, home to one of the first television broadcasts in Germany. Then the Nazis took the building: they bricked in the skylights and kept French prisoners in the attic. The building was shelled in the Battle of Berlin and fell into disrepair after the war. The dome was pulled down in 1980. A decade later, the building was due to be leveled when a group of artists saved it from destruction.

—I thought we should save this old place. And not just because I needed somewhere to work.

I nod. —I thought maybe the damage was from the war. But what are the words above your door?

—*Hier sind sie sicher?* I didn't paint that. I went to Copenhagen for a few weeks and when I came back it was there—

—But what does it mean?

She shrugs. —Here you are safe.

The jeweler walks to the door and holds it open for me.

—Just remember, she says. Keep the brooch.

I walk out of the building trying to make sense of what I've learned. The brooch is from Iceland, a country with no connection to my grandmother that I've ever heard. I cross Oranienburger Straße and sit on a bench, rereading the jeweler's translation in my notebook. Halfway through the paragraph, I shut the notebook and start jogging back toward the hostel.

By the time I cross Rosenthaler Platz I'm moving at a dead run. I enter the hostel and take the stairs two steps at a time. Imogen's letters are in my backpack. It takes a moment to find the right page.

17 October 1916

Dearest –

Eleanor & I went to the London Library today. I picked a tall stack of volumes, but sitting down to them, found myself asleep before ten pages were read. I dreamt of wondrous things – the

stave church at Urnes I told you of, but the famous portals were yet
uncarved, so you drew out your knife & we shaped them together –
you carving one creature & I the other, their bodies linked fast. You
lopped off a piece of the portal as a Souvenir for me, and told me to
guard it well, for we were now as joined as two souls could be. Then
the carillon tolled, for it was time for us to enter the church, but
when you put your hand on the door – I awoke.

I take the brooch out, turning it over in my hands. The silver is cold.
I run my finger over the hard flat eye of the dragon, no wider than a
blade of grass.

If only I'd never seen it, I think. *If only I'd never sent for it.*

I go downstairs to the computers and log on to a search engine. I
hesitate for a moment. Then I type in *Urnes*.

At midnight I lie awake in my hostel bed, listening to the streetcars
halting and starting below, the laughter and voices carried up from the
sidewalk cafés. The other guests in my room come and go, sipping and
clinking beer bottles, rummaging through bags under the half-light of a
bedside lamp, changing clothes and setting out into the night.

The brooch is under my pillow. It is only half a secret now. I've spent
four hours reading about Norse art.

The "Urnes style" of the eleventh and twelfth centuries was the
last of several Viking-age styles of animal art. It is named for the stave
church at Urnes, which lies on a rise above the blue waters of the Lustra-
fjord, an inner passageway of the longest fjord in Norway. The intricate
carvings on the church's north portal depict a writhing snake in the jaws
of a four-legged creature. Here we meet the zenith of a fluid and highly
stylized aesthetic, where animals flail in the embrace of desperate combat,
their curling limbs suggesting a physical fate that is at once dynamic and
irrevocable.

I know I could go back to England or go back to France, or even go back home. But I know I won't do any of those things. Since I got off the plane at Heathrow I've been in a world I hardly recognize. I sense a new set of natural laws at work, but I don't understand what governs them.

The later Urnes style survives in objects created throughout the Nordic world: runestones from eastern Sweden, bronze ornaments from Denmark, silver brooches from southern Iceland. Some scholars believe the creatures represent a Christian vision of the struggle between good and evil. Others contend they depict the Norse legend of Ragnarök, a vision of the end of the world marked by natural disasters and a great battle where gods and men perish alike, leaving two human survivors to begin the world anew. Whatever the inspiration behind the Urnes carvings, in them the viewer recognizes a perverse irony: as each creature clashes against its foe, it becomes more like its enemy, until at last they are intertwined in a death embrace, nearly inseparable from each other—marked by their struggle, but bound by their common fate.

What is the force that guides me toward them? What could you call the thing that pushed Ashley and Imogen together and then pulled them apart? Was it the same force that drove the millions of Europe toward cataclysm, to fight for years against an enemy they had no reason to hate? Next to that Ashley and Imogen were just whitecaps on the sea, the debris of a colossal shipwreck.

Among the exponents of the "modern revival" style was Ísleifur Sæmundsson, a silversmith from the remote eastern fjords of Iceland. Working at a great distance from the art centers of Europe, Ísleifur was notable for fusing modernist influences with Viking age motifs. In his brief career (c. 1925–1937) Ísleifur produced work ranging from sleek Art Deco–influenced jewelry to relatively faithful interpretations of Ringerike and Urnes museum pieces.

I had no business dredging up other people's past. And there was nothing I could do eighty years later about two long-dead lovers who ought to have been long forgotten. Maybe it was kinder just to forget about it, to let everything go to dust. Maybe that was how the world softened a cruelty like Ypres, because Ypres and Regent's Park would look the same after eighty years under the Flemish mud.

I throw back the cover from my bed. I take out my notebook.

What I know for sure:

1. In 1916 Imogen wrote to Ashley mentioning the carvings at Urnes—something they'd evidently already discussed.
2. Sometime in the 1920s–30s an Icelandic silversmith named Ísleifur Sæmundsson made an Urnes-style brooch.
3. The brooch was engraved with Charlotte's initials.
4. Someone gave Charlotte the brooch.
5. It's September 24. I have two weeks left.

Dressing in the dark, I take my wallet from my backpack. I go downstairs to the computers and buy a one-way ticket to Reykjavík.

5 May 1924

Camp II, 19,800 feet

East Rongbuk Glacier, Tibet

The sun ratchets above the valley walls, glinting off the fifty-foot ice cliff that dwarfs the camp. Seated on a circle of packing crates, the climbers breakfast on hot tea and tinned biscuits, the green canvas pyramids of the tents swaying beside them in the wind. Ashley takes a tiny bite of biscuit and marmalade. He starts to gag and gulps from a tin of café au lait to get it down. Beside him the colonel composes a press dispatch into a notebook in small, precise longhand.

Price and Mills chew their biscuits quickly. Price dons the oxygen apparatus for testing, looking alien in his pith helmet and glacier goggles and rubber face mask. He sucks at the gas, grasping the length of India rubber tubing as Mills studies the glass-enclosed pressure dial. Mills cranks the wheel atop the steel cylinder.

—Sixty atmospheres. A wonder it's only half leaked. Feel any different?

Price lifts a mittened hand tentatively. He shakes his head and breathes in deeper.

—Bloody sorcery, Ashley croaks.

The colonel looks up from his notebook.

—You know, Walsingham, when we were last up here Price was forever talking about this chum of his. A climber who was up to all kinds of
adventures in Arabia. I could swear I heard he'd discovered the pyramids
of Giza.

—Is that so?

—And yet, here we are, a thousand miles from civilization, listening
to Noel's bloody tales over and again, and I haven't heard you so much
as mention the desert. And I've promised *The Times* twenty dispatches
from the mountain, and it's twenty dispatches they'll get, even if I have
to write profiles of everyone from Price to the bloody cobbler. So give
me the facts. Were you there or not?

—I was.

—Where?

Ashley clears his throat with a hacking cough.

—All over. From Syria to Aden. A touch into Persia. But the interesting bit was in the south, around the edges of the Rub' al Khali desert.
The empty quarter.

The colonel copies this into his notebook, carefully taking down the
correct spelling of Rub' al Khali.

—Good. And what were you doing there? Archaeology?

—I wouldn't call it that. Epistemology would be more accurate. A
bit of metaphysics—

The colonel waves his pencil threateningly.

—Don't toy with me.

—The trouble is that it's hard to explain.

—You give me the facts, I'll do the explaining. Now why'd you go to
begin with?

—I went to Arabia, Ashley sighs, more to get away than to get
somewhere. I was sick of Kenya and didn't want to return to England.
When I got to Arabia I knew no one, didn't speak the language and
didn't know what I was looking for.

—But you were, the colonel insists, looking for something.

—Later on, yes. I was looking for Iram, supposedly a city of a

thousand pillars, lost somewhere in the empty quarter. It's mentioned in
the *Arabian Nights* and the Qu'ran—

—Slow down. I need to get this down.

—There's nothing to say about it, Ashley protests. I didn't find anything. It was a farce.

—You needn't be testy. I only want the facts.

—The facts, Ashley repeats with a grimace. The fact is that I went
after something that doesn't exist. It's as if we went to all the trouble of
climbing this mountain, nearly killing ourselves and spending piles of
money, and when we got to the top there turned out not to be any summit. Not even a mountain, in fact. Not merely that the summit vanished,
but that it had never existed, had been only the product of one's vanity.
And I knew I was a damned fool and should have stuck to climbing. It's
hardly a story for the papers.

The colonel shuts his notebook. He raps his fingers on the oilskin
cover.

—I'm not coming up to Three today, he says curtly. You and Price
take the porters up with Corporal Tebjir. Mills and I follow tomorrow.
For God's sake, don't let the porters tear the equipment to hell with
those crampon spikes. Mind they keep their feet up as they go.

—Sir.

The colonel squints up at the sun and pulls back his jacket sleeve to
consult his wristwatch.

—You fellows had better get moving. As it is, you'll be in the trough
at midday. Bloody time to be there, but I suppose it can't be avoided.

The colonel looks dubiously at Ashley's broad-brimmed felt hat.

—You ought to wear your topee.

—I'll make do. I've been in glacier troughs before.

—Not this one. No atmosphere up there. That trough catches the
noon sun and reflects it right back at you. Air doesn't move at all. Does
odd things to you.

—All right.

—One more thing, the colonel adds. You'll think of something for me to write about you in the paper, and send it down with the next runner. If you don't want Arabia, fine. But you will give me something, whether it's planting coffee in Kenya or collecting bloody postage stamps.

Ashley and Price unscrew crates of equipment for the journey to Camp III, counting out coiled ropes and crimson flags and hollow wooden stakes. A Gurkha corporal summons the porters for inspection, the line of small and sinewy men standing at attention with puffed chests. Many are missing equipment, supplies lost or stolen hundreds of miles behind in snowblown passes or humid jungles. Two porters have no glacier goggles. Several are without stockings in their boots, and one wizened Bhotia stands barefoot in the snow. Ashley issues new equipment from reserves and gives each man a pair of steel-and-leather crampons.

Price stands on a crate to demonstrate the fastening of crampon straps over his boots, the Gurkha translating all the while. The porters fasten the buckles in unison. Ashley circles among the men. Kneeling and tugging Llakpa Chedi's crampon strap, Ashley grimaces in disapproval. Llakpa Chedi is one of the "Tigers," the strongest porters earmarked to carry loads to the highest camp. At this altitude Llakpa Chedi is a stronger climber than Ashley and both men know this.

Ashley makes a squeezing motion with his hands. Llakpa Chedi smiles benignly.

—Too tight, Ashley mutters. You'll constrict your blood. Frostbite.

Ashley loosens the stiff leather strap and refastens the buckle a few eyelets lower. Ashley looks up at Llakpa Chedi's glittering onyx pupils, his smooth tawny face unmarred by the sun.

—You won't be grinning, Ashley wheezes, when you lose your toes.

Price commands the porters to remove the colored woven garters from their legs. He makes a show of mixing the garters in an empty crate, then lays a garter on each load. The porters heft their burdens, tossing huge rucksacks over their shoulders, crouching and fastening leather straps over their foreheads, entire crates balanced on their spines.

The old barefoot porter coos and breaks into song. Price calls to Ashley from the front of the line.

—I'll lead. You bring up the rear.

The colonel barks encouraging words in Nepali, brandishing an aluminum tent stake like a swagger stick. Ashley stands beside him as the long column threads by, khaki-clad forms disappearing through a cleft in the ice wall.

—Do you ever think, Ashley asks the colonel, that they know something we don't?

—Such as?

—Hard to say. But they seem surer of something.

—What on earth could they know?

—They've all kinds of ideas. They say Price is marked for death. Only Sembuchi will walk behind him and only because Sembuchi's madder than a march hare—

—Rubbish, the colonel retorts. Even you know better than to spread such rot, even in jest.

—Sir.

The colonel sets off toward his tent, the stake clasped behind him. Suddenly he stops and looks back at Ashley.

—Walsingham.

—Sir.

—The porters know they are paid to do this, the colonel says. But we do it for sport.

The line of porters snakes along a valley of white shark's teeth, perfect pyramids of sun-bleached ice. Ashley walks behind the swaying basket of the final porter, the load dwarfing the tiny man as it bobs stride by stride. They have entered the trough. The pinnacles begin as mere stumps at the tip of the valley; flowing down they are shaped by sun and wind, evaporated and sculpted into towering spires, their blue-green glimmer never intended to meet the eyes of men.

The party struggles to find a path. In stifling air they grope for direction, halted by the lip of a bottomless black crevasse. They thread a line among an oval-shaped cathedral of emerald spires, the mirrored surfaces reflecting all bearings back upon them. Abruptly the column halts and Llakpa Chedi runs down to the line to Ashley, breathing heavily.

—Price Sahib says to come.

Ashley ascends the long column at double pace, his heart heaving in spasms. The porters stand with their burdens, sweat streaming down their faces, their eyes following Ashley as he passes. Price waits in the shade of a towering fang-shaped berg, Corporal Tebjir panting beside him.

—Rather far enough for the porters, Price says, don't you think?

—I'd say.

Price turns to Tebjir.

—The porters can rest here. Walsingham and I shall flag the rest of the route and come back down. Mind they don't get too settled.

Price and Walsingham set off alone. They follow a route over black moraine, then a field of powdery snow. Finally they step with crampon spikes onto the arrested river itself, a long azure tongue of ice. Ashley runs his hand along a pinnacle, his damp fingers sticking to the ice. Beneath the crystalline surface are shafts of milky white. He wonders if these are the supporting beams of the spire or mere fissures, the signature of countless tons bearing down upon the trough. Price points his ice axe between a pair of huge seracs.

—This one should go.

The climbers rope on to each other, Price in front, Ashley fixing his waist loop. Suddenly Ashley grins.

—The trouble is that I've left everything to you in my will, Hugh. If you drag me into a crevasse—

—Hush.

They push forward, searching for a route through a maze of obstacles. They stop before vast bergs dropped in the center of their path; they ascend ice cliffs with strange enthusiasm, pleased by the rare challenge of genuine climbing. They hammer wooden pickets up ice walls and string rope through the eyelets, spiking red flags to mark a path. The pennants hang limp in the dormant air.

A searing light reflects off all the ice, the rays passing through the smoked lenses of Ashley's goggles, grinding at his brain in tandem with a sharp altitude headache until the effects are inseparable. His head is humming. It melts in time with the thousand-ton pinnacles, drips in sync with the great icicles, drifts along with the imperceptible slide of the glacier.

They stop to rest among a forest of giant seracs, Price unroping and pulling off his smack. Ashley spikes his ice axe in the snow and sits on a heap of dark moraine.

—Something's on your mind, Price says. You've hardly spoken since breakfast.

—Not worth the effort.

—Come now, Price insists, something's grating on you. What is it?

Ashley swigs greedily from his flask. He corks the flask and wipes his brow, speaking in a dry whisper.

—You remember that first lecture at Kensington Gore? During the war.

Price looks at Ashley with surprise.

—Not very well.

—You were on leave. After the lecture you introduced me to a pair of sisters. Soames-Andersson. I spoke with the younger one. It was right before I went to France.

Ashley throws one leg over his knee and chips the ice from the sole of his boot, testing with bare fingertips the sharpness of his crampon spikes. He says nothing more. Price frowns and peers up the glacier, the summit pyramid looming above.

—Something happened with her? You never told me.

—It didn't last. We had a week together and after I got to France we wrote every day. When I was wounded she came to see me in hospital in Albert. We had a row. She left England. One could say she left to get away from me. That was eight years ago.

Ashley blots his forehead with the sleeve of his wind suit.

—I've wondered what it's like to have it with you every day. I wonder if you live with it, if it becomes familiar and you take it for granted until it isn't love anymore.

Price shrugs. —It's like this place. Some days it's too damned familiar. Other days it's strange and wonderful.

Ashley shakes his head.

—A fine bloody waste, isn't it? Wanting something you can't have. Not wanting what you've got.

—You'll get past it.

The climbers rise and pick up their ice axes.

—Shall we rope up? Ashley asks.

—Probably no need—

—Then let's not bother.

Price looks up the glacier.

—I never knew about the girl. What was her name?

—Imogen.

Price nods. —You never told me.

THE QUESTION

Once an hour I leave the hostel and walk to the pay phone in the middle of Rosenthaler Platz to call Mireille. My flight to Reykjavík leaves at eight in the morning, but I didn't get her e-mail until after I'd bought the plane ticket. *Call me as soon as you get this, whenever you get this.* So I go on calling every hour all night, because if I didn't call on the hour I'd call more often.

It's always the same. I cross the street to the pay phone and lift the pink receiver, dropping a one-euro piece into the slot and resting a stack of coins on top of the phone. The phone hesitates, then connects with a faint ringing that goes on and on. I watch the people coming up and down Weinbergsweg with beer bottles in hand, talking in German or English or Spanish. Mireille never picks up.

By three in the morning everyone in Rosenthaler Platz knows me: the girl at the hostel's front desk who gives me a drowsy smile when I walk out; the burly Turkish man who stands in the door of the kiosk smoking cigarettes; the Vietnamese cook at the all-night Asia Imbiss who has given up trying to wave me inside for a meal, but still grins every time he sees me. All of them know I'm going to the pay phone.

At four o'clock the sky is lightening and I'll be leaving for the airport in two hours. This time Mireille picks up.

—I'm sorry, she answers breathlessly. I went out and my phone died. I just got home and plugged it in.

—You said to call right away.

—I know, but I was going crazy waiting. Claire came over and we went for a walk along the river—

—You're back in Paris?

—Yes. Are you still in Berlin?

—I'm about to leave.

The Canadians from my hostel pass by on the sidewalk. They tap the glass casing of the phone and wave at me. I wave back. Mireille's voice is quieter.

—Where are you going?

I grip the receiver with both hands.

—It doesn't matter. It'll be over in a couple weeks, I can go to Paris if you still want me to—

—So you're still searching, she sighs. Tristan, I'm sorry how I acted at the station. I thought if you went away and I went back to Paris I could forget about all this, but it hasn't worked. I need to tell you something. I should have said it while you were in France, but I was afraid to.

Mireille hesitates. I drop in more coins.

—I believe you about the English couple, she says. But all this about the lawyers and the money. *Ce n'est pas possible.* You need to see that. The first night when you told me about it in the bar, I told myself I shouldn't go to Picardie with you. But when we got to the métro I invited you anyway. Maybe I thought that even if you were a little crazy it didn't matter, because I was just happy to be with you. But now that I know you and I care about you, and I see what this is doing to you—

—It's true. I've met the lawyers.

—But what do you really know about them? If there's so much money involved, why don't they find the evidence themselves, or hire someone to find it?

—The trust says they can't hire anyone—

—And they give you only two months? *C'est fou.* And the letters, it was too simple, as if someone put them there for us to find. Tristan, I don't trust the lawyers. I don't trust their story. And I don't like that you're so far away when none of it makes sense. I wish you hadn't left France—

—I can come back.

—That's not the point. The point is I'm worried and I want you to forget about this search. *Cent millions de francs suisses? C'est une connerie.* You must know that, if you can admit it to yourself.

—I know it's real. Ashley and Imogen are real—

—They may have been real once, Mireille says, but they're gone now. You and I, we're the only part of this that matters. You're worried you'll lose the money if you stop looking, but if you keep going—

The phone makes a beeping sound. I drop in a few more coins.

—What's that? Mireille asks.

—I'm at a pay phone. It takes a lot of coins to call a French cell phone. We don't have long.

—Tell me where you're going.

—Iceland.

Mireille says nothing. I press the receiver against my ear, the last coin in my other hand. The reverse has a picture of tree and the inscription LIBERTÉ ÉGALITÉ FRATERNITÉ.

—It doesn't make sense, Mireille finally says. You know it doesn't make sense.

—I can't explain now, you just have to trust me. If you'd seen what I've seen—

The phone beeps again. I drop in the coin.

—This is terrible, Mireille says. Just come back. I don't care how you get here.

I lean against the phone booth. I don't know what to say.

—You'll come, Tristan, won't you?

The phone beeps again.

—Tell me if you'll come, Mireille says. I need to know if I should wait.

The phone chimes and the line goes dead. Cursing, I slam the receiver down. I walk up the street and wander into a deserted park, circling a pond and trying to figure out what I can do. There doesn't seem any choice.

I go back to the hostel and type Mireille an e-mail, promising I'll come to Paris as soon as I can. The message doesn't come out right, so I keep rewriting it over and over, knowing that I'll miss my flight if I don't leave soon. I click SEND and shoulder my backpack, dashing across the street and into the U-Bahn station.

At a bookstore at Tegel Airport I buy a thick copy of *The Icelandic Sagas* and I sit near the airplane gate, my backpack between my knees. The brooch is in my pocket. I open the book and try to concentrate.

10 May 1924

Camp III, 21,000 feet

East Rongbuk Glacier, Tibet

An inch of powdery snow covers every surface in the tent. Ashley and Price sit on the windward side, pushing their backs against the flapping canvas to anchor it in the gale. Their camp is a cluster of tents pitched below an ice cliff at 21,000 feet, only the thin sheet of weatherproofed canvas separating them from the blizzard. Ashley sits with his legs in his sleeping bag, the gabardine shell stiff and coated with ice.

The wind eases for moment, then rises to a scream, hammering the canvas until Ashley cannot believe only air and snow are striking the tent. The flapping is so hard that nothing but a yell can be heard between them.

—Shall I check the guylines? Ashley bellows.

—No, Price calls. We'd only get more snow.

Their eyes follow the sputtering lantern hung from the tent ceiling. It swings and pitches and the shadows in the tent shift with the wind. They are too exhausted to yell much, but it is too dangerous to sleep. The climbers wait, hoping it will pass.

➤══ ⊂══➤

Half an hour later the wind lowers enough to allow talking. Somervell's face appears in their shelter's door, his eyebrows and beard crusted with snowflakes. He squeezes inside, clawing the snow from his collar.

—What's the verdict? A stroll up to Four in the morning?

Ashley coughs into a dirty handkerchief. He looks at Somervell, whispering hoarsely.

—Hugh's sulking. He left his swimming togs at Phari.

No one laughs. The climbers have been battered by storms for five days, the winds too strong for travel, the nights too cold for sleep. The weather is worse than on any previous expedition and they do not know why. The porters believe the expedition is doomed, that it is being punished by the mountain gods as a warning. Even the British know they will have to retreat soon if the weather does not break.

Price pries open a tin of strawberry jam.

—We must eat something—

He gathers snow from the tent floor and drops it in a tin bowl, dumping the frozen jam on top. He stirs the icy reddish mixture with a large spoon and passes it Ashley. Ashley takes a tentative bite.

—Not half bad.

They pass the bowl around and Somervell picks a book off the floor. *Three Tragedies*. The leather binding is soft from use, the gilding nearly worn off the page ends.

—Surely it's Walsingham's turn?

Ashley shakes his head, touching his throat.

—Not over this racket.

Somervell flips to where they left off in *Hamlet* and begins to read, his voice rising and falling not for theatrical effect but to overcome the changing volume of the wind. Ashley watches Somervell's hand tremble as he reads. They are all shivering.

The wind returns to its previous strength and they can no longer hear. The three men lean into the windward side of the tent, the wind lashing their backs as it rises to a deafening howl. The lamp blows out. It is pitch-black inside, the canvas snapping and fluttering as the Sherpas call anxiously from the next tent. Price yells back in Nepali.

Something hard strikes Ashley's shoulder through the canvas, stunning him. A rock or a piece of ice. He wonders if the tents will tear and he pictures the scene: huge flurries of snow pouring in, the swirling maelstrom of sleeping bags and foodstuffs and equipment, then the tent itself gone, carrying off the climbers or leaving them naked beneath the glow of the clouded moon. It would be death. They are so far from base camp, and base camp so far from civilization, that they might as well be the only men in Tibet, the only men in the world. Price bellows to the other climbers.

—Sounds like Fritz has brought out his Maxim.

Ashley yells hoarsely in the darkness.

—We'll never get to the third act.

Hours pass before the wind calms and Somervell returns to his tent. Ashley lies on his back in the dark, his eyes open. He feels the rock below him jutting into his shoulders. He gets up to realign his kapok mattress, replacing the sleeping bag on top. He lies back down and curses.

—I swear there's a fucking boulder right under me. Who cleared the ground here?

Price chuckles in his sleeping bag.

—It wasn't any sahib. Want to swap places?

—No.

Ashley closes his eyes, listening to the flapping of canvas, a sound of clinking metal. A guyline must have broken from its anchor, freeing the metal fitting to flail among the stones.

—Someone ought to anchor that, Price whispers.

—They certainly ought to.

They fall silent. The unanchored canvas keeps flapping.

—Bloody freezing, Ashley mutters. I don't suppose there's a spare fleabag in the other tents?

—I doubt it. Would you fetch it if there was?

Ashley turns onto his side, trying to avoid the sharpest stones beneath him. Occasionally the wind looses a clump of snow upon his face and he sweeps it off clumsily with a wet mitten.

—You remember, Ashley says suddenly, the girl I was talking about. Soames-Andersson.

—Of course.

—It was my fault she went off. I didn't know what I had, nor how to keep it.

They hear footfalls outside their tent, Somervell walking by to fix the guyline. The flapping ceases. The footsteps pass by again.

—I only wanted to say that, Ashley adds. I'd never said it before.

—All right.

Ashley coughs for a spell and sits up, taking the canteen from inside his sleeping bag. He tugs the cork out and inverts the bottle, but only a few drops trickle into his mouth. The snow has not yet melted. He plugs the canteen and lies down.

—There's more, Ashley wheezes. Something happened before we sailed.

—The girl?

—She sent me a telegram. I hadn't heard from her in years.

—What did it say?

—Hardly anything.

Price shifts in his bag. —Are you all right? Shall I light the lamp?

—I'm fine. I'll clam up.

Ashley has another coughing fit. He hacks some fluid into his handkerchief and lies back down, breathing more freely than he has for hours.

—Maybe you ought to go after her, Price says.

There is a long pause.

—It wouldn't work.

—Perhaps you ought to try anyway.

—Perhaps.

—We really ought to sleep.

—I know.

Ashley coughs and turns onto his back. He feels the sting of an ice fragment melting through his silk undershirt into his ribs.

—How old are you, Ashley? Twenty-eight?

—Twenty-nine.

—That's still young.

—It doesn't feel young.

—Of course it doesn't, Price says. But it might if you let it.

Ashley laughs and the laugh turns into a wheeze. He says good night to Price and pulls up the collar of his sleeping bag, trying to recall the exact words of the telegram. There is the sound of flapping canvas again and he knows another guyline has come loose in the wind.

THE ISLAND CITY

The flight lands at Keflavík Airport, thirty miles from the Icelandic capital. I look out the window as the airplane taxis slowly across the tarmac. The runway is slick with rainfall, the grass a deep rich green.

The halls of the terminal are silent. There are huge circular windows, portholes to the wild country beyond. Collecting my bag from the carousel, I pass through an empty customs gate. At an ATM I withdraw nearly the last of my savings in a currency I've never seen before.

I step outside the automatic doors into the open air. It's bracingly cold. In one day I've gone from autumn to nearly winter. I board an express bus for the city center, but halfway through the journey the driver pulls onto the shoulder without explanation.

The passengers get off and stand around the barren strip of highway, smoking cigarettes or talking in low voices. From each side the black asphalt drops to fields of broken lava crowned with moss and lichen. I pass from the shelter of the bus and the wind strikes me, flapping my jacket and nearly toppling me. The driver leans against the bus behind me lighting a cigarette. He sweeps his hand forward, signaling I ought to walk on.

I step off the road onto jagged slabs of lava, straining to keep my balance as I hop from one stone to another. The fragments are jet-black, the lichen green and brown and orange. I walk twenty yards, then fifty. I swivel around. The lava and lichen stretch out the same in every direction.

Reykjavík is a strange and lonely place. It seems barely a city at all, only an arrangement of colorful houses perched around a bay, their corrugated roofs standing sentry against the driving wind and rain. Dark and savage hills loom above, foreboding the wildness of the country beyond.

One walk along the windswept harbor and I know I'll need a warmer coat. I rummage through an indoor flea market, choosing an olive green German army parka. The elderly vendor accepts my money and peers knowingly at me through thick glasses, as if we share some deep secret.

—It is very warm, she confides.

But when I step outside, I realize the coat barely protects me from the freezing wind.

I'm staying at a new youth hostel on a hill, spotless and shining. On a dining table in the glass-enclosed kitchen I make a list of all the ways I might progress in my search. The list has twenty-three items. I have eleven days until October 7.

I speak to jewelers and antiques dealers, even a curator at the National Museum of Iceland. They tell me little of Ísleifur Sæmundsson, only the same few anecdotes that appear in auction catalogs and surveys of Icelandic crafts, none of which I can read myself. These sources record that Ísleifur was born in 1872 and died in 1936. He made elegant pieces of jewelry heavily influenced by the late Urnes style, but produced few works and seems not to have made his living as a jeweler. He was born in a village called Seyðisfjörður in the Eastfjords—a collection of remote inlets on the far side of the country—but the place of his death isn't recorded, nor the location where he produced his work.

—You're not even sure where he lived?

The curator sighs. —He was a minor jeweler. He probably stayed in the Eastfjords his whole life. Back then, it was nothing but tiny fishing villages. No one cared where he was from—

—But this wasn't even that long ago.

The curator shakes his head.

—We're lucky to know anything about him at all.

I walk to the National Registry to consult records of births and deaths. I speak to people at the Swedish, Danish and British embassies, at Reykjavík City Hall and every relevant bureau of the Icelandic government. I find nothing. It's now September 29: I've got only eight days left, and though I feel a strange conviction that Imogen came here, I know it has no real evidence behind it. If I'm going to leave Iceland, I'll have to leave soon.

At a vast cemetery beside the university, I walk among the chipped headstones, many of them centuries old, the inscriptions illegible, the chiseled characters worn smooth or blanketed in lichen. Because of Icelandic naming conventions, there's a solemn repetition to the names: *Eriksson, Eriksdóttir, Stefánsson, Stefánsdóttir.* I take a few pictures and walk to the newer part of the cemetery to look for Soames or Andersson, knowing this is hopeless.

Early the next morning I ride the bus to the Icelandic Genealogical Society, where I have a long chat with an amiable old man who once lived in New York. He seems troubled by the difficulties of my research.

—You don't know where in Iceland this woman lived?

—No. Maybe in the east.

—And you don't know when she came here?

—I don't know if she came at all—

—So all you have is her name.

—She might have changed her name.

The old man looks at me with sympathy.

—You may never prove she came here, but just the same you'll never know she didn't come. There are too many records. Suppose you knew the name of this woman, and the town she lived in, and when she lived there. You'd search the births and deaths and marriages, of course. But you'd still have the census, the church records, the courts, the tax and property records, the newspapers, medical charts, the passenger lists—

—Passenger lists?

—From the old steamships. Those are worst of all. No indexes, just thousands of names listed by ship. In your case, if this woman came before the war, she must have come by ship. But unless you know the name and date of the ship, it's pointless—

—Where are they?

—Where are what?

—The passenger lists. I want to look at them.

It takes me several minutes to persuade the old man. Finally he takes out a scrap of copy paper and writes the address in pencil.

—If you must, they're at the National Library, near the university.

He lifts the slip of paper, dangling it in the air.

—But if I were a young man again, I'd find a better way to waste an afternoon—

I ride another bus to the National Library, where I page through massive hardbound lists of merchant ships, searching for passenger lines that ran from Europe to Iceland. I learn that the steamship company Eimskipafélag Íslands sailed between Britain and Iceland, with two ships from Leith to Reykjavík via Copenhagen, and another two ships from Hull to Reykjavík. These ships had bad luck. Three of the four were lost to war: the *Gullfoss*, seized by Germans in Copenhagen in 1940, the *Goðafoss* torpedoed by U-300 off the Icelandic coast in 1944, the *Dettifoss* torpedoed by U-1064 near the Firth of Clyde in 1945. At the reference counter I order the microfilm passenger lists for these ships from the 1920s and 1930s.

—And do you know if any ships went from Germany to Iceland?

The librarian furrows her brow, scrutinizing my request list.

—Maybe the Hamburg America Line. But we don't have their

records here. There were other Danish and Norwegian ships that came, I can bring you their lists—

Soon I realize the old man was right. The reels of microfilm are endless and organized only by each ship's port of entry. I roll through them quickly, barely looking at the passenger names, only the vessel names and the shipping lines. I have no idea when Imogen would have come or where she would have come from, but I scroll on anyway. I see that a Danish line called Det Forenede Dampskibs-Selskab ran a ship called *Primula* from Copenhagen to Reykjavík. Its lists were entered in longhand, the columns in English or Danish or Icelandic with the passenger's name, age and sex, the ports of embarkation and disembarkation, sometimes their profession.

Some of the names are familiar. *Gunnar Andersson, 38, Húsavík, Fiskimaður.* I find another ship that called at the Eastfjords, a steamer called the *Nova* of the Norwegian line Det Bergenske Dampskibsselskab. The line ran from Bergen to the Faroe Islands, stopping at Eskifjörður in eastern Iceland en route to Reykjavík. The *Nova's* lists run back only to the mid-1930s. I pull out another box of microfilm and I'm about to change the reels when I see a name at the bottom of the illuminated screen.

Charlotte Derby. 18. Southampton, England. Eskifjörður.

It means nothing. I know it means nothing. An English girl with the same first name as my grandmother traveling to eastern Iceland in July 1936. A coincidence only because the age is right, because my grandmother was born in 1917. But why would she go to Iceland? I lean back in my swivel chair, looking at the ceiling. I imagine Charlotte coming of age in England, boarding a steamer for Norway and then for Iceland to visit the woman she called her aunt, Imogen preparing for her visit and commissioning the brooch from Ísleifur, the initials engraved on the reverse—

It's absurd. Charlotte would have no reason to travel under an assumed surname, and if she did she could just as well have changed her first name. There's also the obvious fact that *Charlotte* is a common

name and common names are bound to occur in these lists, even English names. I scan the lists for familiar names. There's nothing else in
the *Nova*'s lists, but forty minutes later I find an Eleanor M. Cotter, age
forty-eight, sailing from Hull to Reykjavík on the *Goðafoss* in 1934. An
hour later I find a Charles Bell, age nineteen, sailing from Leith to Reykjavík on the *Bruarfoss* in 1929.

I switch off the machine. I'm grasping at nothing, names and dates
and ports pulled out of a hat. There must be dozens of people named
Eleanor and Charles and Charlotte in these lists, and if I looked long
enough I'd probably find an Imogen. I no longer even believe in my own
theories. I take the microfilm reels back to the desk.

Back at the hostel I check my e-mail, but Mireille hasn't written me
back. The only message is from Khan.

> *James and I were pleased to hear of the information you've
> uncovered; we would be interested to see the documents with regard
> to the contact between the two parties in 1924. He expressed
> concern, however, that the chain of research you are following
> cannot lead you to the evidence required for distribution of the
> estate. James reminds you of your time constraint, and he suggests
> reappraising your options before proceeding—particularly as far
> afield as Iceland.*
>
> *As October is fast approaching, I think it would be helpful to
> schedule a call with James at your earliest convenience. Please let
> me know when you are available.*
>
> *Yours Sincerely,*
> *Geoffrey Khan*

I write to Khan that I'm already in Iceland, but I'll call the law firm
soon. Then I log on to my bank account. I have only three hundred dollars left and no ticket off this island. My credit card shows an unpaid

balance of $612, with $88 of available credit. I can't ask my family for money to continue this absurd search. Nor can I get anything from Prichard until I've found real evidence, and anyway he doesn't seem to approve of my trip to Iceland.

I know I should deal with all this by economizing, by organizing my research. But I've lost my confidence. The next morning I realize that all the archives are closed for the weekend. I go back to my bunk and lie there for an hour, feeling close to a breakdown. When I finally get out of bed I stay in the hostel all day, running aimless Web searches and paging through my folder of photocopies, my mood swinging wildly from moment to moment.

At dusk I go to a public pool near the hostel. It's a clear but windy night. An attendant takes a few coins from me and hands me a stiff white towel stamped with the city's logo. I bathe myself carefully according to diagrams posted below the showerheads, then I pull on my pair of cut-off corduroy shorts. I wade into the empty indoor pool, swimming a few laps of breaststroke. Through the windows I see the outdoor hot tubs, their columns of steam curling in the wind.

I'd left Mireille for this. Before I left California I'd even lied to my own father about this trip. The only people I'd listened to were the lawyers and now I wasn't even listening to them.

I rise dripping from the pool and push through the glass doors, sprinting barefoot toward a hot tub. The air is freezing. I plunge into the churning water, floating on my back as I watch the steam lift toward the stars. A few minutes later the jets switch off of their own accord. Above the swirling vapor there is a curtain of shifting blue-green light in the sky.

—The northern lights.

The water laps around me, half of my body freezing and half scalded. I wonder if the lights are pointing in any particular direction.

✦ ✦

Later in the night I walk downtown, swigging gin and tonic I've mixed in a soda bottle. I climb the main shopping street among crowds of young people, picking out a well-dressed group as they turn onto a side street. They go into a ramshackle bar decorated with Christmas lights and painted palm trees. The electric sign says SIRKUS. I follow them in.

It's after eleven and there are only a few people inside. Everyone is dipping glasses of punch from a huge bowl on the bar. I dip myself a glass and sit down. A girl with a doll-like face passes by me and suddenly glances back as if she recognizes me. She's holding someone's hand and she steadies herself with great effort. The girl stares at me and says something in Icelandic. I tell her I don't speak the language.

—You're drinking my punch, she says.

—I'm sorry. I didn't know.

—This is my party, but I don't know you.

—I'm very sorry.

The girl shakes her head slowly, leaning in toward me with a breathy whisper.

—It's my birthday, she confesses. Drink up.

The girl walks on with her companion. They open an unmarked door and disappear inside. I take a sip of punch. It's strong and must have plenty of rum, but it tastes good.

A strange thickness builds in my throat until I begin to feel queasy. I must have drunk the gin too quickly. I go into the bathroom, but as I walk to the toilet stall I glimpse an intruder in the mirror. But I'm the intruder. I lean toward the mirror running my hand along my face, not believing it's my own. My eyes seem wider than I'd imagined, my nose thinner and more pointed. I turn from the mirror and go into the toilet stall, sitting down for a few minutes. But it only makes me feel sicker. Finally I bend over the toilet and throw up, heaving out the whole contents of my stomach. I flush the toilet and sit back down, leaning against the cold metal walls of the stall. My eyes are shut, my head dense with muddled images.

A damp cellar near Polygon Wood in 1917, with no fire and the soldiers wrapping wet socks around their necks to dry; the dark purple wallpaper of the Picardie bedroom, Mireille lying in the blackness with her grey eyes open, listening to my footsteps up and down the hallway; a candle lantern swinging in a snowbound tent on Everest, mittened fingers struggling to write on pages propped over the knees, the pencil skating across the paper; the blood-red house at Leksand, the tin of letters wrapped in paper and addressed to England but never sent; the lapping black water of the Eastfjords, two hundred and fifty miles away, a shuttered window beside the waves.

There's a pounding on the stall door. I rise slowly and wipe my face with toilet paper, unlatching the door. The bathroom is packed elbow to elbow with young men. Someone calls at me in Icelandic. Another person taps my shoulder, but I ignore them and walk out.

The bar is packed now, the air hot and steamy. I check my watch: 2:14. I've slept for two hours. I edge my way upstairs, taking the last empty seat on a couch beside a young couple. They smile at me and move their coats so I can sit. I light a cigarillo. Moments pass and the young man beside me taps me on the shoulder, speaking in Icelandic first, then in English.

—Are you all right?

—Yeah.

—You were sleeping.

—I guess I drank too much.

—That's OK, he says. So does everyone else.

The cigarillo is still lit. I take another drag. My eyes begin to close again, but I sit up straight and try to stay awake. I think about what Mireille said, of what I'm losing by going on with this. It's more than just her, because I can't imagine going back to my old life in California. But I'm also tired of this life.

I'm sick of traveling. I'm sick of searching, sick of questions I can't answer, sick of disappointing Mireille and disappointing Prichard, sick of eating bread and cheese from my backpack and filling water bottles in public restrooms, sick of counting foreign coins, sick of war and dead lovers and the billion cruelties of the past that never, ever could be set right, not by a thousand of me circling Europe for a thousand years.

I collect my coat and go out into the cold. It's a long walk back to the hostel.

✦═ ═✦

15 May 1924

Rongbuk Monastery, 16,700 feet

Rongbuk Valley, Tibet

The expedition has been beaten off the mountain by terrible weather, forced to retreat into the Rongbuk Valley below. They have come to seek the blessing of holy men. They carry gold brocade and a wristwatch for gifts. The true present, the yakload of cement, had been delivered a fortnight before.

They trail past a great stone chorten, its golden paint flaking off in the wind; they file in silence beneath a web of flapping prayer flags, approaching the low whitewashed rooms of the monastery.

The battered men stand in the open court: British, Gurkhas, Sherpas, Bhotias. Climbers, noncommissioned officers, porters, syces, muleteers, cooks, a lone cobbler. Seventy men. In grimed palms they clasp a pair of rupee coins as offerings, rationed out an hour before from the expedition's oaken coffers.

A monk leads the British and their interpreter up a narrow staircase. Unseen trumpets begin a ceaseless drone. The deep note continues without interruption: as one trumpeter exhausts his breath, another begins to blow. The nails of the climbers' boots skid on the stone steps.

Cymbals clash in time, marking the intervals. At first the British can see nothing in the dark, then a few rays of window light upon the worn steps.

—Some of those trumpets, Noel remarks, are made of human thighbones. They've drums made of skulls, with human skin on top.

Ashley peers through a window to a man braying a trumpet on a landing below.

—Looks like brass to me, he whispers hoarsely.

They enter a cramped dining room lit only by a few butter lamps. Amid the blackness they make out an array of small dishes set on a low table. The British sit awkwardly upon cushions on the floor.

—What is it? Mills says. I can't see.

—Macaroni and spices, the colonel says. What else?

The British eat with lacquered chopsticks, the monks replenishing the empty bowls. The colonel glances at Ashley's bowl, shaking his head.

—A bowl and a half, the colonel says. You'll spark a riot. The head lama has been dressing and preparing for two days.

—How many have you had?

—Three, the colonel says. And I'm cooked.

Ashley lays his chopsticks across his bowl. His right leg has fallen asleep and he struggles to find a better posture.

—What's the lama like?

—Damned impressive fellow, Noel says. Supposed to be the reincarnation of a god. Spent thirteen years in one of those hermit's cells in the valley.

Mills lifts his chopsticks to the hovering shaft of light. The red lacquer is chipping at the ends, the wood mottled with indentations.

—Tooth marks, Mills murmurs.

—They're probably older than you, Noel says.

Noel is on his seventh bowl. He grins and keeps eating.

⊷⊏⊐ ⊏⊐⊶

The British file into the small chamber. A low ceiling; the scent of juniper smoldering in an urn. Monks sit on benches beneath huge bronze effigies, blowing horns and pounding drums. A pair of monks hold taut a piece of silk, screening something behind. The interpreter presses his face to the floor in reverence. The English stand silent, clutching their hats by the brim. No one speaks.

Slowly the monks lower the screen. A figure is revealed, fixed in Buddha posture and clad in rich silk gowns, the visage staring past. The trumpets drone on. The face is golden, expressionless, beautiful. The lama perceives the British, but does not react to them. No one speaks.

The screen is raised, the figure obscured once more. The trumpets cease. The British look at one another, bowing awkwardly to no one in particular. They file out of the room.

Now they all feast. The porters drink *chang* and buttered tea and further bowls of noodles. The British hate the tea and claim the yak butter is rancid, but they gulp it down before the monks' eyes.

Ashley is sweating even as his body feels chilled. He excuses himself, navigating a maze of corridors and small chambers until he passes through the front gate into the bright sun. A syce leans against the outer wall, standing vigil over the mules and swinging a whip of yak wool in the wind. He extends his tongue in greeting.

Ashley sits down on a crumbling half-wall, his stomach churning. A few minutes later Somervell emerges from the monastery with a cheerful gait, his hands in his pockets, his scarf flapping wildly.

—Something disagrees with you?

Ashley glances up at Somervell.

—That wretched tea. I don't mind the macaroni, but the stench of that rancid butter makes me sick. And I drank a whole cup, God knows why.

Somervell nods. —Perhaps you'd as well get it out.

Ashley unwinds his muffler, walking a few yards to a cluster of dusty rocks. He bends over and lets the tea come out of him onto the stones. He returns to his seat on the wall.

—Blast, Ashley says. Have you got a handkerchief? My last was nicked—

Somervell hands him a handkerchief and Ashley wipes his mouth.

—We ought to have given them handkerchiefs, Ashley says. More useful than brocade.

Somervell rests his hand on Ashley's shoulder.

—Let me have a look at you. Your face has gone raw.

—No worse than anyone else's.

—Doctor's orders. Indulge me.

Reluctantly Ashley lifts his face to Somervell. His skin is broken and scaled, the color going from pink to red to white.

—Have you shown Hingston?

—No.

—Naughty boy. How does it feel?

Ashley coughs. —Perfect bliss.

—What have you been putting on it?

—The glacier cream. But it runs off in the sun.

—Use the Sechehaye. It's a firmer compound. Been greasing your face at night?

—Yes sir.

Somervell leans back. —Fair enough. Keep it greased. And out of the sun when possible.

Ashley wraps his muffler around his throat. Somervell squints at him.

—Your voice is getting worse.

—Wasn't any good to begin with.

—How's that cough of yours?

—Not too bad.

—It sounds ghastly.

Ashley wipes his face again and folds the handkerchief neatly into a square.

—No worse than yours.

—My cough is wretched, Somervell says. But you've a precondition. Weren't you wounded in the throat?

—That, Ashley says, was in the war. This is a climbing holiday.

—You may have frostbitten the lining of your throat. It could block up and strangle you. If the cough worsens, you must tell Hingston. The colonel too. It's not only for your sake.

Somervell strokes his beard thoughtfully.

—You push yourself too hard, Walsingham. You're very strong, but no one's that strong. It's none of my business, but you can't forever be taking up someone else's slack to impress the colonel, or trying to better Price at every turn. The weather this season has been appalling, and what's worse is that we can't predict it. Sometimes on Everest you simply must turn back. You and Price each make splendid climbing partners, but I worry what you might try together—

—It doesn't matter, Ashley counters. Even if the colonel puts me in one of the summit parties, it wouldn't be with Hugh.

—He'll put you in. I believe you've won the colonel over. He thinks you're mad, mind you, but he knows you're damned fit and keen as mustard. I'd wager the first party will be the colonel and me with the gas, the second party you and Price without. We're to be the capable pair, you two will be the irresistible force. Any idea what the immovable object is?

Somervell shakes his head.

—I don't like this funny weather, he continues, it's worse than ominous. We ought to have packed it in yesterday, but no one wants to sulk back to England as failures a third time. And no one wants to have to come here again. The colonel worries what the press will say, what the committee will say. Everyone expects us to triumph, though they don't know a damned thing about it. Price needs to climb the mountain so he can do his lecture tours, and besides, he must get past Everest before it ruins him. So they need the summit. But I can't see why you should risk your neck in the same way. Do you follow me?

—Certainly.

—Of course, you'll do your duty and more, Somervell adds. All I'm saying is don't let Hugh lead you further than you think you should go. Everest will always be here, she's been here millions of years. This may not be the year. For God's sake, it may not even be possible to climb her.

Ashley looks at Somervell. He extends the soiled cloth to him.

—Want your handkerchief back?

Somervell grins. —Clever fellow. Keep it.

The British are seated on a bench, spectators to a troupe of writhing dancers. Ashley follows the huge grinning masks of the dancers with grim fascination, understanding nothing of the ritual. Noel runs his cine camera; Somervell takes notes of the percussive music on a sheaf of staff paper brought from England. The performance ends and Ashley and Price help Noel pack his camera equipment into cases. Noel puts his hands on Ashley's and Price's shoulders.

—There's something I have to show you chaps.

Noel fetches the expedition's interpreter and they follow an ancient lama through a series of windswept hallways. In a dark passage the lama halts along an inner wall and gestures. Noel kneels beside him.

—It's new. Done since the last expedition.

The lama speaks to the British in a grave voice. Ashley squats beside the painting, making out the great pyramid of Everest, the plume of cloud and ice streaming past its pinnacle. A fallen white man lies below the peak, speared by some mysterious object. The figure is surrounded by demons and barking dogs, by lions and wild men. Ashley turns to the interpreter.

—What is he saying?

The interpreter clutches his dusty bowler hat. He translates in a tentative voice, barely audible over the animated words of the lama.

—The holy lama says you have come to violate the goddess mountain. But the mountain will destroy you.

The lama keeps speaking. The interpreter lowers his eyes into his hat.

—The holy lama says the mountain is very strong. She can take men as she pleases.

Ashley looks back at the fresco. The lions are painted the same color as the snow. The lama is waving at the image of the fallen European, his voice forceful.

—Go on, Ashley says.

—The mountain has forced you back before. She shall force you back again. The mountain can open her sides and swallow men. Against her you are powerless.

Price shakes his head. —They said the same thing last time.

Ashley looks at the lama. Only a few teeth remain in his mouth. His shoulder and arm are bare to the elements, the skin sooted from the smoke of dung fires. He stares back at Ashley without flinching.

—The holy lama asks you something. He asks why you suffer and let others suffer for this pointless thing.

Noel nods to the interpreter. —Tell him we're on a pilgrimage. We've come to the world's highest mountain to be closer to heaven. To be as close to heaven as we can in this life.

Noel comes to his feet grinning.

—Tell the lama I'm fasting and I've given up yak butter until we reach the summit. It's my sacrifice for the pilgrimage.

The interpreter finishes translating. No one speaks. Suddenly the lama bows his head, a lone tooth emerging from his smile. He continues down the corridor, Noel and the interpreter following behind.

Price and Ashley linger beside the fresco, Price kneeling in the dirt. He drags a match tip against the rough wall, holding the flame against the mountain's summit.

—It's strange, Price says. The picture's reversed.

Ashley nods and stands up.

—Probably the colonel wants us back—

Price runs the match along the painted ridge.

—Don't you see? Those are the steps on the ridge. But they're on the wrong side.

—You're right, Ashley says. But let's be off.

Price shakes the match out and drops it into the dust. He follows Ashley down the dim corridor.

—It isn't pointless, Price whispers.

THE RING ROAD

⊸⊜ ⊜⊶

I'm up before dawn in the hostel dormitory, packing my backpack as quietly as I can. It's Tuesday and the estate will pass on Thursday; I can't stay in Reykjavík any longer. I know my leads are worthless: the jeweler Ísleifur Sæmundsson who was born in Seyðisfjörður, the nineteen-year-old Charlotte Derby listed on a steamer bound for Eskifjörður. But both those towns are in the Eastfjords and I'd rather go after something than nothing at all.

A young Norwegian snores on the bunk above me. I wrap my spare clothes protectively around the folder holding the letters, then stuff my sleeping bag and books and toiletries into the backpack, cramming a plastic bag of food into the top.

Outside at the bus stop I wait for a long time. When the bus finally arrives I take a window seat, riding among sober commuters half-dozing or reading the newspaper. We travel north toward the suburbs, passing bright red and yellow houses with shining steel roofs. The clouds to the east are burning off with the rising sun.

I take *The Icelandic Sagas* from my bag and page to the introduction.

The world of the Icelandic Sagas is complex and multi-layered, with the same agents alternately acting as forces for good or evil. The writing style tends towards the terse and impersonal, with little explanation of why events occur. Things happen; fate is rarely questioned. Personalities are shown through action, seldom through analysis. Relationships between individuals are complex, defined by friendship, blood, marriage, and immediate geography.

Certain themes define the Sagas, particularly the contending forces of character, honor, and luck. These devices compete to determine the outcome of the story. Characters must often and at great disadvantage overcome fantastic enemies. Life is short and uncertain; men's worth is determined by glory in arms. Any slight to one's honor or that of one's family must be avenged, whether by blood or money. Men are easily goaded to fatal violence over a perceived insult.

The supernatural plays a major role as well. Oneiric elements are often featured, frequently in the guise of prophetic dreams. The concept of luck is simple, particularly as portrayed in *Njál's Saga*: one is born with a certain store of luck. When that luck runs out, one is doomed.

However subtly it may be posed, a critical question faces the protagonists of the Sagas. Do they have the character to surmount their difficulties, or do they succumb to the vices of avarice, jealousy, pride or cowardice?

The bus approaches the end of the route, the remaining passengers exiting at the final stops until I'm alone. The driver eyes me through his rearview mirror. The bus makes a series of sharp turns and halts in a parking lot. All the doors swing open.

I walk off in the direction where I hope to find the ring road, the main highway that circles the whole island, running along the north coast to the Eastfjords and curving back along the south. I take out my free tourist map of Reykjavík and examine the city's northern periphery, orienting the sheet with my antique compass. The part of the ring road I'm trying to reach is covered by an ad for glacier tours of Vatnajökull.

414 🔑 Justin Go

—You couldn't even call this hopeless, I whisper.

I fold up the map and search for the highway by instinct. An hour of wandering brings me to a long entrance ramp; I choose a spot at the base where I'm visible for some distance and there's a wide shoulder to pull over. I stand up straight and extend my thumb, thinking of my haggard appearance: an army-surplus parka, worn brown pants and muddy sneakers, an enormous backpack. I've never hitchhiked before.

The cars speed by at forty miles an hour, punching gusts of wind at me. I don't look at the faces of the drivers. A sedan passes and its brake lights go red. I swing my bag over my shoulder and sprint up the road.

The first man who picks me up is tall and gangly, his cropped hair graying at the edges. He says he is a troubadour, a traditional entertainer in Icelandic song, and he bellows a few bars as proof of this. His voice is deep and impressive.

—Do you believe me now?

—I do.

The troubadour repairs credit card readers on gas station pumps throughout the country. He is from the Vestmannaeyjar, an archipelago off the southern coast.

We drive through green and rolling hills. The road twists and climbs to higher ground where the moss and dirt have been dusted in soft new snow. There are few other cars.

—The first snow of the year, he murmurs.

The troubadour sings folk songs to pass the time, his huge hands gripping the steering wheel. He tells me the grim tale of a serial killer who picked up hitchhikers.

—Maybe you're the killer, he says, winking at me. But maybe I am.

We stop at a service station straddling the junction of two roads. The troubadour is going the other way. We go into the convenience store and he offers to buy me a hot dog three times before he accepts that I don't want one. His generosity makes me embarrassed about how sorry

I've been feeling for myself. He asks the man behind the counter for a piece of paper and writes down his phone number. He slides the paper toward me, patting a huge hand on my back.

—You should be able to get another ride here. Call me if you get into trouble.

The town of Akureyri lies on the north coast of Iceland about halfway between Reykjavík and the Eastfjords. I get there after nightfall, riding in a young woman's station wagon along a narrow inlet of dark water, the dim lights of the town reflected below. The woman drops me off at the youth hostel. I'd like to keep going, but I doubt anyone picks up hitch-hikers at night.

Akureyri has six thousand inhabitants and feels even smaller than that. The bearded clerk at the youth hostel sits behind the counter turning the knob on an ancient color television. I put my passport on the counter and ask for a hostel bed.

—Took the bus up here?

—I hitchhiked.

The clerk raises his eyebrows, tossing a room key on the counter.

—You're the only one here.

I ask if I can make a collect call. The clerk passes an old rotary phone across the desk. He interrupts his television viewing to stare at me as I ask the operator if I can be connected to England. The secretary at Twyning and Hooper recognizes my voice at once. I'm transferred to Prichard.

—The elusive Mr. Campbell, Prichard says. You're quite the enigma here. Even Geoffrey can't explain what you're doing in Iceland.

—She was here. I know she was here.

—If you'll excuse me, Prichard sighs, you don't know that for certain. This brooch of yours proves nothing. Have you found any other evidence?

—Nothing watertight—

—Mr. Campbell, you've only two days left. And I cannot see how this brooch, or anything in Iceland for that matter, will lead to evidence that connects you to Ms. Soames-Andersson.

—It's all part of the same problem. And it's all I've got to follow.

—No doubt it is, but you won't solve all this by Thursday. In view of that, we've prepared certain arrangements. You recall that I'm forbidden to give details of the Walsingham trust except as necessary. But I can reveal to you now that the standard of evidence required for distribution of the estate is more—flexible, shall we say, than you may believe. In short, we may be able to get somewhere with what you've already found.

—I thought none of my evidence was usable.

—It wouldn't pass muster in court. But the Walsingham fortune is governed by a trust, not a will. It was set up in what we call a 'half-secret trust.' Because a will is essentially a matter of public record, these half-secret trusts were fairly common in Mr. Walsingham's day. A man who wished to leave money to a mistress or illegitimate children would direct in his will that the money be given to a trustee, who would then distribute the estate in accordance with a secret trust, be it oral or written. In this case, Mr. Walsingham bequeathed most of his assets to Twyning as trustee, with instructions for the estate to be distributed according to a secret trust document. That was the document that mentioned Ms. Soames-Andersson. It was out of the question that she be put in the will. We call it half-secret because everyone knows there is a trust, but no one knows what the trust says.

—I don't understand.

—What this means for you is quite simple. The admissibility of evidence is determined by the trustees, not a probate court. And I've spoken with the other trustees—

—Who are they? How could they still be alive?

—I'm afraid I can't tell you who they are. But I can say that the trust document allows for the selection of successors, just as I was successor to Peter Twyning. The point is that provided you return to London tomorrow, the trustees have agreed to evaluate the evidence you've gathered and make a decision from there.

—All the evidence that you said wasn't good enough. Now you're saying it is?

—What I'm saying, Prichard corrects, is that certain allowances might be made.

My voice rises. —Then why didn't you say that at the beginning? This whole time you've been telling me I'm doing everything wrong. But you were the one who told me to follow Eleanor's letter. Well this is where it led me. For two months you've been saying I'm off track, then suddenly—

—Mr. Campbell, Prichard interrupts, I told you all I was permitted to reveal at the time. As for the standard of evidence, I never represented that any specific standard existed. I only encouraged you to seek evidence the trustees might find persuasive. You never found it. The fact that the trustees are prepared to consider your case has more to do with the calendar than any particular evidence you've gathered. They're simply reluctant to pass on the estate so long as a potential heir exists. They're being charitable, and I think you ought to be grateful.

Prichard takes a breath. His voice softens.

—What is far more relevant is what I say to you now. You must return to London. We can arrange your travel and schedule a meeting. I can't promise any result. But I can promise that if you're still out in Iceland on Thursday, the estate will pass on and you'll never see a penny.

There is a long silence. Across the counter the hostel clerk turns the knob on the television. I run my hand across my face, speaking almost in a whisper.

—I don't care.

—Pardon?

—I don't care about the money.

—You don't care, Prichard repeats slowly. Are you sure of that? Have you any idea how you'll feel in ten years, or in forty? Frankly, I don't know that you're mature enough to make such a decision. I don't mean to patronize you, Mr. Campbell. But you're twenty-three years old and you wish to throw away—

—What does it matter to you who gets the money? You're just the lawyer.

—I daresay it does matter. It's not a question of money. Look at the facts.

Prichard exhales sharply. His voice is getting louder.

—Fact one. Ashley Walsingham died alone on Mount Everest at the age of twenty-nine. Fact two. Mr. Walsingham left nearly his whole fortune to Ms. Soames-Andersson, a woman he hadn't seen in seven years. Fact three. Ms. Soames-Andersson never collected the estate. Fact four. Your grandmother never collected the estate, nor did your own mother. Fact five. This law firm learned of a letter connecting you to Ms. Soames-Andersson less than three months before the eighty-year trust expires. What does all this mean to you?

—It's crazy. It doesn't mean anything.

—You're wrong, Mr. Campbell. It means everything. Do you imagine I'm not troubled by the improbabilities of all this? Of course I am, and Geoffrey is, and anyone who ever touched the Walsingham case. But that's precisely why it matters. Perhaps I've grown deranged in my old age, but the meaning is clear enough to me—

—It's just random. It's chaos.

—It is not, Prichard counters. All these signs point to you. The more I've learned, the more certain I've become. Perhaps it's too much to say that Ashley Walsingham died for the money, or that it kept him and Ms. Soames-Andersson apart, or that it hurt your grandmother or your mother. But it seems to me they all suffered something, and only you stand to gain from it. Sentimental old fool that I am, I can't bear to see you throw it away simply to satisfy some mad theory at the extremity of Europe. It isn't fair to you. And it certainly isn't fair to them.

I shake my head, winding the telephone cord around my fingers.

—I can't turn back. I'm getting close—

—You may be close to something, Prichard says. But I doubt it's what you think it is.

No one speaks. Finally Prichard says that Khan will expect to hear from me by tomorrow morning at the latest. I give the phone back to the clerk.

—How far is it to the Eastfjords from here?

—The Eastfjords? Why do you want to go there?

—To go swimming.

The clerk doesn't smile.

—Two hundred and sixty kilometers to Egilsstaðir.

Night falls as I cook dinner in the hostel kitchen, boiling spaghetti with my scarf doubled around my neck to keep warm. I eat alone at the dining table, twirling the pasta onto a fork and looking out the window into the darkness.

Does Prichard know everything, even the things I haven't found out yet? Could he have designed it all? Because I don't know anyone else with the means to have faked all this, even if I can't imagine a reason why Prichard would do it. Who else would have been a part of the deception—Mireille, Desmarais, Karin, everyone I've met in Europe? Did Ashley and Imogen ever exist? Surely it is beyond all notions of luck to have found those letters. Or is the past always there, only waiting for the person who truly wants to find it?

I have to decide tonight. Akureyri has a small airport and if the law firm paid for my travel I could get a flight to Reykjavík and then on to London. Otherwise I could continue east tomorrow and reach the Eastfjords within a few hours. But even if I found more evidence, by then it would be too late to reach London before the estate passes on.

I grab my coat and camera and walk into the town center, following sidewalks among shuttered businesses. I think of the small towns in Picardie, how the shops and cafés were closed but Mireille would describe what they looked like inside. I'd say how cold and lonely these towns were and Mireille would throw her cigarette in the gutter.

This is what you came here for. Not the lights of the boulevard Saint-Germain. This is what you wanted.

Is it?

Everyone gets Paris. But this is just for you and me.

I reach the center of Akureyri, standing in the middle of an empty road. Over the drizzling rain I catch an echo of distant music and I follow the noise to a small bar whose single window is fogged with condensation. I snap a few pictures from the sidewalk, but I don't go in. On the way back to the hostel the lights are in the eastern sky again, swaying like a band of satin in a breeze, the blue-green now frigid with red, the forms changing faster.

My hostel room is cold and empty. The radiator's dial is set to zero. If I cranked the plastic knob, the room would be warm in ten minutes. But I don't turn the knob. I zip into my sleeping bag and switch on my headlamp, lying back with one of Imogen's letters. Past the corner of the pages I can see a little starlight.

6 June 1924

Camp VI, 26,800 feet

Mount Everest, Tibet

There was neither beginning nor end to the night. The light seemed to have vanished days before. The two climbers are not outside to see the last rays of sunset; they huddle in a tiny Meade tent at Camp VI, a heap of stones laboriously stacked to make a six-foot platform on the steep mountainside. At great cost the expedition established this camp within striking distance of the summit. Two days ago the colonel and Somervell tried to climb the mountain with bottled oxygen. They came within a thousand feet of the summit. Tomorrow morning Ashley and Price make their attempt without the gas.

Price forces down a supper of orange marmalade and condensed milk, stirring the mixture in their cooking pot. Unopened tins of meat lie in the corner of the tent, but the climbers cannot stomach anything but sweets. Price spoons the orange-white mixture past his cracked lips. He passes the pot to Ashley.

—You must eat, Price wheezes.

Ashley looks at the pot, the rim crusted with treacle and condensed milk. He shakes his head.

They light the Meta stove to brew tea, but the boiling point is too low and after thirty minutes the liquid is lukewarm and faintly golden. They drink it down anyway, but before they have drained their mugs the dregs at the bottom are frozen.

The climbers speak very little. They cocoon under double eiderdowns bags and massage their hands and feet, hoping to rub some semblance of blood and feeling into their flesh. It is time to sleep.

The tent floor is sloped and jagged. Price is wedged in the lower pocket of the tent wall, pushed flush against the snowy canvas. Ashley is above him. Whenever Ashley's body relaxes he rolls onto the lower climber, collapsing upon Price with indifferent exhaustion. Price jabs his elbow into Ashley's back. Ashley moans and slowly retreats upward. The cycle continues in grim repetition.

The canvas shrieks and flails in the wind, calming slightly before rising to fever pitch. The sound is deafening, a whole screaming sky. There is a stiff thumping against the tent wall and in his half-delirium Ashley imagines that some creature pounds upon the canvas. Price leans into Ashley and yells.

—It's ice, Price bellows. Ice blown off some cornice.

The gusts increase. Each volley is worse than the last, the snow permeating the thin flapping canvas. With every blow further powder is loosed from the roof. Ashley lowers himself deep into his sleeping bag, but its collar is frozen stiff with condensation. At times there is a lull in the wind and Ashley fantasizes that it will calm, but the squall always rises again, only gathering toward a tormenting finale.

There is a wrenching and the canvas collapses upon them. A guyline has torn loose, crumpling the tent in the wind. Price presses his body into the icy canvas, using his weight to feebly anchor the shelter. Ashley gropes for his wind suit in the darkness. He must go outside and refasten the line. The frosted tent roof is draped over his face as he feels for the opening of the gabardine jacket, stiff and dusted with snow. It takes him several minutes to pull on the jacket and trousers, Price ballasting the tent all the while. Ashley thinks the tent might be carried off the slope, but in his dim and distant mind the thought is scarcely troubling.

Grasping in the darkness, Ashley claws the ice from his boots and wedges his feet inside. He sucks his breath in horror. The boots are frozen stiff. He tugs the laces into gangly knots, then struggles to unfasten the icy canvas tapes cinching the tent's flap. He works the ties with cramped white fingers. Finally the flap opens, a jet of snow whirling into the tent. Ashley crawls out into the maelstrom.

The mountainside is howling. The wind shrieks and punches Ashley and he does not rise from all fours, crawling across a slope of icy scree under a purple-black sky. He follows the outline of the thrashing guyline to its source. The line had been rigged to a pair of huge stones weighing hundreds of pounds. The stones have shifted. Ashley clumsily refastens the cord and doubles it back around more stones, stamping his feet as he works with numb fingers. Twice he drops the line and has to fish it from the snow by feeling alone. His toes feel pressed against blocks of ice. The simple task drags on in slow agony.

Ashley knots the line and crawls back to the tent. It takes some time to get inside, for Price has retied the tapes to keep out the snow. At last Ashley ducks into the shelter and collapses onto his sleeping bag, gasping. The cold air sears his lungs.

—Get into that bag, Price yells. You'll freeze.

Price shakes Ashley and tries to pull the sleeping bag over him, but Ashley does not move. It is ten minutes before Price gets Ashley into the eiderdown.

—How are your hands?

—No feeling at all.

Price kneads at Ashley's hands for some time, struggling to restore circulation before frostbite sets in. Ashley's fingers remain numb. Price beats at the flesh desperately and Ashley turns his face in agony, groaning and biting his tongue. He knows that Price's hands cannot be in much better shape. He does not ask.

It is an hour before they lie still in their bags again. Ashley knows he is too chilled to recover any warmth tonight and they are only going farther up the mountain in the morning. He thinks he does not sleep. The night passes between fits of delirium and chilling lucidity, his coughing fits marking the only certain intervals. He is so cold that he burrows his face into the soaked flannel lining of his bag, but the thin air suffocates him and he comes out gasping. Ashley turns onto his side and stares at the icy canvas.

The war has been over for four months. Ashley has been in London for three days. He gives his uniforms to his tailor as scrap and buys three new suits, two in flannel and one in Cheviot tweed. After years of being clasped by a stiff tunic and trousers, the garments feel impossibly soft. On a dismal Sunday afternoon, without invitation, he takes a taxi to the house on Cavendish Square and claps the knocker. He announces himself to a maid. The father comes to the door.

—You say you knew my daughter?

—I did know her.

—What was your name again?

—Walsingham. Ashley Walsingham.

—I'm sorry. I've never heard of you.

Ashley takes a cardboard folio from his coat pocket. He opens it to reveal the portrait.

—Where did you get that?

—She gave it to me. Look at the inscription on the back.

—That's quite all right.

The father's eyes dart around the other houses of the square. He looks back at Ashley.

—*You'll understand our daughter's absence is hard enough without strangers coming here. I don't say you're here to profit from it, but in any case I'm sure there's nothing I can do for you.*

The father shuts the door. Ashley claps the knocker again, but only the maid comes and Ashley quarrels with her pointlessly for several minutes. The maid slams the door. Ashley bangs the knocker again, wondering if he could knock down the door with his shoulder if he ran hard at it. He stands on the porch for another minute, flushed with anger. He returns the picture to his pocket and walks back across the square.

The next week he receives a brief letter from Eleanor suggesting they meet at the Lyon's Corner House on Coventry Street. Ashley goes to the barber beforehand for a fresh shave. He expects the meeting to be some kind of warning, but when he enters the vast dining room and sees Eleanor stand and wave from the table in the far corner, he knows at once that he was wrong. Eleanor forces a smile as he approaches. She looks on the point of tears. They sit down.

—*I've ordered tea, Eleanor says distractedly. I don't suppose you're hungry, Mr. Walsingham? If you wish something to eat, they've quite a menu—*

—*Tea will be lovely.*

—*I've never been in this Lyon's before. It's not so bad, really.*

—*Not at all.*

They fall silent. Ashley watches her across the table and thinks how beautiful she is. She has the same eyes as her sister. The pot of tea arrives and Ashley pours out two cups. He does not drink from his.

—*I'm so glad you're well, Eleanor says. I've thought of you often. Of course, Imogen hardly spoke of anything else—*

—*She's alive, isn't she?*

—*Yes.*

—*But not in England.*

—*No.*

—*Where is she?*

Eleanor folds her hands in her lap and looks away.

—*I can't say.*

—Then why meet me at all?

—I was at the house when you called. I heard Papa talking to you at the door and it made me sick. I thought you deserved more. I know you do.

—Won't you tell me where she is?

—That's not my choice. It's hers. She'd have told you herself if she wished you to know.

—Then it was her decision to go away. Not your father's?

—I don't know, Eleanor sighs. It was Imogen's decision to stay away.

—But why all the secrecy? Why not simply go abroad like anyone else?

Eleanor takes a sip of tea.

—I suppose she wanted to start over. Perhaps she didn't want you looking for her. But it wasn't only you. You know Imogen can't bear to do things normally. Papa's tried to get her to come back many times. But she wanted a new life, and we hadn't any choice but to go along. I can't tell you everything—

—But you've already spoiled the ruse.

Eleanor shakes her head. She looks into her teacup.

—It's gone on long enough. I don't think it matters if I tell you she lives. You knew that already. And she's never returning to England, that's for certain. She's so headstrong, and you're the same, and it breaks my heart to hear you calling at the door. I thought if I didn't see you, you might go on like this for years—

—I'll go on until I see her.

—You mustn't, Eleanor pleads, looking up at Ashley. Probably you could find her, if you looked hard enough. But what then? You'd have forced yourself upon her. She's gone so far to be herself alone. I know it's terribly cruel, but you must let her go.

She smiles a little. —It's peculiar. Imogen said you were always jesting. But sitting before me now, you seem the gravest person I've ever met.

They both drink from their cups and Eleanor pours more tea. She hesitates, straightening her napkin on her lap.

—Perhaps I oughtn't to have come, when I hadn't anything good to tell you. All week I've thought how extraordinary it is that you should go on caring for Imogen for so long, having known each other such a short time. But it struck me this morning that those two facts may explain each other. For in a way, it's been the same in our family. When I was younger I was convinced our parents loved Imogen more because she was so hard to love, because they could never quite have her for their own, not fully—

Eleanor sighs. —I'm sorry. Perhaps it's better if I go now. I wish I had something kinder to tell you, but it's simply not the case. You'll understand this, Mr. Walsingham, and you'll understand I can't see you again.

She stands up and Ashley rises too. He comes close to her, speaking in a low whisper.

—What about the child?

—I'm sorry?

He leans into her ear, his words clear above the clatter of the tea-room.

—She was expecting, but she lost the child. She wrote me as much.

Eleanor shakes her head, her face coloring.

—I don't know anything—

—What happened? Were you there?

—No. She never told me she was expecting. Perhaps she was mis-taken—

—Rubbish. She came all way to the France to tell me.

Eleanor's eyes flit across the dining room.

—I don't know anything. She went mad when she heard you were killed. It was madness that took her to France. After that I didn't see her. I'm sorry, I really must go—

—Please stay.

Ashley opens his palm toward the table, beckoning her to sit back down. Eleanor shakes her head. She looks at Ashley sympathetically.

—You don't need me to tell you this. But I'll say it anyway, if no one else will. You were both children, the two of you. Can't you see that? Imogen was only a child then, and she isn't any longer. You wouldn't even know each *other now. Naturally she cared for you and always will, in some way, and you for her. Only it's in your past now, and her past too, and you can't find that anywhere, however hard you look.*

   —I shan't give up—

   —You are giving something up, Eleanor says. You just don't realize it.

THE SCHOLAR

⊷⊜ ⊜⊶

It takes me three rides to get from Akureyri to the Eastfjords. I ride in unfamiliar cars along the shores of volcanic lakes, pillars of lava rising from their dark waters; I wait for an hour in a misty desert of black sand, the gravel road punctuated only by yellow mileposts.

My last ride is with a long-haired young man who tells me he waits tables for a living. There is a little girl in a child's seat in the back. The highway winds through hills of green moss and brown turf. Twice we have to stop when the girl gets carsick from the twisting road. Finally the highway descends to a valley where the ring road meets a smaller road going east.

—I'm going south, the driver says, but you want to go on toward the sea. A little down the highway there's a small hotel. I could put you there—

—Over here's fine. It'll be easier to get a ride by the intersection.

The driver looks at me with concern.

—Remember, he says, the hotel's just around that bend.

I wait on the shoulder of the eastbound road, kicking stones to pass the time. The rains starts again and soon it's blowing sideways into my hood. I pace the shoulder to stay warm, walking in circles on a twenty-yard strip of asphalt. I'm already wearing every garment I have, all layered in a carefully practiced system. Three T-shirts, two collared shirts and a jacket; two pairs of light pants; two ordinary pairs of socks and one thick wool pair; my parka, a scarf and a knit hat.

The raindrops turn into hail. I turn my back to the wind and the hailstones beat rhymically against my coat, like countless volleys of buckshot. I check my watch. Eighty minutes and still no cars. The hail's rhythm quickens. There's no sign of civilization except the thin band of asphalt.

I'll lose the fortune tomorrow. I've been trying not to think about it, but it's hard to ignore. I kick a black rock off the road, wondering if I'd already lost everything before I left California, if it was always understood that I'd end up shivering on this highway for no reason. Maybe Ashley never had a chance either, not with Imogen and not with the mountain. Maybe no matter what he did the ending was always the same, alone in a whiteout on the tallest mountain in the world. A man has a certain store of luck and when that runs out he's finished. They knew that back then, and we haven't gotten further in all the centuries since.

I turn back to the road. A silver sedan is idling before me. The driver lowers the electric window. He wears wire-rimmed spectacles and he looks to be in his late thirties. He speaks softly in Icelandic, then in English.

—What are you doing out there?

I get into the car. As we accelerate, the driver fiddles with the heater's controls on the dashboard.

—Warm enough?

—I am, thanks.

The ice on my shoulders melts damp circles into my coat. The driver shakes his head.

—What a time to be hitchhiking. I thought maybe you were a ghost standing out there. You're from Germany?

—That's just the coat. I'm from California.

—Sunny California, he murmurs. Why did you leave?

—I probably shouldn't have.

—I would have stayed.

The driver directs the heater's vents toward me.

—It's early in the year for hail, he remarks. You have bad luck.

—I know.

The driver tells me he is a librarian at the university in Akureyri. He grew up in the Eastfjords and he is driving to his parents' house north of Seyðisfjörður. We talk about books and I tell the librarian that I'm reading *Njál's Saga*. He seems pleased by this, so I tell him a little bit about my research.

—Ísleifur, he repeats. I've never heard of him. But I don't know anything about jewelry—

The librarian glances at me.

—One thing I don't understand. Why would this Englishwoman have come here?

—That's the problem. There isn't any reason.

The librarian grins. —There's always one reason to come to this country.

—What's that?

—It's far away from everything.

The librarian lowers the gear, the small engine whining as we climb a steep pass. He remarks that these hills have been inhabited for centuries, though little remains of most settlements but a few stones among the grass. We talk of the myriad stories of mankind both lost and recorded, and of the story that I'm after. The librarian supposes that for every story that is preserved, there must be a thousand others that vanish with the dead from all human memory.

—Imagine if your English couple hadn't written letters, he says. Who would know they had ever existed?

We drive among hulking mountains, black and green ridges with patches of white snow. The librarian says that when he was a child an old woman went after stray sheep in these hills and lost her way. It happened on an autumn day, he says, when thick mists shrouded all landmarks from view. The old woman was a good walker. As dusk fell she wandered deeper into the mountains until she slipped on the rocks and fractured her leg. She could not walk. The nights were long and dark with freezing rain.

—Did she survive?

The librarian nods.

—She was wearing traditional clothing. Heavy wool. It keeps you warm even when wet.

It took the rescuers two days to find the old woman, he says, and when they reached her she spoke not of the vanished animals but of some rare dreams she had beheld, of a secret hidden between the hills and ridges. It was as if she had been lured by the promise of a prize, just as told in legends of the Nykur, a brook horse that tempts men onto its back only to gallop into swirling lakewater until they are drowned.

—The old woman, I say. She lived here when you were young?

The librarian shrugs. —I was in grammar school then. It must have been '77 or '78. But she was no Englishwoman, if that's what you're thinking. She was a Swede, she'd come here before the war—

—Can you turn the heater down?

The librarian ratchets the climate control from red to blue. I ask him when the old woman died, but he says that he isn't certain, because she sold her farm and moved not long after the accident. The librarian repeats that she was Swedish and spoke Icelandic with a Swedish accent. Her husband had died long ago, he says, and she lived here with a caretaker from her own country.

—Can I put down the window for a minute?

—Of course.

I lower the window halfway, feeling the cold wind against my face. We crest the pass and I see the ocean in the distance, the water dark and glassy between the narrow fingers of the fjord. We go around the bend and the sea disappears again.

The librarian looks at me.

—Are you carsick? Should I pull over?

—I'm fine. I'm just needed some air. Listen, did you ever meet this old woman?

—A few times. There were not many people living in this area. I can tell you she wasn't English. I'm sure of it.

—You visited her house?

—Once. I only went to the doorstep.

The librarian explains that his father was a book collector and had bought a personal library at an estate sale. There were foreign books in this library, among these a few volumes in French. His father knew the old woman read French and sent the books over with his son.

A shiver passes through me. The sky begins to pitch downward.

—Can you pull over for a second?

The librarian nods and steps on the brake, stopping in the middle of the road. He switches the hazard lights on, though we've seen no cars since he picked me up. The triangular lamp on the dashboard blinks on and off. I get out and take a few steps off the road, but my foot catches on the lava and I fall, opening a small cut on my hand. I stand up, staring at the bright sliver of blood on my palm.

The librarian approaches cautiously.

—Are you all right?

—Yeah. I just need some air—

I try to calm down, taking slow and deep breaths, looking up at the clouds and trying to fix the position of the sky and ground. I turn back to the librarian.

—What did she look like?

—Sorry?

—The old woman. What did she look like?

—I don't know. Silver hair. Blue eyes.

—Did she take the books?

The librarian shakes his head. He removes his eyeglasses and rubs the lenses with a tissue from his pocket.

—She sent them all back, except for a few. I was pretty annoyed. They were heavy and I had to carry them back.

—Which did she keep?

He shrugs. —It was a long time ago.

The librarian replaces his eyeglasses, watching me with something between curiosity and concern.

—I just got a little carsick, I say. But I'm fine.

We get back into the car. I pull the lever to recline my seat and the librarian puts the key in the ignition. A noise chimes to warn that I haven't fastened my seat belt. The librarian frowns.

—I think it was Baudelaire she kept. Or maybe Rimbaud.

The librarian starts the engine and we drive on toward the sea. I lean against the headrest and shut my eyes.

—The poetry, he says.

7 June 1924

Camp VI, 26,800 feet

Mount Everest, Tibet

The climbers mean to start before dawn, but when the moment comes they do not stir. It would be death to leave the tent. They wait until yellow rays of sunlight strike the canvas, the hunks of frozen condensation melting and dropping on their faces. The wind has all but ceased.

Price sits up in his sleeping bag.

—Sleep at all?

—I dreamt, Ashley rasps. But I didn't sleep.

Price runs his fingers on the slushy canvas walls.

—Weather seems improved. We may have a go after all.

Ashley does not answer.

They move slowly, weak from their night of agony. It takes them an hour to dress and boil water for a thermos of hot coffee. Ashley's mouth is chalky. No quantity of melted snow or tea will quench him. He feels cold everywhere. At last they leave the tent, Price with a coil of rope slung over one shoulder, over the other a small bag holding a vest-pocket Kodak.

Price leads. They traverse a slope of ragged scree, moving toward a sunlit pocket of rock in the distance. The golden rays seem a mirage.

Above them hovers the summit pyramid, the vaporous plume jetting past.

Ashley has trouble navigating the stones beneath him. The twin circles of his vision are vignetted by his snow goggles, obscuring his lower view. He stumbles on the lip of a rock and catches himself with the steel tip of his ice axe. Price removes his goggles, lifting them onto his hat brim for a better view. There is little snow here.

Cutting across the mountainside, the steep slope is within an arm's grasp as they walk. Ashley halts and doubles over, coughing in violent fits. Price waits for him, panting all the while. Price motions to move on, but Ashley glances back, as if waiting for someone.

—Something wrong?

Ashley shakes his head. For a moment he thought there was another climber with them. He treks forward with short strides, straining to make twenty steps before pausing. He makes twelve strides. He leans and pants feverishly. Thirteen strides. He gasps at the searing air, shivering in the sunlight. Price wheezes beside him at each halt.

They reach a patch of névé, snow hardened under pressure into a coat of blue glass. Price pulls down his goggles and swings his ice axe from the shoulders, chipping at the packed granules to carve a step. After a few swings he leans on the axe gasping. He steps forward, fitting his boot into the notch. He begins chopping the next step. The pace is pitifully slow.

—My vision's going double, Price calls. Shouldn't have taken off my goggles.

Ashley's mind is slow and simple. He follows Price through the névé, then frets at each boulder in their path, deliberating over which route requires the fewest steps. In his hazy consciousness he is reassured by the presence of the third climber, and though the apparition vanishes upon close scrutiny, it always returns in time. During gasping pauses he looks absently at the spectacle far below, a flattened array of pinnacles piercing through the cloudbank, whitecaps on a distant sea.

They reach the band of yellow sandstone that rings the upper mountain. A gale begins to howl. They are traversing a line a few hundred feet below the northeast ridge of the mountain, following the slant of this arête steadily toward the final pyramid. Price's pace slows to a crawl. They take a breath for each step, gasping in fits, leaning upon their axes or propping elbows on bent knees. Ashley feels distanced from their predicament, a spectator to his own performance.

Price halts and spikes his ice axe. He waves his hand before his goggles, puffing in exasperation.

—It's over, he gasps. Weather's turning. I'm going snowblind.

The wind whips over their words.

—What?

—It's over.

Ashley shakes his head vigorously. He bellows hoarsely into Price's ear.

—It might go. I've plenty left.

Price fans his mitten at the swirling snow.

—It's a storm.

—I'll go on a bit.

Price grabs Ashley's arm. For a moment they stand eye to eye, Ashley in his green-glass goggles and leather helmet, Price in his brimmed hat, his face covered in an icy stubble of beard. Ashley glances up to the summit pyramid, appearing and dissolving through breaks in the churning whiteness.

—A thousand vertical feet, Price screams. Hours away.

—I'll move faster without you.

—It's impossible.

—I'm going.

Price releases Ashley's arm. He looks at Ashley for a moment. Then he turns and begins stumbling down the tracks in the snow.

Ashley continues up the sloping rocks. The wind reaches a howling fury. He is traversing a face of crumbling slabs, the stones overlapped like roof tiles dusted with snow. Suddenly he skids down a slab, his leg groping for support in the loose powder. He catches his weight with his axe, gasping.

Ashley goes on, gripping the axe in his outside hand and prodding it into the hollows of the rock for balance. He senses the tenuous purchase of his boot nails on the slabs, the uncertain surface concealed by snow. He kicks and hacks at clumps of powder obscuring the tiles. Ashley glances down at the drop. The slope tumbles off to the Rongbuk Glacier ten thousand feet below.

A violent gust of wind roars past, nearly toppling him. The face angles steeply, the slabs now close to his inside mitten. Ashley wades into an immense couloir of soft snow. He sinks in past his knees. The wind is bearing thick snowflakes now and he cannot see far.

He takes the altimeter from his pocket. The needle has swung slightly past 28,000 feet. He looks up toward the summit, but there is only the swirling sky, the air dense with snow. The storm is gathering force.

Exhausted and indifferent, Ashley turns around. He begins to slowly retrace his path. His footsteps are rapidly filling with snow.

Beneath his goggles Ashley's eyes burn with snapping cold, and he truly believes they may freeze solid and splinter. He has been descending for some time in the blizzard, but he does not know how far he has gone. He traverses the scree at a crawl.

The bloody monsoon, he thinks. *Arrived bloody early to get me.*

With each gust the wind goes through the fibers of his garments, delivering a surge of pain like immersion in flowing ice water. His nose and mouth are frozen hard with condensation. His face drapes tiny icicles. Each gasp of frigid air sears his throat and lungs, giving further torment, but he only has to gasp more, his body straining dumbly for oxygen. Ashley has dropped his ice axe somewhere. His goggles have fogged opaque and crusted with ice. He peels them from his face and they whirl off in the wind.

Ashley stops to orient himself, collapsing into a patch of snow. He thinks he may have passed Camp VI, but he cannot be sure. He can see only a yard or two. Suddenly he remembers the altimeter in his pocket.

He holds a mitten in his teeth and pulls out the altimeter with a brittle hand, the metal disk freezing upon his fingertips. He strains to read the dial in the blizzard. The wind gusts hard, smashing him against the scree. His numb hand falters and the altimeter is carried off. Ashley replaces the mitten carefully, stumbling on in his course.

The third climber was once ahead of him, but is coming back to lend aid. The climber comes at a slow but even pace, a rising speck in the whiteness. He has brought a flask of hot tea from Camp V; he carries a candle lantern and magnesium flares, and he knows the way back to the tents. Ashley stops and sinks into the snow, watching the speck approach through whirling flakes. Perhaps the climber whistles and calls through the wind, but Ashley cannot yet hear him.

Ashley blinks heavily, his eyelashes partly stitched together by ice. He rubs his eyes to break the crystals. There is no third climber and he knows it. He waves his mitten before his face, then looks to the side for a long time to clear his eyes, jets of snow lashing him. Ashley walks a few more steps, panting hard. He will take only the shortest break. He leans against the slope. The speck is still approaching, pausing for breath before continuing up.

When the climber arrives he will pour hot tea into Ashley's mouth. He will guide Ashley down to Camp III, tired as he is, where they will feed him soup and put him beneath three eiderdowns. Later they will take him to base camp and thaw his lifeless fingers in warm water; they will call him brave and gallant though he has failed. Then they will leave the mountain and pass down to verdant country: the alpine flowers, the rare butterflies, the rhododendron forests. The first shave and hot bath in Kalimpong; the steamer home. Finally England, greener than he remembered.

Then Ashley will write to say: *Meet me when my train comes in and we shall walk in Regent's Park. I'll be sunburnt still and I'll have a cough, but meet me in Regent's Park and we'll walk again in the French gardens. We will sit by the water and you will tell me what you have done these years. Then I'll know why I wasn't taken by Empress Redoubt or by this mountain or by you. And I can live in England green and rolling, and never wish for anything but what I have.*

Ashley wipes the snow from his face. He has crumpled against the mountainside and cannot rise. He does not feel the cold so much now, only great weakness. The speck quivers in the distance, a hundred yards down the snow slope, the only shape in a surge of white. The third climber is waving at Ashley, growing closer all the time. He will be here soon.

Ashley cannot make himself go. In crazed thirst he stuffs a palmful of snow into his mouth, but the taste is sandy and he gags and spits it out, nearly choking. He begins to curse and moan. He knows well what is happening to him, but he can do nothing about it. *A fine bloody waste,* he thinks. *A stupid fucking waste.* He looks down to his right hand, now a bare white claw, the mitten and underglove lost somewhere behind. Perhaps his teeth will shatter frozen.

Ashley begins to limp down the slope, leaning against the mountainside for support. His clenched hand drags a faint track in the snow. *You can't break me,* Ashley thinks. *You can do anything you like, but you can't break me.*

THE KEY

The librarian drives on through the hills, the road swerving downward, the sea coming in and out of view. My breathing has slowed and I begin to feel calmer. I ask if the old woman might be buried in this area. The librarian shrugs.

—I have no idea. There's a cemetery in the village. It's pretty small, but it's on the way. We can stop by if you want.

The librarian switches on the radio. We turn onto a dirt road and I ask if I can send a text on his cell phone.

—It's to France, I add, but I'll pay you for it. It's important or I wouldn't ask—

—Don't worry about it.

The librarian hands me his phone. I switch the input language to English, typing a quick message to Mireille. We approach a farmhouse on a hill and the librarian suddenly slows down, pulling into a muddy driveway.

—I'm going to ask about the old woman, he says. Everyone knows everyone here.

A farmer in orange coveralls sees us and walks down the

driveway. The librarian gets out of the car. Through the windshield I watch them talking, the farmer pulling off his baseball cap to wipe his brow. The farmer glances at me for a moment, then looks back at the librarian.

Suddenly the librarian's phone vibrates, the display flashing green. I pick it up from the cupholder and look at the number. The country code is 33. I answer the phone. The connection is weak, Mireille's voice coming in and out.

—Why haven't you written me back? I was worried—

—I'm out in the middle of nowhere. I can barely hear you.

—You're still in Iceland?

—Yeah, but I've found something. I'm getting close—

Mireille sighs. —Listen Tristan, I know I've been saying the wrong things, telling you to come back for the wrong reasons. It was a mistake—

Her voice wavers as the phone loses reception. I try to talk back until I'm practically yelling, but I don't think she can hear me. Suddenly her voice returns.

—Meeting you in the bar, and sharing my grandfather's house, and finding those letters. I should have let myself care about you, even if it was dangerous. But now you're making the mistake, because you're staying away. I want you Tristan, but you have to want me too.

—I do.

—Then come back tonight. It doesn't matter what it costs you. You don't need anything once you're here.

—I can't get there tonight. I'm too far out in the country.

—Tomorrow then. I'll meet you at the airport—

Her voice goes out again. I speak loudly into the phone.

—The line's breaking up. But I'll come as soon as I can.

—*Demain*, she corrects me. Please Tristan, just find a way. I'll be waiting—

She says something I can't understand. The line beeps and goes dead. I try calling her back, but the call diverts to a message in Icelandic. I put the phone back in the cupholder, wiping my face with my hands. Outside the farmer is pointing and sweeping his arm as he talks, apparently giving directions. Finally the librarian waves his thanks and gets back into the car.

—I don't know, the librarian says, if that farmer and I were talking about the same woman. He said her name was Östberg, that could be a Swedish name.

The librarian smiles and cocks his head a little, looking amused. He starts the engine and swivels the car around in a three-point turn. We start back down the road, gravel pinging against the car's chassis.

—He said the old woman's still alive.

—Alive?

—According to him she lives about ten kilometers away, at the next fjord to the north.

I sit up in my seat, almost yelling in protest.

—It's impossible. She'd have died decades ago.

—Maybe. But Östberg sounds familiar—

I shake my head, feeling the nausea sweeping back.

—There's no way. If she was in her seventies thirty years ago, she'd be more than a hundred now. It doesn't make sense.

The librarian shrugs. —He said she's very old. Anyway, it's not far from here. We might as well find out for ourselves.

—It must be someone else.

The librarian turns onto a dirt road, shifting into a low gear. The path is an old tractor trail cluttered with huge rocks. We lurch slowly over the bumps, the suspension creaking. My arm is still shaking.

—Don't worry, the librarian says. We're almost there.

The road curves through valleys and drops back sharply to the sea. I lower the window a crack, watching the white swells cresting offshore.

I can't focus on any single thought. I imagine the mad forces that might have conspired to produce all this, the arcane weaving of threads that ends with me on a dirt road in Iceland. It was impossible. It required the gathering of whole constellations, a harvest of countless stars funneled into a single cup and rolled out, a pair of sixes, a million times in perfect succession.

But it had happened. Already I'd seen the proof of it and held it in my hands. And it happened again every moment, for surely the meeting of any two souls required the same arithmetic. If it seemed improbable, maybe that was only my own narrowness of vision. Mireille said there might not be an end to this. But if I could reach an ending, was it possible that the veil would be lifted, that I'd rise to a higher vantage point and see something utterly simple, the purest design of all?

The car dips into a steep fjord. The narrow inlet is flanked by dark mountains, below these a black sand beach, the waves foaming white against the shore. The librarian points down the fjord.

—There.

The house is poised along the finger of water, the windows flush with the ebbing sea. Its cream-colored plastic cladding is immaculate. There is a neat flower garden, a wooden porch. A small waterfall spouts down the sheer cliff behind the house, gushing into a stream that skirts the property. The crags above are sheathed in mist.

We turn onto a smooth gravel driveway and the car stops jerking. The front door of the house swings open. Someone has seen us approaching.

An elderly woman comes out onto the porch, her forearms tucked into her apron. She does not smile or greet us. The librarian parks the car and turns to me.

—Do you want me to come with you?

—I might need a translator.

We get out of the car. The librarian introduces himself to the old woman. The conversation is brief and halting. The old woman walks into the house, leaving the door open behind her.

—She's the caretaker, the librarian says. She's invited us in.

The living room is sparely furnished and impeccably clean. We hang our coats on a rack and sit at a dining table. The librarian talks with the caretaker for some time, his hands folded awkwardly in his lap. Suddenly the caretaker addresses me in English. She has an accent I can't place.

—I'm sorry, she says, I thought you spoke Icelandic. Would you like coffee?

The woman goes into the kitchen and returns with two cups of coffee and a plate of stale cookies. I gulp down the sour coffee, cracking the hard cookies with my molars. The librarian and the caretaker are still talking. She turns to me.

—I understand you've come to see Ms. Östberg. But she's resting at the moment. I wondered if you could come back another time?

I tell the caretaker that it would be difficult to return, because I don't live in this country and have no place to stay nearby. Then I explain that I'm seeking information about a woman named Imogen Soames-Andersson. The caretaker looks at me, and if she has ever heard the name her face does not reveal it.

—I don't know the name, she says, but Ms. Östberg might be able to help you. Perhaps I could wake her. It would be a shame for you to miss her, since you've come so far. We seldom have visitors.

The caretaker excuses herself and goes down the hall. The librarian turns to me, his eyes large and shining.

—I don't think you should go in there. Even if it's really her, you'll never get the money. Let's get out of here—

The caretaker comes back into the room.

—Ms. Östberg is awake. You can see her now, but she'd prefer if you spoke in her bedroom.

I stand, glancing at the librarian, but he only shakes his head slightly, a strange expression on his face.

—Her English is quite good, the caretaker adds, so you won't need anyone to translate. It's the door at the end of the hallway.

I thank her and begin toward the corridor. The woman stops me with a wave.

—I forgot to tell you. The lock on her door is broken. You need a key to open it from the outside.

The caretaker draws an iron key from the front of her apron and hands it to me. It is an old barrel key, as wide as my hand with a long shaft and a tooled bit at the end. A length of ribbon is tied to its eyelet.

I walk down the dark hallway. The wooden floorboards are worn smooth and shiny. I pass closed doors on both sides of the corridor until I reach the door at the end. The key is in my hand.

I hesitate at the door. Then I see the shaft of light on my shirt, a small yellow beam. I wave my hand out of the shadows and the beam fixes on my wrist. It's coming through the keyhole. I put the key in the metal fitting and turn it, feeling the bolt swing smoothly. *Not any more,* I think, *or any less.*

I walk in.

23 June 1924

Schöneberg, Berlin

She watches the shadow of the streetcar glide past on the sidewalk, steel clattering upon iron as the wheels roll over a junction in the grooved tracks. The streetcar halts. The woman studies the white placard displaying the number 8.

She breaks into a jog, pushing down the crown of her hat. A leather portfolio is tucked under her arm; the camera slung over her shoulder bobs against the small of her back. The conductor watches the woman climb onto the streetcar and lean her portfolio against the wooden paneling. She draws out her purse, offering a coin inquiringly.

—*Fährt dieser Straßenbahn nach der Auguste-Viktoria-Platz?*

The conductor takes the woman as French on account of her accent and her strange clothing. He does not care for the French, but he tells the woman the streetcar does stop at Auguste-Viktoria-Platz. He tells her the fare. The conductor is used to telling passengers the fare, for only a year ago under the old Papiermark the fare had climbed to 150,000 marks.

The woman pays the conductor and moves down the aisle, grasping a handrail above her head. An old man stands and doffs his homburg, offering his seat.

—Bitte nehmen Sie Platz.

She smiles, explaining she would prefer to stand. The old man does not believe her, but he taps his hat low over his forehead and sits back down. The woman turns and shifts her weight onto the handrail, staring at a young girl on the seat across from her. The girl wears a white frock, its rounded collar tied by a long blue ribbon; she holds a porcelain doll in her arms, the paint rubbed off entirely from its face. The woman guesses at the age of the child, but in the end she realizes she has no facility for this judgment.

She frowns and looks out the window, studying the faces of the pedestrians on the sidewalk. Her mind returns to the old question of the Teutonic features. Is it only their expressions that make them severe? The Germans remained an enigma to her, and in years past she had considered them a species apart, a people with some anatomical divergence of nerve or gland that accounted for their facility with the problems of this world, the way they systematically solved every obstacle that came along, even the impossibility of their present hardship. She had long admired them for this, differing as they did from her. But was it true? Perhaps there was hardly any difference, perhaps she only imagined how these faces differ from those she might see in Copenhagen or Rotterdam. Her eyes follow the back of a man walking briskly on the sidewalk. Was he a German, and could she tell from the back? There is something familiar in the roundness of his shoulders; the angle of his gray trilby, ever misshapen; the curious rigidity of his gait. Could it be Anton? Of course it could not, for the last she had heard Anton was in Brazil.

She lowers her gaze in distress, studying the cuff of a young man's trousers, the greased crow-black boots of the conductor. She imagines the tram passing the figure on the sidewalk; she pictures the familiar body growing closer, the closest it had been in years and now passed, the distance only gaining between them. Now she is regretful, almost shameful. There was nothing so hateful to her as the fragility of human relations, and love most of all. She had always felt so. As a girl she had never understood the affairs of others, those who had lain with lovers for months and years only to part bitterly, only to pass each other on the street as mere strangers. That was not love, she had felt. That was caprice; that was whimsy. It was not love.

But later it had happened to her too. She had lain with them; they had held each other and promised all they could promise, the past and future alike. And now they were nothing to each other, or as little as two people were who would never speak again. How little remained from such episodes, dimming memories vouchsafed only by scraps of evidence unearthed years later: a visiting card dropped behind a chest of drawers; a pair of earrings in their silken gift box, never worn. She was still fairly young, and yet the affairs of her youth were things hardly remembered, unfocused images she had blurred by trying to picture the same scenes too often. Anton had never been her lover, but she felt the same discomfiture at his mirage, the inevitable embarrassment of the meeting of two people who had once been close but no longer were.

The memories were all that remained. Her life now was an apartment of rented furniture, where even the pictures on the wall were unfamiliar, rented pictures, portraits of dead Junker families and landscapes of the Sächsische Schweiz, a place she had never visited. She had not even a suitcase of mementos to carry with her through the world. But all this was as she had wanted it. It was the life she had chosen.

She had always told herself it would be worse to stay in touch, to trivialize love into trifling acquaintance, where years passed and the letters became fewer and more superficial. Still there were moments of terrible doubt. She woke sometimes from dreams of perfect clarity, trysts with spectral lovers who promised that all histories had been smoothed away, all obstacles removed so that at last they might meet again for all time. These were dreams so perfect in the dreaming that they became nightmares upon waking, for in the morning, in her bedroom, she recognized at once the stark feebleness of her present life. She would be seized by the need to find this specter, to dash to the post office and send a telegram, to board any train or ship or airplane to meet him. She must find him.

Yet in the end she could never do this. There were reasons why they lived apart and the reasons had not dissolved with the years. Besides this, there was always the caprice of human affection: the other people who would come between them, or those who would come in the future if their attachment waned. She could write, at least, a few lines to say she had thought of him. But the only fitting reply to love was equal love; once that was gone, all that remained was the trivial and the tragic. It was better not to write at all, better to remember him only in their finest moment—that interlude where the gilded spotlight had lingered upon them. And so she labored to shake off the dream, passing the day in a haze of murky sadness, waiting for the small but certain pleasures that would reconcile her to this life. Until the dream would come again.

The conductor taps the woman on the shoulder. She looks up and sees the tall spire of the Gedächtniskirche; they have reached Auguste-Viktoria-Platz. The woman snatches up her portfolio, pushing her way off the streetcar onto the square.

She crosses toward the café on the eastern side, weaving among the traffic of motorcars and pedestrians and bicycles. A grimed youth selling bootlaces arrests her on the sidewalk, hoisting his selection before her eyes. The laces are waxed and shiny, in flat or round varieties and varied shades of black or brown.

—*Nur zehn Pfennig*, he pleads.

The woman shakes her head, but the boy persists until she chooses a pair of laces. She has only a fifty-pfennig coin. The boy claims he has no change and in the end she buys five pairs of laces, asking if she can take a photograph of the boy in return. She unslings the camera from her shoulder and the boy asks how he should pose. The woman smiles and tells him not to pose at all.

She extends the leather bellows of the camera and turns a small key to advance the film. Guessing at the distance, she slides the focusing scale to two meters and checks the shutter speed and aperture, screwing her face up to the sun. Plenty of light. The woman holds the camera at her waist and cocks the shutter lever, eyeing the spirit level. In the little

viewfinder there is a reversed image of the boy hefting the bootlaces. She
fires the shutter.

The woman smiles and thanks the boy, folding the camera as she
crosses the street to the café terrace. Under the long awning the morning chill has not yet lifted. The waiters are spraying down the tiled terrace with long hoses, arranging the bentwood chairs and round marble
tables. She pushes through the revolving door into the café. A waiter
greets her and seems to recognize her, pointing to a man seated alone at
a table, his back to the vast mirrored wall that rises to a sculpted ceiling.

The woman hangs her coat on a rack. A disheveled newspaper
waiter passes her with his cargo attached to long wooden rods. The
woman asks which French papers he has, but he has only *Le Temps* and
she shakes her head politely.

She goes to the man seated alone. He is reading a newspaper he
must have brought with him, for it is not on a wooden rod. He does not
see her until she is pulling out a chair.

—*Tu m'as trouvé*, he says, grinning.

The man wears a high-buttoned suit jacket of an unusual cut, the lapels very narrow. His bow tie is knotted into two symmetrical triangles,
his blond hair slicked back with brilliantine. The woman smiles and
tosses the bundle of bootlaces on the table. The man shakes his head.

—*Tu n'as pas une seule paire de bottes.*

The woman smiles and says she has several pairs somewhere,
though it is a long time since she saw them. The waiter comes to take the
woman's order. She asks for a black coffee, then changes her mind and
orders a café au lait instead. The man nods toward the portfolio propped
against a chair. He asks if he can see the prints.

—*Oui*, she says. *Juste après le café.*

The man agrees that perhaps it is a little early. The waiter sets a
white cup and saucer before the woman. With a pot in each hand he
pours the steaming coffee and milk in proportion. The woman urges the
man to continue reading. He lifts the newspaper again.

The woman takes a small sip of her coffee. She picks up one of the flat bootlaces, tying it into an ornate bow. The man glances at the bow and smiles. He lifts his newspaper and refolds it, punching it flat in the center.

As she drinks the woman reads the back of the man's newspaper, a copy of yesterday's *Neue Zürcher Zeitung*. Her eyes pass over an article and she averts her face toward the café terrace. A waiter in a black tie and long white apron is pushing a wide broom across the floor. The woman looks back at the paper, grasping the sheet with one hand to steady it. She tells the man not to turn the page. Her eyes are wet now and she has trouble reading the tightly set Gothic text across the table. She releases the sheet.

—It's no mistake.

The man asks what she said, but the woman says she was only talking to herself. The man folds the newspaper ostentatiously and sets it on the table.

—You wish to speak English?

—No, she says. I'd rather not.

—Do you never miss it?

—Of course I do.

The man frowns. He summons the waiter and orders a second coffee. The woman stares at the folded newspaper, but she does not pick it up. When the man notices her tears he rises and offers his handkerchief. The woman refuses.

—Here, he says. You are making your hand wet.

The woman shakes her head, turning her face to the terrace. The man stands uncertainly for a moment, then returns to his seat. The waiter pours another coffee from the two pots. He notices the woman is crying and looks away, taking the pots back to the bar.

The woman stands as if to go. She wipes her face with the back of her hand, but she cannot stop the tears. The two waiters whisper behind the zinc bar, stealing glances at the couple. The woman picks up her portfolio. The man speaks to her in a soft voice, stopping to glare at the gawking waiters. The woman bites her lip. As the man talks, the woman stares absently toward the plaza. Finally the woman sits down again.

—*Qu'est-ce qui ne va pas?* the man asks. *Il faut me dire.*

The woman takes the man's cigarette case from the table and opens it. She lifts the sprung silver bar and puts a cigarette in her mouth. The man moves to pick up his lighter, but she reaches it first and lights the cigarette and draws a little smoke. She holds the cigarette before her, studying her hand. Her ivory skin is streaked with moisture, a shining droplet in the hollow between her thumb and index finger.

—It's nothing, she says.

THE AIRPORT

The day the estate passed I was on the southbound highway out of Djúpi-vogur, kicking rocks off the asphalt and pacing in circles to keep warm. By the time the sun came overhead it had been three hours since I'd seen a car.

I tried not to think about the money. My shoulders ached from my heavy backpack, so I set it down on the roadside and watched the white seabirds to pass the time. My mind kept going back to my grandmother and my mother. I wondered if people with a hundred million dollars died of cancer as easily as everyone else. Maybe they did. I picked a piece of lava off the roadside and threw it hard toward the ocean.

In the afternoon it grew cloudy and I walked down to the fjord below the highway and ate a lunch of cheese and stale bread from my pack. I lay on the black sand and stared up at the clouds. It was 1:50 now. That made it 2:50 in London. Maybe the estate had passed on at midnight. Or maybe at that moment Prichard was on the phone with a banker in the City, telling him go ahead with the transfers. I thought about Ashley and Imogen seeing each other across a room in 1916, and the letter he wrote her two months later saying that everything he had or ever would have was hers. Soon all that money that had been waiting for eighty years would get mixed up with other money until no one could tell the difference. Soon there would be no reason for anyone to think of either of them again.

I shut my eyes and slept until wind began to rise.

There were no more southbound cars that afternoon. At dusk I went into the village and found a small hotel by the harbor. I asked for the cheapest room and they gave me the key to a dormitory on the top floor with six bunks under a sloping roof. The restaurant downstairs was closed, but I didn't have the money to eat there anyway. With my pocketknife I opened a can of beans I'd bought in Reykjavík and ate them cold, sitting on the bottom bunk and looking out the small window.

I took my notebook from my backpack, hoping that if I read about all the people I'd met in Europe I might understand what I'd been doing here. I wanted to remember Karin and Christian, Mohammed and Desmarais, even the manager at the Berlin post office. Most of all I wanted to remember Mireille. I went through the pages slowly. There was hardly mention of any of them. The entries were about Ashley and Imogen, lists of questions and research topics, the times of trains or planes, the addresses of libraries and archives. I flipped to the day after I met Mireille.

Sept 4   *Paris*

> *Found the painting yesterday—an abstract piece of nothing.*
> *Can't stand to think about the wasted time.*
> *Bought a ticket to Amiens, then wandered the city for one last*
> *night. At a bar in the Latin Quarter met a girl named Mireille.*
> *Stayed up all night with her and her friend—evidently in French*
> *this is called "une nuit blanche." Today we are taking the 1pm train*
> *to Picardie together. If she shows up.*
> *One thing bothers me most—I still have no idea why Imogen*
> *came to France.*

I shut the light off and got in bed. I knew I had to let go of every-thing, but the more I tried the tighter I held on. I kept thinking about the week after my mother's funeral, when my father gathered her clothes to offer to his sisters, and how they all went to the closet and looked at the shoes and coats and handbags, but none of them took anything. I remember picking up a pair of shoes and looking at them. They weren't even real leather.

It was after two when I got out of bed. I turned on the light and pulled out the plastic file with Imogen's letters and my research photo-copies and the papers they'd given me at Twyning and Hooper. I took a cigarette lighter from the lid pocket of my pack and went into the tiny bathroom. I put my notebook and all the papers in the sink. The lighter was in my hand. The envelopes were getting wet from the damp porcelain.

After a minute I put down the lighter. I sat on the tile floor and cried.

Later that night I dreamt I was in Paris. I was meeting Mireille at a mu-seum where her art class was sketching in an atrium filled with marble sculptures. I got there early and saw Mireille at the far end of the atrium, sitting on a bench beside Claire with a large sketchbook in her lap. I de-cided to walk around the museum until her class was over.

In a dark gallery upstairs there were long rows of portraits where everyone looked familiar, though some of the paintings were hundreds of years old. At the end of the corridor there was a picture of a woman I'd never seen before. I recognized her at once. I looked at the picture for a moment, then I walked downstairs. Mireille's lesson was over.

It was raining this morning, but I was out on the highway by six o'clock. Twenty minutes later I was picked up by an electrician in a white van who was going all the way to Reykjavík. My luck had changed again. In the af-ternoon he dropped me off on the highway to Keflavík Airport, and with the steady stream of traffic it only took me a few minutes to get a ride.

By the time I reach the airport ticket desk I've missed the day's flight to Paris. But the agent says she can get me there for 22,000 krónur if I change planes in Copenhagen. The flight leaves in ninety minutes. I have no idea if Mireille will come to meet me.

I unfold the banknotes from my pocket and lay them on the counter along with a ziplock bag heavy with coins. I count it all out, but I'm almost two thousand krónur short. The agent looks at me suspiciously.

—You don't have a credit card?

—It's maxed out.

I dig into my backpack and pull out a twenty-pound note I'd hidden in the lining against the frame. Then I run to the Landsbanki exchange counter and trade the note for 2,500 krónur. I buy the plane ticket and go through security. At a pay phone near the gate I call Mireille, but it goes straight to her voice mail. I leave a hurried message.

—It's Tristan. I'm coming back. I'll be at Charles de Gaulle at five fifteen, Terminal One. It's the SAS flight from Copenhagen. I hope you'll come—

I hang up the phone and run through the terminal to my gate. The airplane is half empty and I have a row at the back all to myself. A stewardess announces the safety procedures in Icelandic and Danish as I buckle my seat belt.

I'm glad there's no one sitting next to me, because I'm dirty and unshaven and it feels like I haven't slept properly for months. My skin is chapped from the Icelandic wind. My hair needs cutting, and my clothes are soiled and wrinkled from weeks stuffed in a backpack, everything scrubbed in hostel sinks with only a hard cake of soap. I wonder if Mireille will come and how she might look at the airport. But the more I try to imagine her the more I get a bad feeling about it, so as the plane lifts off I focus on the things I can be sure of. I try to picture Paris and its parks and boulevards, but it's hard to ignore that in four hours I'll be landing there with no money and nowhere to stay.

At Copenhagen Airport I call Mireille again. Again she doesn't answer. I leave another message and type her an e-mail on a coin-operated terminal beside the food court. Then I sit at my gate and watch the plane

to Paris being unloaded and refueled, my hand in my coat pocket. I can
feel the cold silver of the brooch.

—Ladies and gentlemen, I'm pleased to announce boarding for SAS
flight 559 to Paris Charles de Gaulle—

I find my seat in the second row of the airplane. The middle-aged
woman in the aisle seat watches me stuff my backpack in the overhead
compartment and squeeze by her to the window. A few minutes after
the plane takes off, she closes her magazine and asks me where I'm from.
Her accent sounds Irish.

—An American in a German coat, she says, backpacking all over
Europe. I've heard about these kinds of trips. If it's Tuesday it must be
Paris, that sort of thing?

—Sort of.

—It sounds exciting. What do you think of Europe so far?

I look out the window at the clouds below.

—Of course, the woman adds, it's not for everyone—

—I love it here.

At Charles de Gaulle I'm the first one off the airplane. Outside the bag-
gage claim there's a dense line of people waiting behind the barricade.
Mireille is there.

She leans forward with her elbows propped on the rail, her face in
her hands. When she sees me she straightens up and her mouth opens,
but she covers it with her hand as if embarrassed. She runs along the
railing beside me, appearing and disappearing behind the families with
strollers, behind the chauffeurs holding placards with names on them.
Mireille comes around the end of the barrier and takes my hand.

—*Suis-moi.*

She leads me out of the terminal through the automatic doors.
The autumn air is cool and we walk quickly down the sidewalk. Cars
and buses go past us, stopping to pick up passengers and pulling out
again. Mireille takes me to a niche behind a potted tree. I put my arms
around her and pull her close. I kiss her. Her lips are warm. She smiles

and wipes off a tear and laughs, whispering my name. I put my hand on her face and kiss her again. A line of Mercedes taxis go past us, then a worker pushing a huge train of luggage carts.

Mireille is holding my hand and she feels the thin cut on my palm. She frowns, stroking the wound.

—You hurt yourself.

—I fell down in Iceland. There was lava on the ground. It was pretty sharp.

Mireille lifts my hand and kisses it playfully.

—I'm sorry I wasn't very good at waiting. I just worried you'd never come back. But you did. So you don't have to explain anything—

—I didn't get the money.

Mireille looks at me. Her hair has grown out in the last month and it goes over her ears now. Her gray eyes are pale in the sunlight.

—You were too late?

I shake my head.—It wasn't mine after all.

Mireille nods slowly. She glances at the taxis going past and weaves her fingers into mine, turning back to me. We start down the sidewalk toward the RER trains for Paris. Finally she says,—Then you were right. You got your answer in the end.

—I guess I did.

—What was it?

I reach into my coat and pull out the rest of my Icelandic change, thick brass coins with the image of a fish on the reverse. I hand them to Mireille.

—What's this?

—Three hundred and fifty krónur. Around four euros. It's all I've got left in the world—

—That's not true.

Mireille puts the coins in her pocket. I put my arm around her.

—What's the winter like here?

—Dark and cold, she says. But we'll survive.

EPILOGUE

⤙═ ═⤚

The storm that killed Ashley Walsingham was not related to the monsoon. It had formed three weeks earlier as a low-pressure disturbance above the jewel-green waters of the eastern Mediterranean.

The storm traveled far to meet the expedition. It sailed eastward over the arid plateau of northern Arabia; it crossed Afghanistan, brewing above the snow peaks and Silk Road passes of the Hindu Kush. It skirted the formidable summit of K2 along the border of the Republic of China and the Princely State of Kashmir and Jammu, continuing southeast over the glaciated ranges of the Karakoram.

In late May the disturbance swept east over the immense Himalayan massif, flowing above the peaks now known as Annapurna and Ama Dablam and Makalu. None of these mountains had yet been climbed or even set foot upon by a European. The storm released thick snowfalls and howling blizzards throughout the ranges of the western Himalaya. On June 7, 1924, the storm's full measure reached the northeast face of Mount Everest in the self-proclaimed sovereign Kingdom of Tibet. Mount Everest was the tallest known mountain in the world.

On the same day at the Alipore Observatory in Calcutta, 385 miles south of Mount Everest, the resident meteorologist Dr. S. N. Sen walked outside to take the afternoon's temperature readings, pencil and logbook in hand. It was six minutes until four. The air was sweltering.

Crossing the observatory's back lawn, Sen patted the sweat from his neck and brow with a linen handkerchief, glancing skyward. A few threads of cirrus fibratus strung the eastern sky; the rest was a crystalline azure.

Sen's thoughts returned to the onset of the Asian monsoon. Each day he telegraphed the Mount Everest Expedition with new data, forecasting the probable date of the monsoon's arrival. It was a difficult question. He had to take into account, for instance, the complex interaction of Himalayan and African and equatorial air masses; the retrograde motion of cyclones near the Bay of Bengal; the passage of western disturbances across the subcontinent. One such disturbance ought to reach Mount Everest very soon. Sen had taken lunch at his desk to study the problem, the morning weather telegrams fanned out before him, freshly wired from a dozen surface and upper-air weather stations throughout the Himalaya.

—The fourteenth of June, Sen murmured. No earlier.

Sen reached the Stevenson screen where the thermometers were held, a case of enameled pine with double-louvered walls. He opened the padlock and squinted at the four thermometers inside, appraising tiny gradations between the black bands of the temperature scale. It was 91.2 degrees Fahrenheit.

At the Mount Everest Expedition base camp at the foot of the Rongbuk Glacier, at an altitude of 18,190 feet, Dr. Hingston took the afternoon's meteorological measurements at 4:00 p.m, as he did every day. Hingston was the expedition's medical officer, but he was also a naturalist who observed the climate with genuine interest.

Hingston kept a pair of maximum and minimum thermometers on a wooden provision box under his tent fly, the thermometers fitted in a snap case of morocco leather. He eyed the floating index inside the glass cylinder of the maximum thermometer, the wind lashing the canvas tent fly against his back. Earlier the thermometer's filament had been pushed up to 33 degrees, but the mercury had since fallen to 11. Hingston logged the figures in neat numerals on the green-columned sheets of the meteorological diary.

Next he cradled the cold tube of a Kata thermometer under his armpit for several minutes. He hobbled out among the dirt and gravel, watching the red fluid dive in the wind with one eye on the sweep hand of his pocket watch. Finally Hingston placed a swatch of dark fur on a large stone, suspending a black-bulb thermometer above it. He rested the toe of his boot on the fur and waited for the mercury to rise.

Hingston surveyed his surroundings. The boulders around him had been sculpted by wind over centuries, their surface scarred and striated on the windward side, smooth and glassy on the lee side. They reminded him of coral. Hingston marveled at the diverse conditions that shaped animate and inanimate objects, the legion adaptations of mammal and insect and bird life to this hostile world.

The signs were everywhere. The finches and sparrows that shelter between stones or village walls, or in the warm underground dens of mouse hares, protecting their delicate plumage from the wind; the red-billed choughs that stand with their heads facing scouring gales, anchoring themselves long enough to pick at meager grass. Himalayan butterflies inhabited the most godforsaken places, barren wastelands up to 17,000 feet: these species of *Parnassius* were ill-suited to such elevations, save that they could cower their wings low against the wind, and knew to only fly when the air was calm. Hingston had even seen *Pseudabris* beetles that played dead. Thrown off green stalks of vetch or iris by gusting wind, the beetles would collapse upon the soil as if dead, only to spring buzzingly to life when the weather abated.

Hibernation was a rule here. When the expedition reached the Tibetan plateau in April, the country appeared gray and moribund. But it was only sleeping. A minute universe was saving itself for fairer climes, and Hingston had shown this to the climbers, lifting stones and turning soil to reveal curled caterpillars; dozing colonies of ants; arachnids reclined in hollow snail shells. The design of nature was flawless; the signature of its perfection pervasive.

He raised the thermometer to his face, squinting to read the scale.

—Thirteen point three.

Hingston was very cold. He would soon call for Kami to brew tea.

At Camp III, four thousand vertical feet above Hingston, Colonel Norton lay in his quilted eiderdown sleeping bag composing dispatches to be couriered and telegraphed to *The Times* of London. The wind outside was howling. Suddenly the colonel glanced at his wristwatch.

—Four o'clock, he bellowed.

—Bloody freezing, Somervell called from the next tent. Isn't that specific enough?

—Not for South Kensington.

Somervell hacked out a cough in reply. He crouched in the tent's flapping vestibule and studied a pair of thermometers. He glanced at the red sliver of fluid in the bottom thermometer, then inverted the case to reset the instruments. The metal indices plummeted in the glass.

Somervell recorded the temperature as minus seven degrees Fahrenheit. He estimated the wind speed at fifty miles per hour, which according to Beaufort's numbers would be a force nine gale. It was a blind guess. Somervell knew that winds at sea were hardly comparable to those on a mountain, just as low temperatures in the Arctic were not half so severe as those on Mount Everest, where the oxygen-starved body had no power to warm itself.

Somervell lifted his face to the mountain above. Fractocumulus clouds had swirled over the upper pyramid, sheathing everything in white. Walsingham and Price were somewhere among those clouds. Somervell thought the high camps would drop to at least twenty below in the nighttime, which meant fifty degrees of frost, excluding the tremendous wind.

⬤

Several hours later Hugh Price staggered down the north ridge of Mount Everest, searching for Camp VI in failing light and whirling snow. At 26,800 feet the camp was the highest bivouac ever made by men. Price's vision was blurred and doubled by a mild case of snow-blindness, and he did not see the tent until he was very close, a sagging blotch of green canvas on a shelf of jagged rocks. Price tore open the tapes and dived inside, panting. There was snow everywhere. The canvas walls were screaming in the wind.

Price pulled off his boots and tried to fasten the door flap. It was dark now and it took him ten minutes to knot the tapes, grasping with numb fingers in the blackness. He knocked chunks of ice from one of the eiderdown bags and pushed his legs inside. Snow and ice covered Price's clothing and the lining of the sleeping bag; if his body warmed, the ice would melt and soak him. Ashley's sleeping bag lay beside him in a frozen heap. Price wondered dimly if Ashley could have made the summit. It seemed impossible in this blizzard.

Price sat up and rummaged in the darkness for matches. He must light the lamp and burn magnesium flares to help Ashley find the tent. He felt a tin of café au lait. A compass. An empty water flask. He gasped and burrowed back into his sleeping bag. He was too cold. He must eat something to gain strength, but he felt no hunger, only terrible thirst. There was no water and he was too weak to melt snow on the stove. Price thought of the coming hours and the agony of sleepless visions, the long ticking nightmare of unquenchable thirst and chills and fatigue. He wondered if he would survive it. The second eiderdown bag lay beside him.

When Ashley returns, he thought, *I will give him his bag.*

Price wriggled his sleeping bag into Ashley's and sank toward sleep.

The diary of the head lama of Rongbuk Monastery records that in the third month of the Wood Rat year of the fifteenth *rab-byung*, a party of thirteen European gentlemen arrived accompanied by a hundred porters and three hundred pack animals. The gentlemen bestowed fine gifts upon the lama. They requested his blessing upon their expedition, which sought to climb the tallest mountain on earth for the fame and honor it would bring them. The lama warned the climbers that his country was a very cold one, and only chaste and pious men could survive in such a harsh domain. Nevertheless the Europeans persevered for weeks at their strange errand, erecting seven tents in succession toward the summit. They used iron pegs and chains and plates to challenge Chomolungma, but still they failed. The Europeans returned to the monastery to request a funeral benediction for a comrade who had died upon the mountain. The lama performed the service with great sincerity, knowing that the dead European's soul had suffered untold difficulties for the sake of nothing.

Ashley Walsingham's body has never been found. It is not known whether he died of a fall or if he was benighted on the mountain. There are hundreds of bodies on Mount Everest and they cannot be brought down from their great height. Walsingham did not reach a record elevation, nor did he set foot on untrodden ground. His name is recorded only in the thicker annals of human exploration, and only then as a footnote. Of late these volumes are seldom read and never admired.

It would be decades before men would scale Mount Everest. These men would be a breed apart from the climbers of 1924. They would reach the summit by a different route on a morning of vivid sunshine. They would know the names of their predecessors, but little else of that vanished world, and they would bring to the mountain no magnum bottles of champagne, nor anthologies of poetry or prose, nor stockings or sweaters handknitted and darned, nor scraps of fabric safeguarded through the trenches of Picardie and Ypres. The men who finally climbed Mount Everest would find the mountain less strange than those who had come before, and so it would go on with each generation in turn, until the mystery would shimmer briefly, a last green flash of the setting sun, then cease altogether.

Acknowledgments

Dorian Karchmar, Marysue Rucci, Simone Blaser, Emily Graff, Elizabeth Breeden, Jonathan Karp, Richard Rhorer, Andrea DeWerd, Cary Goldstein, Sarah Reidy, Loretta Denner, Jackie Seow, Ruth Lee-Mui, Christopher Lin and the entire team at Simon & Schuster. Raffaella De Angelis, Jason Arthur, Cathryn Summerhayes, John McGhee and Jeff Kleinman.

Marlene Dunlevy, Ryan Bowman, Eric Bain, Ben Urwand, Emily Cohen, Ryan Wilcoxon, Elizabeth Beeby, Adam White, Leslie Henkel, Alice Brett and Catherine Foley. My father and mother; my siblings Brandon, Alyssa and Lucian.

This is a work of fiction, but it owes its existence to the many lives that inspired it. Wilfred Owen, George Leigh Mallory, Robert Graves, Vera Brittain, Virginia Woolf, Siegfried Sassoon, T. Howard Somervell, J. B. L. Noel, Geoffrey Winthrop Young and F. S. Smythe are among the scores of individuals whose experiences—captured in their letters, memoirs, diaries, poems or other accounts—made me write this book.

I hope I can be forgiven for taking certain liberties with historical events and geography, as well as the people and military units mentioned in these pages. Although I have endeavored to be as faithful to the past as possible, fiction ultimately diverges into a world of its own.

Dr. A. M. Kellas's speech "Notes on the Possibility of Ascending the Loftier Himalaya" is derived from the version printed in *The Geographical Journal*, vol. 47, no. 6, delivered at the Royal Geographical Society on May 18, 1916. Two excerpts from *The Times* of London appear in this book: "Everest Victims: Story of a Grand Lama's Warning" (July 29, 1924) and "The Mount Everest Tragedy: Message from the King" (June 21, 1924); a portion of the latter is extracted as Ashley's eulogy from the King. J. B. L. Noel's 1924 film *The Epic of Everest*, also quoted here, is available from the British Film Institute. The verse that Pritchard recites when he meets Tristan is from Rudyard Kipling's poem "If—"; the online encyclopedia entry for "poste restante," which Tristan reads with Mireille, is from Wikipedia. The article "Post from the Peak of Everest" appeared in the *Daily Chronicle* of February 13, 1924. Dr. Hingston's view of the Rongbuk Valley is based on his chapter "Natural History" in the official expedition narrative, *The Fight for Everest, 1924*, while the account of the lama's diary is derived from E. O. Shebbeare's expedition diary in the Alpine Club archive. I am indebted to Wilfred Owen not only for this book's title, but for the trigger word "mistletoe," which he used in his own letters to his mother—a word too perfect for any substitute.

And to all the people who helped a stranger in his travels—

Thank you.

ABOUT THE AUTHOR

Justin Go was born in Los Angeles. He studied at the University of California, Berkeley and University College London. He has lived in Paris, London, New York City and Berlin.

At present he is at work on his second novel.

⬥ *The* ⬥
STEADY
RUNNING
of the HOUR

JUSTIN GO

ABOUT THIS GUIDE

This reading group guide for *The Steady Running of the Hour* includes an introduction, discussion questions, ideas for enhancing your book club, and a conversation with author Justin Go. The suggested questions are intended to help your reading group find new and interesting angles for discussion. We hope they will enrich your dialogue and increase your enjoyment of the book.

INTRODUCTION

Just after graduating college and at loose ends in San Francisco, Tristan Campbell receives a letter delivered by special courier. It contains the phone number of a Mr. J. F. Prichard of Twyning & Hooper, Solicitors, in London—and news that could change Tristan's life forever.

In 1924, Prichard explains to the young man, an English alpinist named Ashley Walsingham died attempting to summit Mount Everest after willing his enormous fortune to his onetime lover, Imogen Soames-Andersson; but no one came forward to claim the estate. Recent information suggests that Tristan may be the rightful heir, but unless he can present documented evidence within two months, the fortune will be given to charity.

In a breathless race through Europe, Tristan pieces together the story of the lovers' forbidden affair, set against the tumult of the First World War and the pioneer British expeditions to Mount Everest, and he becomes obsessed with the tragic lovers in the process.

Part love story, part historical tour de force, *The Steady Running of the Hour* is a heartrending and utterly compelling debut announcing the arrival of a stunningly talented writer.

TOPICS FOR DISCUSSION

1. The novel's title is taken from a line in the epigraph, a fragment of Wilfred Owen's poem "Strange Meeting." How does the title relate to both Tristan's quest and Ashley's life? Why do you think Justin Go chose it?

2. Of Imogen and Ashley, Geoffrey Khan says, "These were not people like you and me." What does he mean? What were your first impressions of both Ashley and Imogen? Did any of their actions surprise you as you learned more of their love story? If so, which ones?

3. Tristan says of an earlier plan he had for moving to LA, "I talked to Adam about it for a couple hours. In the end all he said was that I always ask for advice so I can worry about it. Then I go and do the thing I was going to do anyway." Do you agree with Adam's assessment of Tristan? Give examples from the book that support your opinion. Why do you think Tristan chooses to share Adam's words with Mireille?

4. Describe the trust that Tristan stands to inherit. How was it set up, and why? Why do you think Prichard is so invested in having Tristan inherit Ashley's estate?

5. Ashley tells Imogen the reason he joined the army: "I was bored at Cambridge. . . . And I was fool enough to worry I'd miss something if I kept out of the war." Compare Ashley's ideas of war with the realities he faces in the trenches. Describe his wartime experiences. Do they change him? If so, how?

6. Mireille tells Tristan, "Even love can sometimes be a mistake, and . . . perhaps this vanished love of Ashley and Imogen's [was] a wasted one." Do you agree with Mireille about Ashley and Imogen's relationship? Do you think they loved each other? Why or why not? Describe the nature of their love.

7. As Tristan delves more deeply into Ashley and Imogen's history, his reaction to Ashley's estate changes. How does it change? What accounts for the alteration in his feelings toward it? Why do you think Imogen never claimed Ashley's estate, despite being named heir?

8. Eleanor criticizes Imogen for "turning away from ordinary choices," saying, "If someone expects something from you, you can't bear to give it to them." Is Eleanor right about Imogen's character? In what

ways has Imogen turned away from "ordinary choices," and what have the results been? Compare the two sisters. How are they different?

9. When a hotel clerk mistakenly thinks Imogen and Ashley are married, Imogen is displeased. "It's just not how I want to think of us," she says. Contrast Imogen's attitude toward marriage with Ashley's. She believes that "one oughtn't give names to what two people are to one another. It only makes it harder to be one's self." Do you agree with her?

10. When Tristan speaks of his plan to leave France and go to Berlin, Mireille is critical of him: "You don't understand what's going on around you." In what ways do his experiences change him—and are they for the better? Why do you think Mireille reacts so strongly to the plan? Is she justified in her criticisms of Tristan? What are some of Tristan's aspects that Mireille disapproves of?

11. While Imogen is in Sweden, she wonders whether she and Ashley had "truly made choices, or had they given in to forces they felt too weak to resist?" What do you think? Did they have choices with regard to their love affair? Both Imogen's relationship with Ashley and Tristan's with Mireille unfold over the course of only a few days. Compare the two relationships. In what ways, if any, are they alike?

12. After the war, Ashley tells Eleanor that he won't give up trying to find Imogen. She replies, "You are giving something up. . . . You just don't realize it." Is she correct? What is Ashley giving up by continuing to search for Imogen? Why do you think he persists?

13. Book 3 begins with an epigraph that reads, in part, "If you are a brave man you will do nothing: if you are fearful you may do much,

for none but cowards have need to prove their bravery." Discuss instances of bravery that occur in *The Steady Running of the Hour*. Do you think Imogen is brave for the way she handles her relationship with Ashley? Why or why not?

14. Duties figure prominently throughout *The Steady Running of the Hour*. When Imogen asks Ashley to leave the army, he tells her he cannot; "I've a duty," he says. Do you agree with his decision to "see this through"? Why or why not? Does Imogen have any responsibilities toward Ashley? If so, what are they? What duties does Tristan have toward Ashley's estate, if any?

ENHANCE YOUR BOOK CLUB

Ashley Walsingham died in an attempt to summit Mount Everest. Learn more about Mount Everest here http://www.history.com/news/7-things-you-should-know-about-mount-everest, and also here: http://en.wikipedia.org/wiki/Mount_Everest.

Ashley believes "it is climbing that makes one feel." What does he mean? Talk about your passions with your book club. What do you do to make yourself "feel"?

Tristan's quest takes him from London to the Somme battlefields and onward to the Eastfjords of Iceland and beyond. Describe the cities that Tristan finds himself in. What would you do in each?

To learn more about Justin Go, and more about the journeys and research he undertook to write *The Steady Running of the Hour*, visit his official site at http://www.justingo.com.

A CONVERSATION WITH JUSTIN GO

The Steady Running of the Hour is your first novel. What has been the most rewarding part of the experience of publishing your book? Was there anything that surprised you about the publication process?

It's incredible just to see the book coming out. I worked on it for seven years, but even in the better periods I had grave doubts about the whole endeavor. When I finally learned the book was going to be published, I felt relieved simply to know I hadn't been crazy all along. You give so much of your life to something like this, but you can't count on getting anything back, not from the world at least. It meant everything just to be able to call myself a writer.

What I find remarkable about publishing is what a long and careful process it is. It's almost like raising a child. When you're waiting for your first book to appear, it can be painfully slow, but the exactitude is what makes it special. In a world where much of what we read was completed within minutes or hours, there's something unique about books. There are more than a hundred thousand words in my novel. I can tell you I looked pretty hard at every single one of them, and other people did too.

As a debut novelist, do you have any advice for aspiring writers? Now that you've published your first book, do you wish you had done anything differently?

I think any aspiring writer should first decide if he or she really needs to do this. Writing novels is probably the longest and most unlikely path you could take toward fame, fortune or even happiness. But if you must write, put everything into finishing that first draft. Be fearless, if only for an hour or two each morning. Until I started writing, I didn't realize how much fear had kept me from the life I wanted. I was afraid to write badly, so I didn't write. I was afraid to be alone, so I didn't move abroad.

Eventually I realized that the only thing that guarantees failure is never trying. If you aren't willing to take risks and sometimes write badly, you'll never discover what you can do. The miracle of fiction isn't producing an adequate chapter that fits into your plot. It's pulling out something from inside you that you didn't know existed. The trick is to keep reaching for that, morning after morning.

Looking back, I wish I hadn't doubted myself so often. A writer, especially a beginner, should be humble and always eager to learn. But it's awful to stand on the brink of giving up. If you're brave enough to write a book, be proud of yourself and keep going.

Like Tristan, you dropped everything to go on a European adventure, quitting your job and moving to Berlin. What motivated you to move to that city? How did you prepare for the transatlantic move?

I lived in Europe on and off after college, but eventually I wound up working at a law firm in New York. It was a good job, and I loved living near my friends. But I felt unsatisfied. I wanted more to my life than an office job, and I felt I had something to give, but I didn't know where to put it.

I started working on the book. I'd tried writing fiction before, but after I developed this story it became more serious. I wrote nights and on weekends. Gradually I realized the book was the one thing I was doing that I really cared about.

A few years before this I'd stopped in Berlin for a few days, and I had been fascinated by it ever after. It was unlike any other place I'd been in Europe—a vast capital full of unpredictable spaces. When you went out in Berlin, you never knew where the night would take you. I thought it would be the perfect place to write a book.

So I saved as much money as I could and quit my job. I left for Berlin with a plot outline, a few rough scenes and three suitcases full of research books. Even once I was on the plane I couldn't believe I was really doing it.

In *The Steady Running of the Hour* the action alternates between World War I and the present. Why did you choose to structure the novel with alternating chapters? Was it difficult to change time frames while you were writing? Or did you write each time frame all at once?

I alternated the chapters because I wanted both stories to progress at the same time, and I didn't want the past to feel too "historical." I wanted both stories to happen in present time, to have the same immediacy. A big question in the book is whether Tristan's life, or anything in our contemporary lives, can measure up to this epic notion of history, the Great War or the Battle of the Somme. But people don't think about history while it's happening. It's personal mythologies that matter—the stories Ashley tells himself about Imogen for seven years, the way Tristan feels about Ashley and Imogen.

I didn't write the book in chronological order. I just wrote scenes when I felt ready. The Everest and war chapters were written last, because I wanted to research as much as possible before writing. I felt so much pressure to get the historical chapters right that it was a relief to write Tristan's chapters, because then I could relax a bit and rely more on firsthand experience.

Anton DiSclafani calls *The Steady Running of the Hour* "an astonishingly vast, meticulously plotted, and beautifully told novel." There are so many twists and turns throughout Tristan's quest: Can you tell us how you were able to plot them out so precisely? Did you know how Tristan's search would end when you began writing?

When I started the book I plotted it carefully. I probably made ten outlines in ten different notebooks. I felt everything had to unfold in a very particular way. But of course I made mistakes, or characters or events changed, and I had to replot things.

As the writing went on I realized that knowing what happens is just the beginning. Next you have to figure out how things will happen, where they will occur among the alternating story lines, which characters will know about them and how those characters will find out. The infinite permutations are enough to give you a headache. Eventually you have to just follow your instinct.

I always had an image of where Tristan's search would end. I had previously gone hitchhiking in Iceland and gotten dropped off at a particular fjord, but then no more cars came. I lay down on a black sand beach and instantly fell asleep, as if I was meant to have some kind of vision. It felt like the end point of the long trip I'd taken across Europe, a destination I'd arrived at without knowing I'd been traveling toward a destination. I knew I wanted Tristan to end there. But what it actually meant for him to reach that fjord—the meaning of that developed as his story grew.

When talking about his research, Tristan says, "All I need is one good piece of evidence, and I keep getting sidetracked. It's hard because . . . every time I got sidetracked I found the best stuff." How did you conduct your research for the novel? Do Tristan's research methods mirror your own?

At the beginning I read very broadly. I got to Berlin with thick surveys of the Great War and Everest and Edwardian Britain. But eventually I realized that specific knowledge was far more useful than historical overviews. I didn't need to know everything about Franz Ferdinand or British Imperial policy toward Tibet. What I really needed was to know what it felt like to be there. So I became obsessed with figuring out such details as what the streetlights looked like in London in the summer of 1916, and what kind of dishes you could get in a good hotel and what the mud felt like in the Somme that November.

A lot of that research was similar to Tristan's. But he never worries about the thing that I found the hardest, which is getting inside a culture. It's one thing to be correct with superficial details. But to be true to an entire vanished civilization—the way people talked or acted, what they cared about, what they shared and what they kept to themselves—it's nearly hopeless. The closest you can get is through what those people left behind, their letters or diaries or memoirs. So I read as much as I could, until I felt neck deep in their world. No amount of research ever felt sufficient. But at some point I just had to close my eyes and imagine.

As Tristan researches the world of Ashley and Imogen, he is often surprised. Did anything surprise you when you were conducting your own research for the book? If so, what?

I was surprised nearly every day. And if I wasn't surprised, I'd feel I wasn't learning enough. It's the surprising things that shift your view of a period, or give you details that later become important. I'd be trying to figure out how long it took to send a letter from the Somme to London, and I would read something unexpected about codes in soldiers' letters. Often I barely noticed those things when I first read them, but they stayed inside me and came out later.

The best surprise was writing something from my imagination, then finding later that it mirrored an archive in a document I had never seen before. It was usually trivial things—I'd imagine Imogen knitting an afghan, or Ashley writing a telegram about Poste Restante letters, or Eleanor ordering certain pigments from Paris. Then I'd read a letter mentioning knitting an afghan all night or Prussian blue pigments or Poste Restante letters. It felt like a small miracle every time it happened. I hadn't done anything special, of course. I'd simply seen a detail elsewhere and it had entered my picture of the period, so I had put it into the novel. But it felt good to be vindicated.

Eventually the line dividing truth from fiction began to blur. I was going to the same places as Tristan and looking up the same things and occasionally finding results similar to what I'd imagined Tristan finding. Sometimes the sense of unreality was so strong I had to remind myself that the letters I was holding were real, that they had been written by real people who had held those pages at the Somme or on Everest. After dealing with so much fiction, the reality of history seemed too much to believe. But it was true.

The climbing sections of the novel are particularly vivid. Did you rely on books or other research to get a sense of what an Everest expedition might be like?

Everest has a wonderfully vast literature—a mythology of its own—but it can be overwhelming. I studied every relevant book I could find, but also photographs, maps, films, newspapers, climbing manuals, everything under the sun. It kept me busy for years. The 1920s expeditions left behind detailed records in the Geographical Society and the Alpine Club in London. There I was able to see things like climber's diaries and detailed equipment lists, as well as many letters.

But I most wanted to understand what it felt like to be up there in a tent in a blizzard, or traversing stone slabs in nailed boots. The official expedition books were fairly dry, but fortunately the memoirs of climbers from the 1920s and 1930s expeditions were often vivid. I also read more recent climbing books, because although the equipment and techniques have changed, the sensations of cold or altitude are largely the same.

Eventually I went to Everest myself, traveling through Tibet to the base camp. It was an incredibly hostile environment—even more cold and dry and windy than I'd imagined. But the mountain was hypnotizing. I could have stared at it for days. Finally I understood the magnetism of it, the reason that men like Mallory kept coming back. Once you've seen Everest, you'll never forget it.

Your characters are so well fleshed out, they feel like people your readers should know. Were they based on anyone in the historical record? How did you come up with them?

History was always the starting point. Ashley is a climber and Imogen is from a very specific background, so I began by imagining the world they would have come out of, the kinds of people they might have known. The best way into this was looking at real people. Eleanor and Imogen seem to have been influenced by Virginia Woolf and her sister Vanessa Bell, the painter, but I didn't do that deliberately. Eventually it just crept in.

In the same way, you couldn't imagine a character like Ashley without the examples of the original Everest climbers, particularly George Mallory. He was such a magnetic spirit that you get the idea all the Everest climbers were men of great artistic and intellectual passion. But they were actually quite different. I tried to get to know all kinds of climbers from the period to broaden the foundation for Ashley's character.

But no matter what your inspiration, characters ultimately just need to feel human. I might decide that Imogen loved Nijinsky's dancing or Laforgue's poetry, or that Ashley was an advocate of guideless climbing. But what really defined Imogen was her passion, a kind of emotional conviction I'd witnessed in certain people in my own life. In Ashley's case, I began to understand him through his humor, a gallows humor I'd often seen in books and letters from the war. I thought Ashley's humor might conceal what he really cared about. So you start with history, but ultimately the characters grow from what you believe about people. And your imagination.

What would you like your readers to take away from Tristan's quest?

The beauty of literature is that everyone can take away something different. I see fiction as a kind of mirror to the world—a human reflection, not a factual one—and I don't think novels should have a single meaning any more than life does. I try to tell a story without telling the reader how to feel about it. The hope is that if you place readers close enough to it—so that they're experiencing what's happening before them—they'll have their own emotions, richer and more individual than anything a writer could impose.

But of course I have my own feelings about Tristan's quest. I spent a lot of my twenties chasing after some grand ideas I'd got in my head. I wanted to see everything, to experience everything. That gave me certain ambitions, but it also made me unhappy, because I was never really satisfied with what was around me.

Tristan is caught between his ideas and his reality. When he starts learning about Ashley and Imogen, everything in his own life seems trivial by comparison. But as time goes on, I think Tristan understands that what draws him to Ashley and Imogen isn't some mythic legacy, but their craving for something greater in their lives, something they were willing to fight for. That's what Tristan wants—to know what matters and go after it. In the end, I think he does that. He has to turn away from the past and that's hard for him. But ultimately he chooses his own life.

Can you tell us anything about the novel you're working on now?

It's set in Europe between the wars, so it pretty much picks up where this book ends. I find the 1920s and 1930s to be the most fascinating period. There was so much political turmoil and at the same time such remarkable artistic achievement. I've been making these huge timelines and the backdrop is astonishing—the publication of *Ulysses* and *The Wasteland* in 1922, the German hyperinflation, American expats flooding the Paris Left Bank, the Nazis and Communists battling in the streets of Berlin, another world war looming.

But that's just the setting. What interests me are the human relationships within that world—what people were like, not only around the centers of power but on the fringes of empires, in the remote corners of deserts or mountains. It's a big story, so eventually I'm going to have to whittle it down to what works best.

I'd promised myself I wouldn't do another historical book, because it's so demanding. But I think the need to anchor things to research also anchors them to the real world, and that's a good thing. I'm trying to get as immersed as I can, as close as possible to experiencing the things I'm writing about. And I'm continually inspired by the people whose books or letters I read—not because they teach me about history, but because they teach me about being human. Maybe one day I'll give up on the past and write about other things. But not yet.